The School for Widows

The School for Widows

Clara Reeve

Edited by Jeanine M. Casler

Newark: University of Delaware Press
London: Associated University Presses

© 2003 by Rosemont Publishing & Printing Corp.

All rights reserved. Authorization to photocopy items for internal or personal use, or the internal or personal use of specific clients, is granted by the copyright owner, provided that a base fee of $10.00, plus eight cents per page, per copy is paid directly to the Copyright Clearance Center, 222 Rosewood Drive, Danvers, Massachusetts 01923. [0-87413-804-3/03 $10.00 + 8¢ pp, pc.]

Other than as indicated in the foregoing, this book may not be reproduced, in whole or in part, in any form (except as permitted by Sections 107 and 108 of the U.S. Copyright Law, and except for brief quotes appearing in reviews in the public press.

Associated University Presses
2010 Eastpark Boulevard
Cranbury, NJ 08512

Associated University Presses
16 Barter Street
London WC1A 2AH, England

Associated University Presses
P.O. Box 338, Port Credit
Mississauga, Ontario
Canada L5G 4L8

The paper used in this publication meets the minimum requirements of the American National Standard for Permanence of Paper for Printed Library Materials Z39.48-1984.

Library of Congress Cataloging-in-Publication Data

Reeve, Clara, 1729–1807.
    The school for widows / Clara Reeve ; edited by Jeanine M. Casler.
    p. cm.
    Includes bibliographical references.
    ISBN 0-87413-804-3 (alk. paper)
    1. Female friendship—Fiction. 2. Widows—Fiction. I. Casler, Jeanine M. 1971– II. Title.
PR3658.R5 S3   2003
823'.6—dc21   2002075005

PRINTED IN THE UNITED STATES OF AMERICA

Contents

Acknowledgments	7
Widows in the Eighteenth Century	9
Clara Reeve: Life and Works	15
Reeve's Widows	49
Chronology of Events in the Life and Times of Clara Reeve	59
Note on the Text	61

The School for Widows

Preface	65

Volume I

Letter I. Mrs. Strictland, to Mrs. Darnford.	67
Letter II. Mrs. Strictland, to Mrs. Darnford.	76
Letter III. Mrs. Darnford, to Mrs. Strickland.	83
Letter IV. Mrs. Darnford, in continuation.	100
Letter V. Mrs. Darnford, in continuation.	117

Volume II

Letter VI. Mrs. Darnford, in continuation.	165
Letter VII. Mrs. Strictland, to Mrs. Darnford.	199
Letter VIII. Mrs. Strictland, to Mrs. Darnford, in continuation.	247
Letter IX. Mrs. Strictland, to Mrs. Darnford, in continuation.	265

Volume III

Letter X. Mrs. Darnford, to Mrs. Strictland	277
Letter XI. Mrs. Darnford, to Mrs. Strictland.	291
Letter XII. Mrs. Darnford, to Mrs. Strictland.	305

Letter XIII. Mrs. Darnford, to Mrs. Strictland.   316
Letter XIV. Mrs. Darnford, to Mrs. Strictland.   323
Letter XV. Mrs. Darnford, to Mrs. Strictland.   331
Letter XVI. Mrs. Strictland, to Mrs. Darnford.   347
Letter XVII. Miss Elton, to Mrs. Strictland.   349
Letter XVIII. Miss Elton, to Mrs. Strictland.   351
Letter XIX. Mrs. Strictland, to Mrs. Darnford.   352
Letter XX. Mrs. Darnford, to Mrs. Strictland.   356
Letter XXI. Mrs. Strictland, to Mrs. Darnford.   358
Letter XXII. Mrs. Darnford, to Mrs. Strictland.   363

Appendix   365
Notes   366
Select Bibliography   379

Acknowledgments

MANY PEOPLE HAVE CONTRIBUTED GENEROUSLY TO THE CREATION of this book. I began and completed the edition while working at the University of Georgia, where I benefited from the careful readings and critical acumen of Tricia Lootens, John Vance, Mike Moran, Anne Mallory, Amanda DeWees, and above all my mentor, Elizabeth Kraft.

T. Keith Dix of the Classics department at Georgia provided some much-needed advice concerning annotations, as did the staffs of the University of Georgia and Emory University Libraries. I have drawn extensively on the resources of the Bodleian Library, the British Library, and the Trinity College Library in Dublin. The staffs of the Suffolk and Essex County Record Offices also provided invaluable (and very amiable) assistance in my search for biographical material on Reeve.

I owe a special debt of gratitude to Tom Keymer, whose guidance throughout all stages of my research and writing made this edition possible. Finally, I would like to thank my parents, William and Joan Casler, for their unfailing support. Muchas gracias también a mi media naranja, por sus consejos sabios y su paciencia infinita.

Widows in the Eighteenth Century

"I DON'T KNOW WHAT THE DEVIL A WOMAN LIVES FOR AFTER thirty: she is only in other folks way," announces the libertine Lord Merton in Frances Burney's *Evelina* (1778), thus putting into words a belief that was widespread in eighteenth-century England. Older unmarried or widowed women fare poorly in eighteenth-century novels in general. Besides Burney's Mrs. Selwyn one thinks of Frances Sheridan's Lady Bidulph, Henry Fielding's Lady Booby, and Jane Austen's acidic Lady Catherine de Bourgh, all of whom suggest that the older unmarried/widowed woman in British society was generally a focus of mockery and derision, if not an unpleasant object to be ignored. In her 1791 novel *The School for Widows*, however, Clara Reeve tells us a tale of three older women whose freedom, autonomy, and personal power increase as they age.

The revolutionary nature of Reeve's representation of widowhood becomes apparent when one considers the prejudices against widows revealed in the English language itself. The word "spinster," initially denoting an older, unmarried, or previously married woman forced to turn to spinning in order to survive, quickly became a derogatory label, and is used as a term of abuse in mid- to late-eighteenth-century novels. The word widow itself is often associated with bad luck, evil, and witchery, connotations that are absent from the word for the male equivalent. Nor are the derogatory associations with the word "widow" specific to English culture. *Almanah*, the Hebrew word for widow, comes from the root *alem*, which means "unable to speak." It is akin to an Aramaic word which means "to be in pain." *Almeuth*, the word for widowhood, means "silence."[1] Thus is the widow connected with powerlessness, helplessness, and the inability to speak. Similarly, *chera*, the Greek word for widow (to which the English word "widow" is also closely related), derives from the Indo-European root *ghe*, meaning "left empty" or "forsaken." *Chera* is also akin to the word *chora*, a noun meaning "region" or "empty space."[2] Similarly negative terms are used to refer to widows in Bangladesh and in India. Indeed, widows are called *rand, raki,* and *randi,* openly abusive and vulgar terms meaning "prostitute," "whore," and "harlot." In one state in the North of India a widow is referred to as *ghoomane phirnaveralli,* or "one who moves around," the equivalent of calling her promiscuous. Another frequently used term of abuse—"one who laughs loudly"—also serves to imply that the widow is unchaste. Similarly, widows are called *daken,* which means sorceress or witch,[3] thus suggesting not only the "lack" or "emptiness" of the widow, or her tendency toward "looseness," but also her inherently evil and actively malignant nature.

Given the biases against widows that thus—from the beginnings of time to the present—manifest themselves even in the languages of these many different cultures, it is not surprising that the social realities of these "lesser" members of society mirror such prejudices. Nonfictional sources of documentary evidence help to attest to the precarious state of affairs for the typical English widow in the eighteenth century. On one hand she had to deal with society's negative perceptions of her, and on the other she was faced with the hard realities of trying to support herself financially after the loss of a husband—something for which she was unprepared by education and upbringing. The great number of organizations for the aid of impoverished widows that sprung into life during the eighteenth century lends credence to the idea that the widow *was* in actuality a second-class citizen, in addition to being considered one by other members of society. William Gordon, in his pamphlet on the plan of a society for making provisions for widows, suggests a system of annuities for life, and writes with some sympathy of the proposed objects of charity. "The painful circumstances in which numbers are involved, when aged, or deprived of that, or those, on whom their support chiefly depended," Gordon writes, "are too notorious to require a recital. But that same Divine Wisdom, which allows and orders the existence of these calamities, has. . .so directed its manner, as to admit of their being greatly alleviated, by the joint endeavours of mankind."[4] Gordon goes on to claim that such circumstances as he describes have risen to the attention of ever-greater numbers of people in England, which has resulted in the birth of "various Societies in *Great-Britain,* which within a few years have multiplied a-pace, chiefly in *London.*"[5] Not only have concerned citizens come to recognize the economic plight of the widow in England, but in the colonies as well, and it is for this reason that Gordon is writing: in order to provide some kind of a guide for fledgling widow's-aid societies in America.

Writing just nine years later, Dr. William Alexander devotes a whole chapter of his ambitious *History of Women, from the Earliest Antiquity to the Present Time* (1779) to widowhood, revealing all of the popular prejudices against widows, and showing himself to be akin to Gordon in his paternalistic attitude toward them. Alexander begins by explaining why women dislike widowhood, which is, he states, because they are by nature weak. "As the state of matrimony is of all others the most honourable, and the most desired by women," he insists, "so that of widowhood is generally the most deplorable, and consequently the object of their greatest aversion."[6] Basing dubious assumption upon dubious assumption, Alexander expands on the widow's supposed incapacity to maintain herself, closing off to her not only the physically strenuous and thus traditionally male avenues of fishing, hunting and farming, but also the possibility of a foray into the world of business, for "to launch out into trade and commerce would require, perhaps, more industry, and more steady efforts of mind, than are consistent with their volatile natures and finer feelings." As I shall soon discuss, Clara Reeve's *School for Widows* belies Alexander's words, portraying women who are not only not "weak," but also possess a business acumen that would put many people—male or female—to shame. Alexander's motive in writing, though, appears to be a good one. He goes on to describe the misfortune of the state of widowhood throughout history, lumping the widow together with the orphan as victims who were "liable to be frequently wronged, oppressed, and plundered."[7] Being either a widow or an orphan, then, is a "dreadful misfortune," and, Alexander implies, one that can only be alleviated by help from outside. Like Gordon, Alexander does not even consider a widow's inner resources to come into the equation.

Also like Gordon, Alexander implies that the widow's status marks her as an easy victim of "rapine and violence," and he places the onus on his readers to help support poor widows in particular, who have more need of protection than those of the upper and middle classes. Interestingly, the aid societies of late-eighteenth-century Britain (for the aid not only of widows, but also of prisoners and certain other categories of the poor) have membership lists that are filled with the names of middle-class widows and spinsters.[8] It is ironic that treatises like Gordon's and Alexander's, which are evidently aimed at an audience of men in an attempt to move them to act benevolently toward the less fortunate members of the weaker sex, seem to have had more effect on female readers—particularly those who were widows themselves—who figured predominantly in the organization and actualization of relief. Upper and middle class widows, left with money and time on their hands, often used it to help their impoverished sisters-in-spirit. In fact, even among the poorer widows there is evidence of a self-reliance and inner strength that belies accounts like Alexander's of what it meant to be a widow. The phenomenon of "spinster clustering"—the grouping together of small numbers of women in order to rent some kind of a shared apartment or house where they could share living expenses and tasks[9]—became increasingly common during the late eighteenth century, suggesting that widows were coming to realize their own inner resources, and the potential of survival through sharing those resources with others in their same predicament.

Not all pamphlets and treatises were as serious in tone as were Gordon's and Alexander's. An anonymous essay printed just at the beginning of the eighteenth century, entitled *The Petition of the WIDOWS, in and about London and Westminster for a Redress of their Grievances,* takes the "problem" of widowhood very lightly indeed. Framed in the form of a petition drawn up by a solicitor for a group of widows, the pamphlet is actually a satire that underscores one of the stereotypes of the widow: her lasciviousness. These "Ladies" are not petitioning the good people of London for economic assistance; rather, they are requesting that the men leave off their slighting of widows (on account of their being "second-hand") and provide the petitioners with the sexual gratification they so lack. Widows have many good qualities that are lacking in younger women, write the petitioners. For example, they are not terribly selective, for "they will sit down content with any thing; and Cripples with Wooden Legs will be cheerfully entertained if they have received no damage in the distinguishing part" (2). Not only is the widow, then, promiscuous, but she is also so desperate for any male company that she will accept what is according to the author a "lesser" man. The petitioners continue with their list of the advantages of choosing a widow, taking issue with those men who insist that widows

"Want several of those Recommendations that set off the sex, ... particularly a Maiden head," and deny many of the popular slurs against marrying widows, such as that doing so is like "splitting upon a Rock where others have been ship-wracked before" (3). Though the pamphlet is a satire, then, it underscores the stereotypical association of widows with accessibility and lustfulness.

Such images as the helpless widow or the libidinous widow are invalidated by Clara Reeve in *The School for Widows*. In her earlier fiction—novels such as *The Old English Baron* (1778), *The Two Mentors* (1783), and *The Exiles* (1788)—Reeve gives very little indication of any resistance to existing social systems: On the contrary, she seems to endorse the status quo at every opportunity. *The School for Widows* is also infused with Reeve's support of typical, accepted ideas of the way society should be run. However, the novel marks a great departure for Reeve with its decidedly nonconformist characterization of the widow.

In eighteenth-century society as in modern times, loss of a husband often meant the loss of both economic and social status for a woman: particularly when she was childless. As Olwen Hufton notes in her discussion of widows and spinsters without family to help them, "All women lived in societies in which marriage and motherhood were regarded as the norm, spinsterhood and infertility as a blight, and in which the notion of the family economy, of the family as a composite unit permitting the sustenance of the whole, was axiomatic. Outside the family was apparently some kind of twilight existence for women."[10] The people with whom Reeve's main characters come in contact in *The School for Widows* are no different from typical citizens of eighteenth-century England in their attitudes toward marriage and motherhood. For the most part they consider the three widows (particularly Frances Darnford and Isabella di Soranzo, who are childless) to be useless members of society, and would cheerfully relegate them to that "twilight existence" which Hufton describes. Reeve's widows, however, will not be so relegated, and instead become arbiters of their own destinies. Reeve thus challenges common perceptions of what it means to be a widow. Granted, the widows Darnford, Strictland, and di Soranzo suffer the same disorientation that is suffered by nearly all widows in every corner of the globe. They experience the same pangs caused by loss of status, limited income, uncertainty for the future, isolation, and depression that other widows experience. They do not, however, simply accept these hardships, but instead choose to fight the status quo, assert their independence, and not only adapt to the shocking change in their lives, but use it to their advantage.

The constant focus on women's resourcefulness that we find throughout *The School for Widows* is also the driving force of many of Reeve's other works, and the reasons for her affinity for the theme become clear when we examine what is known of the life of the author herself.

Clara Reeve: Life and Works

> "I had been skirmishing with Poverty at a distance for some time, and preparing for her nearer approach."
> —Frances to Rachel in *The School for Widows*

THE GENTLEMAN'S MAGAZINE PAID A RATHER DUBIOUS TRIBUTE TO Clara Reeve when she died on 3 December 1807. "Her works," they claimed, "discover her to have cultivated useful knowledge with considerable success; and to have applied that knowledge less frivolously than is frequently the case with female Authors." As she had praised the endeavors of literary women in her writing throughout her life, it is safe to assume that the object of this left-handed compliment would have been at least a little offended at the slighting reference to women writers. In fact, Clara Reeve was a poet, translator, critic, novelist, antiquarian, and woman of letters whose work was widely respected and very popular in her own time. Like many of the women writers of the eighteenth century, Reeve's popularity was subsequently negated or even used as evidence that her works were of an inferior quality, and not worthy of being included in the accepted canon of eighteenth-century British literature. With the recent "rediscovery" and revival of critical interest in many so-called "lost" women novelists like Reeve, the demand for scholarly editions of their novels has increased considerably.

Although primarily known for her critical–theoretical *Progress of Romance* (1785) and her gothic tale *The Old English Baron* (1778), Reeve deserves a re-evaluation on the basis of both recently unearthed biographical material and of her later, oft-neglected novel *The School for Widows* (1791), which reveal that "Mrs. Clara Reeve, Spinster"—as the register of her burial reads—had some decidedly non-traditional ideas about women and their place in society.

> "I have been all my life straitened in my circumstances, and used my pen to support a scanty establishment, yet, to the

best of my knowledge, I have drawn it on the side of truth, virtue and morality."
—Clara Reeve, quoted by Anna Barbauld in *The British Novelists*

Much about Clara Reeve's early life is still unknown, but the shadowy picture of her youth and young adulthood that does emerge is one of financial difficulty and hard work. She was born on 23 January 1729, in Ipswich in Suffolk. Her paternal grandfather, the Reverend Thomas Reeve, served as rector of Storeham, Aspal, and later of St. Mary, Stoke, in Ipswich. Her mother, Hannah Smithies Reeve, was the daughter of William Smithies, who was jeweler and goldsmith to George I. Her father, the Reverend Mr. William Reeve, was rector of Freston and of Kerton, Suffolk, and perpetual curate of St. Nicolas, Ipswich. One of his sons, Thomas, became a clergyman like his father, serving as rector of Brockley, Suffolk, and master of Bungay grammar school. Another son, Samuel, distinguished himself in the navy, becoming a Vice Admiral of the White, and was much lamented on his death in 1803 according to the account of him on a plaque in St. Mary Elms Church, Ipswich, which describes him as "exemplary in the duties of his profession: a man of strict probity, and a valuable friend; a brother justly beloved and most gratefully remembered." He was greatly beloved by all of his family, but especially by his sister Clara, who, in 1804, writes sadly of his death two years earlier. He "was indeed an honour to his family," she grieves, adding "He died vice Admiral of the White Squadron, and after escaping a thousand dangers, died by an accident. He was a man of superior abilities & exemplary character. Beloved—esteemed—& lamented."[11]

The Reeves had eight children in total, of whom Clara was the eldest daughter, and therefore, as Sir Walter Scott writes, it was "likely that it was rather Clara's strong natural turn for study, than any degree of exclusive care which [William Reeve's] partiality bestowed, that enabled her to acquire such a stock of early information."[12] That having been said, it is nonetheless true that Clara's father gave her, like all his children, a healthy respect for education. Clara herself described her father with some affection as an "Old Whig" (i.e., an opposition Whig—not a supporter of Sir Robert Walpole) who made her read parliamentary debates, Greek and Roman histories, Plutarch's *Lives*, and Rapin's *History of England*[13] at a very young age. She also learned Latin, and first became an author with her translation from the Latin of John Barclay's *Argenis* (1621), which was published in 1762 under the title *The Phoenix; or, The History of Polyarchus and Argenis*. Reeve's father died in 1755, leaving his family little other than his house in St. Helen's parish, and she then moved with her mother and two of her sisters, Jane and Sarah, to Colchester.

Reeve's life immediately after the move to Colchester is still a mystery. There are various references to her "straitened circumstances" (Reeve's own letter, cited by Anna Barbauld, among them), the most fascinating being a letter written by a Mrs. Kempe to John Grimston, in May 1778. Mrs. Kempe asserts that Reeve was

> a clergyman's daughter who had a large family and a very small living. She, the eldest, was forced to be a common servant. Her father, finding she had a genius, encouraged and improved it whenever she could be spared from working, etc. She used to steal bits of candle to sit up at nights to read. Thus she went on till she was a woman, and her father died and left her without a penny or the means of earning one, but in the same drudgery she had lived ... her sisters were gone out mantua makers, milliners, etc. In this, her melancholy situation, a lady of fortune—I have forgot her name—took her, where she lived happy a few years, and then the lady died and left her about *40l* a year, since which she has lived with some of her sisters, where she indulges as much as she pleases with her books and her pen.[14]

Reeve's own words, cited by Anna Barbauld, are also suggestive of pecuniary difficulties. Given the Reeve family's financial situation and Clara Reeve's lack of literary output until several years after she moved to Colchester, the possibility of her having been engaged in some kind of domestic service during her early life is a strong one. Cheryl Turner numbers Reeve among those women who were pushed by financial necessity to employ themselves, initially via domestic service, and later as writers or members of the literary profession. Families—like Reeve's—of the poorer clergy were, according to Turner, "potential seedbeds of literary professionalism, combining the probability of education with the possibility of an insufficient income."[15] Reeve was forced to support herself, and she was fortunate enough, eventually, to be able to do so using her literary facility, despite an early life that is indicative of domestic labor and self-deprivation.

The *East Anglian Daily Times* records Reeve as having lived with Edmund Hammond and his sister Esther, of Sparrows' Nest, near Ipswich, for several years. When Hammond died in 1760, he left Reeve a £20 annuity, to be increased to £40 per year on the death of his sister. Since Esther died the following year, Reeve did indeed have the benefit of £40 a year, as Mrs. Kempe suggests in her letter. It may be, then, that the Hammonds were the "[gentleman and] lady of fortune" who rescued Reeve from her domestic drudgery, according to the scenario presented by Mrs. Kempe. Soon after Esther Hammond's death, Reeve began to work on her poetry in earnest.

Original Poems on Several Occasions

Reeve's first collection, which contains an impressive variety of verse types from elegies, to epithalamia, to the first act of an oratorio, was published as *Original Poems on Several Occasions* in 1769. Reeve dedicates the volume to "the Hon. Mrs. Stratford," who, with her husband, "protected and supported" her. Possibly, then, Reeve was so fortunate as to encounter two generous patrons soon after her move to Colchester. The extent to which Reeve did or did not have to labor for the Hammonds and the Stratfords is unclear, but what is certain is that the subsequent years were highly productive ones for her; the implication is that she had a greater command of her own time than ever before.

> What by my talents have I gained?
> By those I lov'd to be disdain'd,
> By some despis'd, by others fear'd,
> Envied by fools, by witlings jeer'd.
> See what success my labours crown'd,
> By birds and beasts alike disown'd.
> Those talents that were once my pride,
> I find it requisite to hide;
> For what in man is most respected,
> In woman's form shall be rejected.
> —from "An Elegy"(1769)

Though this excerpt from the first poem in Reeve's collection indicates a hesitation to acknowledge herself publicly as a writer, the act of publishing *Original Poems* was in fact her first open declaration of authorship. Reeve explains her change of heart in her Address to the Reader, recounting, "I formerly believed, that I ought not to let myself be known for a scribbler, that my sex was an insuperable objection, that mankind in general were prejudiced against its pretensions to literary merit; but I am now convinced of the mistake, by daily examples to the contrary" (xi). The poems that follow this address reveal an author who is alternately sentimental, satirical (her satire on critics asks, "How can I allowance hope, / Where parish-clerks correct a Pope"), rhapsodic (she includes encomia on Shakespeare and Dryden), and admonitory ("To a Coquet, Disappointed of a Party of Pleasure" warns the reader, "rather strive to gain those charms, / Not to a day confin'd! / To beauty's power, add stronger arms, / And decorate thy mind"), moving from one verse form to another with great energy and aplomb.

The poems were well received, and according to Mrs. Kempe Reeve reaped financial rewards from this early success, as the poems brought her £200. This amount does not seem inordinate, considering the large number of subscribers to the volume (over 614, including the Rev. James Fordyce, publisher William Keymer, and Thomas Reeve). Like other female authors during the late eighteenth century, Reeve took advantage of the system of subscription publication, which was rapidly replacing the peerage as the traditional source of literary patronage.[16]

The Old English Baron

> On occasion [Reeve] has soared above [Walpole] to a point he never dreamed of. She touches deftly . . . on the human soul quivering beneath the impulse of vague, apprehensive fear.
> —Christabel Forsythe Fiske, *The Conservative Review*

Soon after the favorable reception of her poetry, Reeve began to try out her skill at another genre, which was proving to be lucrative for women writers: the novel.[17] Reeve was very interested in biography and history throughout her life, and this interest accounts for her fascination with historical fiction, which may have led to the writing of her most famous work, *The Old English Baron*. First brought out by Colchester bookseller William Keymer in 1777, the novel was originally titled *The Champion of Virtue,* and the author listed on its title page was not Clara Reeve but rather "the EDITOR of the PHOENIX;

A TRANSLATION of BARCLAY'S ARGENIS." Samuel Richardson's daughter Martha Bridgen, with whom Reeve had become very friendly by this time, suggested some substantial changes to the novel—including its title—and the resulting product, published as *The Old English Baron* the following year, was the literary event of the season. It became so popular that not only was it translated into French and German, but it was also adapted by John Broster in 1799 for his stage version, *Edmond, Orphan of the Castle*, and was reprinted more than ten times by the century's end.

Reeve's stated aim in writing *The Old English Baron* was "to unite the most attractive and interesting circumstances of the ancient Romance and the modern Novel." She sought to eliminate what she saw as the flaws of Horace Walpole's *Castle of Otranto* (1764). *Otranto*, she writes, "palls upon the mind"—its "machinery is so violent that it destroys the effect it is intended to excite." One must, she claims, keep within "certain limits of credibility" if one is to be effective as a novelist. So, though Reeve is undoubtedly imitating Walpole (she calls *The Old English Baron* the "literary offspring" of *Otranto*), she is also positing her "Gothic Story" as an improvement on his. Walpole, it seems, did not take kindly to the act, nor perhaps to the fact that this, Reeve's first foray into the genre, met with such an overwhelming popular response. His rather acerbic comment to his friend William Mason that "any trial for murder at the Old Bailey would make a more interesting story"[18] suggests that he did not appreciate her insistence upon adding a dose of verisimilitude into the gothic mix.

Whatever Walpole thought, modern critics—Gary Kelly and Jane Spencer, among others—tend to see *The Old English Baron* as pivotal, and credit Reeve with the development of the gothic novel from the supernatural improbability of The *Castle of Otranto* (1764) to the more reason-tempered suspense of Ann Radcliffe's novels. The *Old English Baron* tells the story of Edmund, a young man of noble mien (and, it turns out, noble blood) who is being raised along with the "legitimate" children of the Baron Fitz-Owen (the old English baron of the title, although he is not the main character of the novel; Edmund is). After many ordeals, which include Edmund's spending the night in a haunted chamber, and dream visitations from his true parents, the young paragon of excellence is elevated to his deserved status as heir to the house of Lovel, reunited with

Baron Fitz-Owen, and married to the Baron's beautiful and virtuous daughter Emma.

Reeve's suggestion throughout the novel is that class will tell; though Edmund is made to work as a servant in his early life, it is obvious to all those around him that he is "better than his station," both physically and intellectually. Thus Reeve seems to suggest that class is inborn; despite Edmund's "lowly" early upbringing with the peasant-class Twyfords, the genetic legacy of nobility from the Lovels cannot be hidden. As in her later works, Reeve here emphasizes the stratified nature of a world in which it is imperative that each class maintains its traditional place in order for society to function harmoniously as a whole.

Class conservatism aside, the *Old English Baron* was sufficiently innovative to surprise and delight many readers, and Reeve has been credited with introducing in her "Gothic Story" several conventions which were oft-imitated in subsequent gothic novels: the haunted suite, the ominous dream, and the identifying piece of jewelry, to name a few. Despite its novelty and popularity, though, the *Old English Baron* does not appear to been a very remunerative project for Reeve. Jane Spencer asserts that the novel did not bring its author much money, and that, soon after its original publication as *The Champion of Virtue*, she sold the copyright for a mere £10.[19]

Reeve and the Magazines

Before Reeve became fully ensconced as a professional writer of novels, she followed in the footsteps of authors such as Elizabeth Carter, whose first forays into the public sphere came via contributions to the *Gentleman's Magazine*. By submitting single short pieces of her writing to reputable journals, then, Reeve was in effect testing an established route to publication. Unlike many of the women who contributed to these journals, however, Reeve already had a small reputation for her translation of Barclay, and for her poetry, and soon after *The Old English Baron* arrived on the scene in 1778 that reputation skyrocketed. Thus, her contributions to the magazines were signed, unlike some of her fellow-authors'.

Along with her emergence into the public sphere came a greater awareness of her role as a professional writer, and two important correspondences occurred during the subsequent decade that reveal just how seriously Reeve did take that role. The first public exchange was on the pages of the *Lady's Magazine* in the late 1770s. Robert Mayo sees this incident as an indicator of "the sharp decline of professional standards in the miscellanies ... as a result of the invasion of volunteers,"[20] but it also serves as proof of the seriousness of Reeve with respect to her work and her reputation as an author. The conflict arose after the *Lady's Magazine* published a short extract from Reeve's preface to *The Old English Baron* in 1778. Along with the publication, the editor attached a few sentences in praise of the author, and invited Reeve to contribute any "fugitive or periodical piece" to the *Lady's Magazine*. As Mayo asserts, this was a very strange and public invitation to a novelist who, after the arrival on the literary scene of *The Old English Baron,* was by now much celebrated. Reeve's response was gently critical of the *Lady's Magazine,* but she did accompany that criticism with her suggestion of a new translation of *Les Lettres d'Aza* by Lamarche-Courmont. "In the course of my peregrinations," she writes the editor, "I have met with the *Letters of Aza,* in French, which seem to me the true counterpart to those of Zilia. I translated the first two letters," she adds, "but other things intervening, I laid them aside and forgot them. Your late request suggested a thought, that they may possibly answer your purpose."[21] Her reply to the *Lady's Magazine,* then, would seem to have been the initiation of a transaction between professionals; the magazine's editor had publicly asked for her contributions, and she was responding by sending him sample copy, "in accordance with established publishing procedures."[22] The editor manipulated the situation to his advantage by moving her reply to the column where he placed "Correspondents,"—the portion of the magazine where he regularly rejected or accepted submissions from his many volunteers.

After enclosing the first two *Letters* in her note to the editor of the *Lady's Magazine,* Reeve failed to send additional installments of the series, despite very urgent public appeals by the editor for more. While others have attributed Reeve's silence to a lack of time or literary inspiration, Robert Mayo's suggestion—that Reeve did not respond because she was deeply upset by being asked to compromise herself—is a much more plausible one. The desperate appeals of the wily editor, Mayo claims, "were an attempt to apply public pressure on her to surrender her professional status" (316). Coming to the realization that she, a writer of considerable reputation, was being asked to work *gratis* for "a very lucrative publishing enterprise" (313), she was naturally offended, and abandoned both the project and her public correspondence with the *Lady's Magazine.*

About a decade later Reeve had another very public disagreement—this time with another writer of repute—in the pages of the *Gentleman's Magazine.* Anna Seward (1742–1809), the poet, letter-writer, and so-called "Swan of Lichfield," wrote a letter to the editor in September of 1785 taking issue with Reeve's *Progress of Romance.* Her review faults Reeve for her choices of the "best" novels and romances, and Seward even widens the scope of her criticism by damning Reeve with faint praise, asserting that "though, in her former publications, this ingenious lady has displayed great merit, to none of them the present is inferior."[23] A letter Seward wrote for the January 1786 issue of the *Gentleman's Magazine* is even more slighting of Reeve as a critical thinker. Again dwelling on what she sees as the egregious error of Reeve's claim, in the *Progress,* that Samuel Richardson's *Pamela* is his *chef d'oeuvre,* Seward complains that "the press teems with the monsters of unfeeling criticism," uncharitably numbering Reeve among them. Nor is the rest of the remainder of the letter any less harsh in its judgment of the author of the *Progress.*

> She is ridiculous enough to place Richardson's two immortal works, *Grandison,* and *Clarissa,* below his perishable *Pamela* . . . The *English Baron,* its author well knows, is better written than *Pamela,* that dim dawn of an illustrious genius, and the heart of Clara Reeves [sic], less candid and sincere than her imagination is happy, with the co-operation of that eternal misleader self-conceit, suggested this too common practice of disingenuous spirits, to attempt the degradation of a superior writer, by extolling a work of his, which they know they can *themselves* excel, *above* those *higher* efforts of his genius, which they feel unattainable . . . No person endowed with any refinement of perception, any accuracy of judgment, can think *Pamela* superior to *Grandison,* and *Clarissa* (16).

Disregarding Seward's left-handed compliment of *The Old English Baron,* Reeve was clearly upset by the low valuation of both her ethics and her critical judgment skills, and, as soon as she had been alerted to the existence of Seward's letter by "a friend, who thought [she] ought to know how very rudely [she] was treated in it," she responded to the charges lodged against her in an equally public manner. Writing to the editors of the *Gentleman's Magazine,* she expresses her concern over seeing her name "so freely treated" in the pages of their publication, and, though she admits that she "would rather avoid than seek a contest of this kind," she encloses a measured answer to Seward's criticism to be printed in a subsequent issue. John Nichols and John Bowyer Nichols, the editors of the *Gentleman's Magazine* at the time, eventually published Reeve's rebuttal in February 1786.

She begins by expressing her dismay over being "called to the disagreeable task of speaking publicly in [her] own defense" (117), adding that her hesitation was overcome by the certainty that the charges brought against her by an "unmerciful critic" were completely unfounded. Her attacker (Reeve never mentions Seward's name), she marvels, "charges me with disingenuousness, and a design to mislead the judgment of others; a fault of a much higher nature, which I shall not take to myself while I have the power to prove myself innocent of it" (117). The proof that she gives of her "integrity" and "veracity" is compelling: having been the intimate of Richardson's own daughter Martha for many years, she asked Mrs. Bridgen about her opinion of *The Progress of Romance,* in particular the part relating to her famous father. Bridgen's response having been a positive one, Reeve asks, "Is it likely that the daughter of Mr. Richardson should be less jealous of his reputation than a stranger, who takes, uncalled upon, the liberty to defend what has never been called in question?" (118). Though the writer of the vituperative comments in the *Gentleman's Magazine* is well known to Reeve, she closes with a remark to the editor that suggests otherwise. "You will please to observe, Sir," she closes, "that I have addressed my reply as to a man; for I cannot conceive it possible that so much malevolence, with so little delicacy, could proceed from the pen of one of my own sex" (118). Taking the enterprise of novel-writing so seriously, Reeve thus cannot allow the public suggestion that she is a mere impostor—a fraud with literary aspirations but no critical acumen, without direction or, perhaps most importantly, moral purpose—to stand unchallenged.

Though the magazines gave Reeve the opportunity to cement her status as a professional writer, she nonetheless deplored some of their practices. In the *Progress* she includes a short exchange between her two speakers about the persons who extract portions from new fiction to put in magazines, oftentimes without the permission of the author.

> *Hortensius.* Is it not equally injurious to Authors, to publish extracts of books in magazines and other periodical publications?
> *Euphrasia.* Certainly.—And unless I am mistaken, the method I propose would put an end to these pilfering practices, for so they deserve to be called. (II. 47)

As Robert Mayo notes, Reeve was later to suffer from these dishonest "pilfering practices" herself: In September 1791 *Monthly Extracts* printed a piece called "Memoirs of the House of Marny," which was taken directly from Reeve's just-published *School for Widows* (248).

Such problems were perhaps the incidental consequences of being an author favored by the public, and though Reeve seems to have considered them as such, she was sufficiently concerned with her reputation as a writer and as an inculcator of morals to be extremely cautious in her dealings with the magazines in the following years.

The Later Novels

The Two Mentors (1783) was published during the same year that her mother, Hannah Smithies Reeve, died. After the great critical and popular acclaim that her first novel garnered, it is perhaps natural that her next attempt did not measure up to her readers' expectations. Basically, the tale is an examination of two paths to "education": the education—represented by the Lord Chesterfield–like Richard Munden—a young man gets through immersion in the fashionable world, according to which he is encouraged to give in to any and all pleasures, and the education—represented by the Reverend Jarvis Johnson—that a youth gains through the "private cultivation of social and domestic virtues." Reeve's hero, Edward Saville, chooses the right path, of course, and serves as an example of the true "friend of virtue" to Reeve's readers.

While *The Two Mentors* does contain many of Reeve's characteristic didactic admonitions about the danger of allowing passion to supersede reason, and ends with a typically self-righteous speech from Edward, who reflects, "There is no reliance but upon the friends of Virtue . . . Virtue is the only thing certain upon earth" (315), it is the novel's less upstanding characters that capture the reader's imagination and drive the plot. Though Reeve cannot be said to be espousing the principles of the decadent Munden, she nonetheless makes of him such a compelling, charismatic figure that the virtuous, prudent Reverend Johnson seems a colorless prig by comparison. Likewise her representation of the wicked Lady Bellmour, with whom Edward is initially fascinated, emphasizes the woman's powerful magnetism. Despite the fact that he derides her as "the female Machiavel" (286), he acknowledges that she is attractive ("about 40, fat, fine and graceful") and that her power is such that "when she tries to please she is almost irresistible" (26). The skillful drawing of the less-than-virtuous characters, then, combined with the large amount of dramatic incident makes *The Two Mentors* one of Reeve's most compelling novels. It was widely read in her time, and its influence can be traced in later works; for example, the Bennets, the Lucases, the Collinses, and the Elliots all find their way into the pages of *The Two Mentors*, so it would be safe to assume that one of Reeve's readers was Jane Austen.[24]

THE PROGRESS OF ROMANCE

> It has been the most unfortunate of any of my publications, altho it has cost me more time & labour than any other, and in my estimation it is of more value than all the rest.
> —Clara Reeve to Joseph Cooper Walker

Reeve's next literary endeavor was her theoretical study of the development of the novel, *The Progress of Romance Through Times, Countries, and Manners; with Remarks on the Good and Bad Effects of It, on them Respectively; In a Course of Evening Conversations* (1785), first published by William Keymer in Colchester. As Reeve's own novels show, she was very concerned with the moral duty of the novelist, and using the form of a conversation between friends in the *Progress*, she clearly enunciates her theories on a writer's responsibility, citing Samuel Richardson as being among the best of all authors. "The great and important duty of a writer is, to point out the difference between Virtue and Vice, to show one rewarded, and the other punished," Reeve writes, and she highly favored Richardson's *Pamela*—controversially preferring it to *Clari-*

ssa—for this reason. Given the likelihood of Reeve's having experienced domestic service firsthand, her strong feeling of kinship with Pamela is understandable. "The Originality, the beautiful simplicity of the manners and language of the charming maid," she writes of Richardson's virtuous title character, "are interesting past expression ... There needs no other proof of a bad and corrupted heart, than its being insensible to the distresses, and incapable to the rewards of virtue" (135). Reeve's own knowledge of the life of servitude may have made her see *Pamela* in a much more realistic light than Richardson's average reader. It is this realism that she praises as one of the most important and pleasing elements of the novel. "The Novel," she attests, "gives a familiar relation of such things, as pass every day before our eyes, such as may happen to our friend, or ourselves; and the perfection of it, is to represent every scene, in so easy and natural a manner, and to make them appear so probable, as to deceive us into a persuasion ... that all is real, until we are affected by the joys or distresses, of the persons in the story, as if they were our own" (111).

This is not to say that realism alone is the criterion according to which a novel should be evaluated. Reeve, always concerned with morality, warns against books like Rousseau's *Heloise,* that are "dangerous ... to put into the hands of youth," for they "awaken and nourish those passions, which it is the exercise of Reason, and of Religion also, to regulate, and to keep within their true limits" (II. 17). The warning against allowing oneself to be governed by one's passions comes up frequently in all of Reeve's novels, as well as in her poetry and criticism, and the novels that she praises most energetically in the *Progress* are those in which heroes or heroines display admirable fortitude and rationality in the face of moral temptation (e.g., Richardson's *Pamela,* the work of Madame de Genlis, and the later novels of Eliza Haywood).

Paying particular attention to the works of other women writers, Reeve strives to emphasize the importance and cultural value of what novelists are doing. In spite of the novel's often being an object of derision as a women's genre, Reeve suggests that the form is "equally entitled to our attention and respect" (xvi) with her publication of the *Progress,* which, according to Gary Kelly, works toward establishing "the cultural, intellectual, and literary importance of women in the past."[25]

Although Reeve was quite proud of *The Progress of Ro-*

mance, she apparently did not profit financially from its publication. She accounts for this by faulting the London publishers. "I printed it in the country," she explains, "and my Printer [William Keymer] relied upon his correspondent in town to give it the proper circulation.—The London Publishers will not push a work so printed, because they wish to keep the trade entirely in their own hands."[26] As a result, Reeve suggests, *The Progress* was not circulated at all, and thus failed to garner the commercial success that it should have.

The History of Charoba

> This curious story will sufficiently answer my purpose, if it only furnishes an additional proof that Romances are of universal growth, and not confined to any particular periods or countries.
> —from Reeve's preface to *The Progress of Romance* (1785)

Published in tandem with her *Progress* was Reeve's *History of Charoba, Queen of Aegypt*, an adaptation of an Egyptian romance. Originally included in Murtada ibn al-Khafif's history of Egypt, which had been translated into English by John Davies and published as *The Egyptian History, treating of the Pyramids, the inundation of the Nile and other Prodigies, According to the Opinions and Traditions of the Arabians* in 1672, the story of Charoba told by Reeve is substantially altered, in form and content. It describes the wise and benevolent rule of one of Reeve's trademark strong, single women. Charoba is the daughter of Totis, King of Egypt, a ruler who Reeve tells us was more feared than beloved. When he dies, Charoba is made queen—in spite of naysayers who are set against a female ruler—and as she is ingenious, "of a generous spirit," "of great capacity and ingenuity," and yet also "always endeavoring to prevent the shedding of blood" (unlike her father); she reigns wisely and happily for many years. This blissful existence is destroyed when the aggressive King Gebirus enters Egypt, with the threat that if Charoba does not marry him—thus making him King of Egypt—his army will divert the course of the Nile, causing the Egyptians to die of famine. With the assistance of her intelligent, loyal, female servants, Charoba devises a scheme to best Gebirus, poisoning all of his armies at a great banquet, and finally throwing a "gift" of a fine piece of (poisoned) tapestry over the king's shoulders. Despite his bitter last words against her, the magnanimous Charoba at first accedes to Gebirus's last wish that he have certain words of warning engraved on a pillar ("Whoever is desirous to be great and to prosper . . . Yet, let him put no trust in a woman"), but then decides that she will have her own words engraved instead: "This is the fate of such men as would compel Queens to marry them, and Kingdoms to receive them for their Kings" (132).

Like many of Reeve's female characters, Charoba chooses to remain single throughout her life. Despite receiving many "offers of friendship and alliance," Reeve writes, the queen "remained a virgin to the end of her life," and her successor, Queen Dalica—an equally great ruler—"died also a virgin" (136). Reeve underscores this aspect of the "curious story" of Charoba, highlighting the values of female self-reliance and independence that later figure so prominently in *The School for Widows*.

Reeve's preface to *The Exiles* (1788) describes what was to be her next published novel, a "*Ghost* story" called *Castle Connor—an Irish Story*. The manuscript was sent to London by the Ipswich Blue Coach, Reeve writes, but it was apparently lost, for, "it was never received by the person to whom it was sent." She seems highly suspicious of what is behind this "loss," and takes the opportunity in her preface to warn potential pirates that "if it ever appears in print during her life, under whatsoever form, or with whatever alteration, she will lay claim to it . . . will detect the piracy, and expose the pirates to view" (xix).

She recovered from her disappointment over the lost *Castle Connor* very quickly, however, coming out with the most unabashedly sentimental of her novels, *The Exiles; or The Memoirs of the Count de Cronstadt,* just a year later. A tragic tale of bigamy greatly influenced by the French sentimental writers Prévost and Baculard d'Arnaud, *The Exiles* chronicles—through a series of letters—the experiences of three friends of "cultivated minds and enlarged hearts," focusing on the unfortunate and passionate German, Frederic de Cronstadt. Frederic, whose parents are dead, is reared by his uncle, a man who is obsessed with "chymistry"—that is, alchemy—and who spends his days trying to turn metal into gold, to discover the elixir of life, and the like, instead of caring for the emotional and ethical development of his young charge. Reeve is very critical of this type of dreamer; Robert Bartlett in *Destination* is a similar character, and he comes to a similarly unhappy end.

Frederic's uncle warns him against women, who are "disposed to evil naturally" (53), and threatens to cut Frederic off if he should ever decide to marry without his own approval. Unconcerned, Frederic leaves for his Grand Tour. Crossing through a wood while in Germany, he comes across a woman being attacked, and prevents the rape. The young peasant woman, Jacquelina Volker, is of course lovely and virtuous, and the two promptly fall in love. This is the beginning of Frederic's tragedy, Reeve suggests. In falling in love with a woman of an inferior social class he is upsetting the pre-ordained order of things, and disaster is thus inevitable. Even poor Jacquelina's mother disapproves of the match; there is "no happiness to be found in marriages of unequal stations" (151), she laments. Likewise, Cronstadt's friend Berenstein lectures him on the dangers of marrying into inferior ranks, with a statement that Reeve endorses frequently elsewhere in her writings. "Providence," Berenstein warns his friend, "which governs the world, has ordained a subordination of ranks and degrees of men, which must be preserved; or . . . all would be anarchy and confusion" (54). Berkeley, another of Cronstadt's well-meaning friends (and a mouthpiece for Reeve's theories of behavior), tells the love-struck count that "it is necessary to keep [the passions] at all times in subjection to reason; and if we give them the rein, they lead us astray from reason, duty, and happiness" (245).

Despite all the words of advice to the contrary, Cronstadt secretly marries his Jacquelina, and they have a son. Soon after, he leaves to take his place in the military, where he earns distinction and the attention of his General, who happens to have an unattached daughter. Cronstadt and the daughter—Melusina—are mutually attracted, and the General approves, for the two are of the same class; but the shadow of Jacquelina looms in the background. It is not long, though, before Cronstadt begins rationalizing that he "might consider Jacquelina . . . [his] wife of the left hand, and take Melusina as the wife of [his] rank and consequence" (204). The already disastrous situation becomes increasingly so, and by the novel's end Jacquelina, Cronstadt, and his uncle have all died prematurely, thus supporting Reeve's theory about the need to subdue the passions, and to be ruled by the head instead of the heart.

Three of her subsequent works dealt with a subject always

important to Reeve: education—particularly the education of women. Besides *The School for Widows* (1791), its strange nonfiction sequel, *Plans of Education* (1792), is often directly didactic, and emphasizes Reeve's perennial promotion of sensibility, the social virtues, and egalitarian marriages, while simultaneously suggesting the greater stability and freedom that women can find in the single life.

Apparently, Reeve also became interested in politics at this time, so much so that she felt compelled to write a misguided pamphlet in which she argued against the "anti-saccharites" who refused to buy West Indian sugar because doing so supported the slave trade. This pamphlet, as well as a chapter on the "advantages" of slavery in *Plans of Education* may be attributed to Reeve's sheltered life and total ignorance of the slave trade and its consequences, and to what can only be described as a willful blindness to problems or crises outside of her sphere. For a writer who makes such a strong point of endorsing foreign travel and whose heroes are often described positively as "citizens of the world," her lack of awareness of the evil consequences of slavery outside of England seems unconscionable to the modern reader.

Perhaps a lack of discernment with respect to her friends and kin may be to blame; the information Reeve is working from regarding slavery is gleaned from men and women of her own class (at this stage in her life primarily the gentry), some of whose fortunes are tied up with the trafficking of slaves, and who thus naturally have an ulterior motive for telling her the slaves are "happy and protected." Reeve does not seem to have considered this possibility, or to have questioned her "friends'" account at all, which is unfortunate for her in the eyes of posterity.

One must keep in mind, however, that Reeve's opinion on slavery was a perfectly normal and acceptable one for the time in which she was writing. For example, James Boswell, at roughly the same time (1791), describes his differing opinion on the issue with Samuel Johnson in his *Life of Johnson*. Despite the fact that he and Johnson had several arguments about slavery during which he acknowledges that Johnson made valid points, Boswell's opinion about the slave trade, he says, "is unshaken," and he cannot understand his wise friend's support of the "wild and dangerous attempt" being made "to obtain an act of . . . Legislature, to abolish so very important and necessary a branch of commercial interest" (155). Like Reeve,

Boswell is under the false but apparently widespread impression that the "peculiar institution" is beneficial to its subjects. "To abolish a *status*," he writes,

> which in all ages GOD has sanctioned, and man has continued, would not only be *robbery* to an innumerable class of our fellow-subjects; but it would be extreme cruelty to the African Savages, a portion of whom it saves from massacre, or intolerable bondage in their own country, and introduces into a much happier state of life (156).

Reeve's beliefs on the abolition of slavery, then, though mistaken, were quite conventional for the time.

Again enunciating her political ideas, but combining them with the indulgence of her love for history, Reeve's next novel, *The Memoirs of Sir Roger de Clarendon, the natural Son of Edward Prince of Wales, Commonly Called the Black Prince* (1793), gives a fictionalized account of the history of Edward, while celebrating medieval times and what Reeve saw as the advantages of the feudal system. In her preface she describes her goal in writing *Sir Roger,* which is twofold: to record the exploits of worthy men for her present audience, and to present "a faithful picture of a well-governed kingdom, wherein a true subordination of ranks and degrees was observed" (xvi). Essentially, then, the novel is an exercise in nostalgia for "a better age," carrying an implicit warning against what Reeve saw as the dangerous excesses of the French revolution. *Sir Roger* contains indictments of the beheaders of Charles I, the fanaticism of Cromwell, and Charles II ("unprincipled, extravagant, profligate and abandoned") alike, but the greatest attack is left for "those who would seduce [the poor] to worship the idol *Equality,* which, if it could be introduced, would reduce them to indolence and despondency." These seducers are so dangerous, claims Reeve, because they conceal the fact that that "a true and regular subordination is what makes all orders and degrees of men stand in need of each other, and stimulates them to exercise their courage, industry, activity, and every generous quality, that supports a state and government" (III. 222). Closing with an explicit warning to England against the egalitarian principles of the French revolution, Reeve advises, "Let Britain shudder at the scene before her, and grasp her blessings the closer" (III. 231).

With Reeve's last published novel, *Destination; or, Memoirs of a Private Family* (1799), she returns to her focus on the education of youth, attacking the philosophies of Rousseau and emphasizing the need to guide children firmly in the "direction of their natural capacities." Two of her most appealing and interesting characters appear in *Destination*: retired businessman and benefactor Arthur Ashford, "a true citizen of the world and the friend of mankind," and his ward Arthur Stanmore. As a boy Arthur hates Latin and Greek, and leaves school (with Ashford's blessing) for a life of commerce and adventure in India. Achieving success as a diamond merchant, Arthur is the quintessential Whig; Reeve even has him spouting such propagandistic declarations as "Trade may sometimes be sick, but it can never die" (I. 97). When he inadvertently becomes embroiled in Indian politics, though, Arthur changes his idealistic view of trade. Recognizing the abuse of the natives that is carried out by the East India Company, he antagonizes his superiors by championing the cause of the oppressed "Hindoos" (eventually marrying a native woman) and leaves the Company in disgust, striking out on his own. Ultimately Arthur becomes a prosperous gem-merchant, but his views of commerce are somewhat altered; his dealings with the East India Company have taught him about the abuses that are possible in trade when one of the parties engaged is corrupt. Reeve uses Arthur, though, to represent the "good Whig"—the wealthy businessman who cares for those with whom he trades and works, and who is both culturally sensitive and firm in his religious convictions, for "[Christianity] embraces the whole race of mankind, and universal charity and benevolence are the first proofs of its influence upon the hearts of men" (I.235). Thus, though Reeve makes Arthur a "citizen of the world," she emphasizes that he also lives according to his belief that Christianity is the "true faith."

After *Destination* there may have been another novel, for in a letter to her publishers, dated 1 September 1802, Reeve complains of a long delay in the publication of her "little work, The Story of Edwin." Her friends, she claims, are becoming impatient. Although the manuscript to which she is referring has unfortunately been lost, the surviving letter tells us that Reeve continued her literary output in the years following *Destination*.

Personal details about Reeve's later life are scarce. A portrait of her exists, and the figure represented fits with the description of an Ipswichian who remembered her as "of middle stature, stout in proportion, and having all the appearance of a matronly woman."[27] In a letter written late in her life Reeve describes herself—with characteristic forthrightness—as being

> An old woman, who though not any way deformed, was never handsome . . . Of the middle size, rather square sterned & Dutch built. A round face rather flat & unmeaning, unless when warmed with an interesting subject, but then does not want animation. Dark grey eyes, and hair that was once a middling brown, but now grizzle, and powdered to make it all of a colour. Her style of dress the most plain & simple, and would be nearly that of a Quaker, but does not affect singularity . . . A series of disappointments and mortifications have given a cast of care to her brow, which otherwise would have had more of the look of Thalia than Melpomene.[28]

She was also known for her "very elegant and curious collection of shells,"[29] which had been amassed over a span of thirty years. Writing to fellow collector Thomas Percy in April of 1785, Reeve charts her development from casual collector to avid reader about "marine curiosities," to scientific studier and classifier of shells. The urge to classify, order, and rank seems to have run strong in Reeve, for she is just as adamant about placing each of her shells in the correct species[30] as she is about the ordering of social classes. Reeve thus suggests that any mixing of the categories, or blurring of the boundaries between persons, classes or even objects, results in chaos.

A Continuous Process of Self-Education: Reeve's Reading

> It is incumbent on all parents, guardians, and perceptors, to give young people a taste for good reading, to let them read nothing but what is excellent of its kind, and by thus forming their taste, to teach them to despise paltry books of every kind.
> —Reeve's preface to *The Old English Baron*

Clara Reeve lived a very quiet and unassuming life, as critics and scholars from Sir Walter Scott to Janet Todd are quick to point out, and it is easy to underestimate her work and ideas for that reason. The secluded life suited her, however; it was a *choice* rather than a burden. In October of 1804 she described her solitary existence to her friend, the Irish antiquarian Joseph Cooper Walker (1761–1810), contrasting herself with her sisters who, she writes, "keep much company." She continues,

> I have renounced Cards, and that leaves me in quiet. Ipswich is become a Garrison town, very full of people, every thing in it very dear. I have a tolerable Collection of Books, and am in my third Edition of Spectators. I ought to be thankful that I can read at all, for that is a part of my daily bread.

So vital to Reeve's existence is reading at this time in her life that she sees her books as providing the sustenance necessary for her survival. Indeed, Reeve appears to have read widely and with discernment throughout her life, even during the periods when she was plagued by familial crises and financial worries.

In addition to her beloved *Spectators*; the lifelong interest in history, politics, and biography which began with her early reading of Parliamentary proceedings; Rapin; John Trenchard and Thomas Gordon's *Cato's Letters* (1720–1723); and Plutarch under the tutelage of her father; dramatic work of her own and the previous century seems to have been especially fascinating to Reeve. She was apparently a great reader of Shakespeare, quoting liberally throughout *The School for Widows* from *The Tempest, Othello, Timon of Athens, Hamlet,* and *A Midsummer Night's Dream*. Her novels provide evidence that she enjoyed later and less-canonical plays as well, for, in *The School for Widows* alone, quotations can be traced to James Shirley's *Gratefull Servant* (1629); Thomas Southerne's *Fatal Marriage* (1694); *Hurlothrumbo* (1729) by Samuel Johnson of Cheshire; Edward Moore's sentimental drama about the evils of gambling, *The Gamester* (1753); Moses Mendez's *Double Disappointment* (1760); and George Farquhar's *The Twin Rivals* (1703).

Reeve also demonstrates a knowledge of and fondness for the fiction and poetry of her time. Her admiration for Walpole's *Otranto* (and also her objection to it) has been well documented, and she refers to the "indisputable merits" of his *Mysterious Mother* as well, though she is doubtful about its being "fit to meet the public eye . . . of female youth particularly" because of her belief that "ignorance of vice is certainly one of the guards against it," and that "there are some unnatural crimes that should be thought impossible."[31] In *The School for Widows* she also refers to Sterne's *Sentimental Journey* (1768), and quotes selectively from the poems of Ben Jonson, Alexander Pope, John Dryden, William Shenstone, and especially those of John Milton. Her letters to Joseph Cooper Walker attest to her lifelong fondness and enthusiasm for lyric poetry in particular. The short stories she seems to have read with the most interest are, characteristically, those that are the most concerned with the reader's moral education. The works of Madame Stephanie-Felicité de Genlis (1746–1830)—educator and woman of letters—and the *Contes Moraux* of Jean-Francois Marmontel (1723–1799) figure largely in *The School for Widows*.

The most obvious influence of Reeve's reading on her writing of the novel, though, undoubtedly comes from the Bible. Her virtuous characters pepper their speech with references to specific passages (Genesis, Proverbs, and 1 Corinthians in particular), and Reeve's prose at times takes on biblical cadences, suggesting that her reading of the Bible was so frequent, and so much a part of her daily life, that she had—unconsciously or consciously—absorbed some of the book's stylistic elements and incorporated them into her own writing. Just as she gained intellectual sustenance from her reading of histories or her translations from French and Latin, her Bible-reading seems to have been a crucial aid in sustaining her morally and emotionally, especially in her later life.

Reeve's Retirement from Literary Life: Reflection and Correspondence

In a letter sent just three years before her death, Reeve communicated to Walker her decision to withdraw from public life, which seems to correspond with her decision that "writing for the press is out of the question." She writes as a woman in her late seventies, satisfied with her life and with the quality of her work. Though she will continue "scribbling" (she tells Walker she has several drawers full of manuscripts), she feels no need—financial or otherwise—to continue to publish. Pleased that Dudley Bate, the editor of the *Morning Herald*, has spoken of her in his "list of scribbling ladies, in a way that does [her] honour," she politely refuses Walker's request for additional material from her, telling him "I am satisfied & thankful for the compliment & will not hazard any abatement of it."[32] Despite her insistence that she will not publish again, Reeve retains an active interest in the new publications of other novelists, debating their merits spiritedly with her friend Walker.

This correspondence reveals unexpected aspects of Reeve; she is by turns thoughtful, playful, humorous, and tolerant. She addresses a variety of topics with Walker, clearly comfortable communicating her feelings and opinions to him about politics, history, the state of English society, and the difficulty of dealing with publishers.

Continually returning to this last topic, she complains to Walker about Charles Dilly, whom she says has used her "barbarously," referring to him as "one of the men who have gained by [her] writings, and would starve the Author"[33] and in a later letter as a "Harpy."[34] Her relationship with her next publisher, Thomas Hookham, appears to have been much more amicable, although he eventually comes in for criticism as well. By September 1792 she is declaring herself "very much dissatisfied" with Hookham, and later that same month she even goes so far as to ask Walker to intervene with the publisher on her behalf, for she has already attempted to address her points of contention with him[35] to no avail. "Men of this profession are inclined to treat our sex *en Cavalier*," she writes to Walker, "but to a gentleman they will behave in a different manner."[36] It appears that Reeve's level of satisfaction with Hookham rose substantially in the following months, although subsequent letters still accuse him of showing "unparalleled negligence" and of being "asleep" and "in lethargies" when he ought to be getting her novels out to the public. Never mincing words in her letters to Walker, she makes her conclusive statement on her experience of London booksellers, lamenting, "A woman is under many disadvantages in treating with the London publishers, they are the most insolent, greedy, & oppressive set of men, that can be met with."[37]

She is similarly forthcoming with her friend regarding her political opinions. Nearly always shying away from overt discussion of matters of state in her novels, Reeve occasionally gives the impression that she is blissfully unaware of the political upheaval that is occurring around her. Her letters to Walker paint a very different picture of a woman with definite convictions. Having imbibed certain unshakeable principles from her early reading, including "a love of liberty, a hatred of Tyranny, an affection to the race of mankind, a wish to support their rights & properties," she nonetheless is deeply saddened by the French Revolution.

"My politics are all overthrown," she tells her friend, "France has ruined herself and hurt all the other countries of Europe.—She has strengthened the hands of the enemies of liberty, who will now boldly assert, that mankind are not to be trusted with it." Warning Walker not to go to France, she adds, much discouraged, "They have pulled down the citadel of despotism, the Bastille, and with the materials have built a Bastille for their King."[38] Clearly not hopeful about the prospect of the establishment of a settled form of government in France, she deplores the taking of extreme positions—on either side—and argues in favor of moderation and reason. "I cannot guess," she muses gloomily, "how the mania of the French will end." She is decisive, however in her evaluation of the present form of government in France, proclaiming that "it is not of God, and therefore it cannot stand."[39]

She is equally concerned that the climate of unrest and instability has infected England, where she has observed some of the same inequalities that brought about the revolution in France. "Our wounds here are skinned over," she writes Walker, "and look as if they were healed; but I fear they rankle underneath, and will break out again." Her letters attest to the fact that the political situation was indeed of great moment to Reeve's life; she openly expresses her apprehension to Walker, which reveals just how close she felt England was to an eruption of violence. "I am frightened at the prospect before me, and have thought of putting off my house, and going to board in a family," she tells him, where she feels she might be "under protection in case of dangers of every kind."[40]

Deeply appalled by what she sees as the sorry state of human affairs, Reeve finally is compelled to question the value of her own endeavours on the part of her fellow human beings. Her description to Walker of the process of her disillusionment is a strikingly poignant:

> At our first entrance into life, warmed with the love of virtue and of truth, we think mankind only want to be shewn the light of one, and the beauty of the other, to receive and embrace them.—Alas! The more we know of human nature, the more we perceive the perverseness of it.—Bewildered in the mazes of error, and blinded by passions and prejudices, men shut their eyes against the light of truth, and turn aside to avoid being dazzled by it.[41]

Despite the pessimistic view of human nature that age, experience, and the course of the French revolution, in particular, gave her, however, Reeve continued to read and to write, and to believe that a life spent working in the service of generosity, prudence, self-reliance, and above all reason, was a life well-lived.

The Final Years

> I am now in my native place, where my family have resided several Centuries, & been free Burghers ever since the first Charter, and I believe I am in the Place where I ought to be.
> —Reeve to Joseph Cooper Walker

Loyal and affectionate to family and friends, Reeve had the misfortune to outlive many of those to whom she was closest: her father, mother, and her brother Samuel all died before she did, as did close friend of the family Reverend Samuel Darby. Having achieved a measure of critical, popular and financial success (the last very late in her life), Reeve lived on quietly for eight years after the publication of her last novel. She died, intestate, at the advanced age of 78 on 3 December 1807 in Ipswich, and was buried in St. Stephen's churchyard. In a letter to Joseph Cooper Walker three years before her death Reeve writes of having been ill with "an epidemical complaint" and having grown "old and infirm." Her obituary in *The Monthly Mirror* states that she "had long suffered a painful and lingering illness: and in the early stages of it retained her *literary* perseverance,"[42] thus suggesting that Reeve's lack of literary output for the last eight years of her life was in part due to her poor health.

Reviews and Reception: Popular and Critical Perceptions of Clara Reeve

> The approbation of the worthy and the sensible part of mankind is the first pleasure of my life, and when my labours are thought of value by them, they receive their full reward, and cheer the heart of their Author.
> —Reeve to Joseph Cooper Walker

Reeve was generally respected by critics for her intentions, if not always admired for her execution. Her obituary in the

Monthly Mirror gave her high marks for her "strong, clear, and well cultivated understanding" as well as for her "good principles and correct taste" (451). More recently, her biographer in the *East Anglian Daily Times* lauded her as being a "worthy and talented woman" (1941, #10,764). During her own lifetime, though, she was praised primarily for *The Old English Baron*. The *Monthly Review* called the novel "an imitation of ancient romance" and described it as being "agreeable and capable of rousing the reader's feelings." The *Critical Review* called the *Old English Baron* "no common novel" and, as many others did, compared it to *Otranto*. Many modern critics, however, find fault even with this most famous of Reeve's novels. Mark Madoff echoes Horace Walpole himself when he claims that the world represented in the *Old English Baron* is "idyllic yet dull. Reeve reduces the myth of gothic splendor and superiority until it is insipid." Nevertheless, he adds, the novel "reached a large audience, reinforced earlier gothic work, and acquired a school of imitators," and thus "cannot be dismissed" (337–50). This low estimation seems to be a widely held modern perception of the *Old English Baron*, and of Reeve's work in general. Even James Trainer, editor of the Oxford 1967 *Old English Baron*, faults Reeve slightly for the fear of change, decay, and immorality in society that he implies informed all her novels, often to their disadvantage. Her later works, Trainer explains, "reveal a surprising versatility with Gothic, historical, and contemporary novels, but her increasing determination 'to support the cause of morality, to reprove vice, and to promote all the social and domestic virtues' detracted from her skill as story-teller and frightened rather than attracted her public" (xiii).

Trainer's evaluation of the public's reaction to Reeve's overt support of Christian morality in her novels is highly debatable. Indeed, her moral *intention* seems to be the only thing for which her critics did *not* fault her. Many, like an anonymous reviewer in *The British Critic*, admired her aims, but disliked her technique. "We naturally feel impatient," the reviewer wrote, referring to *The Memoirs of Sir Roger de Clarendon*, "at toiling through what neither informs as history, nor delights as fiction. The morality may be well intended; but morality alone, though itself among the best things, cannot support a novel."[43] This opinion was typical of the majority of Reeve's readers, especially where *The Memoirs of Sir Roger de Clarendon* was concerned.

In other cases, though, critics revealed a sensitivity to and understanding of the uniqueness of Reeve's stylistic approach. The editors of *The Critical Review,* writing about *Destination* in their September 1799 issue, made the assessment that "the incidents, though neither affecting nor uncommon, are so likely to have happened, and the characters bear such a resemblance to many which we meet in the walks of life, that we perused the work with the pleasure of a calm unagitated curiosity" (115). This positive evaluation of Reeve's narrative was shared by the editors of the *Monthly Mirror,* who praise *Destination* for its "interesting and affecting situations," as well as for its "smart" and "often witty" dialogue,[44] though it must be noted that most modern assessments of the novel are less certain about its emotional affectivity.

Another common perception held by both Reeve's contemporaries and many modern critics is that nothing she did after the *Old English Baron* measured up to that first foray into novel writing. The same anonymous reviewer in *The British Critic* who panned *The Memoirs of Sir Roger de Clarendon* claims that after the *Old English Baron*, with novels such as *The Two Mentors* and *The Exiles*, "the name of Clara had lost all its magic, and could no longer attract"(385). Sir Walter Scott, while praising the fact that all Reeve's novels show "excellent good sense, pure morality, and a competent command of those qualities which constitute a good romance" makes a similarly negative comment about the novels she wrote subsequent to the *Old English Baron*, none of which show, he claims, "the possession of a rich or powerful imagination." He continues in this vein, "Her dialogue is sensible, easy, and agreeable, but neither is marked by high flights of fancy, nor strong bursts of passion" (177).

Reception of *The School for Widows*

Scott's comment is partially true with regard to *The School for Widows*, in which the dialogue between the women is unquestionably "sensible, easy, and agreeable," and there are very few "flights of fancy." Indeed, Reeve's characters, Frances and Rachel, like their creator, have little time or inclination to indulge in imaginative caprices. They are too busy making their way in a society that holds older women—particularly those without money—in low esteem. The one character that does indulge her imagination and briefly live in a world of fancy, Isabella di Soranzo, is portrayed as delusional. Giving free rein to the imagination, Reeve thus implies, brings on emotional trauma, at least, and ultimately can lead to total self-destruction, as it almost does in Isabella's case. Frances Darnford's sensible and *practical* presence is the only "treatment" successful in bringing the Italian widow back from the brink of complete mental and physical debilitation.

Frank David Kievitt, in his 1980 article on *The School for Widows*, makes the statement that the novel is "very much in the Richardsonian tradition; as the novel's title implies, Reeve sees the purpose of her novel as primarily one of moral education, offering it to her readers not as a curious story but as a guide to behavior"(84). It is true that Richardson had great influence on Reeve, as he did on many other women writers, including Eliza Fenwick (*Secresy*, 1795), Anna Maria Bennett (*Agnes De-Courci*, 1789), and Elizabeth Griffith (*The Delicate Distress*, 1769). Isobel Grundy, tracing Richardson's influence on women's epistolary novels, explains how many women

> found it congenial to work from his ingredients: authorial invisibility; foregrounded female characters; plots of courtship, seduction (threatened or actual), or married relationships; debate on women's education and the roles of daughters, sisters and wives; a morally educative aim; and naked appeal to the reader's emotional susceptibilities.[45]

Clearly many of these elements are present in Reeve's novels, and glancing references to Richardson throughout *The School for Widows,* in particular, often perform the function that Grundy describes as signaling "a note of toughness and moral rigour amid the torrents of feeling."[46]

While the morally rigorous aspect of *The School for Widows* cannot be denied, to imply—as Kievitt does—that Reeve was unconcerned with whether or not she was presenting a "curious story" greatly underestimates Reeve's awareness of her readers. As she herself quoted from *The Trial, or the History of Charles Norton, Esq.* in the *Progress*, "a moral lesson otherwise dry and tedious in itself, might be communicated in a pleasing dress: as a pill has its desired effect, tho' wrapped in a gold or silver leaf." It was admittedly for this reason that she fashioned her theoretical, critical *Progress* in the form of a lively conversation between friends, and she does not neglect the "silver leaf" in *The School for Widows* either. Although the "curious story" is not perhaps as fantastic or as wildly imaginative as many of the other novels that were produced during the last decade of the eighteenth century—one thinks of Elizabeth Inchbald's *Simple Story* (1791) or Ann Radcliffe's *Romance of the Forest* (1792) and *Mysteries of Udolpho* (1794)—Reeve has clearly worked to make her narrative compelling, and the results are highly successful. The reader's attention is held throughout all three volumes by the tragic but all-too-real events that occur in the lives of Reeve's widows, and by the strength of personality—thanks to Reeve's underappreciated gift for characterization—of the three women.

For the most part, critics applauded *The School for Widows* when it first came out. The 1791 *Critical Review* called the tale "pleasing" and "interesting," commenting on the clear discrimination of the characters. "The events [are] natural and well arranged," the reviewer added, and "the reflections [are] judicious and apposite" (477). Some of those critics who could not find fault with her narrative technique, with her dialogue, or with her character development, though, turned to the "philosophy" behind the *School for Widows* as the object of their derision. The *English Review* for 1792 accused Reeve of presenting a skewed view of marriage. "The very *bead and front* of the story tend to inculcate anti-matrimonial sentiments," claimed the reviewer, noting—with no little sarcasm—that, "two widows, Mrs. Strictland and Mrs. Darnford, have both been relieved by death from unworthy husbands, and studiously avoid any second visit to the pale of Hymen" (70). The same reviewer then goes on to make his gender bias even more overt, by complaining about the way the character of Captain Maurice is treated in the novel. "We cannot conceive," he writes, "by what rules of poetical justice Captain Maurice is so punished. His conduct, save in a few instances, is unexceptionable" (70). Maurice's "unexceptionable" conduct includes beating his friend to death and pursuing that friend's grieving widow. It also includes his driving her nearly mad with his persistence, and his forcing her into a marriage to him that she later (to her great relief) discovers was a sham. Nor is Maurice an adequate father. He leaves his illegitimate daughter with others, sailing off, for years at a time, to foreign climes to seek his fortune. In fact, Frances ultimately agrees to take Maurice's daughter under her wing, and the final picture we get of the poor girl's father is a fleeting one of him preparing to embark on yet another journey. Thus the *English Review* was inaccurate in its evaluation of Reeve's treatment of the Captain. Not only is he free and unfettered (as he would have it) by domestic ties at the close of the novel, but he also does not suffer the usual, harsher fate of negligent parents in Reeve's novels. His only punishment, Reeve suggests, is his exclusion from that happy domestic circle formed by Frances, Isabella, and the other women, and it is an exclusion that he himself indirectly chooses.

An anonymous critic in *The Monthly Review*, taking a similarly condescending tone, also focused on Reeve's representation of gender roles, which he clearly perceived as threatening. He went on to criticize the fact that the novel was "offered to the public under a misnomer, it being rather a School for Husbands; those introduced being represented as very naughty boys indeed, while their spouses, both as wives and widows, are strained up to the best of female characters" (466). Such a comment cannot have been made by one who has read *The School for Widows* attentively, however, for many of Reeve's female characters therein are far from ideal. Several mothers are portrayed as harming their children through neglect or, conversely, through over-coddling. Frances Darnford's own sister is coarse and common in her manner of expression, and seems to have very little sense of familial affection or loyalty.

The *Monthly Review* is perhaps more on-target with the accusation of sentimentality on Reeve's part. There are, without a doubt, moments of heavy sentimentality in *The School for Widows*, yet the example the *Review* offers to illustrate this sentimentality is inexplicable. The passage the critic chooses from the novel is concerned with true friendship:

> Adversity is the test of friendship, the trier and purifier of the human heart; not half its virtues would be known or proved without it. *Yet we still* shrink at the thoughts of suffering; *we shudder* at the approach of poverty, we suppose it to be *the greatest of all evils*. (I. 59)

Such a sentiment, the *Review* implies, is ridiculous, and impractical (467). Again, the critic's response suggests an inattention to the ideas expressed in *The School for Widows* as a whole. Rather than advocating poverty as a higher condition of life than affluence, as the *Review* goes on to claim Reeve does, she has her widows stretch the limits of their strength, endurance, and ingenuity in order to avoid being poor. Poverty for these women, as for most women in England during the eighteenth century, means dependence: a word (and state of existence) to which Reeve reveals herself to be much averse. The core message of the "sentimental passage" criticized by the *Review* is not the idealization of poverty, but rather a warning to those who mistakenly see the path toward true friendship as being a smooth one. Like David Simple, Sarah Fielding's aptly named title character (1744), Reeve's Frances must experience the painful results of her misplaced faith in two "friends"—her husband, and Lord A——, her husband's constant companion—before she comes to the realization that finding a genuinely sympathetic soul is a difficult, often dangerous journey. For all its pitfalls, though, it is nonetheless worthwhile: the negative experiences teach Frances, like David, what true friends are *not*, so that she is ultimately able to recognize what they *are* when she enjoys the "true friendship" of fellow widows Rachel and Isabella.

Recent Criticism: *The School for Widows*

> Those critics who make it their business to discover faults in the writings of others depress the efforts of genius, and injure them in the opinion of those who are incapable of forming a judgement themselves.
> —from Reeve's preface to *The Exiles* (1788)

More recent critics have followed in the footsteps of the reviewers of Reeve's day in misreading the author. Both Kievitt and Elizabeth Bergen Brophy, for example, class Reeve as a novelist of simple and austere didacticism. Not only is this position erroneous, but it is unjust to Reeve as writer, for in revealing only half of the picture it propagates misconceptions about both the woman and her work.

Neglecting the progressive themes of *The School for Widows*—supportive friendship between women and female entrepreneurship, among others—and focusing instead on the way that Reeve represents marriage in the novel, Brophy addresses what she sees as Reeve's hesitation to attack the inequality of marriages during the late eighteenth century. Reeve seems to "draw back," claims Brophy, from "the real dilemma that her novel presents," which she sees as being "the miserable plight of a woman who is, through no fault of her own, trapped in a life of unrelenting unhappiness" (186). While praising the *School for Widows* for the detailed picture it gives of marriage,[47] Bergen Brophy implicitly criticizes what she sees as its tacit acceptance of "the established code of wifely submission" to a husband's authority. Reeve presents us with a pair of marriages—Frances's and Rachel's—in which "a good, intelligent and compliant woman is made miserable by her husband despite her wholehearted attempts to please him" (186), and, according to Bergen Brophy, seems to make no protest against the "established code" that creates such situations. In fact, she assesses,

> rather than challenging the legal and social codes which made such situations possible, the work seems closer to a practical guide, reminiscent of the conduct books, giving counsel to those in like marriages. Accommodation and submissiveness, barring only sinful behavior, make life barely tolerable, and one can always hope to be a widow. (186)

While it is true that much of *The School for Widows* carries the tone of a conduct book, Reeve's main characters are far from being "accommodating" or "submissive" in their actions. The practical guidance that Reeve gives her readers is not to submit to mistreatment, or to tolerate cruelty, but rather to use the greatest caution and wisdom in choosing one's partner for life, so as to avoid the pitfalls of her two heroines. Reeve is openly didactic in her warning to young women about the dangers of marrying inappropriately, and she makes the connection (typical of what G. J. Barker-Benfield terms the "Culture of Sensibility") between a virtuous woman and a man's capability of reform. Granted, there is a certain amount of resignation in her tacit assumption that once badly married, a woman must simply try to make the best of her situation. Realistically, however, the alternatives for women like Frances and Rachel (i.e., women of the impoverished gentry) were unappealing. Divorce was nearly impossible, and willful separation from their husbands would open women up to the slights and scornful treatment of society. (For example, immediately after Frances leaves her husband, she is importuned by Lord A——, who takes her husbandless state as a sign of her easy accessibility and availability). When viewed in light of their available options, then, Frances and Rachel's actions *within* the boundaries of their marriages are actually quite openly resistant to the status quo: both women issue their husbands ultimatums concerning their unacceptable behavior. Frances's husband ignores hers, so she leaves him, while Rachel's husband adheres to her list of conditions (if only for a brief period).

Brophy's belief that Reeve advocates female submissiveness in *The School for Widows* is not unique among modern scholars, but I am convinced that it is a mistaken. Widely accepted perceptions of Reeve position her as morally conscious and religiously orthodox, which she certainly *was*, but also as supportive of female social subordination, which I would argue—with *The School for Widows*, among other writings, as evidence—she definitely was not.

In fact, the network of women in *The School for Widows* is reflective of a growing interest in alternative, feminized societies where women could escape both "patriarchal oppression" and "social and financial restraints."[48] Indeed, the idea of a community of women was hardly revolutionary for the time in which Reeve was writing. Authors such as Margaret Cavendish (*The Convent of Pleasure*, 1668), Mary Astell (*A Serious Proposal to the Ladies*, 1697) and Sarah Scott (*Millennium Hall*, 1762) had introduced the idea much earlier. In their study, *Female Communities 1600–1800*, Rebecca D'Monte and Nicole Pohl bring together recent essays on a number of these fictional projections of alternative female communities that highlight their variety as well as their similarities. Many of the fictionalized representations of these female societies, according to D'Monte and Pohl, share associations of sisterhood, female friendship and companionship, and support networks (12). Astell's *Serious Proposal* is essentially a vision of a female monastery, a college founded on the basis of female friendship and devotion. Scott's *Millenium Hall* offers a full fictional realization of Astell's vision, as does her later novel *The History of Sir George Ellison* (1766).

Reeve's community of women, though, is noteworthy for its complete autonomy. Reeve's women do not rely on any male characters in any way; indeed, they *cannot*, as is shown in the cases of the three widows. Instead, the women use their own inner resources—wisdom, kindness, pragmatism, endurance, in Rachel's case a good sense of humor and in Frances's case a good head for business—to keep themselves afloat after the deluges of their respective failed marriages. The three main "widows" are portrayed as growing more useful as they grow older, thus illustrating an idea about older women that was extremely rare during the period in which Reeve was writing.

Reeve's Widows

> The whole world is a single Lady's Family, her opportunities of doing good are not Lessen'd by encreas'd by her being unconfin'd.
> —Mary Astell, *A Serious Proposal*

THE ENTIRE NOVEL IS NARRATED BY THE TWO MAIN WIDOWS, Frances and Rachel, which again speaks to the idea that Reeve was embarked on a project of elevating the status of widowhood. What better way to propose taking a particular class or group of people seriously than by giving them a voice? By placing her narrative under the control of two widows, Reeve gives them importance and provides them with authority, suggesting to her readers that they are crucial members of society and that they *can* in fact handle power (just as Samuel Richardson had done many years earlier for servant girls with his *Pamela*).

In addition to the clever melding of form and content accomplished by Reeve's use of letters in *The School for Widows,* a sense of verisimilitude is established. As Elizabeth Goldsmith notes in her introduction to *Writing the Female Voice* (1989), commentators have claimed—even since the sixteenth century—that the epistolary genre seemed to be "particularly suited to the female voice" (vii). "Newly educated women could easily learn to write letters," she continues, "and, as epistolary theory became more adapted to worldly culture, women's letters began to be considered the best models of the genre" (vii). Reeve follows a tradition, then, already well cemented by the works of novelists like Richardson (with his appropriation of the female voice in both *Pamela* and *Clarissa*), whose employment of letters by female characters gives credence to Goldsmith's assertion that "the female voice was perceived as the superior vehicle of expression, even when it was not from a female author" (55). As April Alliston notes, after Richardson more than 100 novels were written by women who were drawn to the epistolary form, and many of these are works in which the "primary fictional correspondences are exchanged between female characters" (as in *The School for Widows*), and the reader is commonly inscribed as a woman of similar age and status as the heroine.[49]

The letters written by Reeve's widows are centered in domestic matters, which, as Patricia Meyer Spacks notes, is natural in works that are written by people who are "officially relegated to domesticity."[50] *The School for Widows* does not, however, align Reeve with what Spacks discusses as the circle of "typical" eighteenth-century female epistolary novelists, who "eschew conspicuous forms of emotional drama" (Reeve's novel is full of proposal scenes, violent confrontations, and the like), and contain a "troubling message of despair" and a "demonstration of female ineffectuality" (75). Spacks contrasts this self-confining female epistolary tradition with another, more forward-looking movement, with which she associates Jane Austen and her early work *Lady Susan*. Austen, she writes, "understood letters as voice and as action and understood conventions as capable of manipulation. She imagined possibilities of female power within the sphere of the 'private'" (75)—just as did Clara Reeve. The positive outlook of the widows in Reeve's novel—combined with their humor and their facility with language, sends a message that is anything but "desperate." Indeed, Reeve's novel cautions women against submitting to the feelings of desperation and ineffectuality that can, ultimately, be so debilitating.

The School for Widows presents us with three women who not only survive their widowhood, but who use their new condition to become more productive and beneficial members of society. Reeve does not downplay the difficulties with which a widow living in England during the eighteenth century was faced. After all, Reeve's own mother, Hannah Smithies Reeve, suffered financial difficulties as a result of the early death of her husband, and she may have endured some of the same societal misconceptions about what being a widow meant. Indeed, since Reeve herself never married, it would be valid to assume that much of the knowledge that she reveals about the details of widowhood (particularly her solid grasp of financial matters) was gleaned from her both her mother and her sister Lucia Tozer, who lived for many years as a widow.

For whatever reason, Reeve saw the widow's condition as one that was crucial to society as a whole. In *The School for Widows* she mixes her strong moral message—and at times overt didacticism—with a compelling story and attractive characters, as she was wont to do. The novel is openly didactic in its warning to young women about the dangers of marrying inappropriately, and its warning to older married women to be cautious about those in whom they place their trust. The facet of *The School for Widows* that makes the novel truly unusual is its odd, progressive, and very refreshing representation of the three main widows. For Frances, Rachel and Isabella, widowhood is representative of freedom: freedom to act, to have an effect on the world around one, and more importantly freedom to enjoy female friendship. *The School for Widows* provides evidence, then, that Reeve—this sedate, orthodox, Whiggish spinster from Ipswich—was in some of her ideas two hundred years before her time.

BETWEEN TRADITIONS: *THE SCHOOL FOR WIDOWS*

> The business of romance is, first, to excite the attention; and, secondly, to direct it to some useful, or at least innocent end: happy the writer who attains both these points!
> —from Reeve's preface to *The Old English Baron*

Though some of the ideas expressed in Reeve's novel border on the revolutionary, in many ways *The School for Widows* shares a kinship with other novels that were written during the 1790s, a period in which—as Claudia Johnson observes—sentimentalism and Gothicism combined. The resulting body of novels, Johnson adds, are distinctive primarily

> for their egregious affectivity. In works by Wollstonecraft, Radcliffe, Godwin, Lewis, and Burney . . . emotions are saturated in turbulent and disfiguring excess; not simply disruptive emotions—such as ambition, greed, anger, lust—but ostensibly gentler ones as well—such as reverence, sorrow, even filial devotion—are always and obviously going over the top.[51]

There are moments in *The School for Widows* that are unabashedly sentimental—the description of the sufferings of the Marney family, for example, or the many occasions where Frances's friends praise her goodness with unrestrained emotion—yet Reeve's novel is so tempered by rationality and didacticism that it cannot be spoken of merely as a "sentimental novel."

Reeve fits more easily into Anne Mellor's delineation of a kind of domestic, "feminine Romanticism," which celebrates rationality, and, "taking the family as the grounding trope of social organization, . . . oppose[s] violent military revolutions . . . in favor of gradual or evolutionary reform under the guidance of benevolent parental instruction."[52] The Romantic women literary critics like Reeve thus "laid claim to a revolution in both female manners and cultural authority."[53] They offered readers a new aesthetic, suggesting that literature's cultural role is "to educate even more than to delight, to educate by teaching readers to take delight in the triumph of moral benevolence, sexual self-control, and rational intelligence."[54]

The School for Widows as a Conduct Book

Reeve's many warnings against allowing one's passion to overcome one's reason, and her characters' typical attempts to shape the morals of their young charges by correcting their judgment and their aesthetic tastes (in novel-reading, for example) are thus not merely isolated instances of such ideas. Other women writers—from very different backgrounds and with very different political leanings—were dealing with similar themes and issues. Feminist Elizabeth Inchbald's sentimental-didactic novel *A Simple Story,* published in the same year as *The School for Widows,* carries a similar message in favor of rationality and against the sway of passion. Inchbald's main character, Miss Milner, illustrates the vice of a lack of self-command[55] and its tragic consequences. *The Memoirs of Emma Courtnay* by politically radical Mary Hays, appearing just a few years later in 1796, also takes as its theme the need for self-control, as does Jane West's conservative novel *A Gossip's Story* (1796). The idea of life as a process of education in self-control is present in many of the novels of Frances Burney, as well (*Evelina, Camilla,* and *The Wanderer* in particular).

Such novels illustrate their authors' belief that the cultural role of literature is to instruct the reader, and even within the novels themselves education is a crucial theme. Often, as Anne Mellor asserts, adopting the stance of the mother–teacher, Romantic women literary critics and authors such as Reeve used their writing not only to educate on matters of taste and control of the passions, but also to "advocate new roles and more egalitarian marriages for women . . . [and to] condemn the abuses of patriarchy and the traditional construction of masculinity" (37). *The School for Widows* is akin to novels such as Frances Sheridan's *The Memoirs of Miss Sidney Bidulph* and Jane West's *Advantages of Education* (1793) which focus on the reform or education of a (relatively) young woman by her wiser mother/mentor–figure, and Jane Spencer notes that this phenomenon is typical within the tradition of the women's novel (145).

Critiques of the institution of marriage as manifested in the late eighteenth century are also not uncommon among Reeve's fellow authors. Works as varied as Burney's *Cecilia* (1782) and *The Wanderer* (1814), Charlotte Smith's *Emmeline* (1788) and *The Old Manor House* (1794), Wollstonecraft's *Maria, or the Wrongs of Woman* (1798), and all of Jane Austen's novels take issue with various aspects of marriage. Here again, then, Reeve is working within an already established and widely dispersed tradition of thought. Like Burney and others before her, she is aware of the inequalities and injustices inherent in the institution of marriage in its eighteenth-century incarnation, and *The School for Widows* is thus revelatory of those problems. Like other novelists of the period, Reeve presents her readers with a cautionary tale of what will likely occur if one is not as careful as one should be in one's choice of husband. The important variation on this theme in *The School for Widows,* though, is that marriage (or remarriage) is not presented as inevitable or even necessarily desirable. Working within a novelistic tradition of sentimentality, didacticism and domesticity, then, Reeve nonetheless posits decidedly nontraditional ideas about the roles of women in society.

> " 'Tis Vertue, then, direct Vertue, which is the hard and valuable part to be aimed at in education."
> —John Locke, *Some Thoughts Concerning Education*

The School for Widows is also between traditions in that it is an epistolary novel with a good deal of the conduct book about it. Considering Reeve's preferred reading and her tendency toward didacticism, it seems only natural that her own work owes much to the conduct books of her time. Indeed, the conduct book was so prevalent at the time when Reeve was writing that Joyce Hemlow suggests the period of 1760–1820 might be labeled the "age of courtesy books for women."[56] The aim of such books was usually to set down the behavior and roles that were considered proper to a woman, as is clear from the various titles of some of the most popular of these works. In Steele's *Lady's Library,* for example, are individual titles such as "The Whole Duty of a Woman," and "The Ladies Magazine, or Polite Companion for the Fair Sex." Similarly, endeavours such as *The Female Guardian* and *The Polite Lady: or, A Course of Female Education in a Series of Letters from a Mother to her Daughter* delineate an ideal view of "the nature of women" which is characterized by a "yielding softness," domesticity, and non-participation in the arenas of worldly power or politics.[57]

So common did the phenomenon of the conduct book for women become in the eighteenth century that many different kinds of male writers—from Swift and Defoe, to pedagogues like Thomas Gisborne, to clergymen like Dr. Gregory and Dr. Fordyce—were "compelled to add their wrinkles to the female character."[58] Underlying all of the advice on proper behavior proffered in these works was the idea that religion (rather than custom or fashion) was the basis of both morality and manners. Writers of conduct books thus emphasized that the foundation of "polite and proper behavior" was divine law, as revealed in the Bible, and that the "true lady or gentleman . . . was, first and foremost, a Christian."[59]

From the late eighteenth century on, many conduct book writers decided to take advantage of the increasing public appetite for novels, and turned to that more palatable genre as a new means of sweetening their moral messages. These fictional counterparts to the conduct books, according to Marjorie Morgan, were "infused with the same moral fervor and were replete with characters embodying virtues and manners that would have garnered praise from Hannah More herself" (18). Often compared to Reeve in her penchant for religious didacticism and social reform, More had a similar interest in the education of young girls, as evidenced by her *Strictures on the Present System of Education* (1799), in which she argues for a serious education for girls rather than the training in decorative but useless arts commonly considered "education" at the time. More continued her focus on women as intellectual and moral beings in her widely read conduct book-cum-novel *Coelebs in Search of a Wife* (1808).

The plot of More's work, such as it is, centers around the title bachelor, Charles, who is an inexperienced young man on his first excursion away from home. In the course of his journey,

Charles meets various young women and reflects on the relative merits and faults of each of them as prospective brides. Some of the topics of *Coelebs in Search of a Wife* are common to both Reeve and More; religion, education, marriage, and charitable works figure largely, for example. In addition, some of the criticism levied at More—for instance, that her "moralism impeded the freer operation of her talent for fiction"[60] was also directed at Reeve.

It cannot be denied that *The School for Widows*, like *Coelebs in Search of a Wife,* is a vehicle for morality—a conduct book, of sorts. The values of patience, endurance, diligence, disinterested friendship, charity, and, last but not least, robust Christianity, are driven home by Reeve's main narrators, Frances and Rachel, in a decidedly open manner, without much attention to subtlety. The representation of these same narrators, however, marks one of the main differences between *The School for Widows* and more obviously didactic novelistic conduct books like *Coelebs in Search of a Wife*. More's narrator, Charles, is often attacked by critics as being merely a mouthpiece for the author. Scholars like Mary Waldrop see him as a "self-occupied prig," whose "self-complacency and tendency to pontificate" (xv) make him utterly unconvincing as an inexperienced young man, and prevent the reader from engaging with him in a positive manner. Reeve's Frances and Rachel, on the other hand, are flawed, believable characters. Frances's stubbornness and occasional insensitivity, and Rachel's sometimes overactive imagination and lack of caution when it comes to dealing with her husband are only a few of the failings Reeve reveals in her heroines. Reeve's widows are not "perfect" models, like More's Charles, or Richardson's Clarissa or Grandison, but they nonetheless serve as excellent examples of female resourcefulness, suggesting that *The School for Widows,* not strictly either a conduct book or an epistolary novel, is actually a successful hybrid of the two traditions.

Just as *The School for Widows* resists strict generic categorization, its author is equally difficult to pigeonhole. Though some have tried to place her in a particular "camp" politically, the complexity of her personality makes it difficult to do so. She does not present her heroines as subordinate or self-abnegating, as Marilyn Butler describes such "women moralists" as Jane Austen, Jane West, and Mary Brunton doing. She also, however, does not present her heroines as being overtly revolutionary, as would be expected of a novelist from the politically opposite perspective, so we cannot categorize her among what Butler calls the "reformists": that is, such radical writers as Robert Bage, William Godwin, Thomas Holcroft, Mary Hays, and Mary Wollstonecraft. A deeply religious Whig with a strong belief in personal liberty and individual freedom from tyranny, Reeve problematizes the categories that have been put in place by scholars and critics of late-eighteenth-century literature. Like Frances, Rachel, and Isabella in *The School for Widows*, Reeve was a woman of contradictions. These same contradictions that make her so fascinating to us and allow us to identify with Reeve and her characters call for further scholarly investigation of both the author and her work.

Notes

1. Bonnie Bowman Thurston, *The Widows: A Women's Ministry in the Early Church* (Philadelphia: Fortress Press, 1989), 9.
2. Ibid.
3. Margaret Owen, *A World of Widows* (London: Zed Books, 1996), 21.
4. William Gordon, *The Plan of a Society for Making Provision for Widows by Annuities for the Remainer of Life* (Boston: Joseph Edwards and John Fleeming, 1772), Preface.
5. Ibid.
6. William Alexander, MD, *The History of Women, from the Earliest Antiquity to the Present time* (Dublin: A. J. Hibbard, 1779), 288.
7. Ibid., 291.
8. Olwen Hufton, "Women Without Men: Widows and Spinsters in Britain and France in the Eighteenth Century," in *Between Poverty and the Pyre: Moments in the History of Widowhood,* eds. Jan Bremmer and Lourens van den Bosch (New York: Routledge, 1995), 138.
9. Ibid., 129.
10. Ibid., 122.
11. Reeve to Joseph Cooper Walker, 25 October 1804, Dublin: Trinity College Library, MS 1461.
12. Sir Walter Scott, *Lives of the Novelists* (Paris: W. Galignani, 1825), II:171.
13. Rapin's *History* indicates her father's political leanings. As Henry Fielding suggests by his inclusion of Rapin's *History* in the list of works that characterize Squire Western's irascible sister in *Tom Jones,* it is written from the Whig point of view and is thus highly partisan.
14. Kempe to Grimston, May 1778, *Report on the Manuscripts of Lady du Cane* (London: Ben Johnson & Co., 1905), 238.
15. Cheryl Turner, *Living by the Pen: Women Writers in the Eighteenth Century* (New York: Routledge, 1992), 63.
16. Dunstin Griffin, *Literary Patronage in England, 1650–1800* (New York: Cambridge University Press, 1996), 190.
17. In fact, Reeve states that her usual choice of genre has been primarily

based on its being the most remunerative in a letter written to Joseph Cooper Walker on 29 April 1790. "I have found that Romances & Novels are the most saleable of any thing, & therefore have used my pen in that way," she asserts.

18. Elizabeth Napier, "Clara Reeve," in *Dictionary of Literary Biography,* ed. Martin C. Battestin (Detroit, MI: Gale Research Co., 1985), 374.

19. Jane Spencer, "Clara Reeve," in *A Dictionary of British and American Women Writers, 1660–1800,* ed. Janet Todd (Totowa, NJ: Rowman & Allanheld, 1985), 266.

20. Robert Mayo, *The English Novel in the Magazines, 1740–1815* (London: Oxford University Press, 1962), 312.

21. Ibid., 284.

22. Ibid., 314.

23. Anna Seward to the editor of the *Gentleman's Magazine,* Sept. 1785, 55:454.

24. *East Anglian Miscellany, upon Matters of History, Genealogy, Archaeology, Folk-Lore, Literature &c., Relating to East Anglia,* reprinted from the *East Anglian Daily Times,* (Ipswich, 1940) No. 10, 749.

25. Gary Kelly, *Women, Writing, and Revolution, 1790–1827* (Oxford: Clarendon Press, 1993), 245.

26. Ibid.

27. *East Anglian Miscellany,* No. 10, 735.

28. Reeve to Joseph Cooper Walker, 1 December 1792, Trinity College Library, Dublin, MS 1461.

29. *The Monthly Mirror,* December 1807, 451.

30. "The Cowry is a heavy Shell with a broad lip, but there is a very light Shell, with a thin lip, toothed on both sides, of various colours. And comes from the West Indies, very beautiful, and I think should not be ranked with the heavy Cowry, nor is it near so common," Reeve tells Percy.

31. Reeve to Joseph Cooper Walker, 24 October 1791.

32. Ibid., 25 October 1804.

33. Ibid., 29 April 1790.

34. Ibid., 25 April 1791.

35. Among other errors, Hookham apparently lost the last four folio sheets of Reeve's *Plans of Education,* resulting in its incomplete publication.

36. Reeve to Joseph Cooper Walker, 21 Sept. 1792.

37. Ibid., 29 April 1790.

38. Ibid., 7 September 1792.

39. Ibid., 1 December 1792.

40. Ibid., 14 March 1793.

41. Ibid., 3 October 1793.

42. *The Monthly Mirror,* December 1807, 451.

43. *The British Critic,* December 1793, 388.

44. *The Monthly Mirror,* July 1799, 28.

45. Isobel Grundy, "'A Novel in a Series of Letters by a Lady': Richardson and Some Richardsonian Novels," in *Samuel Richardson: Tercentenary Essays,* eds. Margaret Anne Doody and Peter Sabor (New York: Cambridge University Press, 1989), 223.

46. Ibid., 225.

47. This is most obviously the case in its representation of the economic aspects of marriage, including settlements, jointures, pin money, and the like.

48. Rebecca D'Monte and Nicole Pohl, eds., *Female Communities 1600–1800: Literary Visions and Cultural Realities,* (New York: St. Martin's Press, 2000), 16.

49. April Alliston, *Virtue's Faults: Correspondences in Eighteenth-Century British and French Women's Fiction,* (Palo Alto, CA: Stanford University Press, 1996), 4.

50. Patricia Meyer Spacks, "Female Resources: Epistles, Plot, and Power," in *Writing the Female Voice: Essays on Epistolary Literature,* ed. Elizabeth C. Goldsmith (London: Pinter, 1989), 72.

51. Claudia L. Johnson, *Equivocal Beings: Politics, Gender, and Sentimentality in the 1790s: Wollstonecraft, Radcliffe, Burney, Austen,* (Chicago University Press, 1995), 1.

52. Anne K. Mellor, "A Criticism of Their Own: Romantic Women Literary Critics," in *Questioning Romanticism,* ed. John Beer (Baltimore: Johns Hopkins University Press, 1995), 31.

53. Ibid., 47.

54. Ibid., 45.

55. Marilyn Butler, *Jane Austen and the War of Ideas* (Oxford: Oxford University Press, 1999), 43.

56. Joyce Hemlow, "Fanny Burney and the Courtesy Books," *PMLA* 65 (1950): 732.

57. Elizabeth Bergen Brophy, *Women's Lives and the Eighteenth-Century English Novel* (Tampa: University of South Florida Press, 1991), 12.

58. Nancy Armstrong, "The Rise of the Domestic Woman," in *The Ideology of Conduct: Essays on Literature and the History of Sexuality* (New York: Methuen, 1987), 103.

59. Marjorie Morgan, *Manners, Morals and Class in England, 1774–1858* (New York: St. Martin's Press, 1994), 16.

60. Hannah More, *Coelebs in Search of a Wife,* ed. Mary Waldron (Bristol: Thoemmes Press, 1995), xv.

Chronology of Events in the Life and Times of Clara Reeve

1729	Born on 11 June in Ipswich to William Reeve and Hannah Smithies Reeve; Treaty of Seville signed with Spain; Widespread fatal epidemics sweep England and Wales; Famine in Ireland
1739	War declared against Spain
1741	Samuel Richardson, *Pamela*
1742	Sir Robert Walpole's resignation
1745	Jacobite Rebellion in Scotland; Death of Walpole
1747	Samuel Richardson, *Clarissa*
1753–54	Samuel Richardson, *Sir Charles Grandison*
1755	William Reeve dies; Hannah Smithies Reeve moves with Clara Reeve and two of Clara's sisters to Colchester; Clara Reeve possibly turns to domestic service during this period in order to help to support her family financially; Samuel Johnson's *Dictionary* is published
1756	Seven Years' War with France begins
1757	Edmund Burke, *A Philosophical Enquiry*
1760	George II dies, and George III becomes king
1764	Horace Walpole, *The Castle of Otranto*
1769	*Original Poems on Several Occasions*
1772	Translation from the Latin of John Barclay's *Argenis*
1775	War with the American colonies begins
1776	American Declaration of Independence
1777	*The Champion of Virtue*
1778	*The Champion of Virtue* republished as *The Old English Baron* meets with great critical and popular success
1783	*The Two Mentors;* Death of Hannah Smithies Reeve; Treaty of Versailles between England and the United States
1785	*The Progress of Romance*
1788	*The Exiles*

1789-99 14 July, the fall of the Bastille; Ten-year period of revolution in France, ending with the overthrow of the Directory by Napoleon
1790 Edmund Burke, *Reflections on the Revolution in France*
1791 *The School for Widows*; James Boswell, *Life of Johnson*; Elizabeth Inchbald, *A Simple Story*
1792 *Plans of Education;* Mary Wollstonecraft, *A Vindication of the Rights of Women;* Edmund Burke, *Sketch of a Negro Code* (a proposed plan for orderly abolition of slavery and integration of the slaves into society)
1793 *The Memoirs of Sir Roger de Clarendon;* The Reign of Terror in France; Louis XVI is executed
1795 Napoleon is appointed commander of the forces in Italy
1796 Frances Burney, *Camilla*
1798 *Lyrical Ballads* published by Wordsworth and Coleridge
1799 Hannah More, *Strictures on the Modern System of Education;* Napoleon overthrows the Directory, ending the French Revolution
1801 Truce between Britain and France
1803 Samuel Reeve, beloved brother of Clara, dies in a violent accident; he is thrown from his chaise
1804 December, Spain declares war on Britain; Napoleon is crowned emperor
1805 Nelson's victory at Trafalgar
1807 William Wilberforce, *A Letter on the Abolition of the Slave Trade;* 3 December Clara Reeve dies in Colchester.

Note on the Text

THIS EDITION OF *THE SCHOOL FOR WIDOWS* HAS BEEN PREPARED from the first edition, published in London on the 26 May 1791 by Thomas Hookham and William Miller (See the *Morning Post and Daily Advertiser,* 26 May 1791). Though a few of Reeve's letters to Joseph Cooper Walker (25 April and 24 October of 1791) indicate an interest in becoming involved with a Dublin edition of the novel, I have found no conclusive evidence that her interest was transformed into action.

The Dublin edition of *The School for Widows* (1791) was printed by William Porter for a small group of men; the most prominent of those listed are Patrick Wogan and Patrick Byrne, two Catholic booksellers. As Richard Cargill Cole attests in his study *Irish Booksellers and English Writers, 1740–1800* (1986), Wogan and Byrne were among those Dublin publishers who defended the practice of what many English authors termed piracy. Writing to the *Dublin Journal* (13 July 1784) Wogan and Byrne declared that "Ireland was an independent kingdom and they were only doing what was done in Holland and elsewhere in reprinting [books] in a cheaper format without paying royalties" (7). Given these stated sentiments, it is probably safe to assume that the Dublin edition of *The School for Widows*—in which Wogan and Byrne figured largely—is not authoritative. As a point of interest, though, I have sight-collated the two editions, and have found no substantive variants. Several printer's errors from the London edition were corrected in the Dublin edition, and I have noted these in the Appendix.

This edition retains the spelling, punctuation, italicization, and capitalization of Reeve's original edition. I have made the following changes throughout: the long "s" has been replaced by the modern "s"; running quotation marks have been eliminated, and the use of double and single quotation marks has been regularized. Other emendations made in this edition are listed in the Appendix.

The School for Widows

Preface

AMONG THE PRODIGIOUS NUMBER OF BOOKS THAT GO UNDER THE denomination of NOVELS, the far greater number are only intended as the amusement of a vacant hour. Yet there are some that are written with a better design: namely, to counteract the poison of Fashion, Folly, and Dissipation; to blend together the *utilé* and the *dulcé;* and to impress some moral inferences on the mind of the reader. These last, it is presumed, will always find patrons and protectors.

There has been among the Novel readers, of late years, a rage for SENTIMENT; insomuch that Authors have thought it necessary to recommend their works by this word—*Sentimental* Stories, *Sentimental* Plays, *Sentimental* Tales, *Sentimental* Journeys,[1] &c.

This word, like many others, seems to have degenerated from it's[2] original meaning: and, under this flimsy disguise, it has given rise to a great number of whining, maudlin stories, full of false sentiment and false delicacy, calculated to excite a kind of morbid sensibility, which is to faint under every ideal[3] distress, and every fantastical trial; which have a tendency to weaken the mind, and to deprive it of those resources which Nature intended it should find within itself.

Thus young people enter into life, imbued with false notions and false sentiments: believing it meritorious to have this pretended sentimental turn; liable to a thousand vexations and mortifications; and disarmed of that strength and fortitude which should encounter and vanquish them.

These sentimental people pretend to a more than common degree of tenderness and sensibility, which they carry to the most foolish and ridiculous excesses. There are some who think it a crime to destroy noxious vermin, reptiles, and insects; hornets and wasps, spiders, snails, and caterpillars.

A young girl, about seven years old, begged her mother not to hurt the poor little flea that hopped upon her frock—"For you know, mamma, that we must not kill any thing!"However ridiculous this story may seem, the fact is true. It deserves to be compared with that of a poor lady, whose sensibility was excited by the broken leg of an unfortunate wheelbarrow!

There is a sensibility that ennobles the heart that bears it.[4] It is modest and secret; it never boasts itself, but enjoys it's pleasures, and endures it's pains, in the heart's recesses. It hates and abhors cruelty of every kind: it weeps with those that weep; but avoids all ostentatious display of it's feelings.

False sensibility, on the contrary, is always talking of itself: it complains of it's sufferings, in order to exalt it's merits; and wonders at the hardness and insensibility of others. Yet it is often seen that these very people will turn their backs upon the miseries of their fellow-creatures, and even practise the art of ingeniously tormenting them.

This false kind of sensibility arises from false sentiments: and they are either counterfeited for interested purposes; or, if they are real, they weaken the mind that indulges them. It was a saying of Cato the Elder, "That a virtuous mind, struggling against misfortunes, was a spectacle that the gods beheld with pleasure and approbation.[5]"

Pictures of this kind should be held up to young people, and proposed as models of imitation.[6] They should be encouraged to believe, that misfortunes are not invincible; that virtue will enable them to overcome all difficulties; and that such victories are subjects of honourable triumph: that virtue is active, and gathers strength from exercise; and that indolence frustrates it's own expectations.

The fable of Hercules and the Countryman is a good illustration of this subject: When his waggon was stuck fast in the mire, he kept praying incessantly to Hercules, but never once offered to exert his own strength to help himself.

"Leave off calling upon me," says Hercules; "put forth all your strength, to lift up your waggon. When you have done your utmost, I will come to your assistance." With this moral in view, I have written the following work; which motive, I hope, will be deemed a sufficient claim to candour and allowance, if it should not be found worthy of a warmer plaudit.

It is written more to the heart than to the head. It is addressed to the Virtuous and Candid, to whom I consign it's final destiny.

THE SCHOOL FOR WIDOWS
Volume I

LETTER I
Mrs. Strictland, to Mrs. Darnford.

If Frances Darnford remembers her schoolfellow Rachel Selwyn, she will acknowledge a friend in Rachel Strictland, though she has not been permitted to converse with her under that name. She must have heard that Rachel had changed her name several months before her; but Rachel knew not that her beloved Fanny was married till above a year afterward.

Long have I been separated from all those whom I called my friends; but, at length, Heaven allows us to be united. Banished from society for near ten years, I am restored to my liberty by the death of my husband; an awful and important event, but not greatly deplored by me. Heaven knows what is best for us! I know not *seemings;*[1] I disclaim them.

After being the slave and prisoner of a tyrant for ten years, I feel as does the captive just delivered from his chains. It would be folly, it would be sinful, in me, to affect the part of a disconsolate widow.

The first use I made of my recovered liberty was to enquire after the friends of my youth. One of my guardians was dead; the other was removed to a distant county. My young friends were dispersed here and there, and out of my reach.

I met a gentleman who knew your family; and I enquired after every part of it, particularly the person in it the most dear to me. He told me briefly all that he knew of it—

"Mary Lawson is married to a tradesman in London. Jane is married to an attorney, Mr. Jones, who succeeded her father."

"Tell me what is become of Frances? it is her that I am the most desirous to hear of."

"She was married to a Mr. Darnford, who was said to be a man of good fortune; but he ran through it all in a few years, and then died. All that remained of his estate was entailed on the next male heir[2] of the name; and the widow was left without any provision, and obliged to go out as governess to some young ladies."

"Well, but what became of her ever since?"

"Why, that we do not know exactly. It was said that she kept a school at

W——, and took in needlework beside; but I know nothing certainly."

"Can you tell me who knows more?"

"Perhaps her sisters may."

"That is true; but, where are they to be found?"

"Mrs. Jones lives at N——."

"I thank you, Sir, for this information."

It was a person formerly a clerk to your father who gave me this imperfect account; and he seemed not to know, or care to know, any more.

A few days after, I put myself into a post-chaise, and went to N——.

Mrs. Jones received me graciously, when she thought I came to visit her; but, as soon as she found I only came to enquire after you, she grew stiff and reserved.

I urged her to tell me all she knew. She said, she knew very little more. I begged her to tell me that little.

"Why, really, Madam, it gives me pain to speak of Mrs. Darnford. She was weak enough to give up her settlement[3] and so reduced herself to poverty and distress. After trying to get a maintenance in several ways, she set up a day-school at the town of W——. She lodged with a carpenter's widow, who let her have part of her house. She taught her daughters, and made them capable of assisting her in her school. After some time, she succeeded; and I was told she made it out very well, and I was glad to hear it."

"Good God!" said I, "this a situation for Fanny's sister to be glad of!"

I said this inwardly, as you may suppose.

"Well, Madam, Mrs. Darnford is there still, I suppose?"

"I believe not, Madam. About two years ago, she left W——, where she was well established; and went a wild-goose chace, nobody knows where. It is said she is engaged in a strange undertaking; that she lives in a *haunted house*, and takes care of a *mad woman,* whose husband is gone abroad, and has left his house and his wife to the care of Mrs. Darnford. This is the last account, and this is all that I can tell you of her."

"Very strange, indeed!—But where is this haunted house to be found?"

"Indeed, I do not know: I never hear from her."

"Does any body else know more of her?"

"Mrs. Martin, her landlady, at W——, is the most likely to know; for I am told that she took one of her daughters away with her, and I suppose she may hear from her sometimes."

"I suppose so too; for I hope there are few people that neither know nor care what becomes of their nearest relations!"

"You might have spared that reproach, Madam. The cares of my own family are quite sufficient for me. Mrs. Darnford never writes to any of her relations."

"I dare say she has good reasons for what she does, and what she does not."

"Perhaps so, Madam. You were always partial to her, and now would justify her conduct at every one's expence—I have answered your questions, and I can tell you nothing more."

"I thank you, Madam; I have nothing farther to ask. I will seek out your sister: I will endeavour to be of service to her; and will do the office of a friend, though I am not her relation. Only tell me the name of the person with whom she lived at W——."

I wrote Mrs. Martin's name and place of abode; and then took my leave of Mrs. Jones, who was heartily glad to be rid of me. I ate and slept at the inn where the horses were put up; and the next morning I set off for W——, resolving not to return home till I had obtained more certain intelligence of you.

I slept another night upon the road, and got to W—— by one o'clock. I took an early dinner. The landlady of the White Hart, a sensible and intelligent woman, informed me where Mrs. Martin lived, and sent her servant to shew me the way to her house.

I enquired for her; and was conducted through a neat shop, and into a large back parlour, where sat the good woman in the midst of thirty children, all neatly dressed and well behaved.

At my entrance, they all rose up. I apologized for intruding upon them. I said—"My business is to enquire after a dear friend and schoolfellow of mine, who is also a friend of yours, Mrs. Martin. Her name is Darnford. I am told you are the most likely person to give me some account of her."

"Mrs. Darnford, did you say?—Yes; she is my friend indeed, and the best I ever had in my life. She has been a good angel to me and all my family!"

"When your school is dismissed, I shall be glad of a little conversation with you about this same Mrs. Darnford."

"I will send the children home directly, Madam; I will do any thing to oblige a friend of Mrs. Darnford."

The children were dismissed.

As soon as we were alone, I made my enquiries.

She said it was necessary to tell me how she became acquainted with Mrs. Darnford, if it would not be tiresome to me.

I desired she would do so; for I wished to be acquainted with the history of her own situation, and how she came to be so intimately connected with Mrs. Darnford.

"About seven years ago, I was left a widow, with six children. My husband was a master carpenter in this town; a sober, honest, industrious man, and one of the best of husbands and fathers. He saved money; and had put out his two eldest sons before his death, the first to his own trade, the second to a wheelwright; and he had some hundreds in the funds beside. He left me this house decently furnished, and the interest of his money for my life.

"I had four children to maintain, and wanted to fix upon some way of business to help them and myself, till my son should be out of his time, and succeed to his father's business. I consulted with my friends; but they could not agree in their advice, and only puzzled me, so that I was unable to determine.

"One thing I resolved on, which was to let a part of my house; and I had some thoughts of keeping a shop, and selling a few articles; or else taking in clear-starching and needlework, to employ myself and my daughters.

"I put up a bill at my door—"Ready furnished Lodgings for Ladies of good Character." This was laughed at by some of my neighbours; but I thought it was right, and minded not what people said.

"My youngest boy was a sickly child, and died a few months after his father. My eldest girl was turned of fourteen, and the second thirteen.

"One day, Mrs. Bailey, who keeps the White Hart in this town, sent me word that a lady at her house desired to speak with me. I went directly; and there I first saw Mrs. Darnford, and that was a good day to me.

"Mrs. Bailey said—"Here is a lady who designs to open a school. She enquires for lodgings, to try whether she is likely to succeed before she takes a house to herself. I have encouraged her to undertake it: A school is very much wanted in this town. She is recommended by Mrs. Sorling, and I will answer for her character. She has lived a high life, and deserves a better situation than Fortune has given her; but we never could have met with a person so well qualified for our undertaking. I have recommended your lodgings, Mrs. Martin: we will come and see them; and, if they suit Mrs. Darnford, she will take them."

I thanked Mrs. Bailey for her recommendation, and wished my lodgings might suit the lady. So they returned with me, and looked over them.

Mrs. Bailey made some objections; but Mrs. Darnford, with that graciousness and sweetness which are natural to her, said—"It is easy to rise to better lodgings, Madam; and I know that it is hard to descend to worse. I like the gentlewoman,"—so she was pleased to call me—"I like her character and behaviour. It is of consequence that I should be in a worthy family, who can answer for my conduct. I will fix here for the present."

"I was charmed with the lady from the first hour I was in her company. I saw that she was superior to all that I had seen and conversed with. We talked of the terms. Mrs. Darnford proposed to board, as well as lodge, with me. Mrs. Bailey advised it, as most convenient to all the parties. She settled the terms to our mutual satisfaction. She offered the lady a bed at her house, till her lodgings could be got ready. My daughters and I made haste to get them in order. Mrs. Bailey told every body of the new undertaking, and prepared them to receive Mrs. Darnford with due respect and attention.

"A few days after, my good angel came under my humble roof, and brought with her the greatest blessing of my life.

"She wrote, in a fine and curious hand—A SCHOOL for FEMALE CHILDREN; where Reading, English, Writing, and all kinds of Needlework, are taught in the best manner."

"In a week's time, the school was opened with ten scholars. Mrs. Bailey sent two of her daughters and a niece. She advised every body to send their children without delay, for they never would have such another opportunity.

"The curate[4] of the parish called upon her, at Mrs. Bailey's desire: he conversed with her, and made his report highly in her favour. He said, she had more knowledge, and less confidence in it, than any woman he had ever met with.

"In the course of a month, the school was increased to twenty scholars. Mrs. Darnford had now her hands full of business, and it was daily increasing.

"One day, she said to me—"My good Mrs. Martin, I have something to propose that I think will be of service both to you and me. I will take one of your daughters into my school, and qualify her to be my assistant, if it is agreeable to you and to her."

"I thank you, Madam; it will be an honour to her, and a service to me. I pray God to reward your goodness to us! Only one thing troubles me—Both my daughters love and admire you: they would be proud to serve you. I fear, that whichsoever of them is chosen, the other will be grieved and mortified: she will think herself despised, when she is put to do the houshold work, while her sister is treated like a gentlewoman. I love them equally; and I should be concerned for the poor girl that is rejected."

"Oh, how I love that maternal tenderness!" said the dear lady. "I feel for you the mortification your other good girl would suffer. We must prevent it, by making an alteration in our plan. I will instruct both your daughters: one shall be with me in the school one week, and the other the following. They shall take it by turns to assist you and me; and we will make no difference between them. Will this please you, my good friend?"

"I said, I was only afraid she would think I was encroaching upon her goodness.

"She made my mind easy; and her benevolent scheme was put in execution.

"The school continually increased in numbers and credit; the scholars improved very quick, and their friends perceived and acknowledged it.

"I thought my daughters had been well taught to read and write before; but, when they came under Mrs. Darnford's hands, they made such improvements, that I soon found myself to be a poor ignorant woman, and wished also to become Mrs. Darnford's scholar.

"Her goodness was so great, that she condescended to instruct me after the school hours; and, oh! what delightful evenings have I spent in her company! She deserved knowledge, because she made a wise and good use of it: she taught us our duty, and set us an example of the practice of it.

"She read prayers to us every evening; saying, it was the blessing of God that we must rely upon to give success to our endeavors: and that, putting ourselves under his protection, we had every thing to hope, and nothing to fear; while those who lived without God in the world had every thing to fear, and nothing to hope, either here or hereafter.

"Her conversations were to me as practical sermons, the best and pleasantest that ever I heard. In short, Madam, we grew wiser, and happier, and better, every day of our lives. I shall never forget the blessing I had in her society; nor ever cease to regret the loss of it, though it is for the good of her health, and for her worldly advantage."

Here she burst into tears; mine accompanied them: they were the tears of virtue, that refreshed the heart, and comforted it; and I enjoyed the effects of them.

You, my Fanny, would never have told me these things yourself; therefore I tell them to you, as a triumph over your reserve, and modesty. I claim a share in the friendship of this honest, grateful, worthy woman; whom I will love always, for your sake and her own.

I said—"I rejoice that my dear friend met with a person capable of understanding her merit, and fine qualities. Henceforward, you must allow me, Mrs. Martin, to call you my friend, and to take an interest in all that concerns you and your family."

"You are very good, Madam; I humbly thank you. I can truly say, that nobody can love and honour Mrs. Darnford more than I do, and that all her friends must ever be dear to me."

"Enough, Mrs. Martin, I love and honour your sincerity as it deserves. Proceed with your story, my heart is deeply engaged with it."

"Some time after this I have been speaking of, Mrs. Darnford said to me—"I have another proposal to make you, Mrs. Martin. You have very bad pins, needles, and threads, in your little town. I am thinking that you might sell some articles in the haberdashery way, to a very good account. You have a shop, you need only have some shelves put into it; I will be at half the expence in fitting it up, and I think you will run very little hazard. What think you?"

"God bless you, Madam!" said I: "you are always thinking on something for my good; but how and when can I get them?"

"I will write, in your name, to an eminent haberdasher in London. I will desire him to send the best goods of every kind. I will write your letters, and shew you how to keep your book. One day-book will be sufficient for you, for you must sell for ready money only. You must be very punctual in your remittances of payment, which will induce your dealer to serve you well for his own sake. I shall be a customer to you, so will my scholars; and if your goods are of the best kinds, there is little doubt, that many people will come to the shop of a person so well known and respected as you are in this place."

"No sooner said than done; the goods were ordered, the shop was fitted up, and in less than a month I became a haberdasher of small wares. I sell pins, needles, tapes, thread, silk, worsted for working, and most other articles in this branch of business.

"My demand exceeded my expectations: it increased, and still increases every year; and the profits are now become very considerable.

"Finding that all things succeeded to her wishes, Mrs. Darnford extended her views for me still farther.

"There is yet room in the shop," said she, "for a few more articles. I will write to a stationer to send you pens, ink, and paper, wax and wafers, and school-books for the children. We will make it be known, that you have a good correspondence, and you shall sell books by commission; that is, such books as may be ordered, but not otherwise. We will fill the good shop as full as it will hold, and every little will contribute to make the whole answer your purposes."

"Whatever you please to order I will do," said I; "your will is my law. I may say of you, as the Scripture does of Joseph, that *wherever he went, he did good to those he lived with; and whatsoever he undertook, the Lord made it to prosper in his hands.*"[5]

"She said I was too grateful; but I answered, that was impossible.

"So, Madam, we went on, and our blessings and comforts increased every year.

"In the second year, Mrs. Darnford offered to increase the price she paid for her board, but I would not hear of it. I said, it ought rather to be lessened, considering all that she had done for me and mine. She took my refusal kindly; but it was all the same in effect as if I had accepted her offer, for she was continually making presents to me and my daughters, as if she was under obligations to us.

"In the third year I took a poor girl from the parish, to do the under-work in my family. Mrs. Darnford insisted on paying her wages; and I was obliged to submit, for there was no stopping her generous hand. Every thing prospered with us; my property daily increased; and, at the year's end, I was amazed at my own riches.

"I had now all the business I wished, and the friend that I wanted; I had no occasion to consult any others, for I had my oracle at home."

"Let us stop here, my good Mrs. Martin; you and your daughter must go and drink tea with me at the White Hart."

"Oh, Madam! I hope you will not mortify us so much, as to refuse to drink your tea here."

"No, surely, I cannot mean to mortify or affront you, I like you too well."

"Then you must treat us like Mrs. Darnford's friends."

"Well, I will compromise with you: I will drink tea with you, and you must sup with me; I have ordered a supper with that intention: your friend Mrs. Bailey must make the fourth, and we will talk of Mrs. Darnford."

She consented to this. Her eldest daughter made tea for us, a modest and well behaved young woman. Mrs. Martin told me, that the second was with Mrs. Darnford, and that her youngest was gone to visit a relation.

"Mrs. Darnford's sister gave me a very strange and imperfect account. Pray, does she *live in a haunted house,* and *take care of a mad woman?*"

Mrs. Martin smiled.— "Why, really, Madam, I cannot tell you how that is, but it is so reported. I have asked some impertinent questions; she is silent on the subject, and so is my daughter Patty. She told me I must not mind the talk of foolish people, but she never said positively that it was not true: however, I will tell you all that I know of this, and every thing else relating to her."

"No, you shall not, till you come to it fairly; you shall not anticipate the rest of your story: take breath awhile, and drink your tea."

After tea, we adjourned to the White Hart, and Mrs. Bailey was called in. She told many things of this *strange* Mrs. Darnford, such things as I never should have heard from herself.

Here I shall finish my letter, but I shall begin another tomorrow. While I am writing, I fancy that I am conversing with my friend, and making up for our long separation. By the interest I take in every person and thing that bears any relation, or has any connection, with her, she will judge of the sincerity of her old and faithful friend,

RACHEL STRICTLAND.

LETTER II
Mrs. Strictland, to Mrs. Darnford

SUPPOSE me sitting at a table, with Mrs. Bailey on one side, and Mrs. Martin on the other—Mary Martin opposite—listening to the praises of Mrs. Darnford from all of them, and gaining little circumstances of her life and character that delight my very soul; and more pleased with my company than I could be in the first circles.

I will not offend your ear by reciting all the good people said; I shall only remark, that Mrs. Bailey was more lively and entertaining, but that Mrs. Martin was more serious and pathetic. All that she said came evidently from the heart, and made it's way directly to mine. Mrs. Bailey related an anecdote that pleased me highly.

"The rector[1] of our parish, Madam, is one Dr. Proudly: he is very high and stately; and his lady does not deign to associate with us, the parishioners. Her daughters are always dressed in the heights of the fashion, and they visit none but the squire's family.

"The curate is a modest good man, and kept by his low circumstances from mixing with people of superior fortune. He had seen and understood the merits of Mrs. Darnford. He mentioned her to the Doctor, who resides here only three months in the year, as a person deserving every kind of notice and encouragement. Some time after, the Doctor spoke to her at church, and asked her to drink tea at the parsonage. She went, and confirmed the account they had heard of her. They invited her a second time; then the Doctor asked her, if what he had heard was true, that she understood both French and Italian. She said, it was.

"Should you like to teach my daughter French?"

"She thanked him for his good opinion; but said, her time was already fully employed.

"Could you not come hither of an evening, after your school hours?"

"That is not in my power, it is the only time I have to relax after my labours of the day: I could not undertake more; it would hurt my health, and disqualify me for my business."

"Suppose you take a house to yourself, send away the vulgar children, and take only those of the better kind of people."

"That would be running a great hazard; and, besides, it would be making a distinction that must needs offend those who have trusted me with their children, and to whom I am under obligations; it would be very ungrateful in me, and unjust to them. Excuse me, Sir, it is one of those things I cannot do, were I to gain ever so great advantages."

"Very well, Mrs. Darnford, nobody desires you to do it: if you are satisfied with your situation, nobody wants to take you out of it. I meant to serve you, but it seems you have other friends whom you prefer to me."

"Sir, I thank you for your intentions; but I am so circumstanced, that they cannot be of any service to me at present."

"I have done, Mrs. Darnford; I was mistaken in you."

"The Doctor assumed an air of coldness and reserve, his lady the same; they never invited Mrs. Darnford any more to their house. His lady said many slighting things of her, which I strove to keep from her knowledge, lest it should vex her.

"She said, that Mrs. Darnford was not at all the woman she was represented to be; that she declined teaching French because she was ignorant of it: that she supposed she was some lady's waiting-woman, who gave herself second-hand airs of education and breeding: but it was easy to see what she was, for she preferred low company to that of people in genteel life.

"I was hurt for Mrs. Darnford, but I never minded Madam's high airs, and I wished for an opportunity to let her know it.

"One Sunday, as I was coming from church, she passed by me; she turned back—"Pray, Mrs. Bailey, who is this Mrs. Darnford that you make such a fuss about; and where does she come from?"

"From heaven," said I: "she was sent hither to civilize us and our children."

"She has not taught you good-manners, however, Mrs. Bailey."

"She teaches us, that virtue makes all the difference between one human creature and another," said I. "But she does not invade the province of the clergy, she leaves it to them to teach us humility."

"Impertinent woman!" said she; "she is fit company for you: birds of a feather will flock together."

"True, Madam," said I, "but we are birds without feathers!"—I looked hard at her daughters, who were plumed to the utmost height— "we are as God made us."

"She turned away in anger. I heard her say to her daughters— "Did you hear the saucy woman?" I laughed, and she fretted: so I went away, satisfied with having made her shrink at my touch."

I was pleased with Mrs. Bailey's wit and spirits. I laughed with her. After some other chit-chat, I begged Mrs. Martin to proceed with her story.

"I told you, Madam, that my shop answered exceeding well; we were all successful and happy. The people sent their children from all the villages round about. Mrs. Darnford began to complain that the fatigue was too much for her: she grew pale and thin.

"Several of the principal farmers, parents of the children, used to send a horse, or a light cart, to fetch her on a Sunday to spend the day with them, and to take the air, which she very much wanted.

"One day, she met at one of these houses a seafaring gentleman, called Captain Morris, or *Maurice*, for so he spells his name.

"He said he had a child under his care, and he should like to send her to Mrs. Darnford, and that he would call upon her soon.

"He came the next day; and the more he talked with her, the more he liked her. She asked me, if I should object to take the child as a boarder. I told her, whatever she approved would please me; so they agreed on the price soon.

"A few days after, he brought a young girl about seven years old, called Miss Brady. She had never had any kind of education, and hardly knew her letters. In a month's time, the child was so improved as surprized every body; and Captain Maurice was astonished at it.

"He desired to have some conversation with Mrs. Darnford alone. As I understand, he then told her, that he was so unfortunate as to have a wife that was out of her right mind. That he was very unhappy, and that his house was uncomfortable to him; and therefore he was determined to go abroad again, but wanted to find a person whom he could trust his lady with during his absence. That he had heard an excellent character of her, and what he had seen had convinced him, that she was such a person as he wanted. That if she would undertake this charge, he would make it worth her while.

"She desired some time to consider of this proposal. She consulted me and Mrs. Bailey; who said, it certainly would be a less laborious kind of life for her, but still it might cause her a great deal of care and trouble.

"I could hardly bear the thoughts of losing her; but yet, if she should lose her health, and go into a decline, that would be much worse, and we should reproach ourselves as being accessary to it: so at last we left is wholly to her own determination.

"When Captain Maurice called again, she told him, she must see the house and the lady before she resolved. So he carried her away, and they were gone a fortnight.

"When she returned, she saw us all overjoyed to meet her, and she shed tears while she embraced us. She said it gave her pain to declare her resolution; that she had accepted the trust, and should leave us within a month.

"When our emotions were somewhat abated, she said— "My dear friend, Mrs. Martin, I have one more proposal to make you: I will from this day make you my full partner in the school. Your eldest daughter shall teach the elder scholars, and you can very well teach the younger ones; I hope you will go on as well as I have done. If some few people should take away their children, it would be no misfortune, for we have too many. I shall tell the parents, that I am obliged to go away for one year; and that in the mean time you and your daughters will carry on the school for me. I will certainly return at the time, and see how you go on. If I like my situation, and if the school succeeds with you, I will quit it entirely to you: if either or neither succeeds, we will take other measures."

"And now I have still another favour to ask of you."

"Of me, Madam! What can you ask me, that I can refuse?"

"It is something very dear both to you and to me—It is your daughter Patty: you must let her go with me. I promise that you shall see her once a year, and hear from her oftener. Consider well of it; and if you cannot part with her, I will excuse you."

"We were all melted into tears; we could not speak for some minutes; at last I struggled with myself and gained my voice.

"Patty," said I, "do you decide this point; answer for me and for yourself.

"The dear child rose, and threw her arms round my neck. "I hope," said she, "I have always loved my mother as I ought, and ever shall, as duty and affection oblige me to do; but this dear lady has been the parent of my mind, she has given me a new set of thoughts, and even senses: I feel an affection for her that I cannot describe. If it will not make my dear mother too unhappy, I will follow her to the world's end."

"She went from me to Mrs. Darnford, who embraced her, and again we were silent for some time. At last Mrs. Darnford spoke—

"It is enough; we understand each other. I see your good hearts, and you know mine. The subject is too affecting to us all; let us quit it for the present, we will resume it another time. You are the relations of my soul, and whatever good Heaven has in store for me, you shall share it. Let us separate and recollect ourselves."

"Mrs. Martin wept while she related this scene, and all the rest of us accompanied her. I begged her to proceed with her narration, as soon as she had recovered herself.

"Mrs. Darnford made daily preparations for her departure. She spoke to the parents of most of the children. She wrote a letter for me to shew to such of them as lived at a distance. In it she thanked them for the encouragement they had given her, and the confidence they had put in her. She told them, she had a call of a particular kind, to take the charge of a poor lady, whose mind was deranged; that she had hopes that her company and advice might be of service to her, and trusted that she should be in the way of her duty. She proposed to stay one year certain; at the end of which she would, if alive and able, return again, and either take again the charge of her school, or quit it entirely. In the mean time, she begged, as a favour to herself, that they would continue to send the children to Mrs. Martin and her daughter, whom they would find qualified to go on with them, in the same method which she had used with good success. She recommended them to God's protection, and wished them all manner of happiness.

"As the time drew near when she was to leave us, I had many heavy hours. She said, she would not tell me the week, nor the day, nor yet take any particular leave of us, for all our sakes.

"Miss Brady and my Patty were as lively as birds in the spring; they were not going to lose Mrs. Darnford, but to be her inseparable companions. I often wept by myself, lest my child should think I repented of giving my consent to her going, or Mrs. Darnford should scruple to take her.

"One day, a cart stopped at our door, and the driver enquired for Mrs. Darnford. She changed colour, and said— "This cart is come for our baggage; but we are not going to leave you today, my good friend." I shook like a leaf, but I said not a word. She beckoned Patty, and they went out together: they saw their baggage packed up and sent away.

"She was very chearful all the evening, and said every thing to encourage us to look forward; saying, she hoped we should spend many happy hours together. When she prayed with us, her voice faltered several times; but afterwards she was as chearful as ever I knew her. She bade us good-night, and retired to rest.

"The next morning, when I came down to breakfast, a letter lay upon the table: it was her charming hand-writing, and directed to me. In it she bade me farewell. She said every thing likely to comfort and support me during her absence. She told me, she and her children rose early, and went to the White Hart; they breakfasted with Mrs. Bailey, and went from thence in her post-chaise[2] on their journey, and that they should overtake the cart in their way. She said the kindest and most affecting things to me and my children, and left her blessings and prayers for me and all my family.

"You will guess, Madam, what a heavy day this was to me: however, the duties of my business amused and comforted my mind; and, by degrees, my heart grew lighter, and I set myself to perform the duties of my employment, and to shew myself worthy of the charge she had left with me.

"One thing I could not but observe; she never told me the name of the place whither she was going. I had several times asked it, but she always put it by, without giving any direct answer. She said, I should hear from her within a month; so then, I thought, we should know where to direct our answers. But no such thing came; we were ordered to direct to her, to be left at the post-house, at N——, and she would send a servant to fetch her letters from thence."

Here Mrs. Martin stopped; and your poor friend looked vexed and disappointed.

"So, then, you do not know where Mrs. Darnford lives, and I can neither visit her nor write to her?"

"Not quite so bad as that, Madam. I expect my daughter home in a fortnight; and the carriage that brings her, can carry your letter to her."

"What, then, does she keep a carriage?"

She smiled—"A kind of one, Madam; but not such as would suit you, I believe. It is a light cart, with a seat in it: it carried things from the market, and to the market-town.

"In a fortnight more, it will come to fetch my Patty home; and then it will bring an answer to your letter, and carry another, if you have it ready. You will please to send your letters to me; I will send them one way or another."

"I thank you, Mrs. Martin, and accept your offer.—Pray, did Mrs. Darnford return hither at the year's end?"

"She did, Madam; and she was so much improved in her health, that she gave pleasure to all that loved her, which was all that knew her value.

"I had but three scholars taken away from me; and, thank God! Mary and I have given pretty good satisfaction, though not equal to Mrs. Darnford. But all that we know we learned from her.

"She was pleased to find that the school answered her wishes: she said, she had hoped that, in a year's time, the people would be accustomed to see me and my daughter in the school, and be contented to go on with us, and rejoiced to find it so.

"She refused to accept any part of the profits during her absence, and resigned it wholly to me.

"She did not think it right to make my daughters independent of me: but she advised me, at my own time, to admit my eldest daughter into a share of my business; not more than a third part, because it might afford a provision hereafter for my two younger daughters; also, that if either of them should marry, they should forfeit all pretensions to the business.

"She told me the way to realize my profits, and to employ the money I saved every year.

"I added yearly to the sum my husband had put out; and she made me rich, provident, and easy.

"My eldest son was nearly out of his time. He had been uneasy at my using the shop where he had hoped to exercise the trade of his father.

"I consulted Mrs. Darnford on this subject. She said, you must tell him that your using the shop enables you to provide for him upon a larger scale of business. You must hire or purchase a piece of ground for a shop and timber-yard for him; and you must put him into business handsomely, and not think of laying by money that year. You must give him his board and lodging the first year; and, if that is not sufficient, the second year also. You must assist him till he can stand firmly upon his legs. You must tell him that, after so good an outset, he must depend upon his own industry, and that you have others to provide for as well as himself. When he marries, he must take a house for himself, for you must by no means part with yours.

"She gave me the best advice in all respects; and to this day I do nothing without consulting her, and following her directions in every thing."

"And does she still continue in this unknown situation?"

"She does, Madam; but I know no more of it than what I have told you."

I thanked Mrs. Martin and Mrs. Bailey for their intelligence; and, as soon as they left me, I sat down to writing and preparing a pacquet for your hand.

And now, my dear friend, I entreat you to give me the farther particulars of your health and situation. Is it, indeed, a comfortable one? Are you so engaged to it, that you cannot leave it? Do you prefer it to the company of an old and faithful friend? Answer to all these points sincerely.

My Fanny, I am blessed with two children, and an ample fortune: my boy is hopeful and promising; my girl is the very darling of my soul, and I give up my time and abilities to her education.

I do not like the manners of the youth I have seen since my return to society; you are qualified to direct and assist me in the arduous task. Come and share my heart and fortune, not as a dependant, but as my counsellor and instructress, and my daughter's governess and friend. You must either accept my offer, or give me reasons why you reject it.

I stay one day more at W——, to converse with your worthy friend here. I send my letter by Mrs. Martin's method of conveyance, and expect an answer as soon as possible.

Though entirely my own mistress, I am not without fears of my conduct; and, though I may chuse my own society, I am like the poor Irishman, alone in a throng.[3]

I want a friend, who will neither flatter nor despise me; who will cherish my virtues, and assist me to correct my faults. I know but one person who can supply all these requisites; if she will deign to undertake this generous office, it is I that shall be the obliged person, and not her.

Weigh these things in your own mind, and accept the effusions of a heart, that means more than it can well express; that feels every sentiment of affection, esteem, and confidence, towards you: it is that of your old and sincere friend and servant,

RACHEL STRICTLAND.

LETTER III
Mrs. Darnford, to Mrs. Strictland.

NOT showers of rain to the thirsty earth, when parched with long droughts, were ever more welcome than my dear Rachel's letters to me!

Adversity is the test of friendship, the trier and purifier of the human heart: not half it's virtues could be known or proved without it. Yet we still shrink at the thoughts of suffering; we shudder at the approach of poverty, we suppose it the greatest of all evils.

To those who have been brought up in the bosom of indolence and affluence, it appears so; but I can say of it, as Dryden does of death—"To innocence 'tis but a bugbear dressed to frighten children; pull but off the mask, and it will appear a friend."[1] What advantages have I not received from my trials! They have taught me to know the world and myself; to separate the grain from the chaff of my acquaintance; to gain real and sincere friends, to pity and forgive my enemies.

How dear and precious is a friend, whose affection and fidelity are proved beyond the possibility of doubting! How inestimable are your cares and attentions, your indefatigable enquiries after me! What pains have you taken to get information of every circumstance relative to me and my situation! How sincerely have you been interested for me! I can never sufficiently acknowledge your generous and steady friendship; but I shall wear the remembrance in my heart once and always.

You have a right to be informed of every circumstance of my life and fortunes, of my past trials and my present situation; and you shall have them truly.

You have had a very partial account of me, during my residence at W——; but, as it includes many proofs of gratitude and affection from my friends there, it is very dear and valuable to me.

I am pleased that I know all that you have heard, that I may connect it with the foregoing and succeeding parts of my story. But you judge rightly, that you would never have heard from me all that my humble and grateful friends have told you. I will tell you what remains of my history; and I expect, in return, that you should relate all that has happened to you since our separation.

My present situation is not uncomfortable. I have been enabled to give hope and comfort to an unfortunate lady, who wanted a friend, and who deserved to find one.

When you have heard all the circumstances, you will judge whether I can, and whether I ought to leave her.

Heaven has also given me two children; which, though not mine by nature, are so by adoption. All these are inexpressibly dear to me; and all of them depend upon my affection, cares, and protection.

My eldest sister was married to a woolen-draper and stuff-mercer in London, with my father's full consent and approbation. He carried me with him to the celebration of the nuptials, and to shew me the capital of the three kingdoms. The scene was new and entertaining; I enjoyed it as such. I was noticed as a new face, not yet cheap in the eyes of men. I was followed, admired, and solicited; but I was more frightened than gratified by the attentions that were paid me. My father was attentive to the notices I received: he was very desirous to see me settled for life before he died. He was then in a decline, and I knew it; though he carefully concealed it from his children, lest he should afflict them prematurely.

George Darnford, Esq. was the first man that made me a serious offer. He was young, handsome, gay, and pleasing. There was an air of ease and affluence about him, that pleases the many more than real merit. The first quality strikes the eye, and few people take the trouble to look farther.

At the age of twenty-three he succeeded to an estate of twelve hundred pounds a year, by the death of an uncle. He had been bred to the law; but he disdained business of every kind, and set out in a way that shewed he was likely to lessen his fortune.

My father was transported with joy at the prospect of so handsome an establishment for me: he urged me warmly to accept it, and he hastened the conclusion of it.

I did not dislike the man, but I wished to know more of him before I should make him the master of my fate. My scruples were over-ruled, and my marriage was precipitated.

I was pleased with my husband, and he was extravagantly fond of me. My sisters envied me my prize; but, had they known the man, they would rather have thought me an object of pity than envy.

Our first winter was spent in all the pleasures and dissipations of the capital. My husband was gay, careless, and easy. I was frightened at the expences of our establishment, and soon foresaw the approaching consequences. I studied Mr. Darnford's temper and propensities. I found that pride and indolence were his leading qualities: the first led him into what is called the *best company*, and made him imitate their manners and follies; the second hindered him from looking into his own affairs, and making such reforms and retrenchments as might have retrieved them.

He hated trouble of every kind; and all the time he could spare from the *best company* was spent in eating, drinking, and sleeping; in studying luxuries for the following day, and directing his cook how to dress them; for he was dainty in his palate, and could not eat plain-dressed food.

A proof of his pride he gave me soon after our marriage: he desired me not to visit my sister or her husband often, but by degrees to break with them; and not take it ill, if he refused to go with me into the city, for he had no relish for any *bourgeois* acquaintance; and besides, if it were known that he visited tradesmen, he might be excluded the higher circles.

My brother-in-law soon perceived his coolness, and his motives: it drew upon me the resentment of all his family, without any fault of mine, but a reluctant compliance with his commands.

He staid out very late most nights. At first I sat up for him; but he desired I would go to bed at my usual time.

The evenings I spent alone, were devoted to reading and writing. I had a master three times a week, to improve me in French and Italian. I went into public places, in compliance with my husband's wishes, and never but when he was of the party. I kept up a general acquaintance with such families as he recommended, but I made no friendship: my mind refused to open itself to them; and I found nothing to invite me to esteem or confidence.

When Mr. Darnford came home from his nocturnal orgies, he crept to bed very softly; and wished not to awaken me, but rather that I should be ignorant what hours he kept. Sometimes, if he found me awake, he would apologize, saying—

"My Fanny, I ask your pardon; but I have been in the *best company*, and could not break away before they separated."

At length I began to reply in my own way—I wished he might not pay too dear for keeping the *best company*. I enquired how they spent their time; I declaimed on the mischiefs of gaming.

He was displeased at my remarks; he was judge of his own conduct, and would endure no such monitor.

I rejoiced at the approach of spring. I asked when he meant to leave London.

"Not till after the king's birth-day, certainly!" was the answer; "it would be absurd to think of it."

We had sometimes parties at home, but not very often; I was

always glad when they were over. I saw we were ruining ourselves, and cast about how to prevent it, but in vain.

At length, the birth-day was past. I made preparations for leaving London. He saw that I was impatient to be gone.

He came in, one day, and looked confused and uneasy.

"Madam, I am come to tell you, we shall leave London to-morrow; for I can stay here no longer."

"I am glad of it, Sir."

"So am not I; but it must be so."

"Then I hope you will make it easy to yourself; and I will do all in my power to make the country agreeable to you."

"Do you love the country, Fanny?"

"Yes, I do, especially when you are there."

"Thank you, my dear; but my company has not made you love London."

"I do not love it's vanities and dissipations, it's temptations, it's extravagant expences. It is not the place for people to grow wise or good in."[2]

He smiled—"Do you think the country will make me grow wise and good?"

"I hope so; and I pray that it may."

He shook his head—"Well, say no more of that. I am afraid you are too good and too wise for me."

"Few husbands pay such compliments to their wives; but I will try to deserve them by my conduct."

"Oh, Fanny, you are sly: you do not think I meant you a compliment. You are a good girl, but you are too serious. Don't preach to me, for it does me no good. Pack up your matters, and prepare for your journey."

So saying, he left me; and I lost no time in obeying his last command.

The next day, we left London; and I pleased myself with thinking that he would be all that I wished, when taken away from the *best company*, and obliged to associate with men of reason and principle.

Vain hope! vain expectation! The idle and dissipated always find companions wherever they go. It is not places, but persons, that make the manners of society. Those who complain of the society and situation where Heaven has placed them, are generally the people to be most complained of, who first act improperly, and then complain of the society they fall among, and the places where they reside.

The first month we spent in the country, I was pleased and entertained with a round of useful employments.

Our seat was pleasantly situated, on a rising ground, near a navigable river. On the opposite side were seen woods and lawns, with gentlemen's seats interspersed. It was a charming prospect, that cheared the heart, and delighted the eye. The house was a good one, not new, but airy and lightsome; it was well furnished, neat, and convenient: nothing was wanting, but that the master might be capable of enjoying his own blessings.

He sunk into supine indolence; he lounged about from one room to another, ate and slept, and thought the days too long for him.

I endeavored to inspire him with a love of country amusements. I walked with him, rode with him, fished with him.—He tasted no pleasure in any thing. I read to him, and conversed with him—he went to sleep. He asked my pardon: but reading and talking always had that effect upon him; except in a large circle of company, where the conversation was joyous, and entertaining enough to keep him awake.

I told him, that no man could be happy without some pursuit or employment.—He said, it was true; for the country was cursedly dull, but in London he never wanted employment.

I asked him what employment he followed there?—He could not specify any, but said there was a constant succession all the day and night.

I could have specified the fatal one that was his ruin—gambling: but I forbore it, and strove to lead him gently into the path of reason and of virtue.

I pointed out the study of agriculture.—He despised it, as fit only for vulgar people.

"Gardening!"— "The same."

I told him, that the greatest and wisest of men, of all ages and countries, had not thought it beneath them to pursue these and the like studies.—He left it to them, and had no wish to rob them of such honours.

"What are the honours to which you aspire?"

"A large fortune, that would allow me to enjoy all the pleasures life affords. I hate to be stinted in any thing."

"I will tell you the way to be rich."

"Pray do, and I will thank you."

"By regularity and oeconomy."

"Paltry *bourgeois* qualities! I hate and despise them."

"They are as necessary for gentlemen as for citizens."

"I leave them to citizens and stewards."

"Let me be your steward?"

"Yes, that you may check my expences—no, thank you."

"But, suppose you were running out your fortune, would you not thank a friend that would retrieve it?"

"No; I should think such a friend very impertinent. I would not retrench till I thought fit."

"Then it might be too late."

"Then I will live while I may; and I will hear no more preaching at this time: the sermon is too long."

He run out of the room; and I saw him no more till the evening.

The gentry of the neighbourhood came to visit us. Mr. Darnford received them with coldness and indifference. I tried to make amends by my courtesy and attention.

The clergyman of the parish was, what all ministers ought to be, an humble, modest, courteous man; his wife, a very friendly, good woman: he treated them contemptuously. Had they been like Dr. Proudly and his lady, he would have liked them better.

It was with some difficulty I prevailed on Mr. Darnford to return, with me, the visits we received. He said, he should not be much here, and he cared not whether they liked him or not. His behaviour lessened him greatly with them, and with me also: but he was my husband, and I resolved to do every thing in my power to serve and save him. I exerted all my abilities to please him, and to obtain his esteem and confidence, in hopes he would suffer me to assist him in regulating his affairs, and discharging his debts; but he spurned the idea of it.

In this manner we spent the first months at our country-seat. One day, he came in with a newspaper in his hand—the only kind of reading he loved or desired—

"My dear, I have something to propose, that I hope will be agreeable to you. Ipswich races are next week: will you go there with me?"

"I thank you, Sir, for your kind invitation; but, will it not be attended with too much expence?"

"Leave that to me, Madam."

"You are not offended, I hope, that I wish to spare you in every thing that concerns myself."

"Yes, Madam; you are always checking me, and shewing your own prudence at my expence. No matter! do as you please; but I shall go, whether you approve it or not."

He left me in displeasure, and said no more upon the subject.

The next day, I received a letter from my younger sister, informing me, that my father was very ill, and desired to see me as soon as I could conveniently go to him.

When Mr. Darnford came in, I was in tears. He came to me kindly, and asked what was the cause of my grief, seeming as if he thought it was himself. I shewed him the letter; he read it, and asked me what I meant to do. I told him, I wished he would carry me to my father's, and leave me there, while he went to Ipswich races, and call for me at his return from thence.

He said— "Had you rather spend the time with your father?" I answered, that I should; I thought him in a dangerous way, and should never forgive myself, if I neglected my duty to him, and went in pursuit of pleasure, falsely so called, in my estimation. When I had paid this duty, I would attend him upon the first notice.

He said— "I will do as you desire. I have spoken too sharply to you; and I ask your pardon."

This good-natured apology comforted me. I thanked him for it; and we were again on good terms.

As soon as I was ready, he carried me to my father's. He staid there one night only, and then went on to Ipswich races.

My father told me plainly, that he was going very fast, and that he wished to take a last leave of me. He bade me look upon his death as natural and unavoidable. He wished me sometimes to remember him, but not to lament him. He hoped my husband would be my comforter and protector. He had heard, with concern, that he was too expensive, and that he was addicted to gambling: but he hoped my prudence would be a check to him; and that he would stop in time, for my sake and his own.

My father said, Mr. Darnford had acted so handsomely in making me a settlement of three hundred a year, that he could not tie up the residue he had to leave me: but that he would venture to give him a word of advice when he should take leave of him.

He told me, that his first clerk and assistant, Mr. Jones, had offered himself to my sister Jane, in the hope of succeeding to his business; which would make him as good a match as her fortune required, and her person could expect; and that he had given his consent to the marriage. That he expected my eldest sister and her husband to visit him, after I should have left him. He was sorry to find that they avoided meeting Mr. Darnford and me, and that there was a coldness between us.

I said, that Mr. Darnford had assumed a kind of superiority that had offended them; that I was sorry for it, but could not help it.

My father gave me two bank-notes, one for fifty, the other an hundred pounds. He charged me to keep them safely from my husband's knowledge; saying, I might want them for my own expences.

He took pleasure in conversing with me alone. He had a partiality for me, he confessed, because I most resembled my mother; but he had kept an equal hand, and given us an equal share of his fortune.

He gave me also my dear mother's picture. This, and his other private benefaction, were the only marks of his acknowledged partiality: they were very dear to me, and received with many tears of gratitude and tenderness.

My sisters never loved me, though I never knew the reason. Perhaps they perceived my father's partiality. However it was, I was grieved that they were the only persons who treated me unkindly. My marriage increased their malevolence. My eldest sister had something like a reason: the younger had none. She was jealous and uneasy at my private interview with my father: I tried to conciliate her affections, but in vain.

Mr. Darnford returned at the week's end, to carry me home. He shewed concern for my father's situation. He told him it was a common one, and what all the race of man were born to; it was a lesson of mortality.

He said— "Sir, this is probably the last time I shall see you; allow me the privilege of a father to speak a word of advice to you. I am told that you are very expensive and dissipated; and, worst of all, that you are a frequenter of gaming-tables. This is, of all others, the readiest way to dissipate a fortune, without either pleasure or credit. If you find your own fortune insufficient for you, how will you bear the sting of poverty, and the reproach of having deserved it? How will you sustain the contempt of the world, and particularly of those men who have led you into this vice, and who will be with the first to blame and shun you? But, above all other evils, how will you bear the reproach of your own heart?

"Consider these things, dear Sir, whilst it is in your power to amend them: be just to yourself, and the world will respect you.

"I must assure you, that I did not hear these tidings from your wife, but from some persons who were eye-witnesses of your conduct in London, and who have foretold what I hope will not come to pass.

"You will correct yourself; you will retrench all superfluous expences; you will shun gambling, as the gulph of destruction. As a proof of the good opinion I have of you, I leave the residue of my daughter's fortune in your hands. Consider, it is a sacred trust, and beware how you abuse it. I leave my dearest child in your protection; be good to her, and be good to yourself; that is all I ask of you."

The tear stood quivering in Darnford's eye. I hailed the omen, and felt hope relieving my oppressed heart.

My father held out his hand to my husband. He gave him his own. I kneeled down, took Darnford's hand, and with my eyes implored a blessing.

He gave it most cordially; and it was properly received by us both.

My father was fatigued with this exertion. He bade us retire. He did not wish us to stay and watch the expiring embers of life: he even named the morrow, as the day of our departure.

I took a solemn farewel, and went away with my husband. He saw my grief, and endeavoured to comfort me.

I told him, it was only in his power to comfort me, by obeying my father's injunctions.

He was affected. He heard me with temper. He said, he would try to do better in future, than he had done hitherto: that my father was certainly right; and he would profit by his admonitions.

This hope gave me comfort, and abated my grief for my worthy father.

My father's situation and injunctions had made a faint impression upon the light mind of George Darnford. He behaved better; and even would listen to my advice, and promised to follow it.

My father died within a fortnight after our return home. He left a brother lawyer his executor: which I was glad to hear; for I feared that all our affairs would have fallen into the hands of Mr. Jones, of whom I had no good opinion. But my father's probity and good sense directed him to the best method of doing justice to all his children.

Upon a fair division of his property, my proportion of the residue amounted to eleven hundred pounds. Darnford asked me, how I wished to dispose of it.

I told him, I wished it employed in the way that was the most to his advantage—in paying his debts; which I dared not enquire into, till now that I had hopes to discharge them.

He looked sullen and uneasy, but made no answer.

Soon after, the executor wrote again, to know how and where Mr. Darnford would receive the money.

He ordered, that a thousand pounds should be placed in the hands of an eminent banker in London, and the remainder sent to his house here.

He paid me the compliment of shewing me the letter and his answer, but asked not for my advice or approbation. When I began to enquire, he always stopped me.

I once said— "It is pity the money should lie in a banker's hands, when it might be employed to advantage."

"I shall dispose of it," said he, "when I go to town."

"Have you any thoughts of going thither, Mr. Darnford?"

"I shall go thither when I think proper!" was his answer.

I feared to say more.

There was an house in our neighbourhood to be sold by auction. Lord A—— bought it for an hunting-seat, and furnished it in the cottage style. He knew Darnford, and invited him to dine with him. They commenced an intimacy: a fatal one it proved.

Lord A—— called upon him several times. He was introduced to me, and desired my acquaintance. He begged me to superintend the furnishing of his cottage, and to order what was wanting.

The transient impression of mortality was now worn out. He embraced Lord A——'s friendship with eagerness: he was more with him than at home. His notice gratified his pride, and stirred his indolence: it made him as happy as he desired to be.

My lord swore we were a charming pair, and capable of making the country agreeable at any time of the year. He staid about five weeks at his cottage, and then went to another seat. He desired that we would use the cottage as our own, when he was not there. He hoped we should be very intimate in town, in the winter.

I told him, it was my wish to stay where I was, and not go to town at all.

"The devil it is!" said Darnford; "then, you will stay here by yourself, my dear. I would not live here in the winter, to be lord of the whole country."

"You will settle that point in the mean time," said my lord; "and I will hope to see you at my house, very often."

He took a polite leave, and left us.

After my lord was gone, Darnford lounged away his time, as usual, inattentive to all the beauties of nature that surrounded him: the fields, crowned with the golden harvest; the trees, rich with fruit; and every flower and herb that sips the dew, in blossom; the industrious labourer, singing amidst his toils; the grateful incense which all nature daily offers to her Creator. I tried to open his eyes to these beauties, and his heart to a sense of gratitude to Heaven, for the blessings with which he was surrounded. In vain were all my efforts. The harlots, Fashion and Folly, had got entire possession of his heart, and lulled all his nobler faculties into a profound sleep, from which he would not be awakened.

Darnford now got acquainted with some of the neighboring gentry: he got among some jolly fellows, who loved the bottle. He drank with them; and, when they were elevated with liquor, they discovered, that Darnford was best company when he was so too. They grew fond of him; and he amused himself with them, because he was not within reach of his *best company*, as he called it.

Lord A—— returned in September. Darnford left his jolly fellows, and flew to him. They went out together, and pursued the sports of the field. They commonly dined together, at a late hour. I was always invited to make one at the table; but I had been brought up with *vulgar* ideas, and chose to eat at vulgar hours.

My husband often complained of my vulgar propensities; but he hoped another winter in London would do for him, and felt it, by anticipation: he longed as much for the time.

Lord A—— carried Darnford with him to the October meeting at Newmarket, where they staid a fortnight.

There was a farmer's daughter in the village, whom I distinguished from the rest of the young people. She was sensible and modest, and had a desire to improve herself in reading and writing. She loved my company; and I became her preceptress. When my husband was with Lord A——, she was my constant companion; and my vulgar taste preferred her conversation to that of most of those I had met in the *best company*.

When Darnford was at home, I sent her word not to come to the Hall. I had found him too familiar with one of my maidens; and I feared to trust my good Betsey in his company; for she was "fair, and comely to look on."[3]

When the gentlemen returned from Newmarket, Betsey was

with me. They examined her attentively with their eyes, and asked, where I had found that pretty maiden.

I said— "Where all the good girls should be found—at her father's house."

They told me, they would dine with me. I went out to give orders, and made a sign to Betsey to follow me. I gave her a caution against minding gentlemen's idle talk, and sent her home immediately.

When I returned, they bade me wish them joy; for they had been very fortunate. I shook my head, and said nothing.

"Look here, Fanny!" said Darnford, and took several *rouleaus*[4] out of his pocket.

He threw one into my lap—"There is something, to persuade you to prepare for a journey to London, and to buy new cloaths there!"

"I do not want any, Mr. Darnford: my cloaths are as good as new."

"Oh, but they have been seen, and will be known again: besides, they will be old-fashioned; and you will look like a fright, till they are new-modelled to the fashion."

"If you do not think me frightful, I shall not care what others think of me."

"You are a good girl; but you make every thing a serious matter.—My lord, she has but one fault: she is too good."

"For you, perhaps, Darnford. If I were to marry, I should wish for just such a wife."

I bowed to my lord. Darnford was pleased with the compliment; and they rallied each other.

They dined with me, and invited me to sup with them, at the cottage. I begged to be excused, as their hours did not suit me.

Mr. Darnford spent part of every day with Lord A——, and often the whole, from the hour of breakfast.

I was fond of country amusements. My dairy, my poultry-yard, my orchard, every green plant, gave me pleasure. We might have lived well, out of the produce of our farm; and there might have been money enough to squander away, for any man of a moderately expensive turn: but gaming is a gulph that swallows every thing.

>   ——The world is but a world:
> Were it all yours, to give it in a breath,
> How quickly were it gone!⁵
> SHAKESPEARE.

Lord A—— left his cottage in the beginning of November; and, from that time, I was employed in warding off our fatal journey: I even used artifice to delay it.

I told Darnford, that it was vulgar to go before Christmas; for no people of fashion would be in town. He agreed to that; but, still, it was pleasanter than the country.

I kept it off till the first week in February, well knowing that I was saving so much money as would be idly spent, or thrown away at the gaming-tables.

Lord A—— wrote to Darnford, and offered him his services in town: he offered him an apartment in his own house. This made him fix a day for our journey.

I begged him to be content with lodgings, and avoid all superfluous expences. He would not hear, nor mind me. We must go directly, and nothing should hinder it.

I set out with a foreboding heart. I asked, where we were to go immediately.—"To Lord A——'s. He has invited us to stay with him till we have a house ready."

I did not approve it; but it signified nothing. He would not be told of the impropriety; and I had nothing to do, but to obey.

Lord A—— received us with every mark of friendship and attention. He led us to the upper end of the table; and, in the politest manner, asked the favour of me to do the honours of a bachelor's house, who was proud to see a lady preside in it: he should think himself under an obligation for my assistance.

He told the company who we were, and called Mr. Darnford his friend.

They were all gentleman; and I felt a conscious aukwardness in doing the honours of the table. The vulgar virtue, called *modesty*, hung about me, and told me I was not in my proper place; though Lord A——'s politeness endeavoured to make it easy to me.

Darnford was quite at home, and at ease; and I never saw him more agreeable.

Lord A—— dined at home oftener than usual, in compliment to me. He and Darnford spent their evenings abroad, and never came home till a very late hour.

Whenever they dined at home, there was a circle of company. Sometimes ladies were invited; but they were not such as my mind could acquaint with—gay, vain, dissipated; they only gave me subjects for meditation and vexation.

There was a route,[6] one day. Good Heaven! what an assembly of men and women; who seemed to have discarded nature from their persons and manners, and to be acting in masquerade!

"Surely," said I, "these are not English people!—I must be conveyed into some strange land, where neither religion, reason, nor taste, have any influence."

The women shocked me. There was a boldness and self-consequence about them, that contradicted all my ideas of feminine delicacy: painted, patched, perfumed, powdered,[7] till you knew not of what complexion they were; full of gesticulations, that made them look like actresses who overdo the modesty of nature: in short, made up with all sorts of fashionable materials, till there was not a trace of nature upon them. "It seemed as if Nature's journeymen had made men and women, they disgraced human nature so abominably."[8] I was sick of them. I wished myself any where but where I was, though it was in the *best company*.

Lord A—— had desired me to play for him. I begged to be excused playing at all; but it was not allowed.

I was placed at a table where they played Half-guinea Whist.[9] There was a lady of the party who absolutely stared me down. I never saw, in either sex, such a degree of assurance as she exhibited. The cards relieved me; and Fortune gave me my revenge upon her, for I won all that I played for. There was a kind of jeer upon her countenance, that obliged me to look at her as little as possible; but I shall never forget her while I live.

The gentlemen were polite; and one of them seemed to feel for me. He gave some significant glances at my opponent: his eyes seemed to correct her's; but they, in return, bade him defiance. He was my partner; he perceived my diffidence, and gave me encouragement.

I was heartily glad when this scene was over, for it fatigued my mind.

I offered my lord the money I had won: he refused to take it. I told him, that I would then play no more for him. We had a contest; but he obstinately refused it.

I had cards from most of the company I had seen at Lord A——'s, but declined all their invitations.

Darnford was offended: he would accept them, if I did not. I said, he was his own master; but what made his paradise, was my purgatory.

One day, a nobleman and his wife dined at Lord A——'s. In this charming lady, I saw all that I had looked for in vain in the *beau monde*—good sense, good breeding, and that complacency that accommodates itself to it's company, and makes inferiors easy before it.

This lady opened my lips; and I felt myself honoured and delighted with her conversation.

Lord A—— observed me; and, after they were gone, he said—"I do not ask you, how you like Lady B——: I see, in your intelligent countenance, all that passes in your mind. She is, indeed, good and amiable. Though I comply, in some degree, with the whims of fashion, I know how to distinguish superior merit, and to pay homage to it. I promise myself, my dear Mrs. Darnford, that you will not decline answering Lady B——'s visit. Am I mistaken, or no?"

"My lord, I shall be afraid of you: you can read my thoughts."

"You need not, Madam; for you have nothing to conceal."

Darnford rallied my lord upon his penetration; and said, he had seen many ladies that he liked better than Lady B——.

"Her good qualities," said my lord, "are those of all times, and all countries: they do not depend on fashion. Wherever Lady B—— had appeared, she would have been beloved and respected."

I was pleased with his plaudit: it shewed discernment and judgment.

I have told you, that Darnford spent his evenings abroad—I might have said *nights*; for he seldom came home till four or five o'clock: from words that fell from him undesignedly, I found they were spent in gaming. Sometimes he was unreasonably elevated; at others, depressed. I was dissatisfied with him, and with our situation. I wished to remove to a place of our own. I could not bear that we should be guests, and, as it seemed, dependent on Lord A——. I frequently asked, when we were to leave him, but always received evasive answers. I would rather have lived in a cottage, with peace and a little, than in a palace, with these apprehensions of approaching poverty and ruin.

Some days after, cards were sent from Lord and Lady B——, inviting Lord A——, and Mr. and Mrs. Darnford, to dine with them, in Portman Square. Lord A—— would not suppose a denial possible on our part. Darnford answered for himself and me; and I did not decline it.

Darnford insisted that I should have a new dress on the occasion. I begged to appear in my wedding-cloaths, which were not soiled, nor yet out of fashion: he would not hear of it. He bade me to go to a certain mercer's, and take up new in his name. I told him, I had money by me; and I should take nothing but what I paid for before I wore it. He laughed at my folly and ignorance, but insisted on the new dress. He went with me, and chose it, lest my vulgar taste should disgrace him. It was bought, paid for, and made up against the day appointed.

When I went to the great business of the *toilette*, I found, in one of the dressing-boxes, a compleat set of pearls, of great value, which I was desired to adorn, by wearing them.

I was confounded and uneasy. I ordered my servant to enquire for her master; and, if he was in the house, to send him to me before the *friseur*[10] came.

He was at home, and came in a few minutes. I shewed him the jewels— "Did you purchase them, Mr. Darnford?"

"Ha!—why, no—yes—no matter—what signifies who bought them: here they are, very opportunely."

"Answer me truly, Sir—Do you know who sent them hither?"

"No, not I: they came here of themselves, for ought that I know."

"Very well.—But you see them; and I desire you will enquire who sent them. I will not wear them, till I know whether I ought to accept of them."

"Then, you are cursedly silly. I command you to wear them."

"Sir, I do not think myself bound to obey *all* your commands. You have power to ruin my fortune, and to destroy my peace: but my principles you shall never destroy; they forbid me to accept of presents from any man, except my husband; and I know too well, that he cannot afford to make such presents; and therefore I will not wear them."

"Tal didi-dididum!—Madam, your most humble servant."

He ran out of the room; and came thither no more, till after I was drest and gone into another room.

I did not wear the pearls, but drest myself in my own ornaments. I was uneasy; and grew more so, as I reflected on the dangers that surrounded me. I could not disappoint Lady B——, nor had I any inclination to do it. I resolved to come to an explanation with Lord A——, whom I suspected to have sent this present, and to leave his house as soon as possible.

I should have spent an agreeable day; but, whenever I reflected upon my dangerous situation, I felt, as it were, a string pulling at my heart, and telling me, I had no right to be chearful.

Lady B—— observed, that I was very serious for so young a lady: Darnford told her, it was my only fault.

After dinner, we retired, and she began an agreeable conversation. "I would not," said she, "invite other company, because I desired to have you to myself. I have seen enough, my dear Mrs. Darnford, to wish to know more of you. Let us be good neighbours and friends."

I thanked her ladyship for the honour she did me. I said, when we should be got into a house or lodgings of our own, I should be proud to cultivate her acquaintance; that, at present, we were out of our right place, and aukwardly situated; that I was impatient to remove, and should not be happy till we did.

"You are right, Mrs. Darnford. I commend your prudence."

"May I ask your ladyship, in confidence, what is Lord A——'s character? He is but a late acquaintance of our's. That he is a man of sense and politeness, as every one sees. He is very fond of Mr. Darnford's company; and they are inseparable: but I felt it as an impropriety, that we should make his house our home; and I wish to escape from it."

"I will answer you sincerely, Madam. I believe Lord A—— is a man of honour and principle. He is young, gay, and fashionable; and has been rather free in his conduct, but with discretion. Where he professes a friendship, I believe he is sincere: my lord loves and esteems him. I see that your prudence foresees and guards every point of conduct: I love and honour you the more. You may trust me safely; and, if any difficulties should arise, command my friendship and my services."

After this, we conversed upon many subjects. I found her well informed in all respects, and very polite and accomplished.

When the gentlemen came in to tea and coffee, Lord B—— urged us to stay supper; and we did not part till a late hour.

I was not well all the evening, nor yet easy in my mind, which perhaps increased my disorder. Lady B—— observed me to change colour several times. She asked me to retire from company: I declined it, and resolved to stay where I was. I was rejoiced when the carriage came, and motioned to go. The gentlemen could not let me go alone; and we went accordingly.

I will here conclude this sheet, and sign it with my initials,

F.D.

LETTER IV
Mrs. Darnford, in continuation.

THERE was a trait in Darnford's character, that gave me hope that he would at last hear me and follow my counsels. When I was in health, and at ease, he seemed to be quite indifferent towards me; but, if I was sick or distressed, it seemed to call forth all his tenderness, his love revived, and he was assiduous to comfort and support me.

I had not been well all the day that I spent at Lord B——'s. When I returned home, my sickness returned; and, before I could be undressed, I fainted away.

Never was man more tender and assiduous than my husband at this moment: he assisted my servant to put me to bed, he gave me drops and water, and would have sat up the remainder of the night if I had permitted him.

When he came to bed, I thanked him for his care and attention.

"I could not have thought you were so ill," said he. "Fanny, you looked like an angel to-day, you were well dressed, and were an elegant figure: did you put on *rouge* to-day?"

"No, Mr. Darnford, I never do, nor will I; but, indeed, I had hoped that you loved me for myself, and that my dress was of little consequence to an husband."

"You are mistaken, my dear; it is of great consequence to me; and it gives you consequence in the sight of others, and then I love you the better."

I sighed. I was mortified that this man's weak and frivolous mind should value me more for a new dress than for any internal quality, though I was always neat in my dress, and appeared as became his degree; but my lot was cast, and I resolved to make the best of it.

He asked me often how I did, and what he could do for me.

"I will tell you what will contribute most to my health and chearfulness: take me from Lord A——'s house, and carry me to some place that I can call my home."

"Why," said he, "what objection have you to this house?"

I told him all my objections, and shewed him the dangers that attended me and himself, from living in a state of luxury above our fortune; and his own reluctance to leave it was the strongest proof of it.

I asked him, whether he knew who sent me the set of pearls; he said, upon his soul he did not, but supposed they came from Lord A——.

I asked, if he thought it right for me to accept presents from gentlemen, especially single ones.—He saw no harm in it, so long as the husband knew and allowed it.

I was not obliged to tell my husband, I might have concealed it from his knowledge—He had so good an opinion of me, that he was sure I should act right upon all occasions.

We spent the remainder of the night in these altercations, and did not fall asleep till some time after day-light.

When Darnford told Lord A——, that I had been ill, he shewed every kind of attention and politeness.

He sent several messages, and desired I would not leave my own apartment. I sent word I was better, and should come down to dinner at the usual hour.

He sent to know, whether I would allow him to wait on me in the dressing room. I answered, I should be honoured to receive him there.

I resolved to come to an explanation with him concerning the pearls, which were still in the box, and to speak upon some other points as occasions might arise.

I encouraged myself to act as became me; and, knowing I was right, to put aside disqualifying fears: but, alas! they would rise, in spite of all my reasonings against them.

My lord came directly—he was full of concern for my indisposition; he was polite and friendly, and wished he could do any thing for my service.

I made acknowledgments for his friendship and attention.

After many compliments, I at length introduced the subject of the pearls.

The more sensible I was of their value, the more desirous I was to return them: they were above our degree and fortune, and I could never think of wearing them.

On his side, much sophistry, but no argument.

Supposing they were his present, which he had not yet acknowledged, what harm could there be in accepting the offering of friendship?—it looked like pride, to decline it.

Perhaps it might, but it was the pride of honesty and integrity, which wishes not to accept favours it can never return, and is already too much obliged.

"In what respect?"

"In making your house our home. Excuse me, my lord; but I feel that we are out of our proper place. When people are in our situation, they should not mix with those too much above them.

"Mr. Darnford has a turn for expence, and for dissipation. After living in the house of a nobleman of your rank and fortune, he will find it difficult to descend to his own station.

"I look upon your lordship as his friend; in that light I presume to consult you. He loves gaming, I am afraid he injures his fortune by it. I beg the favour of your lordship to check him, and to remind him of what he owes to himself and family."

My lord looked as if surprized at my plain dealing: he looked down, as if abashed; he was confused, uneasy, and restless. He rose up, and walked about the room, and was silent for several minutes.

He looked displeased; his face was in a glow; and, at last, he spoke—

"When I invited Mr. Darnford to my house, I did not expect to be charged with all the faults and follies he might commit under my roof: it is enough for me, to answer for my own."

"Very true, my lord: but, when he is always in your company, when he looks up to you as his friend and patron, a wife may perhaps be excused for imploring your influence with him; a wife, who cannot be wholly indifferent to his conduct."

My heart was full, I wept involuntarily. Lord A—— came to me, he dropt upon one knee— "Forgive me, dear Mrs. Darnford; I fear I have given you pain; I see your distress, I pity your sincerity. Yes, Darnford does game deeply: I have tried to check him, but in vain. What do you wish me to do more? Tell me what I can do to serve you?"

"I will speak my wishes—Suffer us to go to a lodging more suitable to our fortune and situation, discourage my husband to frequent the gaming table; do this, and I will bless and pray for you for ever!"

"I will, by Heaven, if you insist upon it!—But why will you not stay here till you leave London? I meant it to save expences to him and you: why are you so earnest to leave me?"

"My lord, I see and feel the impropriety: to your good sense, I need not say more."

"You shall be obeyed, Madam: you will not submit to owe any obligation to me. I think I see your motives, and I respect them, though they give me more pain than I dare express. You shall do as you please, but you will leave a sense of your merit engraved upon my heart in strong and indelible characters. Honour me with your confidence and friendship; I swear to deserve them, whatever it costs me."

He went out of the room with tears in his eyes; they seemed those of honour and sincerity. My heart was lighter; it threw off a part of it's burthen. I prepared to meet the reproaches of Darnford, and to depart as soon as possible.

I went down to dinner: Lord A—— behaved more respectfully than ever. As soon as it was over, I retired to my apartment.

I saw Darnford no more till he came to bed, which was earlier than usual. He was in a very ill humour; he reproached me with perverseness and false delicacy; he found my illness was only a pretence to leave the house; I wanted him to go to some dog-hole or another, and to live in my own vulgar style; that I made him slight the friendship of Lord A——, to gratify my own humours.

When he had run himself out of breath, I asked him to let me go to Darnford Hall, and I would leave him at Lord A——'s, till he chose to come home.

No, by G——! I should not have my own humour so far; I should stay in London as long as he did.

I was silent.

After he had exhausted himself and his passion, he cooled all at once; he asked my pardon, and begged me to be friends with him.

I endeavoured to prepare myself for suffering, and resigned myself to it. I got but little sleep for several nights, and looked ill and dejected. He tried to make me change my mind, but I was determined.

We went to look at lodgings; they were all too high for me, and too low for him. At last he took one in Bloomsbury Square, and we removed thither after staying two months at Lord A——'s.

His lordship took a polite and respectful leave of me. He asked my permission to visit me sometimes; I told him I should be honoured by his visits.

He hoped I would sometimes dine with him. I bowed assent.

We went to our lodgings: Darnford was sullen and silent.

I saw very little of him: he breakfasted at home, generally dined with Lord A——, and I saw him no more till his bedtime.

My time was now more my own. I went out before dinner. I visited my sister in the city: she received me very coldly. I asked her to come to me, but she declined it.

She threw out hints of Mr. Darnford's misconduct; that he was ruining himself very fast; that he had thrown them to a distance, and now they would keep it.

My evenings were very lonely and dull, but I had recourse to books: I sent to a circulating-library,[1] and was furnished with all the new publications.

One night, or rather morning, Darnford came home: he threw himself into a great chair, instead of coming to bed. I had slept, and was awake.

I had always a light burning, and I saw that he was much disturbed.

He threw himself about, clasped his hands, and used many gesticulations.

He sighted deeply, and uttered words of anguish— "Cursed luck! D——n the dice! Oh, my head aches! Fanny says true; she is wiser than I. What of that? Shall she reproach my conduct?—O fool! blockhead! ass that I am!—Well, 'tis no matter—A short life, and a merry one, for me!"

"From such mirth as your's, Mr. Darnford, good Lord deliver me!"

"So, then, you heard me.—Don't say another word, Fanny: if you do, I will go out again—I cannot bear preaching now."

"Come to bed, and compose yourself."

"Will you comfort me, instead of reproaching me?"

"I will, Mr. Darnford; and I will pray for you."

"That is kind; for, indeed, I am unable to pray for myself."

I soothed him to rest; but could take none myself, so much had he alarmed me.

He slept several hours, and awoke refreshed. He thanked me for the kindness with which I received him. He wished he had followed my advice: he sighed. He confessed he had lost a large sum of money; he must sell an estate of value: could I forgive him?

I told him, if it was the last sin of the kind, I would forgive it; and, if poverty rendered him good and wise, I would welcome it's approach, and share it most chearfully.

"Do not name poverty," said he: "I cannot bear it."

"I can, Mr. Darnford: it is not the worst of evils. We may, if it is not our own faults, render it a blessing to us."

"You are a blessing to me, Fanny; and I will put myself under your direction."

I was rejoiced to hear him speak so rationally; but I conjectured, that he must have suffered deeply, to be so much humbled.

I questioned him concerning the state of his affairs. He drew back, and would not tell me his true situation. I wondered that he staid at home the whole day with me. I endeavored to entertain him: I read Marmontel's Good Wife[2] to him, to shew him that a woman might be trusted, and sometimes might extricate her husband from difficulties. He shook his head, and was silent.

In the course of the day, he received several letters, and sent answers to them. In the evening, he received one that seemed to make him easy.

"'Tis over!" said he: "I have found a friend!"

"I am glad of it," said I; "but, why will you not treat me like one?"

"Yes, you are my friend; but you could not have done for me what this person has."

I begged to know who it was; but he would not tell me: he changed the subject. He was easy and chearful; and the storm seemed to be blown over for the present.

Lord A—— had frequently invited me to dinner: I went sometimes. He complained of my reserve and shyness. I renewed my solicitations, that he would give my husband good advice, and thus prove himself our friend. He sometimes was angry; at others, he promised to do as I wished him. He said, I over-rated his influence with Mr. Darnford; for he would not be advised, nor reproved.

Darnford behaved well a whole week. He never spent an evening from me: but he would not answer my enquiries; he would not let me know the true state of his affairs.

We dined with Lord A——, without any other company. My lord proposed that we should go to the third act of the play.

Darnford said— "Just as Frances pleases: I am now under her direction."

"I rejoice to hear it," said my lord. "The stool of repentance becomes you well."

"I don't understand that," said he: "I am not pleased to be thought so humble, neither."

"Don't be afraid of being thought too wise, Darnford. I should be proud to sit upon any seat, with such a companion by my side."

I was never pleased with my lord's compliments: I always put them aside. I answered, that, if Mr. Darnford liked it, I would go with them willingly.

The coach was ordered, and we went.

The play was, The Fatal Marriage.[3]—Mrs. Siddons[4] in the character of Isabella—the most heart-probing scene of distress: mine felt it too strongly. Lord A—— observed me; and, in the interval between the acts, he said— "These tragic writers work up scenes of distress, that affect us too deeply; and, what is worse, they punish the most innocent and perfect characters the most severely."

"That is not the present case, my lord: Isabella is not a perfect character."

"No!—What crime has she committed?"

"That of perjury. She was a nun profest; she broke her vow, eloped, and married Biron. Perhaps you never saw or read the whole play?"

"Yes, I have; but I have forgot it."

"Permit me to remind you. Count Baldwin, when she appeals to Heaven, thus answers her—

> "How dare you mention Heav'n!—Call to mind
> Your perjur'd vows; your plighted, broken faith,
> To Heav'n and all things holy.—Were you not
> Devoted, wedded to a life recluse,
> The sacred habit on, profest and sworn
> A votary for ever?"[5]

"Then, Madam, why do you weep for her?"

"Because, though she is guilty enough to be blamed, she is innocent enough to be pitied. Such are the proper subjects of tragedy; and Southern[6] shewed his knowledge of human nature, by selecting them. A perfect character raises our admiration: a mixed one is more common and more natural, and engages our pity and our sympathy."

My lord praised my remarks extravagantly, and said they were of more value than the play.

I told him, I was more mortified than gratified by undue compliments; that it reflected upon his own judgment, as the remarks were common, and not originally my own. He seemed abashed, and stood corrected.

After the play was over, we returned in my lord's coach, and supped at his house.

There was a good deal of light and frothy conversation upon the subject of the play. Darnford asked me, what I should have done in Isabella's situation.—I said, I believed I should have lost my senses, as she did; and in that situation I should not have been accountable for my actions: that our stage abounded in suicides, and I thought it was of bad tendency; that the pride of human nature revolted against sufferings of every kind; but those who professed to be Christians, ought to expect them, and to prepare to meet them.

The gentlemen said, I was too serious: they did not like the turn I gave to the conversation.

We did not part till a late hour. Darnford said, since I liked plays, he would attend me to another, whenever I pleased.

I looked over the play-bills, in order to pick out one that might be likely to make some impression upon his mind, as it seemed now to be fluctuating between right and wrong.

The *Gamester*[7] was announced for the Thursday following. I burnt the play-bill, that he might not see what it was. I did not ask him to go, till I met him at dinner. He said— "With all my heart.—What is the play?"

I asked the servant for the bill: luckily he had not seen it. It could not be found. I said, it was no matter; we would take our chance.

He was always dilatory; but I hurried him, as I wished him to be there before the play began. We got there in time, as I wished.

He was attentive to the play. He sat uneasy upon his seat, and I perceived that he felt it. As the catastrophe approached, he was more agitated. He asked me, who wrote this play: I told him, Mr. Moore. He said, it seemed to him as if I had written it; for it spoke my sentiments. I said, I was proud to think and to speak like this author. The last act was too much for him: he grasped my hand; he trembled— "Oh, God! I cannot bear this!—*Why* did you bring me here?"

I whispered in his ear— "To touch your heart, to serve you, and to save you."

"You chose it, then!—You have torn my heart asunder!"

I answered, in the words of Hamlet— "Oh, throw away the worser part of it, and live the better with the other half!"[8]

"Let me go home!"

"You shall, presently; and I will go with you."

I had ordered the carriage and the servants to be ready, in hopes to get him to go home at the end of the play, that he might not lose the benefit of the impression.

We went home accordingly. Darnford was deeply affected; but he shewed it in a way that proved his inconsistency.

As soon as he began to recover his spirits, he shewed anger against me: I had laid a plot to torment and vex him; he hated plays—they were vulgar amusements; he had not been at any this year, till Lord A—— carried him to one; and he went to this to oblige me, and I had repaid him for it.

I kept silence, and let him run himself out of breath. Then he paused.

I said, if I had given him pain, it was in order to save him from greater; and I hoped there would come a time, when he would thank me for it.

He had vented his uneasiness: he grew sullen, and would not answer.

I went to bed uneasy; and a thousand painful apprehensions came over me. I was going to rise again, when I heard him coming up stairs. He came softly, supposing me to be asleep. He came to bed. He spoke not any more; but I heard him sigh often.

I prayed earnestly, that this impression might lead him to reform his conduct, and to be good and happy.

Ever since we had been at lodgings, there had been a constant succession of people, every morning, knocking at the door. They enquired for Mr. Darnford; they left letters, and messages, and bills: I found they were an army of duns.

Our upper servant was a sober and sensible man. He always seemed unwilling to tell me the business of these people; and he semed[9] concerned for me.

I was preparing myself for the worst that could happen: I expected it, and could not be surprized at any thing.

Several men called on Darnford the next day after the play: he went to them in the parlor, and staid with them some time.

When he met me at dinner, he behaved with his usual politeness, and as if nothing disagreeable had passed. I followed his lead, and endeavoured to entertain and amuse him. I played *picquet* with him in the evening, and was agreeably surprized to find that he semed to have no wish to go from home.

He apologized for what he had said in anger. "Oh, that play!" said he; "I wish I had seen it two years ago: but now it has opened a vein in my heart, and it bleeds to no purpose."

I said, I hoped it was to good purpose, and that he would be the better man ever after.

Still he kept at home.

I asked him to go with me to a comedy; but he said— "No more plays of any kind: I have done with them."

A few days after, I received an anonymous letter, in these terms—

"A PERSON, who knows Mrs. Darnford's merit and character, wishes to prepare her for a cloud that hangs over her head, and is ready to burst upon her. Mr. Darnford has sold all his estates that are in his power to sell; Darnford Hall, and the estates about it, are entailed upon a male heir; and, unless Mr. Darnford has a son, they will go to his cousin, James Darnford, Esq. so that he can neither sell nor mortgage them; but he may anticipate the revenue of those estates, so that they may be sequestered during his life. If this person is rightly informed, Mrs. Darnford will shortly be desired to set her hand to a writing, by which she will give up her jointure;[10] which if she does, she is undone. She is advised to be resolute and steady in her refusal. This warning comes from a friend, who regards her for the sake of her worthy father, and esteems her for her own conduct under the most trying situations.

"BENEVOLUS."

Thus warned, I resigned myself to my fate, and begged of Heaven to strengthen my mind to support it properly.

I conjectured that this letter came from my father's executor; and I was not mistaken. A few days afterward, Mr. Darnford told me, that some gentlemen were to breakfast with him, and desired my company.

He said, he had always found me generous and kind to him, upon all occasions; that he was under some difficulties, and his estates were so tied up, that he could not sell them: therefore he must ask the favour of me to set my hand to a writing, which would enable him to sell an estate that would set him clear of the world; and afterwards, he was resolved to retrench, and to do every thing I could desire of him.

I said, I would consider of it.

"I am thinking of something that will extricate you from your present difficulties. You know the thousand pounds which my father left, were lodged in the banker's hands: use that to free you from your difficulties."

He turned pale, and his lips quivered. He said, that would not be sufficient.

"What, then, do you require of me?"

He was silent.

"You do not, I presume, ask me to give up my settlement, which is all that is left to support me!—You cannot be so base as to ask it!"

He was silent, and in confusion.

"Unhappy man! I will spare you the shame of uttering this request; and I will tell you, if that is your meaning, I will not comply with it: I will keep that, to support you and myself, and to keep us above absolute poverty. Go to your gentlemen, and tell them so."

He retired in silence. He never came home the whole night. I spent it in prayer, and in arming myself with a strong resolution.

The next morning, he came in while I was at breakfast, pale as death, and in much confusion.

I asked, how he did.

"Bad enough!" was his answer.

"I am sorry for it."

"What, Madam, would you advise me to do?"

"Go directly into the country with me."

"I cannot go till my affairs are settled."

"That will never be. I have no other advice to give you."

He went out again, and came home no more all that day and night.

He came to dinner, the following day, with a more chearful countenance. He told me, he had a proposal made him, and came to consult me upon it.

I said, my best advice was always at his service.

He said, a gentleman of very large fortune was going to France and Italy, and wanted a travelling companion; that he had invited him to go with him; that he saw my regard for him was at an end, and that I could spare his company; and therefore he was inclined to go.

I said, he was very unjust and ungrateful, to say so; that I had offered to share his lot in poverty, as well as in riches; that many people were rich and independent with two hundred a year; that I could be easy and contented with it; and, if he would suffer me to manage it, I would promise that he should want none of the comforts of life: but, if he preferred being a rich man's toad-eater[11] to that situation, he was free to pursue his own inclinations, only not to impute it to me, since it was entirely his own act and deed.

It was with some difficulty that I avoided all reproaches; and, in all that I said, only adverted to the future.

In the evening, he went out again, and staid all night. I had many struggles in my own mind; but I left it to him to decide his future situation.

Lord A—— called on Mr. Darnford. He was not at home. He asked for me, and I received him.

He enquired into the particulars of my husband's situation.

I said, he was probably better informed than I was: I only knew that he was ruined.

Lord A—— offered me any services in his power. I thanked him, but declined them.

He called me an inflexible woman, who would not condescend to receive any act of friendship, or to owe an obligation to any one.

I said, I could not wish to owe obligations, and least of all to gentlemen; that I was amply provided for, and as rich as I desired.

He said, Mr. Darnford would go abroad for a few years, till his affairs were, in some degree, retrieved; and that he had recommended him to Mr. Bryanstone, and he thought it would be a pleasant connection for them both; that Darnford had promised him to leave off gaming entirely; that he was now convinced of his errors, and would certainly reform—Did I mean to leave London soon? where did I purpose to go?

"I shall not go till poor Darnford does, which I suppose will be soon."

He begged pardon for his curiosity: he had something to propose for mine and Darnford's service.

I begged him to speak it.

"I have been thinking that Darnford Hall might be let to very good account, ready-furnished. I know a gentleman who is very likely to take it for a summer residence. In that case, I should beg of you, Madam, to accept of my cottage, for this summer at least. I should only come thither as your guest, and at such times only as were convenient to you. Pray consider, before you refuse me the honour of accommodating you for a few months. Do not look offended. I offer it in the sincerity of my heart, and with all the warmth and purity of friendship.

I was inflexible, as he called me; I would not accept any favour from him.

I thought I saw the cloven-foot appear; but I would not let him perceive that I did.

I thanked him for his solicitude to serve us. I approved very much of his proposal to let the Hall ready-furnished. I begged him to mention it to Mr. Darnford, and I would second it.

"But then, Madam, what becomes of you?"

"I shall find a place to board in suitable to my situation."

He tried, by every kind of argument, to induce me to go to the cottage; but in vain.

He looked angry, but prudently restrained himself from

speaking in that style. He went away before Darnford returned.

My husband now was all penitence and humility: he really seemed reluctant to leave me. He begged me to write to him often: he hoped we should meet again, and happier hours would succeed.

He had given me money several times, when he was in a run of luck. I now divided it with him: he swore I was an angel; and he was unworthy to be my servant.

Our parting was affecting on both sides. He went with Mr. Bryanstone to Dover, and from thence to France.

He had sold the chariot and horses, and discharged the coachman and footman. The upper-servant desired to continue with me; but I told him, I should not in future keep a man-servant. I asked if he had received his wages: he said, "No, but he would wait till it was quite convenient for me." I was surprised at the man's disinterestedness; but I paid him instantly.

I next spoke to the landlady, and found she was paid up to the present week. I packed up my clothes and linen; and discharged my own maid-servant, who was much too fine a lady for me.

I kept my other maid, who was the under house-maid when at the Hall, but now was every thing to me: I sent her to the inn, to take places for us in the stagecoach to N——, and in three days time I turned my back upon London.

Lord A—— had called several times— "Not at home!" was the answer. I chose not to see any company not to go any where; but spent my time in preparing for my journey, and in laying plans for my future conduct. Before I left London, I wrote to Lord A——, and kept the copy of my letter—

"MY LORD,

"I CANNOT leave London without paying my acknowledgments to your lordship for the many acts of friendship which Mr. Darnford and myself have received from you. We gladly agree to your lordship's proposal of letting Darnford Hall; and I am impowered to treat upon this subject with any person that it may suit, of which you gave me some reason to hope. I shall be ready to quit it by Midsummer, or sooner, if required.

"Perhaps some part of my conduct may appear ungrateful to your lordship; but when you reflect that I am particularly circumstanced; and that, having imbibed unfashionable principles, I am more solicitous to acquit myself to them, than to what is called the world, or the first circle of it, I hope I shall stand excused. I am, nevertheless, very sensible of the favours which my husband and I have received from your lordship; and am your lordship's most humble servant,

"F. DARNFORD."

I ordered this letter to be sent the morning after I left London, and when I should be out of the reach of all it's dangers.

Darnford Hall appeared unpleasant to me, from the consciousness that it was no longer my home, and that I must seek a new one.

You remember my pupil, of whom I spoke, Betsy Moyle. Her parents lived in an old mansion-house, which had formerly been the residence of an ancient family: the estate, like others, had passed through many different hands, and was now tenanted by these worthy people.

I intended to board with them: I proposed it, and they consented.

They were surprized to hear of the alteration in my circumstances; and feared they could not accommodate me according to my degree.

I chose a parlour and a bed-chamber; and amused myself with fitting it up to receive myself; and my servant, a poor cottager's daughter, whom I had taken as a house-maid. She was now my attendant; the cook remained with me for a time, and I discharged all the rest.

I had my apartment at Moyle's new painted, which made it look light and chearful. I furnished it in the plainest manner. I put a small canopy-bed into the chamber, for my servant to be near me; and I waited with some impatience to hear of a tenant for the Hall.

The rector of the parish visited me: he offered me his services; he invited me to his house, and his wife behaved in the most friendly manner.

This kindness was unmerited by me; for Darnford would never suffer me to be intimate with them, but barely to keep up an external civility towards them.

They had heard that I was going to board at Moyle's; and they offered to take me into their family, if I preferred it. I thanked them for their kindness; but told them I had fitted up an apartment at Moyle's, and agreed with him for my board, and could not go back unless for some powerful cause: that I hoped to be their neighbour there, and to deserve their goodness to me.

At length I received a pacquet of letters from Lord A——, containing one from himself, one from my husband, and the third from the amiable Lady B——. I here enclose them.

"MADAM,

"THOUGH you disdain my friendship, and spurn at the shadow of an obligation to me; I will follow you with my good offices, and do every thing that is likely to give you pleasure. I have seen Lady B——, and we have spoken of you; she loves and esteems you: perhaps you may accept her services, though you reject mine. Strange! that my sex should place me in an unfavourable light; and that her's should entitle her to your confidence!

"I have spoken to Mr. Frampton, and he will soon come down to look at your house; and, if it will suit his family, he will take it. I would attend him, if you would invite me; but I do not expect it, because you shun the sight of me. I am, as much as you will permit me to be, your faithful friend and servant,

"A——."

"DEAR FANNY,

"HERE I am in the city of Paris, which the French chatter of, as if it was the first in the world; but I do not think it is in any degree equal to London. The people I like well enough, for you know we keep the *best company*. I like their cookery; for you know I always loved made dishes:[12] but they give you a loin of mutton, and call it *a roast beef*. The wine is good, and I do it honour.

"I play very little, and only for trifles; but Fortune is always a jade to me. Mr. Bryanstone is reckoned a very fine gentleman; but I do not think him equal to Lord A——. Perhaps he may have more learning than he; but then, in polite accomplishments, Lord A—— is much superior.

"I am sure my lord is my true friend. He has promised to use his interest to get me a place; and then I shall hire a small house near the office I belong to, and we shall live comfortably. I will limit my expences, and you shall be my steward; and I will never play for more than a limited sum: you shall direct me, and advise me, and we will never part more.

"There is a certain Mr. Wilson, Mr. Bryanstone's companion and friend, a clergyman, and very learned and wise in his own opinion. This Mr. Wilson takes upon him to reprove and correct me, and behaves very impertinently to me, and I can hardly bear it.

"When I appeal to Bryanstone, he tells me, I must submit to a man of letters, who knows better than me; and that he prefers Wilson's judgment to his own. They make me appear as if I was very ignorant in comparison of them; and I do not feel myself easy with them: however, I shall bear it for a time, in hope to be recalled, as soon as Lord A—— can provide for me.

"I am sorry, my Fanny, that you are prejudiced against this amiable man; but I hope there will come a time when you will know how to value his friendship. Write to me often; tell me every thing that concerns me to know, particularly about yourself.

"Send your letters, under cover, to Lord A——, and he will forward them to me.

"Keep up your spirits, and hope for better days. Be assured of the constant and inviolable affection of—

"Your faithful husband,
"GEORGE DARNFORD."

PARIS.

"DEAR MADAM,

"I SHOULD certainly have waited on you, as soon as you went to lodgings; but was obliged to leave town at that time, to visit a very dear relation, who was dangerously ill—an aunt, who was so good as to supply the place of a mother to me, at the time when I most wanted one, from my leaving school till I was married. I have had the happiness to leave her quite recovered, and to please myself with the thoughts, that my tender attentions have in some degree continued towards it.

"My cares are now directed to a still dearer object. My lord is in an ill state of health: he is advised to go to Italy. I would go to the world's end to restore him; and, out of question, I attend him, and am his first nurse and companion.

"The first time I saw Lord A——, after my return to town, he told me of the surprizing alteration in your circumstances and situation. I was very much concerned for you. I saw, from the first moment I knew you, that your mind was not easy, and I judged that you were unfortunate, but not blameable. I forbear to speak my opinion of Mr. Darnford, because he is your husband: I hear he is gone abroad with Mr. Bryanstone; but what becomes of you in the mean time? Will you do me the favour to give me your company while I stay at my country-seat, and to go with us to the Continent? Consider of this proposal, and be assured that it comes from the heart.

"Lord A—— is mortified, that you will accept no favour from him. He shewed me your letter to him before you left London. I comprehend your motives, and honour you for your guarded conduct. You can have no such scruples towards me. Permit me the honour to be your friend; and, under that title, accept the trifle I enclose.

"My lord unites with me in every sentiment of esteem and friendship. Direct to me in Portman Square; and believe me truly, dear Madam, your sincere friend and humble servant,

"LOUISA B——."

Here, my friend, I will conclude my enormous pacquet, which I shall send by Patty. During her absence, I shall be preparing another, which I shall send to W——, by the person who fetches her home.

You must make me the return of your own story, from the time of our separation.

I am, yours truly,
FRANCES DARNFORD.

LETTER V
Mrs. Darnford, in continuation.

I ANSWERED Lord A——'s letter first. I thanked him for his kind attention to Mr. Darnford's interest. I told him, I was ready to receive the gentleman, as soon as was convenient to him to come down; that my principles did not allow me to invite single men to visit me in my husband's absence; I hoped he would excuse my frankness, or else that he would impute it to my vulgar prejudices, which were not to be subdued.

I enclosed a letter to Darnford, which was as follows.

"I AM surprized, Mr. Darnford, that your past misconduct, and your sufferings in consequence of it, have not corrected that light and frivolous turn of mind which gives all it's attention to trifles, and neglects things of the first importance.

"What signifies it to me, how you eat and drink, or what cloaths you wear? You play still, then—and for trifles, because you have not money to play deeper: great virtue and self-denial in that!

"Your utmost ambition is to be in a state of dependance on others. This is a mean and abject spirit.

"I had hoped you were studying how to be industrious and independent; to retrieve the time and fortune you have so cruelly mispent.

"You were bred to the law: perhaps, if you had practised it, you might now have been in an easy and comfortable situation; but the addition of your uncle's estate made you vain, idle, and dissipated.

"You are still young enough to pursue your original destination. Put yourself under the direction of some lawyer of eminence; study hard; be honest and diligent. Pursue this course, and you may retrieve your fortune and character, and become a good member of society.

"If you do not, but continue idle and expensive, you will become the contempt of all mankind, as I perceive you are to your present companions.

"Come home to me, poor, honest, and industrious, and I will welcome you to my arms, and to my heart: but, if you continue in your present sentiments, I will seek my fortune by myself.

"If Lord A—— should provide for you in the way you mention, take notice, that I will not live with you in London. I hate the city, and defy all it's temptations.

"I beg you to find out some other method of conveyance; for I do not chuse that all our letters should pass through the hands of Lord A——.

"You value yourself upon keeping the *best company*, who have led you to dissipation and ruin: but you have not yet learned wherein consists the true spirit of a gentleman; it is, in being superior to every thing mean, selfish, and unworthy.

"Learn and confess this truth, and I will call myself your faithful and affectionate wife,

"F. DARNFORD."

I should have told you, that Lady B——'s letter covered two Bank-notes, of fifty pounds each.

I paid my best acknowledgments for her unmerited friendship and kindness. I declined her proposal, because I feared poor Darnford would have need of me, and I could not give him up entirely.

I would not refuse all her favours, and therefore I kept one of the notes, but returned the other, assuring her that I was not in want of money, nor at present likely to be: I wished to preserve her invaluable friendship; and there might be a time when I might be permitted to converse with her personally. In the mean while, I begged her to honour me with her correspondence.

I wrote to Counsellor M——, my father's executor. I told him my past and present situation; I desired his advice and assistance in regard to letting the Hall, and what price I should ask for it.

He answered me, very kindly, that, as soon as I knew when the gentleman would come down, I should let him know, and he would meet him there.

Mr. Frampton wrote word by his steward, that he would come to Darnford Hall the following week. I gave notice to Mr. M——, and he came the day before.

Mr. Frampton brought with him another gentleman, and his steward, who was an attorney.

They talked over the business with Mr. M——; and, after some altercation, Mr. Frampton took the house for three years certain, ready furnished, with all the land about it, the farming stock and cattle, and every thing upon the premises; conditioning to leave every thing, in all respects, as good as he found it.

I had before-hand taken a few necessaries for my own use, and sent them to my new lodgings, where every thing was prepared for my reception; and I agreed to give up the house the week following.

Mr. M—— assured me, that Darnford had still many debts unpaid; but he did not know the extent of them. He advised me to set apart the rent of the Hall and farm; and, at every year's end, to pay off so much of the debts.

I begged him to enquire into them, and to send me an account of them.

I offered to pay him for his services; but he resolutely refused to accept it, saying, he was over-paid by the satisfaction it gave him to serve a daughter of Mr. Lawson, whom her relations had abandoned to her ill fortune. He desired me to consult him as often as I should have occasion.

As soon as the gentlemen left Darnford Hall, I removed into my new lodgings, where I was joyfully received by Mr. Moyle and his family. My old pupil desired to receive new lessons from me; and her two sisters envying her advantages, I taught them all.

I thought I perceived in myself a talent for the education of youth; and I resolved, if I should be reduced to indigence, to undertake something of this sort.

I read many books of this kind; I wrote remarks on them; I drew plans of seminaries of education. In short, I endeavoured to qualify myself for this employment; and one of my plans was afterwards realized.

I was not unhappy in this situation, excepting when Darnford came across my thoughts. I pitied him, but could no longer esteem him: and I confess, at times, something too much like contempt for him arose in my mind; but I checked it, and resolved to fulfil my duty, however painful and distressing it might be to me.

Mr. Frampton's family came to the Hall. They had acquired a fortune in India. They were proud and stately, assuming the style, and expecting the homage, of princes.

If Darnford's pride gave offence, think what these, his successors, gave! It put people upon enquiring after their origin. They discovered that Mr. Frampton and his wife were both adventurers: that they were nursed in the bosom of Indigence; and that, being raised to affluence, they knew not how to behave to others, less fortunate, but not less deserving, than themselves.

I doubted whether to visit them or not: my pride came to my assistance, and turned the scale. Should I keep back from visiting them, it might seem as if I thought myself of too inferior a degree to aspire to their acquaintance. They shall not think so; I will shew them the contrary.

Oh, my friend! how often does pride turn the scale of our actions! even the best have too often a tinge of it! *"Pride is the Serpent's egg, laid in the hearts of all, but only hatched by fools and wicked men."* Would one think this sentence was written by a madman, in the midst of a thousand follies and impertinencies? Yes, it was; but crazy Johnson,[1] the author of Hurlothrumbo: yet many rational men have never said any thing so good in their whole lives. Many endeavour to conceal this quality; but it will always break out at some time or other. I think it better to confess mine, and to claim the allowance due to ingenuousness.

The latent seeds of pride being thus stirred up, I visited the Framptons.

Madame was a large woman, with a look of self-consequence about her, that impressed an idea of itself upon common beholders. She affected a kind of dignity that imposed upon them; but, to those who looked beyond the surface, she seemed a vessel of pride, whose reverberation proclaimed it's emptiness. Had a modest and diffident mind inhabited that body, it would have been overlooked; but the consequence it gave itself, made it be distinguished; and she was called a fine woman.

Mr. Frampton was very like, for a man, what his lady was for a woman. *"A man of my fortune! a man of my consequence!"* were the words oftenest in his mouth: and he seemed to despise the house, as not suitable to a man of his fortune, though it was known that he had lived in a cottage in his childhood, and wanted most of the comforts and conveniencies of life.

The great couple had two sons, and three daughters. They kept a private tutor for the young gentlemen, and a French governess for the young ladies; and they were to be fashionably educated.

The eldest daughter was the copy of her mother.

The second had a look of modesty and good sense, but was brow-beaten and kept back, lest she should obscure the merit of her elder sister. This was, in fact, of great advantage to her, as it obliged her to take some pains to make herself agreeable.

The third daughter was a disagreeable, chattering, impertinent thing, whose tongue never lay still, and yet never spoke to any purpose.

The boys were forward, ignorant, and under-bred.

This is a brief sketch of the family.

They received me with a kind of insolent condescension, which seemed to say— "Though I am your superior, I will deign to take notice of you." I have met with this behaviour often, since I was in reduced circumstances.

Mrs. Frampton told me of the absurd pomp and state in which she had lived when in India; the number of attendants by which she was surrounded; her various dresses, her fine palanquins,[2] her jewels, and ornaments. Every thing that she had met in England was poor and mean, in comparison. Then, the great people that visited them in London; the respect that was paid them by every body: in short, that they were a family of the first consequence, and had expectations of being ennobled.

I wished that she had a printed catalogue of all her superlatives, to have given to each of her visitors, to have spared her the trouble of detailing them, and them that of hearing them.

She seemed to recollect herself afterwards. She found I expressed neither surprize nor admiration, and that all her magnificence was lost upon me.

She let me know that I was a very early visitor. When the cards were brought, I begged to be excused playing; and, as soon as they were set down to Whist, and their attention fully engaged, I took leave, and retired, heartily tired with my visit.

One day, the week following, Mrs. Frampton and her daughter called upon me. They were attended by one of those hangers-on with which they were perpetually surrounded; a made-up thing, that called itself a *gentleman*.

The ladies invited me to dine with them on the Thursday. I thanked them for the honour they did me, but begged leave to decline it. I told them, that I was an old-fashioned woman, and that I adhered to early hours of eating and sleeping; that fashionable hours did not agree with my health, spirits, or situation; that I could not disturb the family I lived with, nor break the rest of any of their servants.

They were surprized to hear me talk in this way; for they understood that I had lived in the *world*.

"Yes, ladies," said I, "so I have, for seven-and-twenty years; yet I never conformed to the manners of the fashionable part of it. I am sometimes thought singular in mine; but I do not wish to be thought so. I only live to my own feelings and principles. I do not pretend to impose them upon others.

"You will not, then, dine with us, *Mistuss* Darnford?" (she spoke it thus.)

"I had rather breakfast with you, Madam, if you will permit me."

"Well, do as you please. We breakfast at twelve; but every body comes and goes as they like; and the things stand upon the table till two, or after."

"I will wait on you, Madam, on Friday, if it is agreeable."

"Yes, do; come on Friday. You must see my daughter's ingenious works, and hear her play on the *forte piano*, and such like. I am told that you can draw and paint, and write very well: and you must make acquaintance with my young folks;

for I hear a very good character of you, and that you had no share in your husband's extravagance."

I made no reply to this compliment, as she thought it.

My room was neat and plain; but it was ornamented with my own drawings and paintings; and my husband's picture, done by myself, was over the chimney. They seemed surprized at the execution of them; and I found they knew little or nothing of the arts they talked of.

I wished not to offend the Framptons: therefore I went to breakfast with them on the Friday.

They received me in the dressing-room, where I used to breakfast, and pursue my little works of fancy.

They were surrounded by a set of parasites and hangers-on, who fed them continually with flattery so gross that none but such self-admirers could digest it.

Among these was a young man of a superior kind. He looked and spoke like a gentleman; and his compliments had an air of irony, which I wondered they did not perceive. His name was Wilmot.

After breakfast, Miss Frampton was requested to play and sing. She did both very poorly; but she was praised above measure. Her mother said, she only wanted a little more courage; but I thought she had no such want.

The second lady played an easy lesson much better than her sister.

I was asked to take my turn, but declined it.

Mr. Wilmot urged me. I said, I could not play after Miss Frampton. He looked at me with an expression that I understood plainly, but did not seem to do.

There was an air of freedom and familiarity in his manner, that did not please me; and I determined to discourage it.

Mrs. Frampton commended my skill in drawing, and my pictures. Mr. Wilmot begged he might be permitted to see them. I said, that, during my husband's absence, I received no visits from gentlemen.

"With us, you will suffer him to call upon you," said Miss Frampton, who seemed to look on Wilmot as her admirer.

I was pressed to spend the day; but I chose to return by Mr. Moyle's hour of dinner. Mr. Wilmot offered to attend me home, but I would not suffer it.

The next morning, he called on me, but was not admitted. He left a nosegay of the finest flowers. From this time, I was disturbed with the continual visits of this Mr. Wilmot, who sent me a nosegay every morning.

I never saw him but when he came with the ladies from the Hall. He then saw my drawings and paintings. He did not praise them extravagantly; but, turning to me, he said, in a low voice— "Merit like yours, Madam, is superior to flattery, and above praise; but I pay that homage which it best deserves." He put his hand upon his heart, and bowed gracefully.

The ladies were attentive to the pictures, and he observed it. His behaviour to me was very different from his attentions to them: it was respectful and modest; and shewed politeness of manners, and an improved understanding.

Some days after, in a walk to the Street, as it was called, Mr. Wilmot overtook me. Sally Moyle was with me; for I never walked out without some companion.

He accosted me politely; and, after some conversation, he begged me to permit him to visit me. He said, he had often been honoured with the acquaintance of accomplished women, and wondered that I should be scrupulous of receiving him.

I answered, that I was particularly circumstanced; that my husband was gone abroad, and I had my character to guard by myself; that I was not blind to merit; that his company and conversation would be very agreeable to me, if Mr. Darnford was at home to share them with me; but, in my situation, I ought to abstain from all appearance of evil.

He confessed that my conduct was right and commendable, but lamented the effects of it.

He ridiculed the Framptons with some humour. I rallied him upon his behaviour towards them, and his applause of Miss Frampton: I said, what could I think of his sincerity?

He answered— "Try it by your own, my dear Madam. Why did you say, you could not play after Miss Frampton, and deny us the pleasure of hearing you?"

"I can answer you fairly, Sir. Supposing I do play better than Miss Frampton, (which is more than you can know) would it have been wise in me to excel her, and to raise her envy and jealousy, and perhaps to incur the resentment of the whole family? I did not wish to shine at their expence, nor to attract notice: it is my wish to shun it; and I beg you so far to comply with it, as not to be seen in my company without that of the family."

He said, he would obey me, whatever it cost him; and he would shorten his visit to the Hall, for that reason.

As soon as we came within sight of the Street, I took leave, and begged him to return.

He retired with great reluctance, and often looked back after me.

I had many invitations to the Hall, but declined them as often as I could without offence. I forbore to walk out on an evening, excepting in the grounds belonging to Mr. Moyle's farm.

I amused myself with various employments. I enjoyed the beauties of nature; and observed them, in their respective seasons, with encreased reverence and adoration.

I had several letters from Darnford. He complained of my severity; he protested against the law, as a dry and disagreeable study; he grew tired of his company; they ridiculed his manners and character; he was tired of this new mode of idleness, and knew not what next to try; but he could not find any employment or resource.

Darnford's letters came always under covers from Lord A——. I made short answers, and such as any person might see without injury to either of us; recommending integrity, industry, and independence.

I received a letter from Mr. Wilmot, as follows—

"MADAM,

"EVERY word of yours goes directly to the heart; and I feel more concern to acquit myself to you, than to any person living. You accused me of insincerity: I will endeavour to clear myself of this charge, before I leave this country. I came to Darnford Hall with a design to pay my addresses to Miss Frampton. I had been told, that she was an accomplished and amiable young woman; that her father would give her twenty thousand pounds in his life-time, and a farther expectation at his death. I confess that the latter consideration was not without it's weight; but it was not sufficient to induce me to give my hand to Miss Frampton. I hope I have too much honour and principle to marry a woman whom I cannot esteem. During my visit at the Hall, I saw a woman whom I admire above any I ever saw in my life; and, was she at liberty to accept my vows, I would offer them to-morrow. I am denied the liberty to visit her; but she shall see my heart, before I bid her an eternal adieu. Her honour, and her peace, are dearer to me than my own. May she be happy, whatever becomes of me! She is peculiarly circumstanced: and so am

I; who see a gem of inestimable value thrown away upon a man who is insensible of it's price, and unworthy to possess it. I beg you, Madam, to tell this charming woman, who is well known to you, that I shall never cease to love her, to bless her, and to pray for her, so long as I have any existence. May every blessing Heaven can bestow, light upon her head!—So prays, and departs, her admirer, friend, and servant,

"J.C. WILMOT."

This letter gave me pain: I wished I had never seen it. I will confess to my friend, that I never saw a man more to my taste than Mr. Wilmot. There was soul in every glance of his eye, and grace in every motion and attitude.

I rejoiced when he left the Hall, and wished never to see or hear of him, from that day forward to the end of my life: yet he would sometimes intrude upon my thoughts.

I left London the 20th of May, and spent my time as I have related, during the months of June, July, and August; on the last day of which, I was surprized by an unexpected visit from Mr. Darnford.

I suppose that I received him coldly; for he complained of it, saying— "I thought my Fanny would have been glad to see me, after so long an absence."

"I should be glad to see you, Mr. Darnford, if you were come to any end or purpose. Are your affairs finally settled?"—No, they were not.

"What, then, do you propose to do?"—Lord A—— had a place in his eye, and was soliciting for him: in the mean time, he had given him an apartment in his house; they were come to the cottage, and should go a-shooting on the morrow.

"And what next are you to do?"—No reply to that.

"Lord A—— hopes you will come to us at the cottage, and spend a few weeks there."

"Indeed, I will not."

"Then I shall live there all day, and come to sleep with you here."

"No, Sir, I do not consent to that. If you were the occupier of the meanest cottage, and lived as a cottager ought to do, I would be your companion, and your servant; but, while you are a voluntary dependant and hanger-on to others, I refuse to share your lot. Seek your fortune in your own way, as I will do mine in another."

He seemed vext and mortified: yet he kept talking to, and playing with, two young spaniels which he brought with him; and sometimes addressed himself to me, at others to them.

I was sitting at a desk; and he saw I had been writing.

"You are writing, perhaps, for the press."

"I do not know that. While you are educating puppies, I am endeavoring to qualify myself to educate human creatures. Perhaps Lord A—— will promote you to be the master of his dog-kennel."—I was damnably severe; it was more than he could bear.

"Yes, you can bear worse things than that. You could bear the contempt of Mr. Bryanstone and his friend; yet it did not stimulate you to aim at activity and independence."

"No, Madam; I left them because I could not bear such treatment."

"And you come home to the same situation with Lord A——."

"Well, Madam, what then? Do you wish to see me a day-labourer?"

"The poorest husbandman[3] in the village is a better member of society, and a more respectable man, than you, Mr. Darnford."

This made him angry. I wished to stir the lethargy of indifference. I preached, as he called it, till he went away; saying, he hoped, the next time he called, to find me in a better temper.

The next day, at noon, Lord A——'s servant brought a leash[4] of partridges, and the following note—

"LORD A—— and Mr. Darnford request Mrs. Darnford's acceptance of their morning's game. They will do themselves the pleasure to sup with her, at nine o'clock, if not forbidden. To them it will be a dinner, as they shall not return home till near that hour. They desire Mrs. D—— will provide nothing else."

I sent word, I should be glad to see them. I almost repented of my harshness to Darnford; and yet his indifference to his own affairs provoked me to speak as I did.

In the evening, Lord A——'s servants brought a French pye, fruit-tarts, six bottles of wine, knives and forks, &c.

The butler said, his lord begged I would excuse this liberty, knowing that my conveniencies of this kind were left at the Hall. I was not pleased with this freedom; but I would not quarrel with him: I would allow it once, but forbid it the next time it was offered.

They came between eight and nine. Darnford paid me as much respect as if I had been a duchess. "Lord bless me!" thought I, "if this man had married a shrew, she would have had more influence over him, and perhaps might have used it to better purpose."

Lord A—— addressed me with his usual politeness, and paid me many compliments on my good looks, and afterwards upon my lodgings: he had heard they were mean ones; but I made every place delightful that I honoured with my presence.

I begged him to wave compliments, and to speak the plain language of the country to a poor cottager like me.

I was rather constrained in my behaviour, and kept them at a polite distance.

They talked of the sports of the field, the goodness of the season, and such kind of subjects.

Darnford enquired, how the family at the Hall had behaved to me. I said, very well; they had paid me every kind of civility.

He said, they complained of my shyness, and wished to have more of my company. I replied, that I neither liked their hours, their style, nor their manners; and I wished to keep at a civil distance.

"Ah!" said Lord A——, "you know too well how to keep those you do not like at a distance."

"That is better, my lord, than being too obtrusive and familiar."

"No danger of that from you, Madam; but much to those who aspire to your friendship, without sufficient merit to deserve it."

Darnford blamed me for being so shy, and so hard to be pleased.

The gentlemen did not leave me till twelve o'clock, though I gave them many hints that it was time; and that I thought it cruel to keep servants up late, especially those that worked hard all the day.

Lord A—— hoped I would return their visit soon. I curtsied, and was silent.

Darnford called upon me most days: he brought me game, and shewed me as much attention as when he was courting me for a wife.

I felt pity and concern for him. "If," said I, "this man's understanding is not strong enough to shew him the errors of his conduct, perhaps he is more to be pitied than blamed; and yet, by the same way of reasoning, one might excuse and extenuate every fault men can be guilty of. Right and wrong may be known by almost every degree of understanding; and every man may know and practise the great duties of morality, and the social and domestic virtues."

Lord A—— sent a card by Mr. Darnford, requesting me to fix a day to dine at the cottage, and to name my own hour.

I accepted this compliment, because I intended to avail myself of it, by not going as often as he should invite me: I therefore named the hour of three.

Lord A—— received me with politeness and respect. He wished I would eat with them often: poor Darnford complained that I kept him at a great distance, and wished to enjoy my company more frequently.

I wished that poor Darnford had more prudence than to make Lord A—— his confidant, especially in what concerned me; but I must be the more cautious.

After the first visit, I was urged to go to the cottage almost every day. I exhausted all my stock of contrivances to evade it, and at length was obliged to give a positive denial. Darnford argued, persuaded, wheedled; but all to no purpose.

I was invited to meet Lord A—— and Mr. Darnford at the Hall. I made the same rule of conduct; to go once, that I might not seem to slight their favours, but not to go a second time.

I heard, that Mrs. Frampton said I was an odd kind of woman; I was so reserved, she could get nothing out of me, and that I was very affected and conceited; that Mr. Darnford was a very genteel and agreeable man, and that Lord A—— was charming and delightful.

Miss Frampton drest at him, and played and sung; and her mother displayed all her accomplishments to no purpose. The cruel man shewed no signs of admiration or attention; he did not deign to flatter or compliment; he was dumb, blind, and insensible; he seemed devoted to the sports of the field, and Beauty spread her nets in vain.

I copied some rare and curious drawings. I worked embroidery with my pupils: I contrived to have them shewn to the Framptons, and offered to be sold, as the works of an Italian artist and his wife.

They bought them at a good price; they took down those done by the Miss Framptons, and put these up in their places.

Afterwards, they told all that had not seen the others, that they were done by Miss Frampton, and the former ones by the younger daughters.

Lord A—— was obliged to leave the cottage sooner than he intended: he offered it to Darnford, who was to stay there till either my lord returned, or else till he went to town, and then he would let him know.

Darnford tried all his powers of persuasion to induce me to go to him at the cottage; but I was firmly resolved against it: I strove to make him sensible of the impropriety of it; but his *nonchalance* was equal to my inflexibility, and neither could convince the other.

He grew tired of living alone at the cottage, though he was always a welcome guest at the Hall.

He saw me almost every day, and I never refused him my company. He reproached me for the coldness of my behaviour, and I set against it the absurdity of his.

One morning early, I was surprized by a letter that informed me he had left the country, and I might direct to him at A—— house in London.

What I could not prevent, I submitted to; and I expected nothing but a continuation of folly and misfortune.

Darnford wrote me several letters: I answered them very briefly. He told me, I no longer loved nor cared for him: I replied, that when he should forsake his vanities and follies, and live like a man of reason and principle, he should find an affectionate and faithful wife in me; that I should not cease to pray for that time, nor to make his honour and interest mine upon all occasions.

He went to London in November; the Framptons in December.

I employed my time in reading, writing, drawing, and needle-work.

I grew fond of gardening; and, amidst my various avocations, the days were too short for me. I visited nowhere but at the rector's, and at a gentleman farmer's in the same parish. I had been skirmishing with Poverty at a distance for some time, and preparing for her nearer approach. I tried the experiment of selling my little works of fancy; and found it would do as an aid, but not as an entire support.

I had monies by me, which I carefully kept as resources; and I would not allow myself to spend a penny idly, for I made no doubt I should have calls enough upon me in future.

Darnford wrote me word, that he had been very ill: that he

came home late in a heavy shower of rain; that he had caught cold, and had a good deal of fever. Lord A—— was out of town at the time; that he sent for his lordship's apothecary to attend him, and he was now getting better; that he wanted money to pay the apothecary's bill, and if I could spare him some, he should be obliged to me.

I had long expected this demand, and was prepared for it. I sent him a bank note for ten pounds. I was convinced, that if I sent him more, he would squander it away, and that small sums were best for him.

He thanked me for it, as if it was more than he expected from me.

One morning, the 10th of February, when I came down to breakfast, I found two letters upon my table; one under a cover from Lord A——, the other a post letter.

The first contained two letters that follow here—

"MADAM,

"I AM concerned to be the messenger of bad tidings. At my return to town, I found Mr. Darnford under confinement, within the rules of the Court of King's Bench. His creditors have made repeated applications for payment; they laid in wait to arrest him; but, by advice of an attorney, he has thrown himself into a place of personal security. I have lent him money at different times to a considerable amount; and am advised not to go any farther, as there is no likelihood of repayment. I send his dinner every day from my own table, and will perform every act of friendship that prudence will allow. I am sorry, for your sake, that there is no better prospect before you; but you will not permit me to be your friend. By desire of Mr. Darnford I send the enclosed; I am, Madam, your most humble servant,

"A——."

"DEAR FANNY,

"I AM sorry to inform you, that my creditors have been very urgent with me to settle accounts with them. I have consulted an attorney, and he has advised me to live within the rules of the King's Bench,[5] and so to keep them at bay till I can pay them. I am here, and very ill beside: if you were with me, I should be more comfortable; but I have no reason, nor no right, to expect it. I confess, that I only am to blame, and that you deserve a better lot: however, if you would be so good as to come to me, it would be very kind indeed; but do as you think best, and I will resign to my unhappy fate.

"Lord A—— is my best friend; he visits me, and sends me every day provisions from his own table, and bids me hope for better days. Let me hear from you, if I cannot see you; and believe me always, yours most affectionately,

"GEORGE DARNFORD."

"MADAM,

"I HOPE you are prepared for misfortunes, which threaten to be of no short duration. Your husband has thrown himself into the rules of the King's Bench, and his creditors will not accept of any thing short of the full payment of all his debts. I make no doubt, that you will be urged again to give up your settlement, in order to set him free; and I fear you will not have courage enough to refuse it. If you come to town, call upon me, and don't scruple to consult me on any occasion; I shall always give you my advice freely, and you may command my best services. Bear up, and take courage; Heaven will support and reward those virtues which it permits to be the most severely tried: I am convinced of your merit, and of your fortitude, and that you will come out like pure gold, that is tried and purified seven times in the fire. I am always, dear Madam, your faithful friend and servant,

"D—— M——."

These letters did not overset me: my mind seemed to collect itself, and to bear up against evils which it had not deserved, and could not avoid.

I sat down immediately, and wrote to my husband—

"DEAR MR. DARNFORD,

"YOU have a right to call upon me to come and share your troubles, as I have shared in your prosperity. It is my duty to attend you, to nurse, to comfort and support you. Expect me in a few days, not to condemn or reproach you, but to perform all the most tender offices of love and friendship, and to convince you that I am, most truly, your affectionate and faithful wife,

"F. DARNFORD."

I put this letter into a cover directed to Lord A——, and wrote a very brief note as follows—

"MY LORD,

"I THANK you for the information you have given me, and beg the favour of you to send the enclosed to Mr. Darnford without delay. I am your lordship's most humble servant,

"F. DARNFORD."

I thought it unnecessary to write to Mr. M——, as I hoped to see him shortly.

I sent my letter to the post, and then packed up my clothes and linen; and the day following my servant went with me to N——, and we went to the stage to London the day after.

When we arrived at the inn, I took a hackney-coach,[6] and went directly to the King's Bench rules. I enquired the way; and, after some difficulties, found out the place where my husband was, in a sorry lodging, and laid upon a bed.

I got a porter to carry my portmanteau, and my servant carried her own box. I lost no time till I found Mr. Darnford.

He was so surprized at my expedition, that he hardly believed his own eyes. He received me with transports of joy: he called me his good angel, his only love, his only treasure. I was too good, and he could never deserve or repay my kindness.

I desired him to be composed; I was come to share his lodgings, but he must tell me where to get a bed for my servant. I sent for the landlady. Darnford told her I was his wife; he asked her to provide a bed for the servant, which she promised to do.

I desired her to procure us some refreshment. Darnford sat down with me, and ate a few mouthfuls: he drank a glass of wine; his eye was brightened, his countenance cheered, and he seemed another man.

I had brought sheets with me, and aired them before I put them up. When my maid had taken some refreshment, I assisted her in making the bed, and putting the room into some order, for Darnford had only a casual attendant.

I sat down, and was conversing with my husband, when Lord A—— entered the room. He seemed like one thunderstruck; he could not speak presently.

Darnford cried out— "Here she is, my best and dearest treasure! You said, she would not come; but she is better than you or I could conceive. I have her now, and I will never more part with her."

Lord A―― coloured; he looked uneasy; he tried to assume a more chearful aspect, but it was not easy or natural.

" I rejoice to see you, Madam. I was surprized; I did not think you could have been here so soon: this is kind, indeed!"

"I am only performing my duty, my lord: there is no merit in it; for it was likewise my inclination to attend my husband."

"Mrs. Darnford cannot possibly lodge here," said my lord.

"Indeed I can, and will, my lord: wherever my husband lodges, I chuse to be."

"That was not always the case, Madam."

"It is the case now, my lord: I come to nurse him, and I trust that office to no other hand."

Darnford gazed at me with unusual tenderness: he grasped my hand, and looked with an air of triumph.

Lord A―― looked confused and gloomy; and I could not think what ailed him.

He soon left us, as if to conceal his uneasiness. Darnford spoke highly of his friendship and affection. I said, we must consider whether his actions would prove them; for my part, I was not convinced that we owed him any obligation, but I would not just then enter upon the subject.

I shared my husband's homely bed; and we slept more comfortably than we had ever done in Lord A――'s palace, *"with all appurtenance and means to boot."*[7]

Darnford was full of acknowledgments for my coming: he had not been so happy for a long time.

"If my company really contributes to your happiness, it is in your power to have it constantly."

"Certainly I wish it, and would do any thing to obtain it from you."

"I will shew you the only way. Give up your expectations and dependance upon Lord A――; go with me into the country, and live in a cottage: I will love you better than ever I did, and study to make you happy; I will decorate our little cottage, and make it a paradise."

"But, how is it possible, when I dare not stir beyond the Rules?"

"I will make it practicable. I will give up my settlement voluntarily, which I refused upon compulsion. We will live upon the rent of Darnford Hall; and, if any thing more is wanting, these hands shall furnish the means for it. It will be my honour, and my pride, to reclaim from ruin the man whom Heaven has made my partner and companion for life."

He seemed to reflect upon what I had said: it seemed to give him pain.

"Oh, Fanny! what have you said?—Give up Lord A——! my patron, friend, and benefactor! the man upon whom all my future hopes depend!"

"The man who has led you into the path of ruin; into dissipation, extravagance, gambling; and who has now got you into fool's paradise."

"Give up Lord A——, leave London, and bury myself in obscurity!"

"Better than being buried in sloth and slavery. Oh, Darnford! think that Heaven speaks by me; that it warns you of the dangers that surround you; that it once more shews you the path of peace. If you slight the offer, it may never again come in your way. Consider well; for, perhaps, your fate depends upon your answer."

He was silent. He walked backwards and forwards in the room. His complexion, which used to indicate health and chearfulness, was now grown sallow and unhealthy; his body emaciated; and his step weak and tremulous.

The tears trickled down my cheeks, my bosom heaved with sighs, to see the alteration.

I urged his health as a motive; I said, that the country air, sobriety, and temperance, would restore his health, and his morals: he would see, that happiness did not depend upon affluence and luxury, but upon peace of mind, and health of body; that more real happiness was to be found among the middling and lower degrees of men, than among those distinguished by rank, title, or fortune.

I spoke with earnestness, till my voice faltered. Darnford saw me affected: he came and embraced me.

"Oh, my Fanny! what can I do?"

"Comply with my proposal. You ought to accept it with transport, instead of reluctance."

"Oh how can I promise what, I fear, I shall not perform!"

"Not perform!—Then, do not promise. But, you mortify and distress me. I have only one more argument to urge. If you decline my offer, and chuse to remain in your present wretched and shameful situation, you will entirely forfeit my esteem and affection, and I will give you up to your fate; I will leave you to your well-chosen patron, and will seek my own fortune, and earn my bread by my own industry. This is my fixed resolution. Consider of this till to-morrow, and then give me your final answer."

We were both silent for some time, and seemed afraid of speaking to each other.

I ordered stewed mutton and broth for our dinner, to be ready at three o'clock. Just as we were sitting down to it, a man, drest like a cook, came in, followed by a servant with a basket. He set on two covers; and the servant set on two bottles of wine, with all other appurtenances of the table. When they had finished their business, they went away.

"This is from Lord A——," said Darnford; "from that generous friend, whom you desire me to renounce!"

"I do not wish you to be ungrateful, or unjust, Mr. Darnford. It would be easy for you to give such reasons for retiring as Lord A—— must approve. I should find no difficulty in appealing to him; and perhaps I may, if you will not: but I shall urge it no farther just now."

Darnford urged me to eat. I kept to my mutton and broth, and did not touch either of the other dishes.

Darnford exclaimed— "Good God! how strong some people's prejudices are!"

"Very true, Mr. Darnford. The same exclamation suits me, as well, at least, as it does you. I wish to shew you, that I can be contented with one dish, plainly drest; and I think it best for health, as well as cheapness."

He was gloomy and uneasy.

"Will you drink a glass of wine with me?"

"Yes, I will, notwithstanding my prejudices; and I wish both yours and mine may be cured by time and reason."

He drank about a pint of wine, and would have drank more; but I begged him to take care of his health, and restrain himself.

He said— "I thank you, my love, and submit to your restrictions."

"Oh, that you would, Mr. Darnford! they should be only those of duty, reason, and prudence."

Our day passed away heavily; for neither of us was pleased with the other. I urged Darnford repeatedly to comply with my proposal, but could not get a positive answer.

He received several notes in the morning, and wrote answers to them, but would not tell me from whence they came.

About three o'clock, Lord A—— came. He accosted me with

his usual ease and freedom: he hoped I had recovered the fatigues of my journey. I, on my part, hoped his lordship was well; as I thought he seemed indisposed the other night. He coloured; said, he was not quite well that night, but was now perfectly so: he was come to dine with us, if I did not forbid him. I feared, it was we that were to dine with him, and was sorry to be so expensive to him. He wished I would not think of such trifles, which were nothing between friends.

Between three and four, the dinner came; three covers, a soup, and two others; a boiled, and a roast, with wine, &c.

After dinner, we conversed on various subjects. Lord A—— introduced that which was next my heart: he wished we could find some means to extricate Mr. Darnford from his disagreeable situation.

I felt myself, as it were, inspired. I took the lead. I told Lord A—— of my proposal to my husband; and I called upon him to second me.

He seemed surprized. He applauded me warmly: he said, I was one of the best of wives, and of women; and that Darnford ought to think himself the most fortunate and happy of men.

"You think, then, my lord, that he ought to promise me to perform the conditions I have mentioned."

"He must, he shall perform them," said he: "I will answer for him."

"Do you hear that, Mr. Darnford?" said I.

"Yes, I do," answered he: "I will do whatever Lord A—— and Mrs. Darnford require of me."

"Then he is to go into the country with me, and to make his home there: that is the condition I make."

"I agree to it," said Darnford.

Lord A—— seemed overjoyed that we were agreed; and I began to think myself mistaken, and that he was really our friend.

Lord A—— left us at nine o'clock, being engaged to spend the evening; and I was most compleatly deceived: my suspicions were lulled to sleep, and I went to bed contented and easy.

The next day, Mr. Darnford's attorney came to him several times. The writings were preparing, by which I was to give up my settlement, and Darnford was to be set at liberty.

I was full of hopes, that he would be reclaimed from his follies; and, in time, would be all that I could wish or desire him to be.

The creditors and the lawyers met, and discussed the subject. The estate in Essex was to be sold as soon as I should give up my right in it: they agreed to accept it as the last dividend; and, although it should not amount to the full sum, they promised to give a discharge.

They met a second time at our shabby lodgings. Lord A―― was present. It was supposed, that the estate must be sold to a disadvantage. Darnford and I both gave up our right in it: I signed it chearfully; but I dropt a tear upon the signature.

Lord A―― seemed affected: he rose, and held his handkerchief to his eyes.

He said― "Be of good cheer, Mrs. Darnford. This is a necessary thing. Better and happier days will come forward afterwards."

"I fear not, my lord: I have now little to expect, or hope."

The estate was to be sold at Garraway's.[8] It was advertised; and we were to wait till all was finished.

After the gentlemen were gone, Lord A―― endeavoured to keep up my spirits: but I was fully sensible of the sacrifice I had made.

Lord A―― promised to attend the sale, and to be a bidder: he hoped it would not be disagreeable, if he should be the purchaser.

"Surely not!" said Darnford. "I had rather it should fall into your lordship's hands, than any man's living."

I said nothing: it was a matter of perfect indifference to me.

The day came when the estate was sold. Lord A―― was the purchaser.

He came to us with joy in his countenance. He took a hand of each of us― "The estate is in the hands of your friend; he has given a fair price for it; your creditors are satisfied; and you will soon be released from this odious place. I wish you would come to my house; but I know Mrs. Darnford's scruples too well to expect it. You must have a lodging till the creditors have signed the releases; and then you will go whither you please."

"Darnford, you must fulfil your promise. I have something to propose for your service, before you leave town. At present, I only call to tell you these particulars. I am engaged to-day, but will dine with you to-morrow. Farewell!"

He beckoned Darnford. He followed him out.

When he returned, he looked thoughtful and uneasy.

I asked him, whether he had heard any thing to vex him. He said, no; nothing but what he knew before.

I questioned him farther, but could get nothing from him, though he was still uneasy.

Lord A—— sent word, that he should dine with us at half an hour past three. I begged of Mr. Darnford to tell him, I desired he would not alter his hours in compliment to me; that I knew he usually dined at a late hour, and I could sup very well at his hour of dinner.

"You may tell him so yourself, my dear," said he: "you will have the same opportunity."

"Darnford, there is something that dwells upon your mind: I wish you would tell it me at once. I expect nothing good; and, I hope, am prepared for the worst."

He paused—hesitated—and then—"No," he said, in a drawling way; "nothing to vex you, I hope, my dear."

Lord A—— did not come till the dinner was served up, by his own order, as usual. He looked gay and elevated, but a little hurried.

I told him what I had before said to Darnford. He said, his hours were always adapted to those of his friends, and begged me to say no more upon the subject.

After dinner, I asked, whether I might not look about for a lodging: I hoped Mr. Darnford would soon be at liberty.

Certainly he would, my lord said; but I might as well stay here a few days longer.

I answered, that I cared not how soon I left London, and reminded Darnford of his promise.

He had not forgot it; he did not want to be reminded of it— "I will go into the country, if you insist upon it."

"I do insist on it."

"Well, I will keep my word; but I will not promise to live there always: I will not be a prisoner, Madam."

"The promise runs, that you shall make it your home, Sir. I do not mean to make you my prisoner, nor to hinder you from going wherever you have a proper call."

"Very right, Madam," said my lord: "I hope to be able to settle this point for you. Darnford shall go down with you into the country. There is a house ready to receive you. I offer you my cottage: I will either give it, or lend it, or let it to you—which of them will best satisfy Mrs. Darnford's unreasonable scruples; and I will never come there but when you shall invite me."

"My lord, I cannot accept it: you know I have often declined it. We are already under too many obligations to you; and I cannot, will not, encrease them: I will not go to the cottage."

"You will not receive an obligation from your friend! Surely, there is more pride than principle in this refusal, Madam?"

"Perhaps there may: but it is a pride I will never part with; a pride that you cannot but approve in your heart, whatever circumstances may induce you to speak against it."

He coloured, and looked confused. He rose, and walked to the window: he seemed to be trying to harden his heart.

He then came to me, and renewed his attack. He kneeled to me; he took my hand in both his. I observed that he trembled. He urged every argument to make me accept his offer: he disclaimed all kind of obligation; it was he that should be the obliged person, and he would study to return the obligation.

I wrapped myself in my integrity, and remained inflexible.

At length, he grew angry; he talked of obstinacy and ingratitude. Darnford kept a sullen silence; but looked uneasy and confused.

"Why do not you speak for me, Darnford?—Speak, as becomes the husband and the master."

He was still silent.

"Well, Sir, I leave you to use your influence with your wife. I have put you into a way to fulfil your promise to her; and now, I insist upon your performing YOUR PROMISE TO ME!" He took his hat, and went out of the room, with resentment in his countenance: he did not bow to either of us, and he clapped the door after him.

"What is the meaning of this behaviour, Mr. Darnford?—What promise have you made to my lord?"

"Be composed, my dear; I will tell you by and by; you are now too much affected."

"Affected, indeed!—Oh! God, support me!" I burst into tears.

Darnford drank two or three glasses of wine, as fast as he could pour them down: he brought a glass to me, and begged me to drink it.

My indignation rose: I dashed the glass out of his hand, and broke it.

He stared at me, but did not speak; he went to the table, and drank more wine.

"What mean you, Sir? to intoxicate yourself and me, in order to suppress your feelings?—Tell me all that you have to say, at once; for I can no longer endure the agony of suspicion and suspense. Speak now; or I will leave you, and never see your face again!"

"I will, presently: be composed, then, and I will."

I took the bottle from him; he seized another, and he looked flushed and furious. He seized that in my hand: I was terrified; I retreated to the window; I sat down, and shed torrents of tears.

He tried several times before he could speak plainly— "I have to tell you, that it is in your power to make yourself and me happy, and restore us to ease and affluence."

"Tell me the means, Sir; but look that they be honest ones, or else they will make an everlasting breach between us!"

He went on— "The estate lately sold will be again settled upon you and yours; the cottage will be given to me unconditionally; and, because you have scruples about accepting an apartment at my lord's, a lodging will be taken for us both, while we stay in London; and, whenever you please, I go with you to the cottage."

"These are the proposals you have to make me! and this is the promise you made to Lord A——! You did well to stupify yourself with wine, before you explained yourself, otherwise you could not have supposed I should accept them."

"You must accept them, my dear; we have no other resource."

"Speak on, Sir: say, the conditions of this obligation?"

"Why, only that you should be generous—and kind—and grateful to Lord A——."

"I believe, I understand you. Base—unworthy—unprincipled man! I cannot find words to express my resentment. After having made away a noble fortune, you can reduce your wife to indigence, and then sell her, as your last resource!"

"No such thing, my dear: I would not part with you for the world."

"What, then, would you share me with another?—More and more base and shameful!"

"Now, don't be so angry! I would not part with you; I would live with you, and preserve your reputation: nobody would dare to wag a finger against you, while I supported you; and, if I winked at some liberties between you and my friend, who could blame you?"

"Lord A—— is a master in contrivance; that I allow. He has made this infamous proposal through you, in order to render you perfectly contemptible in my eyes; and he has succeeded. If I were inclined to listen to his proposals, the first article should be, that you should never more come in my sight."

"Now, you are very unreasonable, Fanny; but you know better. I am your husband, and your master, and you shall live with me, and you shall do as I please, and go where I please. So it don't signify talking any more; for I am tired and sleepy, and—and—" He gaped, and nodded, and fell back in his chair.

I prayed to God to give me courage and resolution. Now, one effort for liberty! for virtue! for virtuous poverty!

I called my maid: I bade her go up stairs with me. I packed up my clothes, and put on my riding-dress; I made my servant do the same. I bade her call a hackney-coach; she had the luck to get one soon. I made the coachman help her to carry the portmanteau down stairs, and to put that and her box into the coach.

I left Darnford in a sound sleep: I prayed that God would give him repentance, and a sober mind.

I then stepped into the coach with my maid, and bade the coachman drive to the inn from whence the N—— coach set out.

My agitation supported my spirits; I hardly knew where I was, when I arrived at the inn. I asked for two places, and luckily secured them.

I ordered a bed, and threw myself upon it in my clothes; and bade my maid lie down by my side. Happily, my fatigue served me in lieu of an opiate; and I slept till we were called to rise for the coach.

I found myself greatly refreshed, and set out chearfully on my return to peace and the country.

While I was on my journey, the various objects amused me; but, when I came to the inn, and was in a state of rest, a torrent of reflections poured in upon me, and awoke the pain in my heart. My husband, by his base conduct, had made a divorce between us; I had no longer a friend, or a protector, in him; I had no resource for myself; without friend or fortune, what was to become of me?

Lord A—— had justified all my fears of him; the mask was taken off: I saw a regular plan of conduct, that was to end in my ruin. I was out of his reach at present; but, after all the pains he had taken for me, it was not likely that he should give up the pursuit: I had, therefore, still reason to fear his machinations. I must not stay at Mr. Moyle's; I must seek some other asylum, where neither my husband nor his patron were likely to find or to pursue me.

My maid observed, that I looked very ill; she begged me to

take some refreshment; she feared I had met with something to vex me. I told her, she guessed truly; but I would strive to overcome it. I ordered something for her and myself, and took enough to support nature.

I went to bed early, and spent a miserable night in reflections upon my melancholy situation.

Want of rest made me rise early. I went out, and walked about the town: the streets were empty, and the inhabitants were at rest. "They are free from those cares that oppress me," said I. "The husbands protect their wives, instead of betraying them; and the wives repose securely in their bosoms!"

There is an Italian proverb, that says, "The tongue will strike against the hollow tooth."[9] The adage holds true: people oppressed with sorrow apply every thing they see and hear to their own sufferings.

I saw, at an inn, a printed advertisement, that a broad-wheeled waggon was to set out, at ten o'clock, for J——, to carry goods and passengers. I enquired, whether two places could be had? It was to pass through our village, and to stop at the public-house there. I took two places, and then hastened back to the other inn.

I wakened my maid, and made her dress, and breakfast; meanwhile, I told her how we were to go home. The poor girl wept.

"Oh, my dear lady!" said she, "times are changed indeed, when you go home in a stage-waggon!"[10]

"They are so, my good Hannah; but let us keep up our spirits, for they must support us under our troubles. I shall no longer want a servant to attend me; but you shall stay with me, till you can meet with an eligible place."

"I would serve you for nothing, Madam, rather than any other lady for great wages. I hope you will live to see better days; and, when you are able, you shall pay me what you think I deserve."

"I thank you, my good girl; your fidelity cheers my heart; but, indeed, I have no hope of better days: all my fortune is gone; and I must, perhaps, seek a service for myself.—Don't weep, my girl; you weaken my heart, and I wish to harden it. Go, and get a porter to carry our baggage to the inn; and, as soon as he comes, we will go: let us lose no time."

When she was gone, I wept, and found myself relieved.

She soon came back; and we went to the inn, and took our places in the waggon.

There were several merry and happy mortals among us: they laughed, and sung; my poor Hannah and I wept, and were silent.

After a few hours, the waggon stopped in sight of our village. We got out here, and ordered our baggage to be left at the public-house, and I would send for it.

We got home by Mr. Moyle's dinner-time; and I was welcomed by all the family.

Mrs. Moyle and her daughters enquired after Mr. Darnford. I said, he was better in health, but ruined in his circumstances. That he was in hopes of a place, and therefore he staid in London; but I chose to return to the country.

After our greetings, I retired to my apartment, and to my painful reflections. I thought on the surprize Darnford must have felt at my escape. Perhaps, he might expose me, and himself, in the public papers: this thought terrified me; and I resolved to write to him, in order to prevent it. I did so immediately.

"SIR,

"THE infamous proposal which wine encouraged you to make me, has cancelled all ties between us, and made an eternal separation. I did not think myself safe with you, and therefore made my escape while you were in a state of intoxication, and in a lethargic sleep in consequence. I warn you to beware how you mention to any one what passed between us; otherwise, I will expose you to the world in your true colours.

"I leave you to pursue your own measures. You are worthy of the patronage of your noble friend, and he of such a parasite. I leave you to each other.

"I am seeking an asylum in the arms of virtuous poverty! I have no doubt of earning my livelihood, and my slumbers will not be broken by the reproaches of guilt. This state I prefer to all that affluence and luxury can give me.

"I came to London to do you service, and you have requited me by the basest ingratitude. May God give you repentance! and may it be soon enough to be of any benefit to you. Farewel, for ever!

"F.D."

The next question was, how to send it? Under cover to Lord A——? Should I say any thing to him? Why not? I had done nothing to be ashamed of. Perhaps he might think that Darnford connived at my escape, and deprive him of his protection. Perhaps he might throw him into prison, for he was still in debt to him. At last, I resolved to write a few words under the cover—

"MY LORD,

"I AM now, God be praised! in a place of peace and safety. Lest you should think Mr. Darnford connived at, or allowed of my escape, I think it proper to tell you, that he served you too faithfully, and that he threatened to oblige me to comply with your infamous proposal. Your lordship's schemes have at length succeeded. You have rendered my husband despicable in my eyes, and effected an eternal separation between us. In this, if your heart will permit you, you may triumph; but the other part of your designs, I trust, will never be compleated. God will give me grace, to prefer virtuous poverty to guilty affluence, as long as he gives me life and reason.

"I have only to request you to give the enclosed letter to your friend; and tell him, I never desire to see again his handwriting, or yours.

"F.D."

I felt a kind of satisfaction after writing these letters. I am afraid there was a degree of revenge in it. I enjoyed the uneasiness the two friends had felt on my account; and I was gratified by letting them see, that I despised them, and all their machinations.

I told Mrs. Moyle and her daughters, that I was reduced to a state of poverty; that I was, moreover, persecuted by an enemy; and that it was necessary for me to leave her house, and to conceal myself in some obscure place, where I was not known, for a time; that, if I should hereafter be enabled to emerge from this situation, I would return to them, in preference to any other place; and I begged them to enquire after such a situation for me.

They were greatly concerned. Mrs. Moyle took pains to convince me, that I should be safer under her roof than any where else. I said, being so well known in this village, it was impossible for me to be concealed in it.

She gave way reluctantly; and I was obliged to be resolute, in order to persuade her to look out for another situation.

In a week's time, she told me that a servant, who formerly lived with her, had married an husbandman in an obscure village; that he was the bailiff, or overlooker, of a farm for another man, and lived in a decent kind of farm-house; and, she believed, would be very glad to take a boarder.

I thanked her for the intelligence, and began to contrive how I should get thither.

Mr. Moyle kept a kind of chaise-cart, which was at that time exempted from the taxes, before the long arm of Power had deprived the industrious farmer of this convenience. Mrs. Moyle proposed to go with me to visit Mrs. Styles. Her eldest son was to drive us.

The next day, we went in this manner. I told Mrs. Moyle to call me by the name of *Smith*, and begged her son to be cautious of mentioning me by any other.

It was a tiresome journey, through bad roads; and I was glad to get to a resting-place. The house was decent, the mistress was civil, and we agreed upon terms.

I would fain have staid here, and let my baggage be sent after me; but Mrs. Moyle urged me so warmly and tenderly to return with her, that I could not refuse her. She said, her daughters would break their hearts, if they were not to see and take leave of me; and poor Hannah would think it hard to be discharged by any other person than myself. I consented to return, and told Mrs. Styles to expect me one day in the following week: so we were jumbled back in the same manner we came.

Mr. Moyle's family shewed every mark of affection and concern to part with me; and Hannah wept incessantly.

I thanked them for their affection and fidelity. I begged them not to weaken my heart by their tenderness; that I found this parting too painful to myself, beside other burthens which I must bear.

I set about packing up my cloaths and linen, and preparing for my departure. In looking over some writings, I found a paper, with these words written upon it— "MY DEAR FATHER'S LAST GIFT." This was a welcome treasure; for I had forgotten it, my mind had been so much engaged by the alterations in my circumstances.

I began to lay plans for employing it in some way of business, and in a scheme that I shall explain hereafter. I bought a plain stuff gown, to wear in common; and took two calico ones, to wear occasionally.

I begged Mrs. Moyle to let me leave all the best of my cloaths at her house, and also the furniture of my apartment, till I should be settled in some way of life.

She gladly consented; saying, she would keep them as an earnest of my return. I paid for my board and lodging, and also my servant's wages.

These good people would fain have had me remain in their debt; but I would not consent. I had never wanted money, having saved most of what I had received since I married; and now I found the benefits of my frugality.

I visited, and took leave of, the worthy rector and his family. I told him of my reduced circumstances; and that I was going a long journey to visit a friend, and it was uncertain when I should return. I thanked them for all their civilities, and prayed for their welfare and happiness.

I took a friendly leave of all my neighbours, and had the pleasure to find myself beloved, and my departure regretted, by all the village.

I settled a method of intercourse with Mrs. Moyle. She was to send any letters to me, under cover, directed to *Frances Smith*, to be left at an inn at B——; and Mrs. Styles's servant was to fetch them on a market-day, and to carry mine in the same manner.

Two days before I left Mrs. Moyle, a letter came from J——, directed to me. Lord A—— had used the art to get a friend to direct the cover, lest I should return it unopened. The contents as follow—

"DEAR MADAM,

"NOTHING was ever so welcome as your letter, notwithstanding it's severity; because it brought the good tidings of your health and safety. Never were two poor devils so wretched as Darnford and me, at your cruel and abrupt departure. We feared that you were fallen into greater dangers than those you wished to avoid, which were merely ideal and imaginary. We were half distracted; we had no clue to trace you by; we feared every possible evil; but, thanks to Heaven! you are well, and in charming spirits, though you spend them unmercifully upon those who love you best, because they best know your value; and one of whom would spend half of his fortune to obtain the return of your friendship and confidence.

"Darnford is very ill: he drinks too much wine; I tell him so; and I take the bottle from him, and preach temperance every day. Now you are found, I hope he will be easier, and take care of his health. We conclude you are at Moyle's: we beg you to continue there. We promise that you shall not be interrupted. Do not go farther, out of any fears that your fancy may suggest. I know the respect due to you too well to offend you by intruding upon you; and I will convince you, in spite of your prejudices, that I am not unworthy of your friendship. Darnford is afraid of you: he dares not write, after your prohibition. I am bolder, because it is in my power to prevent your suffering what most people think an evil; and which you, in a cooler moment, will, I hope, be convinced of, and will suffer your friends to preserve you from it.

"Lady B—— is gone with her lord to the south of France; and from thence she goes to Italy. She desired me to present her compliments, and to send you the enclosed; which I have now performed.

"Darnford says, he loves you better than himself; and wishes incessantly for your company, and your assistance.

"Let us hear from you soon. Tell us, that you are well; that you forgive our attentions to your ease and interest, and our efforts for your happiness.

"Your friend and servant,
"A——."

I make you a present, my friend, of this fine letter. You will draw many inferences: I shall only offer one—It is a generally received opinion, that Virtue is bold, and Vice timid. This may be true in some cases; I can only say, that I have seen the contrary in every case that has come within my knowledge: that Virtue has been timid, and wanted help to support her own innocence; and Vice assured and impudent, so as to stagger those who judge only from appearances.

I offered to hire a cart, to carry myself and my baggage; but Mr. Moyle would insist upon my accepting his vehicle. His son offered to drive me; and my old pupil, Betsey, gave me her company, and would stay a fortnight with me, till I was used to the place and the people.

When Betsey left me, I seemed to be quite alone, and felt as if I was placed at the world's extremity. I was, for the first time, among people I could not converse with, and also was obliged to do many things that I was unaccustomed to; but the thought that I was in my duty, made them easy and pleasant to me.

I now recollected a great omission I had been guilty of: I had neither called upon, nor written to, my worthy friend, Counsellor M——. I wished to consult him upon my present situation, and future establishment. I had leisure enough to repair my fault; and I sat down, and wrote to him—

"SIR,
"I AM afraid you will set me down in your list, as unjust and ungrateful; but I shall endeavour to acquit myself of this charge. My time and attention have been so much engrossed by my husband's ill health and unfortunate situation, that I could think of nothing else. I have acted against your advice and injunction; and therefore I have hardly the courage to address you now.

"I could not see my husband sick, and under confinement, without doing every thing in my power to set him at liberty. I could not be rich myself, and suffer him to be poor, and a prisoner. You expect that I should have acted thus, and are prepared to allow for it.

"Mr. Darnford is in London, and in expectation of getting a place by the interest of his friends. London does not agree with my health, or my principles: I have therefore determined to seek my fortune in another way.

"I have, for some time past, been preparing for what has happened, and endeavouring to qualify myself for gaining a livelihood by my industry and ability.

"I have thoughts of opening a seminary of female education; and I beg your advice as to the place and manner which may be the most eligible, and the most likely to succeed. I have sketched out several plans of this kind, which I shall lay before you; and I have found out means to put one into execution.

"The last time I ever saw my dear father, he gave me a noble present; and he bade me save it for some future exigency. I have saved great part of the monies I have received; but I take no merit in reserving this; for, in truth, I had forgotten that I had such a sum that I could strictly call my own. With this I can furnish a house. I have, beside, some furniture at Mr. Moyle's; and I think I may open a school with as good an expectation as most others have done.

"I depend upon your advice and patronage before any other. Let me hear from you soon. Direct to me at Mr.

Moyle's, as usual. I am, dear Sir, your obliged friend and servant,

"F. DARNFORD."

I had brought a good many books with me to Styles's; and I found, in reading and writing, a resource against my misfortunes.

I should have told you, that Lady B—— sent me a charming letter, under Lord A——'s cover, and a note for fifty pounds, which she said was before my own; and desired me to write, and send my letters through Lord A——'s hands. She little thought of the part he had acted.

I spent three months in this retirement. It was not pleasant, but use made it tolerable to me. I hoped one day to emerge, and to mix with conversible people; the want of which made my greatest trouble, especially of an evening, when my mind was tired of reflecting.

In the month of August, I received the following letter—

"MADAM,

"BY desire of Mr. Darnford, I write to inform you, that he is very ill, and is thought to be in a decline. Dr. H—— attends him; and my lord does every thing in his power for his recovery. He begs the favour of you to write a few words to comfort him, and to say that you forgive him for his behaviour when you were last with him. He does not wish you to come to him, for reasons that, he says, you know without his telling them. I write without my lord's knowledge; and therefore, Madam, if you write to Mr. Darnford, send it under cover to me, at Lord A——'s. I am, Madam, your humble servant,

"JAMES COVELL,
"Under Butler to Lord A——.

"You may get some person to direct your letter for you."

I was concerned, but not surprized, at the contents of this letter. I wrote an answer; and sent it, by a special messenger, to the post at J——.

"I AM very much concerned, Mr. Darnford, to hear of the bad state of your health; but I am pleased to find, you think that your faults stand in need of forgiveness.

"I dare not flatter, nor deceive you; but I wish to lead you to sincere repentance. I truly forgive you for all offences against myself: but you have an account to settle at an higher tribunal.

"You have made it impossible for me to come to you at Lord A——'s; but if you will, even now, throw off your fetters, and come to me at Mr. Moyle's, I will receive you as my husband—will nurse you with the most tender care and attention, and do every thing in my power to save your body and soul. The worthy rector of your own parish will attend you, and assist my endeavours; and we shall be proud of our penitent, and anxious to lead him into the path of virtue and of peace.

"Let me intreat you to comply with my request. Believe that Heaven warns you, by me, to shun destruction, and to secure your recovery.

"Write to me, or let your friend Covell write; and I will meet you at Mr. Moyle's at your first notice, and will convince you that I am still

"Your faithful wife,
"F. DARNFORD."

I directed as desired, and wrote in the cover these few words—

"MR. COVELL,

"I THANK you for your attention and humanity to my poor sick husband. I beg you to give him the enclosed directly, and to send me his answer as soon as possible. I pray Heaven to reward your kindness, and grant that you may never want a friend to repay your good offices.

"F.D."

I wrote to Mrs. Moyle; I told her, that my husband was very ill, and that I had invited him into the country, for change of air. I begged her to let my bed be constantly aired, and that she would let me have a garret for a servant; and, if Hannah was not engaged, to let her know, that I should want her attendance; and, if any letters for me should come to her house, to send them immediately by a special messenger.

Having discharged this duty, I prayed incessantly for Darnford's return to me and virtue; and waited impatiently for an answer to my letters.

Ten days after my letter went to the post, I received one directed by Lord A——, and sealed with black wax. My heart foreboded the contents—

"MADAM,

"Mr. Darnford expired two hours ago. I could not have written to you at this solemn moment, but to ask a necessary question. I take upon me the sad task of performing the last duties to my departed friend; which obliges me to enquire, whether you wish to have the body interred in the village where lie the remains of his ancestors, or whether I shall see it deposited in the parish where he died. I beg you will make no scruple of declaring your wishes, nor of commanding all the services of your afflicted friend and devoted servant,

"A——."

I was deeply affected, though not surprized, at this awful event. I gave some hours to grief and meditation.

"Poor, unhappy man!" said I: "Is this the end of thy career, at only twenty-nine years of age?"

I was awakened by the contents of the letter: it demanded an early answer. I had no friend to write in my name. In spite of delicacy and disinclination, I must use the pen myself.

This was, indeed, a heavy task to me; but I could not avoid it. After some consideration, I wrote as follows—

"MY LORD,

"It is a dreadful aggravation of my sorrows, to be obliged to address you at this time: yet, your attention to your deceased friend calls for my acknowledgment. I leave the circumstances attending the last duties entirely to your lordship. Oh, my lord! Death is an awful preacher! May he touch your heart properly, and lead you to reflection upon mortality, which is the certain lot of all men; and to a timely preparation for it! Which is the wish and prayer of

"F. DARNFORD."

When the confusion of my thoughts was somewhat abated, I considered, that I should have some points to settle with Mr. Darnford's heir; who would probably come to the Hall, to take possession of it: that no one had any right to molest me; and I might return to Moyle's, and stay there till I had settled my plan of life.

I discharged my board and lodgings. I hired a cart; and a peasant drove me back to Moyle's. The family were rejoiced to see me. I told them what had happened: they wished and hoped I would fix with them; but I had no such intention. My mind spurned the idea of living upon casual support; and I resolved to exert my abilities, and to eat the bread of industry.

I expected a letter from my friend and counsellor; and I would wait for his advice and direction.

A few days after my return to Moyle's, I received the following letter—

"MADAM,

"I AM ordered, by James Darnford, Esq. to inform you, that he is heir at law to all the effects of your late husband, George Darnford, Esq. and that he will come down to Darnford Hall within a week: also, that you have no right to take away any thing from the house aforesaid. Mr. Frampton has bought an estate in another county, with a larger house upon it, suitable to his family, and has given up his agreement to the said James Darnford, Esq. and he purposes to reside there himself. I am ordered to desire you to prepare to give an account of all the effects of the deceased George Darnford, Esq. as monies, plate, jewels, and all other effects whatsoever. I shall attend Mr. Darnford to the Hall; and then I shall wait on you. In the interim, I am, Madam,

"Your humble servant,
"ROGER RACKHAM."

This mandate gave me great uneasiness. I resolved to write again to my good counsellor; but the next day brought me a letter from him—

"DEAR MADAM,

"I AM not surprised at the contents of your letter. I expected, that you would be persuaded, or threatened, into such a measure; yet I cannot but wish you had held out a little longer: Providence was hastening to your assistance; and it would have been out of the power of any one to have urged you to set your hand to your own ruin. It is done, and cannot now be helped. Let us, then, look forward.

"It gives me pleasure to find you laying plans for your future establishment: I honour and esteem you the more; but I am not willing that you should engage in any hazardous undertaking.

"You say, that you may open a school with as good an expectation as most others. Very true: but who can assure you, that those expectations will be answered? I have known ladies, as well qualified as yourself, undertake this business, and fail of success. I have seen others, with no other requisites but conceit and assurance, succeed to admiration; and, by the help of *able assistants*, send out their pupils veneered over with external accomplishments, that strike the eyes of superficial observers more than solid virtues and principles.

"Beside this, schools are fluctuating and uncertain; a parcel of gossips will sit in judgment upon them and their conductors. Schools are talked up, and talked down, by those who know nothing of the requisites, or the real government, of them.

"Parents are weak and partial: in that case, they are offended that their children are excelled by others. Are there others, who are careless and indifferent toward them? They will exonerate themselves of all blame, by throwing the whole of their faults upon their preceptors and governesses. The conducting of a seminary of education is an arduous and laborious undertaking; it is not duly estimated, nor sufficiently rewarded. Those who devolve upon others the important charge of education, do not sufficiently consider their obligation to those who discharge it faithfully, and who are to acquit *themselves* of a most serious duty to society in general, and to their families respectively.

"You see, my dear lady, it is easier to overthrow a plan, than it is to erect one. I will, however, try to lead you into a path, where you shall not hazard all your property; nor yet be so bound and fettered, that you cannot get away if you dislike, or are unhappy.

"A baronet's lady has enquired for a person, properly qualified, to be a governess to two daughters, and her niece, to whom she is guardian. She asked me to recommend one. I told her, I would look out for her; and I thought it likely, that I might meet with such an one as I could honestly recommend.

"You were in my thoughts; but I would not propose it without your knowledge and approbation.

"Let me know, as soon as you have resolved, lest another should step in before you.

"I shall say nothing of the late event, but that God knows what is best for us.

"Depend upon my friendship at all times, and give me your confidence upon all occasions. I am, dear Madam, yours sincerely,

"D—— M——."

I wept over this letter. "God be praised!" said I, "I have, then, an honest and sincere friend, who scorns to flatter or deceive me. In telling me, he thinks he can honestly recommend me, he says more than flattery can. How different is the language of sincerity from that of adulation! yet, how few know the true value of it!"

M. Marivaux observes, justly— "Charity is never magnificent in it's gifts, and that such are always to be suspected of some latent design: in like manner, Sincerity is always modest in it's professions, and frugal of compliments."

I resolved to answer my friend's letter without delay; and to enclose Mr. Rackham's in mine.

I asked Mr. M——'s advice, in regard to him and Mr. James Darnford. I thanked him for his kindness and attention to my welfare and interest. I begged him to recommend me to the lady, and I would endeavour to deserve his credentials. I asked for a speedy answer, with his directions for my behaviour to Mr. Darnford's heir.

A few days after, came a second letter from Mr. Rackham—

"MADAM,

"It is reported in town, that you have been weak enough to give up your settlement; and that the estate in Essex has been sold to pay your husband's debts. If this be true, my friend, the present Mr. Darnford, is highly injured; for this estate would have devolved to him upon your death. In that case, you cannot expect any favour from him; and I warn you, at your peril, to take any thing from off his premises.

"You must give up every thing belonging to the family, or else you must go to prison. Take your choice. Do not offer to go from Mr. Moyle's; if you do, you will be arrested. I shall be with you soon, and will tell you farther particulars. Your humble servant,

"ROGER RACKHAM."

I should have been terrified by this letter, but my reliance upon my friend gave me courage: I depended that he would not suffer me to be arrested, or insulted, and I despised these threatenings. I sent this letter also to him, and begged his advice and direction. I was soon put out of my pain by his answer—

"DEAR MADAM,
"I KNOW the fellow who sent you these impertinent letters. Do not let them frighten you. I will be with you in a few days, and will protect you from insults of every kind.

"D. M——."

On the third day of September I received a brace of partridges, and a note—

"LORD A—— begs Mrs. Darnford's acceptance of the first birds he has shot; and desires to know when he may wait on her."

ANSWER— "Mrs. Darnford is much indisposed, and admits no men visitors."

I gave a general order, to admit no man but the rector.

Mr. Rackham called, and was told, I saw no company.

Lord A—— and Mr. Rackham came again the next day, and received the same answer.

I told Mrs. Moyle, I expected a friend from London: and begged her to accommodate him with a room in her house, if possible; and to order her servants not to mention it, as it would be only for a short time.

She was so kind as to do what I desired; as, indeed, she always did.

It was my design to accompany him back to London; and I was busied in preparing for my departure. My mourning for my father was nearly as good as new; I only made up a travelling dress.

On the sixth of September, my worthy friend arrived; and I received him with joy and gratitude.

He informed me, that the lady was prepared to receive me,

and was now expecting me; and that I might return with him in his own carriage.

Mr. Rackham called again, a few hours after. Mr. M—— desired that he might be admitted.

He came in. He was surprized to find Mr. M—— with me.

"Sir, you know me," said my friend; "and I know you also."

He bowed, and looked confused.

Mr. M—— went on— "How dared you, Sir, to write two such impertinent letters to this lady?"

"Sir, I beg pardon, I was acting for my client."

"Yes, Sir! acting the part of an incendiary—of a villain!—Go, Sir! I will speak to your client myself; I have nothing to say to you!"

He was going, but Mr. M—— called him back— "Stop, Sir: Is Mr. Darnford at the Hall?"

"Yes, Sir; he came last night."

"Then, tell him, I will wait on him tomorrow morning—And, for you, Sir, I forbid you to trouble or disturb this lady any more, at your peril! You are what a sensible writer calls— "a worm, or maggot of the law; bred out of the rotten parts of it."[11] You live by stirring up strife and litigation. I shall acquaint Mr. Darnford with your character, and warn him to beware of you—And, now, you may go about your business."

The man sneaked away, crest fallen, and ashamed.

"A rascally pettifogger!" said Mr. M——. "I know him well enough: he has done some very bad actions. My eye is upon him; and, the first opportunity he gives me, I will expose and punish him."

The next morning, after breakfast, Mr. M—— went to the Hall.

While he was gone, I received a letter from Lord A——

"I AM told, that Mrs. Darnford receives no men visitors; and I am informed that, last night, a gentleman came to Mr. Moyle's, in his own chaise; that he was well received, and that he lodged there.

"I am farther informed, that James Darnford, Esq. came yesterday to the Hall; that he brought with him an attorney of bad character, and that they threaten to give trouble to Mrs. Darnford.

"These intelligences incite me to write to her, notwithstanding her former prohibition. Will she avow a falshood? Will she admit one man visitor, and exclude all others?

"This morning, I learn, that her visitor is a gentleman

learned in the law; and that she consults him, in regard to the proceedings of James Darnford and his attorney. This I can allow, and approve: but I beg to be admitted to the consultation, as her friend; I have a right to expect, and to demand it.

"Your husband, Madam, upon his death-bed, recommended you to my care and protection; he desired me to be your friend: in regard to him, you ought to permit me to perform my promise and my duty.

"I shall be happy to meet Mr. M——, and to second every thing that he can offer for your service. I know his character, and respect him as I ought. I will wait on you and Mr. M——, the moment you permit me; and convince him and you, that I am, Madam, your faithful friend, and humble servant,

"A——."

This was a vexatious and provoking letter. In appearance, it was all fair and honest friendship; and, unless I told all my reasons for avoiding Lord A——, it seemed prudery and folly to refuse his company and assistance.

I did not care to quarrel with him; and, as I was going to be out of his reach, I thought it most adviseable to be upon terms of external civility with him.

When my good friend came in, I shewed him the letter, and desired his advice how to act towards him.

"You have refused to see him?"

"Yes, Sir, I have."

"Was it on account of your widowhood? or, do you mean to avoid his company in future?"

"I do: to avoid him for ever!"

"Then you will not accept any favours from him?"

"No, certainly. I would sooner receive them from the parish."

"Then, I am sure, you have good reasons for it. Your conduct has always been right hitherto, and I give you credit for it. This letter looks fair enough; but you know the man, and can judge of his honesty."

"But, Sir, he was my husband's friend; and supported him in his sickness, and paid the last duties to him."

"Well, well, I see your difficulties; I guess from whence they proceed. Suppose I was to call upon my lord, and make a kind of apology for your refusing to see him; and thank him for his polite attentions, and all those sort of things? Then he would let us be at quiet for a few days; we should be gone, in the meantime, and then he might be pleased or angry, and nobody care for it."

"My dear Sir, you would oblige me inexpressibly by so doing. What should I do without such a friend!"

"Say no more, child. Did not I come hither to serve you? If you did not employ me, I should have come to no purpose. I will go directly."

He did so; and staid till my dinner was waiting for him.

He came in, rubbing his hands— "Well, Madam, I have pacified my lord for the present. He is very angry that you will not see him, nor accept his offers; but I see there is more at the bottom than what appears upon the surface. Come, let us dine. I am sorry to have made you wait, but I could not get away sooner."

I thanked him heartily for all his goodness to me.

As we sat at dinner, he kept telling me how he had managed with Lord A——.

"He was very stately with me at first: he thought it strange, that I should be admitted to visit you, and even be lodged in the house with you, while he was denied admittance to your presence. I said, there might be reasons for both.

"I should be glad to hear them," he said.

"Why, my lord, I am an old friend of Mrs. Darnford's family; I was her father's executor."

"I knew not that," said he.

"I desired her to consult me, whenever she wanted my advice or assistance. She had received two impertinent and threatening letters from James Darnford's attorney: she wanted me to protect her from their attacks."

"Very right, Sir: she is indeed obliged to you; and I thank you for assisting her."

"But, secondly, my lord, I am an old fellow; she can have nothing to fear from any obligation to me. Your lordship is young, handsome, and accomplished." (I thought it right to smooth him over a little.) "The lady is young and engaging also. Were she to be under obligations to you, her gratitude, and her sense of your merit, might put her into a dangerous and trying situation." (He looked down, and shrunk from the touch.) "But, supposing your lordship's honour and her virtue to be invulnerable, the world might think otherwise of your connection: and her character, which is unquestionable, might suffer; and that would do her more injury than your assistance could do her service."

"He changed colour several times, and seemed uneasy in his seat.

"He said, that, if he might be honoured by your accepting his assistance, there was no occasion for the world to take cognizance of it: things might be managed so discreetly as to conceal it from notice.

"She could not conceal it from herself, my lord; she respects virtue, more than appearances. I think her right to decline your favours: it is from principle, not from pride or prudery."

"By Heaven!" said he, "I think it is from both."

"Then you justify her conduct, and give a reason against yourself."

"He started. I came too near him: he did not recover it immediately.

"Sir, you do not do me justice. I wish you to understand me better. I was Mr. Darnford's *friend*: he recommended his wife to my care. But pray, Sir, tell me what Mrs. Darnford intends to do with herself?"

"As her *husband's* friend, and as *her friend,* I will tell your lordship. She has been endeavouring to qualify herself to assist others in the important department of female education. She purposes to open a school by herself, or else to be governess to one or more young ladies, in the family of their parents. I have advised the latter; because it is less laborious, and less hazardous also."

"I cannot bear that a woman of Mrs. Darnford's merit and accomplishments should be condemned to such a degrading situation."

"Why not, my lord? Where is the degradation? It is this active and industrious temper and mind, that makes me her friend; I love and honour her for it. Had she sat piping and whining, as many people in her situation would do, and expected Heaven to rain down riches into her lap, I should, perhaps, have pitied her; but I should not have stepped forward to her assistance. Such people are ready to accept other kind of assistance, which is far more degrading. I respect that noble and independent spirit, which finds resources within itself for every thing. Heaven looks with pleasure upon a brave spirit, struggling with misfortunes, and rising above them: it's talents are exerted, it's virtues are proved, and conscious rectitude supports it with fortitude and firmness; while virtue prepares for it an eternal reward. I honour and respect Mrs. Darnford too much, to offer her pecuniary assistance; it would offend her delicacy, and my own: but I will follow her with my friendship and services, till I see she has no farther need of them."

"Oh, my generous, noble friend!" said I. "Your good opinion excites me to strain every nerve, and make every effort to deserve it!"

"Now, don't interrupt me," said Mr. M——, "let me tell my story out—

"I made this noble lord turn pale, and red, and pale again, in the course of our conference.

"I rose up to come away; but he took my hand— "Let me intreat you, Sir, to persuade Mrs. Darnford to accept this cottage; to live here, as the person to take care of it, with only one servant to attend her, or more, if she pleases; in short, to live here in her own way."

"At your expence, my lord?—No: I cannot persuade her; because I think her right to refuse it."

"He tried every argument; but I found means to confute them all.

"He tried what anger would do. I was as angry as he. Then he wheedled and coaxed me. I made several efforts to leave him. I said it was your dinner-time. He urged me to dine with him; but I refused positively. Finding it was to no purpose to urge me farther, he suffered me to take a polite leave of him."

"Oh, my dear Sir! let us go to London—let us go directly!"

"Patience, my dear lady!—I shall be as glad to go as you can be, but I must first settle your affairs here.

"Your cousin, James Darnford, Esq. is a mean, shabby fellow. He talked much of his claims upon all the effects of his kinsman. I told him, there was another claimant. He seemed frightened, and asked who it was?

"Mrs. Darnford, Sir. She has a lawful claim to one-third of all the personalities[12] of her late husband. I will enumerate them—The goods and furniture of this house; the plate, linen, &c. the farming stock, and utensils; and the crops now upon the ground. The whole premises, with these things upon them, were let to Robert Frampton, Esq. for the sum of two hundred pounds *per annum*. The year's rent is due, and, I suppose, you have received it; but you must account for it to me, in behalf of Mrs. Darnford. I am her lawyer, and I demand it for her."

"Darnford, and his attorney, stood aghast. They looked at each other, and were silent.

"I went on— "I have made a kind of estimate, in my own

mind, of her share of these personalities. If you will pay Mrs. Darnford the sum of one hundred and fifty pounds, she will give and sign releases, and all will be settled quietly: but, if you take this fellow's advice, and go to law for it, you will spend as much, and perhaps more, than the whole is worth; and you will have to pay the costs of suit, and nobody but this man will be the better for it. I profess plain dealing. I tell you nothing but the truth. Consider this point, and give me your answer as soon as possible."

"Mr. Darnford talked a great deal of nonsense and impertinence, which I shall not repeat. He offered twenty, forty, fifty pounds.

"I refused to accept any thing less than my demand. I desired him to consider farther, and give me his answer to-morrow morning.

"You may have your baggage packed up, to-night, if you please: if I finish the business in the morning, we may set out for London in the afternoon; but, if otherwise, we must wait till the day after. I will draw up the releases myself, this evening, and have every thing in readiness. Get me pen, ink, and paper, for that purpose."

Thus did my generous friend act for me; and with as much activity and dispatch as possible. He wrote all the evening, and every thing was ready for signing the next morning.

As soon as breakfast was over, Mr. M—— went to the Hall, with his papers in his pocket.

Some time after, Lord A——'s servant called, with his Lord's compliments, desiring to know how I did, and inviting Mr. M—— to dine with him at four o'clock.

I sent word, that Mr. M—— was gone to the Hall upon business, and would be engaged there most part of the day, and that I was much as usual.

I packed up all my mourning, cloaths, and necessaries, and had my trunk put into Mr. M——'s chaise, and was ready to go at a minute's warning. I discharged my servant Hannah; to whom I gave a written character, such as she well deserved, and such as most people would accept.

I took leave of Mrs. Moyle and her family; telling them, I should leave them very soon, and begging them to say nothing of it till after I was gone.

I waited impatiently for my friend's return. At one o'clock, he sent me word, he should dine at the Hall, but would be with me by six o'clock. This I took for a hint, that he would set out with me at that hour.

Mr. M—— came back at half an hour past five o'clock.

"Well," said he, "what did you think of my staying to dine at the Hall?"

"I thought it a good omen, Sir, that you would finish the business, and that we should set out on our journey this evening."

"You guess well. Your kinsman and I understand one another; and I verily believe, that fellow instigated him, or he would not have given you any trouble. I have got the sum I demanded from him. And, pray, get all your money together; and, when you get to London, you shall buy stock with it, and let it accumulate for hereafter. While you are young, I hope you shall live upon your own earnings; but, when you go down the hill, it is good to have a resource. Come, give me some tea; and I will order my servants to get ready, if you chuse to set out tonight."

"If it is not disagreeable to you, Sir, I am quite ready."

The tea was drank, the chaise was got ready, and we went as far as N—— that evening. We supped and slept there; and, the next day, we went forward on our journey.

We slept at Rumford[13], and got to Lincoln's Inn Fields by noon the day following.

Mr. M—— told me his management with James Darnford. I found he had pleaded my cause with that eloquence which only appeared when he was warmed with his subject; for his common conversation was blunt and plain.

This excellent man took my monies, and bought into the Long Annuities[14] for me. I believe he added to the sum; but he concealed it so cunningly, that I could not be certain of it.

He gave me the Bank securities— "Here," said he, "keep these safely. Twenty pound a year is a good fortune to those who had nothing before; and you will find it a pretty addition to your salary.

"You are to have fifty pounds a year. I have settled all things for you with Lady Haughton. You shall call upon her to-morrow morning; but you must finish your week with me, before you go there entirely."

I was going to express my gratitude and respect; but he stopped me.

"I won't be thanked, nor I won't be flattered. Be my good

child, and I will be your good father: that is enough for us both."

The next morning, Mr. M—— carried me to wait on Lady Haughton. She received us in her dressing-room. The young ladies were with her.

There was an air of condescension about the lady, that had pride and insolence in it; and humiliated, while it seemed gracious to me.

The young ones whispered and laughed aside; which convinced me that they were ignorant and ill-bred, and foreboded an unpleasant task to the person who should undertake to inform and instruct them.

Mr. M—— presented me to Lady Haughton. He reminded her of what had passed between them; and told her, I was the person he recommended.

My lady gave a nod of approbation: the terms were mentioned, and agreed to; and the Monday following named for my reception into the family.

Mr. M—— treated me with the greatest kindness and hospitality; and I left him with reluctance. He would not suffer me to express half the gratitude I felt for his goodness. He took a paternal leave of me; and I went to my new destination.

And now, my dear friend, I will make up this enormous pacquet. Our ploughboy will take it with him to W——. I hope to hear from you, at his return home with my Patty. I shall go on writing in the mean time.

I have kept a journal; and that enables me to be as minute as you find me, for I have little more than to transcribe.

You must tell me some particulars of your past situation. You speak very disrespectfully of your husband, and I expect you to account for it. He has left you an ample fortune, and the care of his children. This proves that he esteemed and put confidence in you. He must have had good sense and penetration, to have understood your merit.

With every sentiment of esteem and friendship, I am, dear Madam, your faithful friend, and obedient servant,

FRANCES DARNFORD

P.S. I will contrive a way to send my pacquets to W—— once a month, and receive yours in return.

Volume II

LETTER VI
Mrs. Darnford, in continuation.

HOW comes it, my dear friend, that, at first sight of a person, we receive a favourable or unfavourable impression? It is sometimes just, but as often the contrary: it ought not to be relied on. Yet, there is a something like intuition, which attracts kindred minds, and repels discordant ones, and which we cannot understand nor account for.

It is certain, that I felt something repulsive from Lady Haughton and her children, and that this presentiment was fully justified.

The young ladies had been under the tuition of a French governess, who had taught them airs and graces, self-confidence and vanity; but they were ignorant of those graces which attend on Virtue and her pupils only. They had received no instructions relative to religion, or morality: they were proud and conceited; full of remarks on the weaknesses and imperfections of others, entirely ignorant of their own.

I behaved with all the politeness I was mistress of to them, in hope to excite theirs in return; but it had no effect: my politeness to them was their due, and a thing of course; but theirs to me was unnecessary. I was a reduced person, and received wages for my attendance on them; which made me a dependent, not much above a servant.

These things were more implied than expressed; dropt at times only, but so as to render it impossible to mistake their meaning.

I strove to merit their confidence, before I should demand it; but they were shy of conversing with me: they would talk aside, in a half whisper, laugh and sneer among themselves, but seldom allow me any share of their conversation.

At length, I told them, it was reckoned a mark of ill-breeding, and desired them to forbear it. They did it so much the more, and in defiance of me.

I read French with them: they could chatter away among themselves; but they knew little or nothing of the grammar, either of French or English. I offered to read history: they objected to it, as dull and dry, and only fit to set them asleep.

I proposed the Spectators.[1] They were only fit for children.

Poetry—morality—essays. Nothing pleased them.

I introduced the Theatre of Education by Madame de Genlis.[2] This was new, and they seemed to pay some attention to it.

The first pieces were for children only. I desired them to look out for one they liked, and to translate it into English. They did not like the trouble of it.

I mentioned this book to Lady Haughton, spoke highly of it, and begged her to use her influence with them, to oblige them to read and translate it.

She heard me with indifference; said, she could not insist upon it, but would advise them to read it, if agreeable. Miss Morton, her niece, was in her fifteenth year; her daughters were in their fourteenth and thirteenth. It was too late to treat them like children; though, in knowledge of every kind, they were as backward.

I recommended the other works of Madame de Genlis; the Tales of the Castle, which I gave to the young ladies; Adelaide and Theodore, which I begged Lady Haughton to peruse, as a system of education.

The young ladies were neither entertained nor improved: it shewed them defects in themselves, which they had no inclination to amend; it reproved their pride, vanity, and indolence. They were offended, and vented their spleen and ill-humour upon me. My lady thought the other work a very impertinent satire upon parents and guardians.

I endeavoured to instruct them in the outlines of religion and morality. They either gaped over them, or else talked aside while I was reading.

I introduced books of a serious kind: Fordyce's Sermons to Young Women;[3] The Father's Legacy, by Dr. Gregory; A Father's Instructions, by Dr. Percival; Madame de Lambert's Advice to a Son and Daughter; Mrs. Chapone's works, and several others; without effect.

I thought it my duty to tell them theirs: they only flouted me.

"To what purpose, ladies," said I, "was I brought here, if you will not suffer me to be of any service to you? I wish you would tell me what I can do to oblige you."

"Why, then, Madam," said Miss Morton, "you must do as Mademoiselle Bourdiere did with us. She did not teaze us with dry lessons of morality; but she read us little stories, full of fun and humour; she translated some short things, and let us copy them, to shew my aunt and uncle, and their friends; she entered into all our little parties; she played with us, danced and sung with us, and always spoke well of us; she taught us to make a little learning go a great way, and to display what we did know to advantage; she made us love her, and be satisfied with ourselves. If you would do so, we should live well with you."

"Then, she was exactly like Dorina, in *The Spoiled Child*;[4] a comedy that I will read to you, as a lesson. But, ladies, I cannot act as she did; my principles forbid it. I have undertaken an important charge, and I am obliged to perform the duties of it. I am accountable to your friends, to you, and to myself; and I cannot be pleased with myself, if I do not. But, beside, I have heard Mademoiselle was discharged disgracefully: is it true?"

"Poor Mademoiselle! She had a little misfortune."

"That is, a little child: is it not so?"

"Surely, Madam, that is no business of yours; and beside, you, that are so perfect, should be above scandal."

"That is no scandal, that is known to every body: but, setting the *little* misfortune aside, she was a very improper person to have the care of young ladies. Suffer me to read you a pretty comedy of Madame de Genlis, in which you will hear such a person treated as she deserves."

I read the Spoiled Child to them.

They were sullen and gloomy. They could not have any pleasure in such books as only served to point out to them all their faults.

"If you will not hear them, how can you amend them?"

They did not desire to hear of them. "Then, I can be of no use to you. I will talk with my lady, and tell her so; for I cannot take her money, and lose my own time, to no purpose."

"Just as you please, Madam!"

I had a conversation with Lady Haughton. She was not convinced of the deficiency in the young people's education. She said, when girls were almost grown to the stature of women, they were no longer to be treated as children; that her children were thought amiable and accomplished by as good judges as myself; and she would not suffer them to be made unhappy, in order to teach them what they had no desire to learn.

I asked, what service I was to do them in this situation?

"Why, I want you to sit with them when I am otherwise engaged, and when their masters attend them; and, if you do not like this, Mrs. Darnford, you may leave my family whenever you please."

"It will be very easy, Madam, to find a person qualified for this office; a servant may do it: but I could not be satisfied to receive a salary for doing nothing."

"I acquit you of that; and I have no desire to part with you—But, do as you please, Mrs. Darnford."

She left the room.

I went, the next morning, to my worthy friend and counsellor, and told him all that had passed. He said, these were disagreeable circumstances; but he advised me to bear with them till I could meet with something more eligible, and he would be looking out for me in the mean time.

The young ladies no longer kept any terms with me. Authorized by my lady, they treated me with insolence and contempt.

I no longer took any thought for their improvement, but waited with some impatience for my release.

Sir Gilbert Haughton was an inoffensive, peaceable man; an admirer of his lady's wisdom: who submitted quietly to her government; and, in return, she suffered him to enjoy the run of his own house. He appeared as the master of it when she received company; and he actually kept the key of the cellar, and overlooked the butler.

His conversation was confined to the wind and the weather: I scarcely ever heard him speak upon any other subject, any farther than an affirmative, or a negative.

He was courteous to every body. He generally saluted me with civility; saying—"A fine day, Madam;" or—"An easterly wind, Madam," &c. He seemed to go beyond his usual bounds, when he heard I was going to leave the family.

I had answered him in his own way, and paid him more attention than he usually received; and, I suppose, that pleased him.

When the family met at dinner, after the usual compliments of the day and the weather, Sir Gilbert said—"I hear you are going to leave us, Madam. I am very sorry for it."

I bowed, and was silent.

My lady drew her mouth on one side. The young ladies tossed their heads, and smiled scornfully.

Sir Gilbert said—"May I know the reason, Madam, of your leaving our family?"

I answered—"Sir, it is because the young ladies have no farther need of my assistance."

My lady frowned—"You are very inquisitive, Sir Gilbert. What signifies it to you, whether Mrs. Darnford goes or stays?"

"Nay, my lady, I only asked the question: I hope there is no harm in that. Mrs. Darnford is a very well-behaved woman; and I should think you would not get one more proper."

"Surprizing!—How come you to know her qualifications?"

"Not I, Madam: I don't pretend to know any farther of people than their behaviour."

"Well, then," said my lady, with a jeering laugh, "be pleased to know, then, Sir, that Mrs. Darnford chuses to leave us, and to go where her merit is better understood."

"Enough, my lady: I am satisfied."

The young ladies whispered and giggled all dinner-time. Every eye was upon me; and I was glad to retire from the parlour.

My worthy friend had called in the morning of this day, to tell me of another lady who wanted a governess for her children. In consequence of which, I declared my resolution of leaving Lady Haughton the following week; and though she was influenced by her children, she was displeased at my departure.

I dragged on three miserable months in this family, with every external of what contributes to ease and comfort, but without one happy day. I had no society, and was not permitted to converse with myself. Some days before I left it, I received the following letter—

"LORD A—— TO MRS. DARNFORD.

"Why, Madam, do you still fly me, and reject my services? To what cause must I attribute your inflexibility? The ties between Darnford and you are dissolved, and nothing but shadows remain to hinder our being united in the bonds of an indissoluble friendship: yet still you fly me; and, in so doing, own that you fear me. This fear I must investigate: there are two causes from which it may arise; either you hate me more than others, or else you love me, or fear that you may love me.

"Oh, that I dared to believe the latter! I will no longer bear this cruel suspense; I will come to an explanation with you.

"That I have loved you long, you know too well; otherwise you cannot reconcile your behaviour to the rules of politeness, which you observe to every body but me, who would risk every thing to contribute to your happiness.

"You have fulfilled every duty to your husband, under the most trying circumstances: what remains farther? I loved George Darnford; he was a good-natured, careless fellow, most agreeable in company, and over a chearful glass. I tried to check his passion for gaming. I tried to extricate him from the troubles he brought upon himself, but in vain. I followed him with my friendship to the last, and I paid the last duties to his memory.

"I am free to pursue my own views; you are free also: but you have a proud and indomitable spirit, that spurns the idea of an obligation.

"Oh, but you cannot forgive nor forget my proposal in your husband's life-time! You admire the wisdom and virtue of the old Romans; yet some of them did such things. Cato, the austere Cato, lent his wife to his friend Hortensius, and afterwards took her again.[5]

"We are no longer in this predicament. I only make this reference to the past, to induce you to forgive, and think no more of it.

"All times and people have had their prejudices: these have, in time, given way, and were succeeded by new prejudices of different kinds.

"From being over strict in their principles, they have gone to the other extreme, and become too relaxed and profligate. In all moral objects there are two extremes; and there is also a medium.

"A state of concubinage is by no means so immoral or disgraceful as your very strict people represent it.

"The Book which you venerate, and I respect, is of a more tolerating spirit in this particular. I forbear to produce instances, but refer to your own memory and observation.

"And now, Madam, I will once more make you a proposal, which I beg you will honour with your serious consideration; and, when you have made up your mind upon the subject, let me know your determination.

"I will settle the farm in Essex upon you and your heirs, irrevocably: I bought it with this view, to restore it to you whenever you would deign to accept it. The cottage shall be yours, and a pretty little parcel of land about it, lately purchased; which, together, make a farm sufficient to amuse and employ one who delights in rural occupations.

"These I mention as resources only in case of accidents, and a barrier against the *foul fiend* whom you have lately paid court to, while the arms of your friend were impatient to receive you, and protect you from his detestable approach.

"I invite you to share my fortune and my heart; to live where it pleases you. If you chuse to visit the Continent, I will attend you to any part of it. My house in town, either of my seats are at your service: all are yours; and I am yours, when and where you chuse to command me.

> "Come, Rosalind! Oh, come! for without thee
> "What pleasure can the country have for me?
> "Come, Rosalind! Oh, come! my farm, my kine,
> "My tender flocks, my fields, and all, are thine."[6]

"I chuse to explain myself so, that we may fully understand each other. I make no dark and obscure promises of future recompence.

"I should not like to have my name set at the top of a lamentable ballad, shewing how the base man seduced the nymph under the promise of marriage.

"I treat with you as a free woman; one who knows the world, and has sense enough to despise the censure of it, and who lives to her own feelings.

"I do not expect you to be very explicit in your answer. Only say—"*I shall go to the cottage in the month of May, and enjoy the beauties of the Spring;*" or, "*I should like to go to France,*" or "*to Italy;*" or, *any time and place where you chuse to spend the summer.*" Only give me the *hint* I sigh and long for, and I will fly to meet you with all the warmth and tenderness of love and friendship. I am, dear Madam,

"Yours—all yours—and only yours,

"A——."

"Direct your answer to me in town; I shall not leave it till I hear from you. Pray do not consult Counsellor M——, but make me your counsellor."

My answer will be the best comment upon this letter. I wrote it at a leisure moment, in the morning, before I came to breakfast—

"MY LORD,

"FEW women have been so peculiarly circumstanced as I have. I have no friend to refer to in a case of delicacy; I must, therefore, speak for myself.

"Your letter is a master-piece of art and sophistry. I shall answer it with sincerity and plain dealing, in order to put an end to all future correspondence between us, once and for ever.

"Your lordship may think me prejudiced or precise, or whatever you please, when I declare, that I would rather fall into the arms of the *foul fiend* you have described *Poverty*, than accept of a deliverance by indirect or dishonest means, such as are contrary to the principles I profess, which have hitherto been my guide and my counsellors.

"Lest you should think your arguments unanswerable, I will venture to reply to them: a puff of wind is able to overthrow them.

"The man, who could endeavour to seduce the wife of his friend, and to make her husband accessary to her seduction, is the last man I would chuse for my counsellor, friend, and protector.

"You have taken up an idea in your defence that is false and groundless.

"The Romans were not guilty of such vile actions: they respected the holy rites of marriage; they divorced their wives for adultery, and sometimes for a mere suspicion of it, as in the case of Caesar's wife Pompeia. Cato the Younger did not lend his wife upon the urgency of his friend Hortensius: he divorced his wife, Marcia, and she was solemnly married to Hortensius. Her father Philip, and Cato, were present at the marriage, which was celebrated with the consent of all parties. Cato did not receive Marcia again till after the death of her husband Hortensius: then, indeed, he was re-married to her; he put the highest confidence in her; he put his children and family under her care, when he followed the party of Pompey, and went over to Africa.

"Pray observe, that I do not defend this action of Cato's; I only put in upon a fair basis, according to the testimony of Plutarch and other historians. In this light, it does not bear the least resemblance to any part of your lordship's conduct; and I beg that you will inform yourself better, before you compare your character with that of Cato.

"Your appeal to the sacred writings is still less excuseable.

"You have not distinguished between the Old and the New Testament; to confound them together answered your purpose better.

"The Mosaic law was local and temporary: that of the Gospel, immutable and eternal; calculated for all times, and all people.

"The former allowed a plurality of wives, as it has always been customary in the Eastern countries; but I never knew that it allowed a woman to have two husbands. I profess the religion of the Gospel, and hold myself bound to observe it's laws. It signifies nothing to me what was allowed by former legislators; I submit to the laws of my own religion, and my own country.

"I am, however, persuaded, that if Cato had been born under the Christian dispensation, he would have been a strict observer of it's laws.

"Thus far, my lord, in answer to your arguments. For the rest, I thank you for your generous and charitable intentions towards me; which, I make no doubt, you think do me honour.

"I forgive your prejudices, as I hope you will mine: but they are so different, as to render it impossible for us to live together; and, had you really offered me your hand, with your heart and person, I could not have accepted it.

"I respect your sincerity, in disdaining to raise expectations you never intended to fulfil. I wish all men, that hold your opinions, were as honest in this respect.

"As I have fully made up my mind, and have taken my final resolution, to decline your lordship's proposals, I beg that our correspondence may here be concluded.

"I wish your lordship every good in present and future; and remain,

"Your most humble servant,
"F.D."

I did not send this letter till the day I left Lady Haughton's, that my lord might have no clue to find me at my new destination.

Lady Haughton behaved with more politeness the day I left her, than during the whole time I resided there: she wished I could have made myself agreeable to her young people; she believed they had been too much indulged by their late governess; but it was now too late to begin a new method. She wished me better success in future.

"I spent a few days with my friend Mr. M——, before I went to my new appointment.

During that time I heard a very indifferent character of Mrs. Ilford, to whom I was engaged.

A lady, who visited Mr. M——, told me she was a very bad mother; that she loved some of her children, and hated others; that she was proud and ill-natured, envious and spiteful; in short, that she was a very disagreeable woman to live with.

Mrs. Langston did not spare her, nor, indeed, any body; for she seemed informed of every one's ill qualities, and made no scruple to declare them.

Mr. M—— advised me not to go to Mrs. Ilford's, but to wait for something more eligible. He said, Mrs. Langston saw a great deal of company, and might hear of another situation.

I answered, that I had given my word, and would make the trial; I thought it could not be more disagreeable than that I had left.

Mrs. Langston said, she would be upon the look-out for me; and, if she heard of any thing more agreeable, she would let me know.

I have a good mind to give you a short sketch of this lady's conversation.

"I like you well enough to endeavour to serve you—but, good Lord! to see what luck some folks have! There was Susan Brittle—she had singed the wings of her character, spent the greatest part of her fortune, and was at her last shift; when old Lady Bilson lost her companion, and was seeking out for another. Mrs. Martlet goes and recommends Sukey, and cries her up for a nonpareil. Lady Bilson took her without farther enquiry. Sukey put on airs of prudery and preciseness; followed my lady to the Tabernacle; read books of theology to her all day; watched with her all night when she was sick; and pretended a great affection for her. Behold! in three years time, the old lady stept aside, and left Susan three thousand pounds, and all her cloaths, linen, and jewels. Well—there was poor Mrs. Pilgrim, as good a creature as ever lived, went from one place to another, and could find no rest for the sole of her foot, but was obliged to go and live in Wales, and board for fifteen pounds a year.—Depend upon it, my dear, I will do all I can to serve you; but luck is all: give us luck, and you may throw us into the sea."

"By your account," said Mr. M——, "the young woman

earned her fortune hardly enough; but I would not wish my friend to sacrifice to luck, as you call it. I would have her exert her own merit and industry, and rely upon God's blessing upon them."

"Well, and so she should, to be sure; but, in spite of all her merit, and all your wisdom, there is such a thing as luck, depend upon it."

There is a specimen of Mrs. Langston for you! I shall not let her say any more at present; perhaps I may speak of her in future.

I went to Mrs. Ilford's without any expectations; for I was out of luck, as Mrs. Langston said, and I had resolved not to pay court to Fortune.

Mrs. Ilford was exactly what she was described: she was the mother of six children, all lovely and promising; three of them she loved, and the other three she disliked.

Mr. Ilford was a plain, blunt man; with a good understanding, very little cultivated. He saw his wife's faults, and told her of them rudely, but he had no malignity in him: with good-nature and courtesy, he might have been persuaded to any thing; but peevishness and thwarting made him ten times worse.

With an honest, worthy husband, a plentiful fortune, fine children, and every thing that is wished and desired, Mrs. Ilford was a most unhappy woman.

She was one of those wretched mortals that extract misery out of every thing about them.

She was desirous of giving her children a good education: they were handsome, and amiable, yet she was never satisfied with them nor their doings; she studied to find faults in them.

She was always changing her servants; she put no confidence in them, and they had no affection for her.

With all these miseries in her mind, I really believe, she meant to act rightly; but her unfortunate temper cast a shade upon every thing; and she thought she was making herself miserable, and every one around her.

The eldest son was at a public school: one of his mother's cares was, lest his morals should be corrupted; and in this there was some reason.

The eldest daughter was put under my care: her mother thought her the superior to all the rest in genius and abilities of every kind; but in this she was mistaken.

The second daughter was a sweet, amiable girl; lovely, modest, and ingenuous. She was discouraged and depressed, in order to give consequence to the elder; and she received many advantages from this discouragement. She was the darling of all the family, but the mother; who could not bear that she should be distinguished.

The next child was a son, a fine manly boy, rather rough in his temper, but of a docile and generous spirit, that might be excited to do any thing by praise, but was hardened by undue punishment. I desired to have that child under my care, as well as his sisters.

The next was a girl about four years old; the youngest a boy under two. The eldest daughter was just twelve years old.

I put my pupils into training, tried their capacities, and was pleased to find they had been well initiated in their own language, and were docile and agreeable in their dispositions. I taught them with pleasure, and put Mrs. Barbauld's Lessons[7] into the hands of the little girl.

Mr. Ilford asked me, what I thought of his children?

I spoke of them as they deserved; and he heard me with great satisfaction.

"You do not, then, find any of them deficient in understanding?"

"Not in the least, Sir; but I shall be a better judge some time hence."

Mrs. Ilford had taken it into her head, that Miss Anna, the second daughter, and James, the second son, were inferior to all the rest; this was the reason of Mr. Ilford's enquiry, and I was soon perfectly convinced of the contrary.

When I had been a month in this family, I received the following letters. The first was from Lord A———.

"MADAM,

"You are a proud, ungrateful, saucy woman, unworthy of my love or esteem. I leave you to your fate; to that Poverty, which you prefer to my friendship. I hope, and believe, you will one day repent of your behaviour to me, when youth and beauty are gone, and no man will give himself any trouble about you: then you may regret the friend that you have lost. I have done with you for ever! Farewel!

"A———."

"P.S. I shall leave London in a month. If you should repent of your behaviour within that time, you may let me know."

The second was from the youngest Miss Haughton—

"MADAM,

"ONE of your late pupils is very desirous to ask your pardon, for her share of the impertinent treatment you met with at Lady Haughton's; and the more she thinks, the more she is ashamed of it.

"Since you went away, I have read the first volume of the Theatre of Education, which you left behind you; and I have received both pleasure and advantage from it.

"I should take it as a very great favour, if you will have the goodness to lend me the other volumes: I will take the greatest care of them, and return them all together.

"I have, in a manner, put myself to school to these books, and hope to make some amends for the time I have lost.

"I remember your instructions, and observe them as much as is in my power. I am sensible that we all wanted them, and might have improved by your company and assistance.

"You must know, Madam, that my cousin and sister were determined to persuade mamma not to take another governess; and they would never have forgiven me, if I had not joined with them in this, and all other things; or else I was desirous to have behaved better to you in all respects.

"I will send the person that brings this, to-morrow at this time; and beg you will send the books by her, if convenient.

"I should be still more obliged to you, if you will recommend such books as you think will be agreeable and improving to me; and I will save my pocket-money, and buy them as I can afford.

"I beg pardon, Madam, for giving you all this trouble; but I have such an opinion of your goodness, as to believe you will excuse it. I am, Madam,

"Your humble servant,
"BELIZA HAUGHTON."

The third letter was from Betsey Moyle. The contents were to this effect—That her mother, and all the family, missed me very much, and were very desirous to hear of my health and safety; that they hoped I was situated to my liking, or else that I would come into their country again; that her mother had lately met with an old friend, who lived near the town of W——; that she was informed they wanted a person of ability to open a school there; that such an one, well recommended, could not fail of success; that her mother had heard me wish for such an employment, and she thought, perhaps, this might suit me.

She begged I would excuse the liberty, and that I would answer her letter. I resolved to consider this proposal well before I replied to it.

I wrote an answer to Bell Haughton's letter. Her messenger called the next day, and I sent it with the books, as desired—

"DEAR YOUNG LADY,

"It gives me very great pleasure to know, that the time I spent at the house of your parents was not wholly lost; that you have remembered my instructions, and have taken the generous resolution to finish your own education. I shall be happy to do every thing in my power to assist your studies for this laudable purpose. I send the remaining volumes of the Theatre of Education; and request your acceptance of the whole set, as a token of friendship and remembrance: and I will give you a list of books, such as may be of use to you.

"Be assured that I have forgiven, and almost forgotten, all the disagreeable things that passed at your house: it is to themselves that your friends have done the greatest injury, and I wish them to repair it as you have done. I am, dear young lady, your affectionate friend and servant,

"F. DARNFORD."

LIST OF BOOKS

Madame de Lambert's Advice to a Son and Daughter.
Mrs. Chapone's Works.
Mrs. H. More's Sacred Dramas, and Search after Happiness.[8]
A Father's Legacy. By Dr. Gregory.
A Father's Instructions. By Dr. Percival.
The Ladies Preceptor.
The Geographical Grammar.
A Short History of England. Question and Answer.
A Roman History. By Goldsmith.
A Grecian History. By the Same.
Theatre of Education. By Madame de Genlis.
Tales of the Castle. By the Same.
Fordyce's Sermons to Young Women.

Mason on Self-Knowledge.
Moore's Fables for the Female Sex.
Cotton's Visions.
Telemachus, in French.
Cyrus, in French.
Spectators, well translated into French.
Sacred History, selected from the Scriptures. By Mrs. Trimmer.
The Bible—A Chapter every Day.
The Guardian.
The Rambler. By Dr. Johnson.
The Adventurer. By Dr. Hawkesworth.
The Idler. By Dr. Johnson.
Spectacle de la Nature.
Mrs. Carter's Poems.

The first month I spent at Mr. Ilford's rolled away smoothly. The second, not so well. The third, Mrs. Ilford began to vent her ill humours upon me. I loved the children; they began to improve under my tuition: I took pleasure in their company; I hoped they would repay my cares, and that even their mother would be satisfied with them.

Mrs. Ilford generally found fault with them the whole time she staid in the room. If she could not see any thing in their behaviour, their cloaths bore the blame—a spot on James's cloaths, Anna had dirtied her frock, Ellen trod her shoe aside.

I heard her with the greatest composure. Even this displeased her: I did not pay regard enough to what she said.

I answered, that I had so high an opinion of her good sense, that, when her children were good in material points, she would not mind trifles.

"What, then, Madam, do you think they are without faults?"

"I think nobody is happier in promising children than you are, Madam. There is not one among them of which I should not be proud to be the mother."

The children smiled upon me; the mother pouted, and left the room.

Another time, when she was making comparisons in favour of those to whom she was partial, I would not allow of them.

Did I see no difference among them! Were they all exactly alike!

"No, Madam; I do make some distinctions: I think Miss Ilford sometimes wants a check, and Miss Anna wants encouragement; but that both of them will, under proper government, be good and amiable."

"So, Madam, you make a point of contradicting every thing I advance, in order to shew your superior judgment! I ought to know my own children best; what should hinder me?"

"Partiality blinds you, Madam. I am impartial, and will endeavour to do my duty to all of them."

"Do you dare to tell me that I am partial?"

"Yes, Madam, I dare: I heard so before I came hither; but you have sense to correct yourself, otherwise I would not take this liberty. When you reflect upon the consequences of letting this appear to the children, I hope and trust you will excuse me, and be convinced of my sincere attachment to all my pupils."

She flew into a passion, and said some rude things. I was calm, and made no reply. She recollected herself, grew cooler, and said, if she must not speak of the faults of her children, she must get a governess who knew the respect that was due to their mother.

I bowed—"Whenever you please, Madam, if you cannot bear with my sincerity."

She left me in anger.

When we met at dinner, I behaved as usual; and she recovered herself enough to treat me with civility; and, beside, she did not wish that her husband should take cognizance of the matter, well knowing he would decide against her.

Some time after, I made James read before his parents.

Mr. Ilford took him in his arms, praised and caressed him.

"You are very much improved, my boy; and are greatly obliged to your governess."

"Yes, papa, so I am, because she loves me, and speaks kind words to me; and then I strive all I can to do better."

"There, Madam, do you hear that?"

Mrs. Ilford frowned, and looked angrily at me.

"What, then," said her husband, "are you sorry that your son is improved? I suppose you are, by your behaviour to Mrs. Darnford.—Well, then, Madam, I thank you for us both, and am delighted that my boy does so well."

I took the children away, and left the parents to finish the scene.

Mr. Ilford spoke the truth. His wife was really displeased at the improvements of those children she did not love. She wanted the others to surpass them in all things; and, though they did well, that was not sufficient. She accused me of putting them backward, and the others forward. She was unreasonable and unjust. She made my duty uneasy to me; and I began to think of leaving her: yet my love for the children made me unwilling to part with them.

I sometimes dined with Mr. M—— on a Sunday. He was one of those old-fashioned men who dine early on that day, that their servants may attend the public worship of God, thinking their obedience to his laws the best security for those duties they owed to their masters. This suited me also; for I held the same opinions with him.

One day, I met Mrs. Langston there; and she was curious to know how I went on with Mrs. Ilford. She thought I staid longer than she expected. I told her, I had some thoughts of leaving her, and enquired whether she knew of any thing more eligible for me.

"Why, yes, I have heard of several; but I do not know whether they will suit you. There is old Mrs. Batson wants a companion; and there is Mrs. Gumly wants a governess for her daughters. I will enquire farther, before I recommend them to you, child. My maid is very intelligent: she finds out people's characters; she knows Mrs. Gumly's servant; she shall sift her well; and I will let you know the result as soon as I can."

When Mrs. Langston was gone, I said to Mr. M—— "I would give something, Sir, to know your opinion of that lady."

"Why, Madam, it is not very different from your own: but I find her of as much use as a newspaper; she knows every body, and every thing. Sometimes I want information, and she gives it me: how she gets it, I know not; but I seldom miss of obtaining from her the lights that I want relative to names, families, and characters. She has some good qualities, and has done service by her recommendations. She is a kind of nomenclator;[9] and I refer to her as I do to the Red-book."

"Do you think she is likely to be of any service to me, Sir?"

"Not unlikely. Come and dine with me next Sunday; and you shall hear what she says."

In the course of the week following, Mrs. Ilford had teazed me almost out of patience. She wanted to get rid of me, but wished the motion to come from me. She found that Mr. Ilford had a good opinion of me, and was pleased with the children's improvements. If she dismissed me, he would not fail to blame her; but, if I desired to leave the family, she fancied she could turn the blame upon me. The poor woman took more pains to do wrong, than it would have cost her to do right.

The next Sunday, I met Mrs. Langston again at Mr. M——'s. After the customary greetings, she took up the thread of her discourse, and run it off till she came to the end of the clue—

"Well, my dear, I have been very diligent in making enquiries upon your account. I will begin with Mrs. Batson. She is old, and rich: so far is very well; but then, she is as covetous as Old Elwes.[10] She loves nobody but herself: yet she loves good living, but will not let others have their share. She had sometimes a chicken, or a bit of fish; a single sole, or a flat fish of any kind; or half a pound of salmon, or any thing that is nice. Now; I will tell you the rest of her establishment—She keeps three maid-servants, and two men; but the coachman is at board-wages; and lives with his family. She buys a quarter of mutton every week, and has it cut out into pieces as it is wanted; so they live upon mutton and mutton through the year. She has a large side-board of old-fashioned plate, which is set out every day, as if for a feast; but it serves only to put you in mind of good dinners, and create an appetite, without gratifying it. I dined with her one day, to meet a relation of us both: there were four of us; and I will tell you our dinner. At the top, a pair of soles—small ones they were too; at the bottom, a whole loin of mutton; on one side, three scollop-shells of potatoes, beat up with milk; on the other, an ordinary rice-pudding. After dinner, three bottles were set on the table; one was Madeira, the second Port, the third raisin-wine, made at home. When she is alone with her companion, she drinks a pint of Madeira to her own share: and the companion drinks two glasses of raisin-wine; which, I dare say, is not a bit too good."

Mr. M—— laughed—"Where do you get intelligence of all these *minutiae?*"

"No matter where: I warrant them true. I have not done yet. Mrs. Batson has a tolerable piece of ground, for a London garden. It is divided into two large beds, and a gravel-walk between them: one is full of cabbages, the other of potatoes; the borders are full of pot-herbs and onions. There is always either a large cabbage, or a dish of potatoes, at her table, to eke out the mutton; and the servants are not stinted in these articles. If she leaves any thing of the top dish, she gives it the companion; but she must not ask for it."

"Enough, enough of Mrs. Batson!" said Mr. M——: "let us hear no more of her."

"Yes, one trait more, and I have done: she expects her companion to sit with her all day, and to read her to sleep at night."

"Now I say *enough*, too," said I. "I will not be Mrs. Batson's companion. I cannot bear to have my rest broken: the vexations of the day are sufficient for me."

"Well, I thought so," said Mrs. Langston. "The poor girl that has left her, is quite worn out, and sinking under it. For all this service, she gave her thirty guineas a year; and she paid for her washing out of it.

"I have got another character for you, as good as Mrs. Batson."

"Reserve it, then, till after dinner," said Mr. M——: "it is ready by my watch." He led us into the dining-parlour, and postponed our subject till tea-time.

When we returned into the drawing-room, Mr. M—— said—"Come, Madam, give us your other character; but, pray, make it as brief as you can."

"Well, so I do always: I love brevity as much as any body. Mrs. Gumly is the wife of a cheesemonger; not one of your tip-top folks, but a retail-dealer in butter and cheese."

Mr. M—— laughed—"Well said, Madam Brevity!"

"She had a few hundreds to her fortune, which made her husband's outset. She had an only brother, who went with a merchant abroad into Spain. He had abilities for business; and behaved so well, that he succeeded his master, acquired a great fortune, died a bachelor, and left it to his sister, Mrs. Gumly. There is a story told briefly, I hope!"

"Very much so, Madam!—Proceed."

"This great fortune overwhelmed Mrs. Gumly; and, as it came by her, she took the lead, and the good man, her husband, marched under her command. They disposed of the shop immediately, hired a house at the west end of town, bought a villa in the environs, and lived among the gentry. This good couple have two sons, and three daughters. The eldest son is sent over to Spain, to settle his uncle's affairs; and with him a very clever young man, who understands business of every kind. The youth is thrown among men, and stands a chance to be one. The father does not want sense, and has judged rightly with regard to his son. There are three tall, gawky girls, whom the mother wants to have qualified for the new society they are to appear in. The eldest is full sixteen years old, ignorant, aukward, and vulgar. Mrs. Gumly had thoughts of sending them to school; but the girls cried, and begged they might not go. She was advised to take a gentlewoman into her family, to instruct the young ladies in all the forms of polite life; and she thinks this the only knowledge worth acquiring. Mrs. Gumly thinks fortune is given people in order to enjoy all the comforts and conveniencies of life; and this, she believes, consists in fine cloaths, good eating and drinking. She keeps an over-plentiful table, loaded with dainties of every kind, good wines and liquors of all kinds; and thinks herself honoured, if the neighbouring gentry will partake of them. She admits no tradesmen's wives into her house: they must be *born gentry*, to be worthy of her notice. A person of quality transports her; and she is ready to fall down and worship titles, pomp, and fortune. The husband insists upon being her steward, and keeping an account of their income and expences. By this prudent conduct, he will hinder her from out-running their fortune: but she gives dinners and suppers continually; and there are always people ready to run after her, and to flatter her vanity. She wants a person, as I have told you, to educate the young ladies, her daughters.— Now, my good Mrs. Darnford, what think you of this office? I believe I have interest sufficient to introduce you, and get you accepted. You would live a life of ease and plenty; and, I believe, she would be easily satisfied."

"I confess, Madam, that these advantages have no temptations for me. I wish the lady I am to serve, to be a judge of the duties of my office, and an eye-witness of the manner in which they are discharged. Ignorant people neither praise nor blame in the right place: it gives one neither credit nor satisfaction to serve them."

"Give me leave to say, you are very difficult, Madam. There are many people would catch at this last offer. You might do as you pleased; and, by a little address, you might govern the whole family of Gumly."

"To those who wish to make advantage of the vanities and follies of others, such a situation might be desirable; but I could not excuse myself for using such means of advancement."

"You are too scrupulous. Half the world live by the vanities, follies, and artificial wants, of others."

"That is true, indeed," said Mr. M——. "Mrs. Langston speaks like an Oracle."

"Would you, Sir, advise to pursue this kind of conduct?"

"Not if you mean to lay your sins at my door: I have enough of my own to answer for. Don't say, I advised you to act thus."

"Then, I am answered. I have a good mind to lay before you

a proposal that has been made to me lately; which I have a greater inclination towards than any of those you have heard."

"Come, tell us, then: I like to see the workings of your own honest mind."

"I am invited to open a school in a small country town, or perhaps in a village near it, where such a thing is much wanted."

"I do not consent," said Mr. M——, "to your running any hazard. Keep together the money you have got, and try to increase it."

"I think," said Mrs. Langston, "it would be descending too much. Surely, your present is a much genteeler employment."

"I had rather enjoy the comforts of life, than the vanities. I am tired of your genteel people: and think, by descending a step lower, I shall keep better company; that is, more rational people, who will be more likely to do me justice. I have had no society, no communication of mind to mind, since I came last to London.

"Lady Haughton was too proud to converse with me: her children scoffed at and ridiculed me. Mr. Ilford I must not converse with, lest his wife should be angry with me for loving his children. Mrs. Ilford dislikes me, because I am not partial, like herself. Mrs. Langston has given me such information as is equal to an actual trial of the two families she has described. I am very much obliged to her, as much as if I had made the experiment.

"I read Shenstone's School-mistress[11] lately, and thought I could be contented to be like the good dame he described: surely, it is better than to be a slave to the humours and follies of those in higher life. I never was ambitious, and am now sick of the gaudy vanities and luxuries which are coveted by the many."

"I honour your virtues; but I think you are too humble. You are too young to give up the world as yet: try it a little longer; perhaps it may have some good in store for you, to make amends for the past."

"Aye, do, my dear," said Mrs. Langston; "wait a little longer, before you give up the town and the world, as Mr. M—— says. I will look farther, and try what I can do for you."

"I thank you, Madam: I am much obliged for your endeavours to serve me; and I will wait till I hear what your enquiries will produce."

Thus far my journal goes. The rest of our conversation, I suppose, was common, and uninteresting.

Mrs. Langston was shrewd and penetrating. She had a knack at painting characters, and gave a perfect idea of the persons she described. She knew a good deal of the world, and was too compliable with the ways of it: but she had some good qualities; and, where she liked, she was sincere: she was as severe to those she disliked, and they were the greater part of the world.

Mrs. Ilford shewed her bad temper more and more: but I resolved to wait till I should hear from Mrs. Langston; and, if she gave me no hope of a more eligible situation, to try what the country would do for me; and this was always my favourite scheme.

In a few days, I received a billet from Mrs. Langston, as follows—

"DEAR MADAM,

"LADY Mary Cormack drinks tea with me next Thursday. I desire you will meet her. She wants a governess for her two nieces, of whom I shall soon know more. She is said to be proud and stately, but has some good qualities. She is generous to indigent gentry, but has no charity for plebeians. She has heard a good report of you, and is desirous to know you. Pray, do not seal up your lips before you come; but speak, that she may *see* you,[12] as one of the philosophers said: I forget his name. Believe me always

"Your sincere friend and servant,
"E. LANGSTON."

Mrs. Ilford now began to play the tyrant: she teazed me incessantly; she scrupled my going to Mrs. Langston's for an hour or two. I told her, she must look out for another governess, for that my patience was exhausted.

She was surprized at my sincerity.—"You reckon yourself well-bred, Madam: you give me such proofs as I did not expect."

"I am sorry, Madam, to be obliged to speak so plainly. It is painful to me to say disagreeable things; therefore I cannot contend with those to whom it gives pleasure."

"Meaning me, I suppose?—More proofs of your good-breeding!"

"Good-breeding must give way to truth, Madam. I wish you

may meet with a person endowed with many more requisites than I possess, and that your treatment may equal her merit; and then you may be happy together. Adieu, Madam: I am going to Mrs. Langston's, and will come back as soon as I can conveniently."

I curtsied to her, and left the room.

Lady Mary was all, and more than all, I had heard. She uttered her opinions freely, and wondered that people could be found that differed from them. She thought kings should be under no controul, and subjects were born to submit to every tax and oppression that could be laid upon them. In like manner, this fine doctrine was to descend, in gradation, to all the different ranks and degrees; every different one was to be kept within certain limits, which they were not to pass on any account. The nobility were a kind of demi-gods, who were to be worshipped by all the inferior ranks: the gentry to exert their superiority over their inferiors. Tradesmen were to be kept at an awful distance. Mechanics and servants were useful in their places; which, in her system, were but little above the quadrupeds of the earth. The greatest crime, in her estimation, was for the nobility and gentry to intermarry with those of the lower orders; and she did not think even wealth a sufficient excuse for such degradation. She thought the common people were either rogues, cheats, or fools; and actually said, that servants in general were without common sense.

Mrs. Langston cast many arch looks at me, and made signs for me to reply.

Lady Mary applied herself to me, and seemed to expect my assent to all that she had said.

"Come," said Mrs. Langston, "let us hear your opinion; I guess that it is not the same as Lady Mary's, and therefore you are backward to declare it."

"You guess truly, Madam," said I: "but I do not wish to obtrude my opinions in contradiction to her ladyship's; I am content to wear them in my own bosom."

"Oh, but I expect you to answer me," said Lady Mary: "for I think all the regulation, and the conduct, and the propriety of life, depend upon observing these subordinations; and, therefore, I should like to hear what can be said against them."

"I do not presume to speak against them," said I; "but I should wish to preserve a distinction that is superior to them. Degrees of subordination are necessary; I look upon them as such: but there are degrees of merit in every one of these, that are superior to every temporary distinction. The gifts of God are impartial and universal. Beauty, strength, understanding, every endowment that is truly valuable and respectable, are dispensed equally to all ranks and degrees of men. Merit is not limited to any set of people, but is to be found every where. When I consider these truths, I learn to love and respect my fellow-creatures; not according to their birth, fortune, or station in life, but according to their degree of virtue and merit. There is a gentry, and a nobility, of God Almighty's making; and to them I bow down, and confess my inferiority: while to the temporary distinctions of men I pay only the external marks of respect, for the first I reserve the homage of my heart. It is not our virtue that gives us these temporary distinctions; it is not our fault to be without them: they serve, however, as a criterion of the hearts of those who possess them; and prove whether they are worthy of them, by the use they make of them towards those above and below them; and they are accountable for them both to God and to men."

"We have got a philosopher, Mrs. Langston. She speaks well, and there is something in what she says; but nothing that can set aside the distinctions of honour and gentility, and regulation and propriety."

"I do not wish, Madam, to set them aside; I only wish people to make a right use of them, and not to estimate them above their value."

"Education makes the great distinction: I hope you give that it's just value?"

"I do, Madam: but here I make a great distinction between external and ornamental accomplishments, and internal qualities, which may be called the education of the mind. The first are by no means to be neglected; but to the second the chief attention should be paid."

"You seem to set but little value upon the first; which shews the difference between people of birth and breeding, and their inferiors."

"There your ladyship is right. These, indeed, are the chief distinctions: for human creatures are made of the same materials; they come all alike from the hand of the Creator, and are formed to manners and characters, by the various methods of education, and the examples of those with whom they live."

"So, Madam, you are, then, a leveller! All human creatures are equal, in your estimation?"

"I believe they are so in the sight of God; and I believe what his word says concerning them."

"Pray, do you think there is any difference in the breed of horses and dogs? or, do you think they are all naturally equal?"

"I think there *is* a difference; and I wish people in general were as attentive to the breeding of the human race, as they are to dogs and horses."

"You allow there is a difference: why not in the human species?"

"If the same attention was given to the human race, it might have some, but, I should think, not equal, effect. Much might be said upon this subject: I am not equal to the discussion of it. I will only ask your ladyship, whether you have not seen as many beautiful persons in the lower degrees of life, as in the highest? and, *vice versa*, as ordinary and ugly persons among the quality and gentry, as among the peasantry of the land?"

"In particular cases, I have; but not generally."

"That is fairly answered. Perhaps your ladyship may not have extended your observations sufficiently to decide this point; they may have been confined to those of your own rank in life."

"Perhaps I may not. But I think it is best for people of quality to believe that it is so, for many reasons; particularly, that young people may not marry with their inferiors."

"That is a reason of the first magnitude!"

Mrs. Langston and I both smiled, and looked at each other.

"You smile," said Lady Mary. "You think it of no consequence?"

"Very well, Madam. I should think it likely, that a person who held your opinions, might connive at a connection of this kind."

"For myself, Madam, I can answer. I should be extremely concerned at a clandestine marriage in a family I was engaged in; and I should do every thing in my power to prevent it."

Mrs. Langston said—"I dare say you would: I think I can answer for your honour and fidelity."

"Your opinions, however, I can by no means approve. They are such as have a tendency to overthrow those distinctions, that I consider as the basis of society; and your pupils might imbibe them."

"I should think it my duty to lead them to aspire to such virtues and principles, as should give them a real, and not an ideal, superiority."

"I should chuse they should have both: that they should support that pride of birth that becomes their station; and that honour, dignity, and propriety, should regulate their actions."

"I apprehend they are not inconsistent with the principles I avow."

"In my opinion, they are. I do not want my children to think every body their equals, nor to put themselves upon a level with them. No, Mrs. Darnford, you shall not have the care of them!"

"As your ladyship pleases. I do not wish it, unless you can approve of my principles; which I can never deny, nor be ashamed of."

"Very well, you may keep them to yourself: they will do for the lower kind of people; I dare say they will approve them."

"Upon my word, Madam, Mrs. Darnford has not done herself justice; she is qualified in all respects for the office she undertakes. Your ladyship desired her to speak upon this subject."

"Very true, Mrs. Langston; and she has shewn me her opinions. I am, indeed, obliged to her: I ought not to be offended."

"I certainly could not mean to offend your ladyship: I only answered your sentiments, as desired. I could have said much more, and expressed myself more strongly and decisively."

"Could you, indeed?—All is over with me; so you may now say what you please, and I will not be offended."

Mrs. Langston said—"I wish to hear some of your stronger arguments."

"I will only mention one or two, and them briefly.

"When we consider the infinite distance between the Creator and any of his creatures; and that he deigns to preserve, protect, and provide for them all; we conceive that no human creature can be degraded by an intercourse of humanity, and even friendship and affection with the lowest of his fellow-creatures; because no inequality, between man and man, will bear any degree of comparison with that of the creature with it's Creator."

"That cannot be denied," said Mrs. Langston.

Lady Mary was silent.

"Nothing can do so much honour to a creature, as to resemble it's Creator in such of his attributes as are imitable. When we raise and cherish our fellow-creatures, we most resemble our Creator."

"I agree to that, with all my heart and soul," said Mrs. Langston.

"So do I, in a degree," said Lady Mary. "I would contribute to the support of the lowest creatures, but I would not make them my companions."

"Not generally, Madam; no more would I: but, among those whom we call the lowest *human creatures*, there may be many whom *I should not disdain to make my companions* for their benefit and service."

"I would give them my money, but not my company!" said Lady Mary, disdainfully.

"Now, Madam, I must beg your patience, while I affirm, that the Greatest Personage that ever honoured this world with his presence, chose his friends and followers out of this order of people."

"Who could that be?" said Lady Mary.

Mrs. Langston looked, as if surprized at my freedom with her ladyship.

"Surely, I need not name Him!—It was HE, *who knew what was in man.*"[13] (She seemed confounded.) "He chose his Twelve Apostles from among them; and those who succeeded the Apostles, those who propagated the Gospel, and it's doctrines, were plain, illiterate men. The rich and noble were passed by; and integrity of heart and manners were the qualities that were chosen in preference, to be the Instruments, in the hand of Heaven, to accomplish this great work. Their MASTER told them, that "*God had chosen the foolish things of this world, to confound the wise.*" He enjoined humility and benevolence, as the characteristics of his religion, and enforced them by his own life and practice. I could recite many instances, very severe upon the rich, and the proud; but I forbear them, and only just mark the outline, and leave the rest to the memory and reflection of my hearers. I have done."

Lady Mary was silent some minutes. At length, she spoke—"Now, you have laid a heavy hand upon me, Mrs. Darnford: I feel it as much, or, perhaps, more, than I should have done from the pulpit; indeed, I feel it too much to reply to it. But, though what you have said is indisputably true, we are too much the slaves of custom, to obey in practice what we acknowledge in theory."

"Now, I acknowledge, in my turn, your ladyship's ingenuousness; and, in reply, I presume to say, that the practice of all the Christian duties and virtues is consistent with the highest accomplishments which human nature can attain. I presume, also, that your ladyship would not wish that your children should reach them, at the expence of their Christian hopes and expectations."

"You judge me fairly, and truly; and yet, you have made me unsatisfied with you, and with myself. I find you too wise for me; we should not do well together. I am used to have people about me that submit implicitly to all my opinions and directions. I should be lowered in my own eyes, and in those of my young people. I shall, however, reflect upon all you have said, and I hope I shall be the better for it."

"Now, I trust, you are come fairly to a compromise," said Mrs. Langston; "and you will, at last, part with a good opinion of each other."

"I have a very high one of your friend," said Lady Mary; "and I wish her success in life may be equal to her merits."

Mrs. Langston complimented Lady Mary on her ingenuousness. We fell into conversation upon general subjects, and parted upon better terms than we met.

Mrs. Langston blamed me for speaking so freely; and said, there was no occasion to declare my principles. I answered—That, as I never deceived any body, I thought it right that we should understand each other before we came together; which was much better than that we should discover disagreeable things afterwards, and part in disgust and dislike—That Lady Mary began with me in so high a tone of pride and insolence, that I could not but reply; if I had not, she would have thought me of a base and abject disposition—That I should have dared to speak such truths as these before people of the highest rank; and to say, with David—"*I will speak of thy testimonies before kings, and will not be ashamed.*"[14]

"I like your notions, I like your principles, but I could wish you to comply with the prejudices of people in upper life: let them pay for them, they well deserve it."

"That, Madam, is a point upon which I cannot agree with you. I cannot take advantage of their vanities and follies; I leave that to others that can."

"But, then, you must not associate with the better sort of people."

"Yes, I will. I will go a step or two lower, to find a better sort of people."

"Oh, fie upon your wit! I see you are incorrigible. Well, you must do as you please; but my good wishes will follow you."

I took leave of Mrs. Langston, and returned to Mr. Ilford's.

The family had supped, and were retired to their apartments.

The servant who attended the children followed me into my chamber. She told me, that her master and mistress had had words together, and it was about me; that William heard his master say—"You will never get such another: I insist, that you shall ask her to stay, and that you treat her as she deserves." My mistress cried sadly, and went up stairs, to avoid seeing you, Madam; and I heard high words between them afterwards."

"Is this known to all the family?"

"No, Madam; only to Mrs. Nelson, Mr. William, and me."

"Then, pray, let it go no farther. I am determined to leave the family soon. I could not bear that the principals should differ upon my account."

"As to that," said the girl, "my mistress will always find something to make her uneasy: she is never long pleased with any body."

"I am sorry to hear you say so. It becomes you to conceal the faults of those whose bread you eat, and not to expose them. Nobody is perfect. Perhaps, Mrs. Ilford is more to be pitied than blamed."

I sent the servant away, and went to my rest.

The next day, there was an altercation between Mr. and Mrs. Ilford, and myself.

Mr. Ilford blamed his wife, in severe terms, for her behaviour to me, and to every one before in my office. She was humbled, and seemed conscious of her fault. I said every thing that could excuse her to her husband. He urged me to stay; but my resolution was fixed, and I told him so. Would I stay till they could get another person? I could not promise that; I might be engaged within that time: but I would enquire for them, and let them know, as soon as I should fix the time of my leaving London; for I intended to settle in the country.

After Mr. Ilford left us, Mrs. Ilford thanked me for excusing her to her husband. She owned, and lamented, her unhappy temper; and said, she should be sorry to part with me. I pitied her most truly; and said, I hoped, as she was convinced of her error, she would endeavour to correct it; and that my successor might find the good effects of it.

I dined at Mr. M——'s on the following Sunday. He and Mrs. Langston were never tired of laughing, and rallying me on my interview with Lady Mary Cormack.

"After all," said Mr. M——, "I believe we must make our friend wear the breeches, and get her ordained; for she preaches to a miracle; and she would soon be followed, and become popular."

"Now, I must differ from you in opinion," said Mrs. Langston. "Her doctrine is too humiliating to become popular: she should offer something as substitute for virtue, which requires too many sacrifices and labours; and hold out an infallible key, that will open a short way to heaven, without taking any pains for themselves. This is the way to be popular."

"I give up all the honours you offer me," said I: "I will no more preach, reason, or remonstrate, either to nobility or gentry. I am going to become a country school-mistress; and I shall be fully employed in discharging the duties of that office."

They asked me, when I thought of leaving London. I said, very soon, but I had not yet fixed the time.

Mrs. Langston said—"You must not go into the country till your charming month of May invites you. Leave Mrs. Ilford and her children; come and spend the remainder of your winter with me, who know how to value your company."

I thanked Mrs. Langston for her very kind invitation. Mr. M—— approved it: and said, he wished I might meet with something better within that time; for he did not heartily agree to my present scheme, and yet he could not heartily oppose it.

Mrs. Langston said, she had that in her eye, and should not lose sight of it.

I thanked my good friends for their solicitude for my happiness; but, in my heart, I embraced my own little rural scheme. I thought of a cottage upon a green; a few straggling houses in view; the parish-church at half a mile distance; a number of sweet children around me; a little maid, and a little dog, to attend and guard me; a rude paling round my house; a bit of garden, that I could cultivate myself; and a thousand other comforts and conveniencies. I thought of it all the day, and I dreamed of it in the night.

Mrs. Langston made enquiry. She heard of a young woman, lately teacher at a boarding-school, and dismissed to make room for another person related to the principals. She recommended her to succeed me at Mr. Ilford's. I privately advised him to put Master James to a good school; which he did directly. The children wept at parting with me. The parents behaved with politeness; and Mr. Ilford paid me more than was due to me.

I left them, and went to Mrs. Langston's, where I spent a month idly, but not unpleasantly.

During this time, I called on my sister frequently. She received me coldly; and upbraided me with my weakness, in giving up my settlement. I told her, that I acted according to what I thought my duty; and, was I again in the same situation, I should probably do the same. She said, that was defending my folly by obstinacy, and I deserved all that should follow.

I wished to find a friend in a sister; but I sought in vain. I informed her of my intention to open a school in the country. She coldly wished me good success. She had four fine children; two of each sex: my heart yearned towards them; but they were not permitted to be acquainted with me. It gave me a pain to be so received; and, at length, I gave over calling on them.

I wrote to Mrs. Moyle, desiring her to let her friend know, that I should soon come into the country; and that I intended to open a school, as she had advised, and I would be with her next month.

Mrs. Langston was a smart little woman, turned of fifty, very active and alert. She lived in Clarges Street, Piccadilly. She had a key to the Green Park, in which she walked every day when the weather would permit.

She used to walk till she was tired, and then sit down upon a bench, and observe all the people that passed, as in review, before her. She would give me the history of most of them; and never seemed so happy as when she was thus engaged.

There was a good deal of acuteness in her remarks, but they were chiefly on the left-handed side: I took the liberty to tell her so. She laughed, and said, those were the least mistaken who remarked upon what was wrong; for that most of the apparent good qualities were put on to answer purposes to themselves, and to deceive others.

"Then, Madam, I wish to be deceived as long as I live."

"Pho, sho!—You are not deceived: you only fancy so. You can see as clearly as I do. I was pleased to see you take down that saucy woman of quality; only, for your own sake, I wished you could have condescended to flatter her vanity: you might have lived in affluence; and you and I might still have laughed in our sleeve.—Oh! but you have scruples about it!—Well, "I will laugh where I must," as Pope says;[15] and you may look grave, if you please."

But Pope says likewise, that we should "be candid where we can."

"Well, so I am, sometimes, where I cannot help it."

I shook my head: she laughed at me. More company came

forward: she began a new history, which lasted till a new subject came up to us.

Mrs. Langston was too familiar with her servants. Though I contend for the natural equality of human creatures, I do not hold it wise to do this: we expose to them all our weaknesses; and they either ridicule, or take unfair advantages of them. We ought to be gentle and kind to them; but it is seldom that we can make them our confidants with prudence and safety.

Mrs. Langston's motive of confidence was an insatiable curiosity: her servants were her spies; they were daily picking up stories of their neighbours; their mistress gave too much attention to them, and thus was supplied with intelligence.

She kept two maids, and one manservant, or rather boy, and used to talk to him all the time he waited at dinner and supper. My eye reproved her, I suppose; for she replied to it's remarks.

"I can manage boys," she said: "but men are stubborn things; I will have none of them."

"Do you not put yourself in the power of this boy's tongue?" said I: "may he not report to others what he tells to you? Boys are not naturally discreet, Madam."

"A fiddlestick! I can keep him in order well enough: he finds a good mistress of me, and will not get a better easily. The rogue knows when he is well, I warrant you. I do not expect my servants to have a disinterested attachment to me: it is all cant and nonsense. I feed them well, and pay them well; and they serve me well, in return. I seldom change: my maids all marry away; and, if my boys behave well, I put them to a trade when they grow to be men. This is my method; and I have not found any reason to repent it."

We walked constantly in the Park every morning. We saw company in the afternoon. There was another source of intelligence: people knew Mrs. Langston's turn, and they brought her fresh supplies frequently. She read the daily papers, and commented upon them: they were her study, and she exercised her faculties in remarking upon them. On Sundays, she went to church in the morning, and sent her servants in the afternoon. She dined at Mr. M——'s, and returned home to supper. Once a month, she hired a coach, and returned all her visits. This was her manner of life, which she seldom altered or varied.

One day, as we were sitting on a bench in the Green Park, Lord A—— passed by us. He caught a glimpse of me; he turned his head, and looked again. He soon came back; he stared rudely at me; then looked at my companion, and again walked away.

"That is Lord A——," said Mrs. Langston. "Oh, you know him, I perceive!"

I was confused and uneasy. I dreaded her curiosity, and her sarcastic turn.

"Yes, Madam, I know him too well: he was my husband's companion, and called himself his friend; but he led him into expences, and bad company, and was one of the causes of his ruin. Let me return home: the sight of him gives me painful reflections."

"You ought to look *him* out of countenance, and not he *you*. Sit a little longer: I will go with you presently."

Two genteel men passed by us, in earnest conversation. As they drew near, I perceived one of them to be Mr. Wilmot, who was a visitor to the Framptons, at Darnford Hall.

A second confusion seized on me. I held down my head, that I might not be known. He passed me without notice.

I told Mrs. Langston, I was not well, and wished to be at home. She rose, and leaned upon my arm. In our way to the door, Lord A—— passed us a third time. There was a smile of contempt upon his countenance. I was glad to retire from his observation. We went home directly; and, as I entered the house, I saw Lord A—— in the street, walking slowly. He passed the house, soon after we entered the parlour, unnoticed by Mrs. Langston. I soon recovered from my sickness, which was entirely owing to my confusion.

I resolved to leave London as soon as possible. I heard not of any situation more likely to suit me than those I had tried; and I resolved to see whether the country would not render me happier.

When I dined with Mr. M—— the Sunday following, I declared my resolution to leave London in the course of the week.

He gave me his kind advice, and paternal admonitions—"Do not hazard your little pittance in any great undertaking. Do not take a share of any other person's school: partnerships are dangerous, unless you are perfectly acquainted with the temper and qualities of the person you engage with. Hire a lodging ready-furnished: let it be a genteel one; that may give you some credit. Ask a handsome price, such as may pay you for your trouble. You shall not keep a dame's school, like Shenstone's, though you use the poetical licence in describing it; but such as may induce the principal people in the place to send you their children. Let me know how you go on, as often as may be convenient; and my best wishes and services will always attend you."

Mrs. Langston shewed concern at the thoughts of losing my company, and invited me to visit her in my winter vacation.

I thanked them for the good offices I had received from them both, and promised to acquaint them with my good or ill fortune.

I called on my sister, and bade her adieu; on Miss Beliza Haughton; on Mrs. Ilford. This last regretted my departure, and wished me to return to her. I was convinced that her temper was unalterable, and feared it might spoil my own.

A friend of mine wrote the following distich on this subject—

> "The sullen gives you pain; the angry smart;
> "But, 'tis the teazer, only, breaks the heart."

I sent Mrs. Langston's servant to take a place for me in the coach. The evening before, I felt, for the first time, a kind of petty distress, at going by myself to the inn, and to sleep there alone. Imagination called up a thousand terrors, and set them in battle array before me.

I called on Reason to support me, and to vanquish these ideal enemies—Was I not in England, in London, whither so many people come every day, to do their business, upon which their livelihood depended! This fear was a weakness that must be conquered, arising from false indulgencies, and being constantly attended by others.

I resolved to overcome it, and I did. The same method pursued, will always succeed!

I slept three hours at the inn; I then rose, and made myself ready for the coach. I went in it to J——, and from thence, in a stage-cart, to Mr. Moyle's, where I found myself an expected and welcome guest.

I staid there a week; during which time, Mrs. Moyle wrote to her friend, Mrs. Sorling, the farmer's wife whom I have mentioned. She received an answer, recommending me to Mrs. Bailey, at the White Hart, at W——.

I went there the following week, and took lodgings with Mrs. Martin. You know all that passed there; and I now unite the foregoing part of my story with your account, which is told very much to my advantage.

I wait to hear from my friend, to hear all that has befallen her, and to know how much further her curiosity extends. I do not refuse to gratify it, if she desires it; but I am impatient to know every circumstance that concerns her.

When I have read your pacquet, I will prepare to answer it. I am in hourly expectation of that, and my other adopted daughter, Betsy Moyle: she, Patty Martin, and Charlotte Brady, are as my own children.

With every sentiment of friendship and affection, I am, dear Madam,

Yours faithfully,
FRANCES DARNFORD.

LETTER VII
Mrs. Strictland, to Mrs. Darnford.

I CANNOT write like you, nor make fine similes, nor metaphors; but, in the plain and simple language of the heart, I will say, that nothing can be more welcome than your letters to me.

Oh, my friend! how much have you suffered! how steadily have you persevered in the path of rectitude and honour, in spite of allurements on one hand, and discouragements on the other!—Yes, you are the heroine; and I am ashamed to mention my trials, which seem light (although I once thought them very heavy) in comparison with yours: yet, you desire to know my past conduct; and, perhaps, it may be necessary for me to relate them, in order to vindicate myself, in your eye, for speaking disrespectfully of my husband.

You know that I lost both my parents in my childhood. My guardians were men of prudence and oeconomy: they sought for a man of the same character, to whom they might transfer their charge; and thought that, in giving me to such an one, they had discharged their whole duty.

They recommended Mr. Strictland to me, as a young man of uncommon prudence and sobriety; one who would increase my fortune, while others were spending and dissipating theirs.

He kept a large farm in his own hands, and cultivated his lands to good account. He studied agriculture, and made improvements in it beyond any of the farmers who surrounded him. They ridiculed him; but, like the Athenian miser of old,[1] he clapped himself, while others hissed him.

The idea of a farm did not displease me. I admired the poetical descriptions of a rural life, and thought the wife of a shepherd must be a happy creature.

Mr. Strictland was a healthy, rosy-faced, well-looking man; very plainly dressed; not a trait of the gentleman about him: he looked like a decent farmer, dressed in his Sunday cloaths. There was nothing to attract, nothing to disgust one.

I had no bias towards any other man: I thought I could like him as well as any other lover; and, after I had engaged myself to him, I gave him the preference that was due to a husband.

His father was a miller, a mealman,[2] and a farmer. He acquired a good fortune, and brought his son up with his own ideas and sentiments. Knowing his birth and education, I ought to have made allowances: perhaps, I did not, so much as I ought; if so, you shall be my confessor, and enjoin me a penance equal to my offences.

I married Mr. Strictland without any reluctance, and without passion: I had none of those violent emotions that make so great a figure in poetry and romance. I had a preference towards my husband, and I resolved to fulfil my duty: I aspired to nothing higher than a state of tranquillity.

Mr. Strictland had shewn many indications of a mean and sordid mind during the time of his courtship to me; but they were either concealed, or smoothed over, so that I took no notice of them.

On the evening before my wedding-day, as we were drinking our tea at my guardian's, Mr. Wotton's, Mr. Strictland was called out, and told, his servant desired to speak with him. Mr. Wotton followed him, and they staid out some time. Mrs. Wotton sent the footman to tell them their tea would be cold: they sent word, they should drink no more.

They went through the hall, and into the garden.

I heard Mr. Wotton say—"I tell you, Sir, it is d——d shabby of you; I do, and will resent it!"

Strictland spoke low; and they were soon out of hearing.

Mrs. Wotton and I sat in surprize what could be the matter.

They did not come in till the lawyers came, and they were called in to sign the marriage articles. They seemed then to be friends; but Mr. Wotton's countenance wore marks of anger, though subdued.

I knew not the cause of this till some years afterwards; but I relate it now, as a trait of my husband's character, that prepares you to expect all that follows.

Mr. Strictland kept a chaise-cart, that served to carry his

butter, fowls, and pork, to the next market-town, one day in the week, and carried home articles for the use of the family. It carried sometimes himself, and sometimes his servant, to country markets, with samples of corn, and other articles of his business: in short, it was of great service to him, both as a chaise and as a cart. This vehicle he had new painted green, and ordered his servant to bring it to my guardian's house, intending to carry his bride home in it. Mr. Wotton expected to have seen a new and genteel carriage, and was shocked at the sight of this family convenience. He told Mr. Strictland, it was a shame, that a man with fifteen hundred a year, and several thousands in the funds, who was going to marry a girl with near six thousand pounds in her pocket, should think of carrying his wife home in a cart. He was very angry, and was not soon appeased. They talked it out in the garden: he made Strictland ashamed of his meanness. He pacified him, by saying, he waited to see the event of the Bill then before the House of Commons, and whether they would lay a tax upon the chaise-carts; and, as soon as that was decided, he would buy a chaise; that, in the mean time, he would keep me a saddle-horse. He desired him to say, that the cart came for my baggage; and he would hire a post-chaise to carry me home. They had just settled this point when they were called in to sign the articles.

The next day, we were married. We dined at Mr. Wotton's, and went home in the afternoon. It was five and twenty miles to Mr. Strictland's house; the roads very indifferent; my spirits depressed; and I wept several times, but concealed it as well as I could.

My husband's conversation was chiefly on his own superlatives. His house was an old one; and he liked it the better, for he hated every thing that was fashionable. The furniture was old, and he preferred it to more modern. His father purchased the estate, and the old mansion was thrown into the scale. It was supposed, that he would pull it down, and build a new one: but, as it was strong, and in good repair, he had no such intentions; for, he believed, it would outlast two modern built ones. He had an old housekeeper, who had lived with him and his father ever since the death of his mother: she was an industrious and faithful servant, and overlooked all the others. He went on, describing every servant, and their offices.

I found, he kept only two maid-servants beside; one of whom was dairy-maid; the other, cook; and both were house-maids occasionally: but I perceived there was nobody to wait upon me.

When I first saw the house, my heart sunk within me: I thought of all the haunted houses I had ever heard or read of—An old brick mansion, with Gothic windows, with square panes diamond-wise, and plaister divisions in the windows; a large porch in the center, with a seat on each side, and an iron balcony over it.

"You are welcome to my house!" said my husband; and saluted me so that his servants might have heard him. He then gave a loud whistle; and a parcel of clowns[3] came out, and offered their services. They were followed by an old woman with a sharp pair of eyes, and her nose and chin were like nut-crackers: she curtsied, and bade me welcome home.

"Here, Mrs. Gilson! I have brought home your mistress: do you shew her the way to her apartment, while I give some orders to the servants."

She had a small candle, in a flat candlestick, that gave a winking light, to discover a large, gloomy hall, paved with black and white marble in squares, with old oaken wainscot; and the Twelve Caesars frowned upon me all around: a large open chimney, adorned with carvings in wood, of frightful grotesque figures, and foliages of various kinds. The furniture was suitable: large wooden chairs, rudely made; and oaken tables at each end.

I just took a cursory view of these antiquities, and followed Mrs. Gilson up the great staircase, which was good old wainscot; and the stairs were rubbed brown, and polished highly, so that you might chance to fall down them, without taking great care how you stepped.

When we came to the top, we entered a long gallery, out of which were doors into the bed-chambers, which were separated; and every one had a small dressing-room adjoining—Old-fashioned beds, almost up to the cieling, with tassels of various colours.

Mr. Strictland's apartment was really the most comfortable-looking room I saw. There was a dressing-room next it, which, I was told, was for my use. The chairs were modern; but there was an old toilette-table, with a petticoat of point lace; the looking-glass in a black japan frame, and boxes of the same.

I adjusted my hair, and set myself in readiness to go down, when I heard Mr. Strictland's voice upon the stairs, calling me to supper; to my surprize, for it was not yet eight o'clock.

I met him in the gallery, which was full of pictures, that looked as if they were taken out of Noah's Ark. All together, they struck me with a sensation of fear, though I knew not why, unless that they looked like the ghosts of the former inhabitants of the venerable mansion; and I feared to be left alone with them.

"Pray, Sir," said I, "are these the portraits of your ancestors?"

"No, my dear; they belonged to the family of whom my father purchased this estate: they are very ancient; they serve to cover the walls as well as any thing else; I seldom look at them. Come, supper waits for you."

He led me down the stairs, and into the common parlour, where the cloth was laid. And here a new surprize awaited me. Five different dishes were brought in by as many servants, in order that every one might stare at his new mistress, while she was gazing at the plentiful supper. At the top, a pair of chickens boiled; at the bottom, a great loin of pork; on one side, a very large plumb-pudding; on the other, a dish of potatoes; and, in the middle, a huge buttered apple-pye.

I stared at the supper. Mr. Strictland said—"We do not often cook a joint of meat for supper; but this is a wedding-night, and I give my servants a treat, and I tap a hogshead of beer that is a year old next month. The chickens are designed for you, Madam, and I hope you will do them justice."

I was not in an eating or a drinking humour; yet I affected both. I saw that my gentleman expected a chearful compliance with all his commands. I tasted his October,[4] and his made wines; and was in a fair way to be tipsy, when Mrs. Gilson came in, and offered to attend me to my apartment.

Here ends the history of my wedding-day.

Mr. Strictland took upon him the *master* from the first minute I entered his house: he never asked me, whether I chose to do this or that, but he commanded me to do so or so.

The honey-moon is said to be generally happy; mine was spent in fear and trembling. I feared the house, the master, and every thing around me.

Mrs. Gilson saw my situation, and pitied me. She gave me the best advice, and encouraged me to look forward.

"I see, Madam," said she, "that this house is not much to your liking. Pray do not let my master perceive it; he is partial to his house, and proud of it; endeavour to like it, and, in time, you will be used to it. He will be gratified by your compliance with his humour: he is particular, but he has many good qualities, and he will improve upon farther acquaintance; but he will not bear any kind of opposition. I have lived with him a long time, and he is a good master to me, and, indeed, to all his servants, and I hope he will prove a good husband."

"I hoped, Mrs. Gilson, that he would have made some distinction between his wife and his servants; he speaks to me as if I was one; nay, he speaks, generally, as if he was angry."

"That is only his way, Madam; do not mind it: he loves you, I am sure; and, when you know each other's good qualities, you will do them justice. Let me beg you to appear chearful, and to seem pleased with every thing."

"I thank you for your kind and well-meant advice; I shall endeavour to profit by it. I am truly sensible of your merit, and I thank Heaven for sending me so sensible and discreet a servant!"

"I thank you, Madam: as far as my poor ability extends, you may depend on every thing that can contribute to your happiness."

"I do find, already, that your goodness abates the horrors of my prison."

"Dear Madam! how strongly have you expressed yourself! You do not yet know what you call a prison: you seem afraid to walk out of one room into another!"

"Very true, Mrs. Gilson, and so I am. This house resembles all the haunted places I ever heard of. Pray, is it not haunted; or, at least, reported so?"

"Dear heart, Madam! you have too much good sense to believe such idle stories!"

"Not I, indeed. I could believe any thing you could tell me of it."

"Then I shall take care of what I do tell you. Come, Madam, permit me to shew you the rest of the house. My master is in the fields with his workmen; he will not be at home till dinner-time: let us go over the ground-floor; you have not yet seen the best rooms."

"I followed her down stairs, into the great hall I have already described. There were two doors at each end. On the right-hand, one into the common parlour, and one into a passage which led into the kitchen and offices. On the left-hand, two more, exactly opposite to the others; which opened into three parlours in the other wing of the house.

They were large, dark, and gloomy; old wainscot, in small

pannels; with old high-backed chairs and tables, to match the rest of the furniture.

The third was, indeed, a large and well-proportioned room, and handsomely furnished in a suitable style. The chairs were covered with a rich damask silk, with stuffed backs and bottoms; the window-curtains the same, and both fringed with a silk fringe of the same colour; a very large looking-glass, in a Japan frame, ornamented with a gold foliage; the tables of the same; on each side the great table, two high stands for candles, of the same japanned work.

But the principal ornaments of this drawing-room were some very fine portraits that hung around it; two of which made so strong an impression upon my mind, that nothing could ever erase it; and I can at any time bring them before me. One was a gentleman in armour, except his head; his helmet lay upon a table beside him; he seemed about the age of thirty; his look expressed dignity, virtue, and complacency; he looked like the patron and protector of all that had need of his assistance. The lady, on the other side the great glass, was somewhat younger, and exquisitely beautiful—and, to my fancied sight—

> "Love, sweetness, goodness, in her aspect shin'd
> "So clear, as in no face with more delight!"
> MILTON.[5]

She was dressed richly, in embroidery on a white ground, which seemed to rise above the ground, so that you might take it off with your hand. Her neck and arms were adorned with pearls, and her dress trimmed with them. I gazed on these two charming pictures till the tears gushed from my eyes, and I felt as if I was soliciting their protection.

"Oh, my dear Madam!" said Mrs. Gilson, "what is it that affects you so?"

"It is those divine portraits; they are another and different race of people from those I am obliged to converse with. I feel as if I was hardly worthy to be their servant; yet I could offer them my service, if they would deign to accept it."

"You are very fanciful," said she; "but I have heard say that they are very fine, and your behaviour convinces me of it."

"Yes, they are more than fine; I could almost worship them. But, pray, Mrs. Gilson, can you tell me who they are?"

"Why, they were some of the gentry that were formerly owners of this estate. There are boxes full of papers, in some of the upper rooms, that make mention of the names of many of them; particularly three, that old Mr. Strictland said were of very ancient and noble families. One was Montfort, that were once Barons of the land; another was Roscelin; and the third was *Marney*, if I remember right."

"All noble and ancient names, Mrs. Gilson; but I wish to know these, that I might honour them."

"To my thinking, you have paid them honour sufficient.—But, pray, Madam, cast your eyes upon the prospect from these windows, and then tell me whether that is not a fine look-out; lay prejudice aside, and see whether it deserves to be despised?"

"No, indeed, it may well be admired!"

"Well, then, I hope you can find something to be liked in this house?"

"This is a fine room, and well furnished: nevertheless, I confess, I should find more comfort in a modern room of half the size, furnished only with deal tables[6] and rush-bottomed chairs—but this is only to you, Mrs. Gilson. I will endeavour to like the house; and I shall visit this room often, for the sake of it's inhabitants."

Mrs. Gilson conducted me back to the hall, and went after her business; and I prepared to attend my lord and master at dinner, at one o'clock.

It was his custom to rise at six, and go into to the fields; he came in to breakfast at eight, he dined at one, drank tea at five, supped at eight, and went to bed between nine and ten o'clock.

If his meals were not ready exactly to his time, his voice was heard to resound through the house: but his servants were generally very punctual.

I made an excuse for not going to church the first Sunday; but there was no excuse that could be admitted for the second.

I asked where I was to get one to dress my hair? I was told there was no such person in the village. I said, I was used to have a servant to attend me, and to dress my hair. My husband told me, he liked my hair best as Nature had dressed it; and as to other folks, it did not signify whether they liked it or not—Mrs. Gilson would attend me as well, or better, than a young girl.

I was forced to dress myself, and make a virtue of necessity. I found we were to be trundled along in the chaise-cart; so I dressed accordingly.

An aukward boy, one of the under-servants, ran before us to open the gates: he had a green cape put upon his coat, which, I suppose, his master intended as an apology for a livery.

Thus attended, we made our appearance at church; and you will easily believe that my mind was not elevated by pride or vanity on the occasion. Perhaps, a state of humiliation might be more proper, and more suitable to the duties I was to pay, as they were free from parade or ostentation.

After the service was ended, the worthy rector, Mr. Elton, and his wife, came up and paid us their compliments. Mr. Strictland answered for us both.

Mr. Elton said, that he and his family intended to wait on us in the afternoon to tea, if agreeable.

Mr. Strictland said he should be glad to see them. Poor *I* was an insignificant monosyllable, that had no kind of meaning. We got into our chaise-cart, and trundled home again.

I asked Mr. Strictland which room I should receive company in?

"Why, in the common parlour, to be sure. I have never used them since I was master of them. However, you may sit in one of them, if you have a mind. But the evenings grow cold now; and, I think, the common parlour is most comfortable."

I agreed that it was so, as I found a fire was not to be mentioned.

In the afternoon they came; and, soon after, a Mr. and Mrs. Southgate, a gentleman farmer, who lived at the distance of a mile. He was Mr. Strictland's most intimate friend: I say, *most intimate*, because he sometimes consulted him in the way of business; for, in reality, he had no ideas of friendship or intimacy, but thought all pretensions to them proceeded from interested motives.

He had lived alone in the world, and all his views were centered in himself; and he married to perpetuate the idea of *self* in a race of his own.

Mr. and Mrs. Elton solicited our acquaintance; they hoped we should be good neighbours; half a mile was a short walk in the country, and they wished to see us very often.

I bowed, and looked at Mr. Strictland. He was silent.

By their looks to each other, I saw that they were no strangers to his character.

Mrs. Elton said, she had two daughters about my age; they longed to find a neighbour in me, and she hoped I should find them worthy of my friendship. Mr. Strictland and Mr. Southgate talked of their crops and their managements. Mrs. Southgate was silent and acquiescent.

Mr. Southgate mentioned a chaise to be sold at the squire's in the next parish, and he had some thoughts of buying it; but he, like Mr. Strictland, waited to see whether the chaise-carts were to be taxed or not.

Mr. Elton said, they need not to doubt of that, for they certainly would; but, whether that were so or not, ought to make no difference to Mr. Strictland, for his fortune set him above such considerations.

He shook his head.

"Why, Sir, people of less than half your fortune keep carriages!"

"Well," said he, laughing, "do not I keep carriages enough?"

"No, Sir; you want one more, for the use of your lady."

"All in good time, Sir. There are many people that set up carriages, and lay them down again: I should not like to be one of those."

"No fear of that," said Mr. Southgate; I wait till yours comes out, before I presume to let mine appear. I only aspire to a one-horse chaise; but yours ought to be a post-chaise, and that of the handsomest kind."

"Thank ye, my good friends, for your generosity in my behalf. I hope you will keep it for me."

I need not tell you who said this.

Their remarks shewed me the opinion they had of my husband; and he was so gratified by their compliments to his wealth, that he forgave their advice and implied reproofs to him.

Several other respectable farmers, and tradesmen in the parish, wished to visit Mr. Strictland and his bride—but here his pride, ever the companion of meanness, shewed itself.

The first man that called on him, he received in his kitchen, and asked him to drink some of his October; but never asked him into the parlour, nor offered to introduce him to his wife. This man was affronted: he made his report to the rest, and they all resented it; but knew not whether it was Mr. or Mrs. Strictland that had rejected their acquaintance, and threw them to such a distance.

Mr. Strictland was in no hurry to return the first visits. I took the liberty to remind him that such visits were always returned early. He said, he would do it for once; but he did not mean to be always receiving and paying visits; he had something else to do.

I was pleased with Mr. and Mrs. Elton, and their family, and wished to cultivate their friendship. The two eldest daughters were charming girls: to cultivated minds they added that simplicity of manners, more engaging than all the factitious[7] accomplishments of upper life. My heart felt the attraction; and I longed to be intimate with them; to make them my companions; to have them work, read, walk, and converse with me, and to form a little select society: but I dared not hope that my monarch would allow me so much liberty. However, I resolved to have a trial or two, before I gave it up entirely.

It was a month, at least, before I had seen the whole of my territories; I mean, my husband's; for I had no power over, or in them. When Mrs. Gilson had leisure, she shewed them to me; for I had not the courage to go over them alone.

There was a suite of bed-chambers over the best parlours, furnished in the same antique style; the last, over the drawing-room, was furnished with crimson velvet, but in a forlorn and tattered state: there were some pictures in it worthy of notice; particularly one of an old lady that looked very cross, but well painted.

"I will not chuse this for my bed-chamber, Mrs. Gilson; that old lady looks as if she would bid me get out of it."

"Good Lord, Madam! what strong notices you take of every thing!"

"So much the worse for me: if I neither liked nor disliked strongly, I should be a much happier creature."

"Do not dislike us, Madam. I do not despair of seeing you very happy here."

"Ah, my good woman! I wish I could believe or hope so!"

She shewed me many odd places, nooks, and closets, that had not been looked into for many years. I felt glad when I got through them, and went down a pair of stairs that brought me into a passage that led to the kitchen and offices one way, and the other into the great hall.

I told Mrs. Gilson, I was glad to get out of that apartment.

She smiled—"One would think, you knew by inspiration all that has been said of it."

"Tell me," said I, "tell me all."

"Why, some silly people have said, that it is, or was, haunted; and others, as silly, have believed them."

"I should be one of the last sort: I thought of it all the time I was there. Can you tell my any thing more?"

"That old lady you observed, Madam—."

"Walks out of her frame at midnight, constantly, does she not?"[8]

"You make me laugh; but I am glad to see you so pleasant. They say, she walks through these rooms every night, and shuts the doors hard after her."

"Oh, I believe it all; but I shall never go there to be convinced of it. If your master wishes to get rid of me by a short way, he need only shut me up one night with that old lady, and she will dispose of me before the morning."

"Good God! what a thought! I wish you loved my master well enough to believe, that he studies to do every thing to promote your happiness."

"I wish I could believe it. However, you may see that I have a very good opinion of you, or I should not have spoken so freely. I will try to love the house, and it's master; but it depends upon him to bring it to pass."

We went over the offices, which were large, neat, and convenient; and I returned to my own apartment, thankful that it was really the most habitable and comfortable of any in the whole house.

One day, Mr. Strictland led me over his grounds; he shewed me some very agreeable prospects; his grounds were, as I have since understood, in high cultivation, well fenced, and neatly kept. I was no judge of this; but I praised and admired as much as I could, sometimes in the wrong place, and sometimes in the right.

He seemed pleased with me and himself; so I took the opportunity of asking leave to invite an old friend and school-fellow, *Frances Lawson* by name, to come and spend some time with me.

He puckered up his face into a thousand wrinkles—"No, Madam; I do not approve of it."

"And why, Sir?"

"Because I do not like female friends and confidants: they often make differences between man and wife; and I wish my wife to have no other friend and confidant than myself."[9]

I said no more. He frowned, and grew sulky; and we had little more conversation of any kind on our way home.

I asked him, whether he could play picquet?—"No."

"Cribbage?"—"No."

"Backgammon?"—A very loud *"No."* I shrunk into myself, and was silent.

Another time, I urged him to keep me a servant to attend me: he thought Mrs. Gilson was good enough to wait on me. I said, she was too good, and that I scrupled to let a person of her years and merit wait on me; beside, she had business enough upon her hands, without this addition. He did not like a fine-lady servant in his house.

"No more do I, Sir; I want only a cleanly and humble girl about me. I have always been used to have a servant to myself; and I did not expect that my conveniencies would be lessened by marrying a man of your fortune."

"I will consider of it; but I don't like it—I tell you, I don't like it."

"That may be a reason to you, Sir; but it is none to any one else."

"May be so: but I am the person to judge of that; and what I like, is, and shall be, the law in this house."

"Alas for me! I find it so to my sorrow!—You are more despotic than the king of France."

He swore a great oath, and went out of the room, muttering, that he was, and would be, the master in his own house.

I fretted sufficiently, as you may suppose. He saw me in tears; but they had no effect on him.

Oh, Frances! your husband could not bear to see you weep! A good-natured man cannot see the woman he loves weep, unmoved; but an ill-natured one will chide her for that grief which his harshness and cruelty have occasioned. Let every woman take care to know the temper of the man she marries. Of all the requisites, let good-nature be the first; it is the basis upon which woman must build her happiness: I have paid dear for my experience.

I was naturally of a chearful temper. There is a happy elasticity in the human mind, that bends like a bow under the hand of Tyranny; but, as soon as that force is withdrawn, it recovers it's strength, and returns to its original state: so my mind rose, at times, and resisted the affronts it received.

I had heard of women who had dared to oppose their husbands; of those who had gained the victory over them; and of those who had assumed the reins of government, and ruled over their husbands. The latter I detested: I wished for nothing more than a kind and gentle master, who would indulge my reasonable demands, and check me in what was improper and unreasonable.

Mr. Strictland used to go to a market-town three miles off, and to a club there every Wednesday, and did not come home till ten, or sometimes eleven o'clock.

I asked his permission to invite one of the Miss Eltons to spend the day with me, during his absence. He answered, frowningly—"No!" he did not like female gossips.

"I never supposed that you meant to shut me up here, and debar me from all society."

What did I mean by society?

"What you and every body else mean by it; the word is well understood, and wants no explanation; what you are now going in search of, and what is denied to no one else but me."

"Hey day! you can use your tongue, Madam, upon occasions."

"Yes, Sir, I can; and I use it to tell you, that you are cruel and unjust to me. I have never asked any thing unreasonable; and I have had every request of mine refused. Had I known, or could I have supposed, you would have shut me up here, and denied me all kind of society, I would never have come within these doors. Would to God I never had!"

I burst into tears. I threw my hands upon the table, and my head upon them. He finished buckling the straps of his boots; and then he came and threw his arms around me, and would have caressed me, to make amends for his insult; but I pushed him from me, and ran out of the room; for my heart rose against him.

He sent Mrs. Gilson after me, telling her what I had said, desiring her to try to reconcile me to my lot; and he mounted his horse, and rode away.

My anger got the better of my grief; which was a lucky circumstance. I ranted like a queen in a tragedy. I said, I would no longer submit to such usage, but would write to my guardians, and desire them to fetch me away, and protect me from my tyrant.

Mrs. Gilson let me run myself out of breath: she then threw in her kind and prudent counsels.

She said, that, by striving against the stream, I encreased my own distress; that, if I would submit to my fate, and condescend to soothe Mr. Strictland's humour, I might, in time, soften the harshness of his temper, and bring about many things; but opposition would only harden and encrease it.

She pitied and soothed me with a true maternal tenderness; and she saved me from desperation, and from taking a rash step which I meditated.

From resenting warmly, she brought me to be cool and reasonable; but I settled into grief and melancholy, which she could not cure.

She promised to speak to her master.

"For," said she, "he will sometimes hear reason from me."

Mrs. Gilson left me when she saw me composed. I ate no dinner; but I made Mrs. Gilson drink tea with me, and sit with me some time afterwards.

I went to bed early; and, soon after, I heard Mr. Strictland's whistle in the courtyard: and, angry as I was, I was glad to hear him; for I thought his company a kind of protection against the goblins of a strong imagination.

He did not come up stairs till near an hour after; and my fancy was employed in supposing him so much offended, that he would not sleep with me, but go to another bed.

I had lighted a candle in my room, which was in lieu of a companion; but, as soon as I heard my husband coming up stairs, I put it out, and counterfeited a sound sleep, to avoid speaking to him.

He came to bed softly, for fear of waking me, and rose in the same manner.

When breakfast was ready, he sent Mrs. Gilson to ask my company. She said, he was sorry to have vexed me so much yesterday; and begged me to forgive him, and to speak kindly to him.

I said, when he should acknowledge himself in fault, I might forgive him; but I doubted whether he thought so or not.

I went down stairs with a resolution to support my spirits, and not to give up my cause till I was compelled to it.

When I entered the room, he met and embraced me—"Forgive me, Rachel, the pain I gave you yesterday! Mother Gilson has been schooling me in your behalf: she says, you were very uneasy all the day. I did not mean to vex you; and I am sorry you took it so."

My foolish heart fluttered so, that I could not speak presently; but my tears spoke for me.

He led me to the table, and asked if he should make the tea for me.

I bowed, but said nothing; for I dared not trust my voice: but my heart was cheered by his behaviour, which shewed more tenderness than I had yet seen.

As soon as I had recovered my voice, I said—"Sir, I desire that you will send to Mr. Wotton's, for my book-case and my harpsichord; for, as I am denied the blessings of society, I shall have need of every resource beside."

He seemed to consider of it; and then said—"I will, my dear, the first opportunity; that is, when I can spare the waggon and horses."

I thanked him, and was cheered by his compliance; for it was the first request of mine that he had seemed to grant.

He behaved with complaisance to me the whole day, which I received gratefully; and this calm lasted several days; but then he returned to his altitudes again, and was as despotic as the Grand Seignior.

We went on this way for several months. I was married the first week in September; and he had not found an opportunity to send for my book-case and harpsichord till the beginning of December.

The day before, Mr. Strictland told me that he should send for them on the morrow, and seemed to think he had conferred an obligation upon me.

I went up stairs into my dressing-room, and wrote to Mr. Wotton as follows—

"DEAR SIR,

"I OUGHT, long before this time, to have paid my acknowledgments to you, for your paternal care and goodness to me, from the death of my parents to the day of my marriage. From that day, I have been kept like a prisoner, forbidden to write, or converse with any of my friends. Mr. Strictland will not allow me to make acquaintance with any of the very few conversable neighbours this village affords. He says, three or four times in a year is often enough to visit, or be visited. I am allowed to walk about this old rambling house, and to converse with the pictures with which it is furnished. I have hardly yet got over my fears of walking alone from one room to another. Yet, all these things I could bear, and use myself to, if my husband was good-natured, kind, and companionable; but indeed, my dear Sir, he is neither of them. He treats me like a servant, and speaks as if he was always going to chide me. Once or twice, he has roused a spirit that I did not know was in me; and I have been upon the point of running away from him, and enquiring my way to you. Now, Sir, I beg that you will, as soon as you can conveniently, come over hither, and talk to Mr. Strictland: perhaps, you may prevail upon him to treat me better, or else to let me go away from him, and live in some obscure way, upon what allowance he will agree to make me; for I shall not live long here. I am very unwell: I lose my rest, and my appetite. Mr. Strictland seems to care very little about me; and, I hope, he will be prevailed upon to part with me, without much difficulty. With my best wishes and regards to Mrs. Wotton, and all the family, I am, dear Sir, your unfortunate ward, and humble servant,

"RACHEL STRICTLAND."

I gave this letter to Mrs. Gilson, the last thing before I went to bed; and charged her to give it to the servant who was to go with the waggon, for he was to set out early in the morning; but to take care not to give it him before Mr. Strictland.

Having thus guarded all my points, I went to rest, and did not dream of the storm that was to burst over my head the following day.

When I went down to breakfast, Mrs. Gilson came in hastily. She lifted up her hands and eyes; and, in a low voice—"Prepare yourself for——"

That instant, came in her master, with his face in a flame, and every feature in motion.

He threw a letter at me, saying—"There, Madam! there is your answer from Mr. Wotton!" It was my own letter.

He stormed and raved like a madman: he abused me all to nought. How dared I write to Mr. Wotton, and call him hither, to be a judge over him in his own family? He vented an hundred epithets of rage and contempt against me, Mr. Wotton, and all his family.

I was terrified; but I let him run on till he was out of breath. In the mean time, I got spirit enough to answer him.

"I am neither afraid nor ashamed to own all that I have said to Mr. Wotton: I would say the same to all the world. You have used me cruelly and unjustly; and I will complain to Heaven and earth!—Why did you marry me? to torment and distress me? to have a wife to vent all your ill-humours upon?—What have I ever done to deserve such usage? I have only been too tame and humble to you; and that has made you worse and worse. You have used me basely and ungenerously: you were conscious, that you deserved that I should complain of you; and, therefore, you had the meanness to open my letter to my guardian. You have gained a new means to triumph over me. I despise you more than ever; and I would rather die than live with such a man as you are!"

Here I sunk down in a swoon, and lay senseless upon the floor.

It was now his turn to be terrified. He called Gilson: she soon came in. They raised me, and seated me in a chair. Mrs. Gilson supported me; Strictland stamped, and tore his hair, like one distracted; Gilson called out for water; and the whole house was a scene of confusion.

As soon as I recovered my senses, I called out—"Take away that man who has killed me! take him away, and let me die in peace!"

Gilson begged me to compose myself. I felt an unusual pain; and it seemed to restore my spirits.

I said—"I am taken very bad: I know not what ails me; but, I believe, I am dying. Put me to bed, and let me have none but my own sex about me."

Strictland offered to approach me: he shook like a leaf.

I pushed him away—"Begone, man! do not touch me!"

Gilson, and the cook-maid, led me up stairs, and put me to bed. My pains continued; and, in an hour, produced an effect which I neither foresaw nor understood, till Mrs. Gilson explained it to me.

She went to her master, and told him what had happened, and desired him to send for the doctor: so they called the apothecary and accoucheur[10] of the village.

Strictland was in agonies: he was disappointed of his hopes; which, I believe, afflicted him still more than my sufferings.

"Compose yourself," said Mrs. Gilson: "thank Heaven, it is no worse; I feared you would have had her death to answer for. All will be well: but you must turn over a new leaf; for she will not bear your ill-treatment any longer."

He swore, he would do any thing I desired, if I would but forgive him. He sent away a servant for the doctor, and would fain have then come up to me; but I sent word, if he wished me to live, he must keep out of my sight, for I could not bear it.

The doctor came. Mrs. Gilson told him all the circumstances: and, moreover, that I had heard news that affected me, and occasioned a great agitation of mind; and, she thought, I wanted something that was both comforting and composing, to set me to rest.

He sent me a draught, to take at night. He told Mr. Strictland, that I must be kept quiet, and not be disturbed; and, in a few days, I should be well.

That poor man, the martyr of his humours and passions, spent a miserable day, and restless night. Mrs. Gilson begged him to wait till I was better, before he came before me. She blamed him, and soothed him, by turns; for he was really an object of pity.

Finding that I had a good night, and was out of danger, she began to plead for my pity and forgiveness of her master. My resentment was not abated: I refused to see him, or to hear of him.

"Supposing," said she, "that you had really been in as much danger as you thought yourself, would not forgiveness have been a duty? Would you wish to leave the world in a state of hatred or malice with any person? Do you stand in no need of forgiveness yourself? Where is the person living that has not sinned?"

She went on—"You cannot repeat the Lord's Prayer, unless you forgive those that have offended you."

"Have I not cause for resentment?"

"I do not deny that; but the Scripture says, *Let not the sun go down upon your wrath; be angry, but sin not.*[11] A true Christian must forgive the greatest injuries, or he is not worthy of the name."

"Oh, my good woman! you are wiser and better than I. You know, and practise, every Christian virtue. I will do what you require of me; but the sight of your master will ruffle me; I cannot talk with him at present."

"Stay till you are better first: I do not insist upon it to-day. My master is so much vexed and humbled, that it grieves me to see him: he has neither eaten nor slept since he saw you. Send him some words of comfort presently; and let me tell him, you will see him as soon as you are able."

I was silent.

"Come, my dear mistress, tell me what I shall say to your husband?"

"Tell him, that I forgive him what is past: but, if I live, I will be parted from him."

"That is not forgiveness: I will carry no such message."

"What can I say?"

"Shall I say, that you forgive him, and will see him as soon as you are able?"

"Yes, you may say so: but—"

"No *ifs* nor *buts*: we must do our duty."

She went away, lest I should draw back, and left me to my own reflections; which were sufficiently painful, with respect to the past and the future.

She came back in an hour, with some broth she had made, and urged me to take it. "My master sends his love to you, and thanks you for the kind message; and he says, he will deserve your forgiveness, and very soon give you proofs of it, as soon as you will allow him to see you."

I begged her to say no more upon the subject at present. I asked her to bring me a book.

"Not I, indeed," said she; "I hope I know better."

"Then, you must talk of something to entertain me. Now, I think of it; pray, tell me your own story, and how you came to live with Mr. Strictland."

"Lack-a-day! my story is not worth your hearing."

"I am certain it is better than my own uncomfortable reflections."

"If you say so, I will tell it you. But you must not brood over uncomfortable thoughts: I can see much happiness in store for you, and better prospects than you have had since the day you married."

"Or else they must be very gloomy!" said I.

"Now, do not talk so: you grieve my heart."

"Come, tell me your story, then."

"I will," said she, "directly.

"My parents were shopkeepers in this village. They sold almost every thing, and got a very good livelihood. My brothers were idle and unthrifty youths; they wanted to be of genteel professions; they made my father spend all his savings upon them. My sisters and I had what is thought a good education here in the country: we were taught to read and write, and the first rules in arithmetic. We served in the shop, and were of use to my father. My mother performed the duties of the house.

"My eldest sister and I kept the day-book; and, in the evening, my father used to transfer it to other books. He understood his business well, and would have raised a fortune, but for his prodigal sons.

"My mother died under fifty years of age. She lived not to see the misfortunes of the family, which came on soon after. My eldest brother broke his indentures, and ran away: he went to sea; and we never knew what became of him.

"The second followed his example: he went several voyages to India; and he gets his bread, and that is all.

"My father met with several losses: people ran away in his debt; and he got into trouble, and went backward every year.

"There was a young man, who had served his time, in a great town, to a draper and grocer. He made love to my eldest sister. My father let him into his affairs, and consulted him what he should do.

"Mr. Dixon had good property to put himself into business. He agreed to take my father's shop and stock off his hands, and to pay him a sum annually for his life; which my poor father gladly accepted. He married my sister, and keeps the shop unto this day."

"Well, but, Mrs. Gilson, you tell me nothing about yourself. Had not you a sweetheart, as well as your sister? I think you are a widow."

"Yes, Madam; so I am. I had a sweetheart, a farmer's son; as honest and worthy a man as ever lived. His parents disapproved of our courtship, because my father could give me no fortune.

"An uncle of his died, and left him two hundred pounds. He hired a farm, and went into it: but, alas! he had not sufficient to stock it.

"We married the Michaelmas after. We strove hard for a livelihood; but, somehow or other, we were unlucky in all our undertakings.

"Our corn was spoiled, our cattle died, and nothing succeeded with us.

"My husband died seven years after our marriage, (I verily think, of a broken heart) and left me, with one son, and a ruffled skane,[12] to get through as well as I could.

"My wish was, to pay every one their due, whatever became of us; so I gave up all we had into the hands of a gentleman, and it was sold to pay the creditors: and all were paid to the last shilling, and there was fifty pounds left for me and my son.

"My sister and I loved each other dearly. She and her husband took us into their house for a time; but I scorned to hang upon another for support. I resolved to go to service, as soon as I could get a place that was suitable to me.

"My husband's relations were all people of good property; yet they could stand by, and see his widow and son in a state of indigence, and never reach out a hand to save us from sinking under it.

"Mr. Strictland bought this estate. His wife died soon after he came to live here. He wanted a housekeeper, to be over his servants: I was recommended to him, and he accepted of my services; and I have lived here five-and-twenty years.

"The old gentleman was a kind master. After his death, I continued with his son; and, I can truly say, I have been a faithful servant to them both.

"I resign myself to the will of Heaven: I see many others worse off than me; I am thankful for the good I receive, and patient under the evil."

"Excellent woman!" said I; "thou art content with a little, and patient under thy ill-fortune. What a lesson to me!—But, what became of your son?"

"He is living, God be praised! He is all my care, and all my hope, in this world."

"What situation is he in?"

"He is a farmer's servant. All that I could spare went for his board and education: he is qualified for an upper servant, and will soon, as I hope, be a head man; that is all that I can hope for him: but, if he is a good man in his station, he is all the same, in the sight of God, as if he was in a higher, and I am thankful for it."

"I thank you for your story; it is that of Christian patience and peace, under sufferings and misfortunes; I will endeavour to profit by it."

"My good mistress, I am very much attached to you; I am sensible of your merit, and that your situation is unpleasant; but I think, most of us increase our sufferings by our own impatience: by our submission and resignation, we blunt the edge of them. I would fain teach you the lesson of patience, which I have learned myself; and then I shall think I have done you good service."

I was affected by her good sense and humility; it reconciled me to my fate, and humbled me in my own eyes. I felt, that I had increased my sufferings by my passion and resentment. I looked up to Heaven, and begged pardon for my impatience and petulance: I prayed for patience and fortitude; my mind was softened towards my husband, and more at ease with myself. I went to rest in more tranquillity than I had known since I went to Woodlands.

The next day I was much better.

I loved Mrs. Gilson better every day: I was resolved to go to her school of patience, and to practise those virtues, which shone in her through the veil of adversity.

The third evening after my illness, Mrs. Gilson begged of me to see her master before he went to rest: she was so earnest, and so right in her remonstrances, that I could not refuse her. She went and fetched him.

He was so humbled, and so dejected, that I felt pity for him; and yet, my heart said, that he well deserved it.

He kneeled down by my bedside; he seemed unable to speak for a minute. At last, he sighed deeply, and said—"Can you forgive me?"

I answered—"Yes, I do: but you have another forgiveness to ask. Wretched are they who suffer their passions to be their masters! You have suffered for it; so have I. You have been in the wrong; I have not been without blame. Let us pray to God to forgive us both!"

He said—"Amen, I pray God!"

Mrs. Gilson repeated her Amen with fervour.

Mr. Strictland said—"Now, I shall go to bed in peace, and hope to rest there." I said—"I wish you a good night, Sir!"

"I thank you, my dearest! thank you! You are too good to me; but I will hope to deserve it."

"Come, Sir," said Mrs. Gilson, "you must not stay here too long: let me light you to your chamber."

He kissed my hand, and retired to rest.

Gilson came back, and slept with me as before. She thanked and praised me for my behaviour; and I went to rest in peace and tranquillity.

As soon as Mrs. Gilson perceived I was awake, she thus spoke—"My dear mistress, I have been thinking, that you might believe me very partial to my master, by my earnestness in his behalf. I thought I was in my duty, and that needs no apology. You have fulfilled all my wishes, and my hopes of you, by your behaviour last night; and now, I will be the counsellor on your side.

"My poor master is sufficiently humbled. Before his temper rises again, for Nature will return to it's bent, I advise you to make some terms and conditions with him, and to obtain such things as may contribute to your ease and comfort. He will refuse you nothing at this time: but think well of what you ask; and you may lay a foundation of future peace."

"I thank you, my good friend, for your wise counsel. I had

once intended to make but one condition, which was that of a separation; but you have shaken my resolution. I will try him once more; and I will shew you the terms I shall offer."

She was pleased with me, and I with her.

She went down stairs, and I set my mind to work upon the important subject. After I had breakfasted, I rose, took my pen, and wrote as follows—

"ARTICLES OF RECONCILIATION BETWEEN
MR. AND MRS. STRICTLAND."

"MRS. STRICTLAND thinks she has been most unworthily treated. She had once resolved, at all hazards, to acquaint Mr. Wotton with every part of Mr. Strictland's behaviour to her, and to request his assistance to make articles of separation. Upon farther consideration, and reflections upon the duties of her situation, she consents to forego, or, at least, to postpone, such intention, if Mr. Strictland will agree to the following conditions.

"I. Mr. Strictland shall be very punctual in the payment of the allowance stipulated by Mrs. Strictland's guardians, for her cloaths and pin-money;[13] viz. Fifty Pounds a year; and shall not, in future, put her to the disagreeable necessity of asking for it.

"N.B. The first quarter is now due.

"II. Mr. Strictland shall allow his wife a servant to attend upon her; for she cannot bear that so respectable a woman as Mrs. Gilson should attend upon a young woman under age, unless in particular cases, where her skill and tenderness are required. She can never enough acknowledge her care and kindness in the present case. Mrs. Strictland does not wish for a lady-servant, but only an humble, decent, and cleanly girl, about her person; and she will pay her wages out of her own allowance.

"III. Mr. Strictland shall allow his wife to visit and be visited by such gentry in the neighbourhood as are of unexceptionable character: particularly the family of the Rev. Mr. Elton, whose friendship she is very desirous to cultivate. Mr. Strictland has an acknowledged right to except against any improper acquaintance, and any person to whom he may have any particular dislike or objection.

"IV. Mr. Strictland shall permit his wife to write to her

friends; especially to her guardians, and the friends of her family.

"V. Mrs. Strictland requests, that Mr. Strictland would behave to her with complaisance and kindness, till he discovers her to be unworthy of it; and to use himself to habits of courtesy: she presumes, that it will promote his happiness as much as hers. She requests him to forgive all that he has seen amiss in her; and she truly forgives all that is past on his side; and wishes these articles may be the foundation of future peace and unity between them."

When Mrs. Gilson came up again, I read the articles to her: she was pleased with them upon the whole, but objected to some passages. She advised me to scratch out, *"at least, to postpone,"* in the first article, and I complied; but I would not alter any of the rest. I desired her to give them to her master as soon as he came in.

After dinner, he sent to desire my leave to wait on me.

I pitied poor Gilson, for being obliged to trudge up and down stairs so often; but she said—"Never think of it, Madam: I can never be better employed than at present."

I sent word, I should be glad to see him; but it went against the grain: however, I could not now recede; and I resolved to fulfil my proposals.

He came, with a more composed aspect than I had seen him wear for a long time past, with my paper in his hand. He bowed to me, and looked as he used to do when he courted me for a wife. He asked after my health, and thanked God that I was getting well.

He saw my pen and ink upon the table: he took it up, and wrote under my articles—

"I AGREE to every thing my dear wife has proposed. Witness my hand,

"JONATHAN STRICTLAND."

He gave the paper into my hand: he bowed; I curtsied; and you never saw a politer nor better satisfied pair.

I thanked him for complying with my requests; and he thanked me for making the conditions so easy.

He then took out his pocket-book, and gave me a Bank note for twenty pounds.

I thanked him; but said, I had rather he would pay me is cash, for I could not change the note.

He said, there was no change wanted: he desired me to accept the whole; for, as I had charged myself with the servant's wages, I ought to be enabled to pay it; and, that he should pay me the same sum quarterly.

I thanked him, and prayed inwardly that this humour might last; for I feared it was too good to hold long.

He asked my leave to drink tea with me. I said, I was obliged by his company.

Old Gilson wept for joy. She had never seen any thing like it before; and could hardly believe her eyes.

After tea, he said—"To-morrow is Wednesday, which is club-day: if it is agreeable to you, my dear, I will send to ask Miss Elton to spend the day with you; that is, if you are well enough to see her."

I was agreeably surprized at this proof of his sincerity in regard to the articles. I answered with caution, lest he should think I preferred Miss Elton's company to his.

I said, if it was agreeable to him, it would be so to me.

He left me at eight o'clock. He left me easier and happier than I had been ever since I was the declared mistress of Woodlands.

Gilson and I had a long gossip afterwards. The good woman promised me much happiness, from my prudent conduct and her wise counsels; and we went to rest with our hearts at ease.

The next day he called on me, and took an affectionate leave before he went to his club. He told me he had sent for Miss Elton, and that she would come to me soon.

I began to hope that he was, indeed, convinced of his fault; and that he would, in future, be a kind husband to me.

Miss Elton came early, and I spent an agreeable day in her company.

I told her, I was permitted to cultivate her friendship, and that of all her family, and I desired to see them as often as possible. She brought the compliments of her family. Her father desired to know, whether I loved reading. I said, I had suffered much for want of my books; but they were lately arrived, and I should be glad of her assistance to arrange them. Mr. Elton had desired his daughter to tell me he would lend me any of his books; as, he supposed, I should not find any to my taste at Woodlands.

She told me, her sister Kitty offered her services to help

nurse me; and that she was jealous, lest her sister should engross my favour. I desired to see her in a day or two. Miss Elton would eat with me in my apartment: she was obliged to go home early in the evening, but promised to see me again soon.

I went down stairs a few days after, and lived again in the family way.

Mr. Strictland was very good for several weeks; but, as Mrs. Gilson foretold, Nature would return to it's bent: however, his behaviour was more tolerable, upon the whole, from that time; and, though he broke out in passions and ill humours occasionally, yet he always recollected himself, and paid more attentions to me.

I have shewed you his character in it's two extreme points, his worst and his best behaviour, that you may judge him fairly.

I desired Mrs. Elton to look out for such a servant as I described. She recommended a young woman, who then wanted a place, a cottager's daughter in the parish. She came to me the week after, and has lived with me *unto this day,* as good Mrs. Gilson says.

From this time, I saw the Elton family often. On Wednesdays, I had always one or two of them to dine with me; and I made excuse to see them, at their own house, as often as I dared. They were a family of love and unity, and every virtue resided among them.

Mrs. Elton came sometimes with one of her daughters: her company gave me entertainment and improvement.

One day, when we were chatting upon various subjects, she gave me such advice as I shall never forget; for it made my situation more than tolerable.

"My good neighbour," said she, "by your account, you listen to Mrs. Gilson, and are grateful for her good offices: will you permit me to offer such advice as myself and my children have profited by?"

"Yes, surely, Madam; and I shall be thankful for every instance of it."

"You are here in a large and lonely house, and have found it gloomy and uncomfortable; and, though you are sometimes lively and pleasant upon the dark rooms and old pictures, I perceive that they have taken hold of your imagination. I will give you a receipt to make them familiar to you, and to make you forget they were ever formidable to you."

"I shall be truly thankful for your receipt, Madam."

"It is only this. Use yourself to a constant habit of employment: reduce it to a method—Such hours to your first duties; such to needle-work; such to reading; such to music; such to writing; such to exercise, to walking, to gardening. Thus your time will be filled up; there will be no room for idle or gloomy thoughts, and you will find the days too short for you. If there should be any time to spare, I will tell you of another employment, that is both pleasant and profitable."

"Dear Madam, what is that?"

"It is spinning flax, or hemp. Myself, my daughters, and my servants, do more or less of it every day, as we have leisure from our other duties. We spin all our sheets, table-cloths, towels, and kitchen-linen: it turns to a very good account, and it makes us pleased and happy in ourselves."

"I shall be proud to be your scholar, Madam, if you will take the trouble to teach me."

"That I will, with pleasure; and my daughters will be ready to assist me, when I cannot attend you myself."

"I put myself to school to you, Madam; but you must get me the apparatus for this employment."

"I will get you a wheel, and all things necessary; and one of us will come and teach you, whenever you will send to us."

They got all things in readiness, and I began the week following; and this proved a most pleasant and profitable employment. It relieved me from that ennui of which so many complain; and it gratified Mr. Strictland, who was pleased to say—"I am glad to find that my wife is good for something:" and it confirmed the Eltons in his favour.

One New-year's-day, Mr. Strictland invited the families of Elton and Southgate to dine with him; and he allowed me, in conjunction with Mrs. Gilson, to order the dinner.

It was in the old English style; plentiful, but not elegant, and every thing good in it's kind.

Another day, he gave a dinner to all his workmen.

We returned the visit to our neighbours; and this was the only invitation we gave or accepted through the year.

The general course of our housekeeping was this. We killed a hog one week, and a sheep another. Mr. Southgate killed a sheep once a fortnight likewise: half our sheep went to his house, and half his sheep to ours. We had plenty of pork and mutton, as you see; but seldom any thing else. Sometimes a piece of lean beef, of the inferior parts; and then it was fat pork and lean beef to eat together, like ham and chicken. We had plenty of garden-stuff in our own grounds, and puddings and dumplings within-doors.

This might be called good housekeeping; and so it was, in fact: but to me, who had been used to another kind of table, it was disagreeable, and it was a long time before I could relish it.

I used to ask for a chicken sometimes, but Mrs. Gilson dared not kill one without her master's orders; and his manner was so ungracious, that I dared not ask favours of him.

I grew used to the house and it's master, as Mrs. Gilson foretold. I recovered my health, but my spirit was not quite restored, nor yet quite subdued; but I reconciled my mind to what I knew to be my duty.

Thus I went through the first year of my marriage. The second brought with it an increase of my blessings and comforts: Heaven sent me a dear child, which I received as it's best gift. Strictland was overjoyed at the birth of a son; for he, like other men, wished to continue his family: he had expressed a desire, that he might fill the old house with a new race of his own.

Mrs. Gilson was so good as to nurse me herself. She said, she would never yield that office to any other; for it was her pleasure.

She, too, enjoyed the birth of my son, as if it had been her own—Now, she should see all her wishes accomplished: she should see her master and mistress happy.

A new set of ideas, cares, and employments, succeeded this event. I nursed my son; and this office was both a duty and reward. The child grew, and answered all my hopes; and new I began to find myself at home.

In the summer-time, I used to walk in the fields, and I improved the garden. I made a green-house of one of the uninhabited parlours, and filled it with exotics of various kinds. I never failed to visit the two charming pictures, and my heart paid them in involuntary homage.

Mr. Strictland was naturally rough and surly. He had chiefly lived at home, with no other company but his servants: he was accustomed to command, and to carry a high hand over those under him. His marriage, and the birth of his son, softened him a little. When he thought my life in danger, he was concerned deeply; for his conscience reproached him with his ill behaviour to me, and he would make his peace with both upon any terms. Nevertheless, Nature would return again to it's bent; he had never been accustomed to check or restrain himself, and he scorned that any other should.

One day, he came in with a pleasanter look than common—"Rachel, I have done something that will please you. I would not do it to please Mr. Wotton: what I do, shall be of my own accord."

"What have you done, Sir? Tell me, that I may thank you for it."

"I have brought a carriage—Come, and see it."

"A post-chaise, Sir?"

"No, d——n it! No, rot it!—Not a post-chaise!"

"Lord bless me! How should I know what it was?"

"I understand you! Nothing will serve you but a post-chaise!"

"You are very unkind, Sir; I meant no such thing."

He flung out of the room, and went scolding into the court-yard.

Mrs. Gilson came in. She asked, what had put him out of humour?

I told her all that had passed; and added, that he seemed always seeking out for something to be angry at, and to quarrel with.

"You cannot alter Nature, nor I neither," said she. "Come along with me, for he wants you to see the chaise, and he will be pleased again."

I followed her into the court-yard. He was getting into the chaise, to try the horse. He drove it round the court-yard, and seemed to vent his ill humours upon the poor horse.

He saw me and Gilson observing him, and drove up to the porch. He jumped out, and came to us.

Mrs. Gilson said—"A very neat chaise, indeed, Sir; and the head is very convenient to keep off a shower of rain."

"Yes," said he; "and Sorrel goes well in it, and looks well in the harness, don't he?"

Mrs. Gilson admired it; and asked me, if I did not think so?

I said all that I could think of in it's praise. He was gratified, and came into the house in as good a humour as usual.

I could never be sure of the temper he was in; but was obliged to guard every word I spoke, as if before a court of justice. I am afraid my dear friend will blame me when I confess, that it was always a holiday to me when he went abroad.

The next year, I brought forth a daughter, who was most welcome to me; but her father set little value upon her. He was one of those *wise* men who thought women a drug,[14] and that they were hardly worth rearing.

I saw, in my daughter, a future friend and companion; one, upon whom my wearied heart might rest it's cares, and from whom new hopes and expectations should arise to cheer my latter days.

A second son was born to me, and a second daughter; but they were cut short by the scythe of Time, in an early stage of childhood. The two elder are living, and the dear objects of my hopes and cares.

Mr. Strictland was angry at their deaths; and with me, because I did not bring stronger and healthier children.

While my last child was in a state of infancy, Mr. Strictland met with an accident that hurt his health, and was, perhaps, the latent cause of his decline and death.

He was a breeder of horses; and he sometimes broke them in himself.

He had a very fine colt, that promised to be a capital horse: he was very high-spirited; and his master was proud to see that he would be managed by none but himself.

One day, when he was engaged in this employment, the colt threw him, and he lay some time as dead.

When he revived, he spit blood and it was supposed that he was much hurt inwardly.

He kept his chamber three weeks. Mrs. Gilson and I nursed him alternately; for I had my babe to attend beside: but, I trust, I was not wanting in my attention to my husband.

He was exceeding fretful during his confinement. His doctor, who knew something of his disposition, advised him to keep himself composed and quiet; for that every thing that ruffled his mind was bad for his internal complaint.

He expressed great resentment against the colt; and said, he would give him a good trimming, the first time he got across him.

I said, I hoped he would never get upon his back again.

He replied—"What signifies your hopes, or your wishes? It shall never be said, that man, woman, or beast, got the better of me."

The doctor smiled; I shook my head, but I durst not speak. And so ended this scene.

Mr. Strictland was as good as his word. As soon as he got abroad again, he gave the colt a good trimming. "There!" said he, "I hope I have taught him to know his master!"

I took warning by the lesson, and bore in mind, that he was my master also.

He was fond of his children; but he could not bear with their little childish ways, nor with their cries, and other noises. He would send them away out of his hearing, for he could not bear their cursed noises.

Strictland had many disagreeable qualities; but he had no vices. He was sober and temperate, chaste in his manners and conversation. He was industrious and frugal: this last degenerated into avarice, which excited him to accumulate wealth, which he never enjoyed; and, doubtless, it would have increased upon him, had he lived to old age.

I had a strong and lively imagination, which is generally accompanied with a degree of enthusiasm towards it's favourite objects. Whatever I love, it is with warmth; and I know that there is a little romance in my composition.

I am going to apologize to my friend for an adventure which her cool and steady judgment may, perhaps, condemn: and yet it has given me one of the greatest pleasures of my life; and, I hope, I shall never have cause to repent it.

One day, I heard the smack of Mr. Strictland's whip, as if he was using it improperly; for he did, sometimes, condescend to inflict manual chastisement upon his younger servants. I heard, also, the shrieks of a young voice, that touched my heart.

I went into the court-yard, to see who was the subject of his wrath.

I heard him say—"Go, you young dog! If ever you dare to come begging here again, I will flog you within an inch of your life."

The child went away crying and sobbing bitterly.

I went on to the outward gate, and met him. I asked him, who and what he was; but he could not speak for crying.

I saw, at a distance, leaning against a tree, an old man, very ragged, as was the boy, and with every sign of poverty and wretchedness.

The man beckoned the boy, as soon as he came in sight.

I gave the child a penny. The man bowed to me, in token of gratitude.

He came forward. I beckoned him to come nearer. He came up to me with humility and courtesy.

I spoke to him—"I want to know the reason of Mr. Strictland's displeasure against this child, and what he has done to offend him?"

"Nothing," said the boy: "I have done nothing but ask his charity."

"Did you say nothing to provoke him?"

"I said, I had a right to ask charity at that house, if all others refused me. My grandfather bid me say so."

"Alas, Madam!" said the old man; "if you knew who that boy is, you would pity him. Your countenance shews all that is good and gracious. I am sure you would pity his unhappy fate."

"Who is he, then?" said I.

"He is the right heir of this house and estate, if every one had his own."

"You surprize me! What is his name?"

"Reginald Henry Marney."

"I wish to hear this story. But I must not tarry here longer: if Mr. Strictland should see me conversing with you, he would be angry. Go away, friend. Come again on Wednesday, at noon-time. Do not come to the house, but wait till I come to you here. I wish to know this child's story: I pity him indeed, and wish to do him service; but I must first be convinced that he is what he pretends to be."

I gave the man a shilling, and bade him go out of sight as soon as possible. He prayed for blessings upon me: he went away; and I returned to the house.

My imagination had now a fine subject to work upon: it wove a thousand romantic webs, and then broke them in pieces; but still, all my fancies bore some relation to the old pictures. I wished impatiently for Wednesday, that I might hear the story.

I thought Mr. Strictland later than usual: I watched every minute. As soon as his back was turned, in came Miss Elton.

I had given a general invitation to the family, that whichsoever of them could be spared on Wednesdays, should spend the day with me.

She saw that I was reserved and absent; for I was weighing in my mind, whether to trust her with the secret, or not.

She asked, what ailed me; saying—"I fear I come unseasonably."

"No, that you cannot do: but yet, I am under a difficulty."

She smiled—"If I did not know you well, I should think you had made an appointment, and that my coming interrupted it."

"You have hit it, my dear; I have made an appointment, and was debating with myself, whether to take you into the party, or not. Can you keep a secret from all your family, and from every other person, even your parents?"

She looked serious for a minute, and then said—"If it is an honest one, and will injure nobody, I will."

"Oh, Nancy! I can hardly forgive that *if*. Trust my honour and integrity for that, and make me a solemn promise of secresy."

She did so; and then I took my hat and cloak, and said—"Follow me. I am waited for."

She did so, and we went to the place of appointment.

I soon saw the old man and the boy, sitting upon the ground, by the road-side. I beckoned them to follow me to a seat at some distance, where I sat down, with Miss Elton by my side. I made the boy sit down on the ground, at a little distance. The man stood near me.

I bade him relate the story he had promised; but warned him, to have a strict regard to truth in all that he should say.

He made me a bow that was above his degree, and began as follows—

"I suppose, Madam, that you are Mr. Strictland's wife?" I nodded.

"You have shewn a noble mind; and I will tell you our story.

"My good lady, you have, doubtless, heard, that your mansion, called Woodlands, and the estate round it, have been in the possession of many great and noble families.

"The Montforts were once the first barons of the realm. They withstood the tyranny of kings and priests, and were the guardians of the rights and liberties of the people.

"It passed from them to the Roscelins, by a female branch; and, in like manner, from them to the Marneys.

"The heiress of the Roscelin family was married to Sir Reginald Marney. His picture, and that of the lady Isabel, his wife, are now hanging in one of the parlours at Woodlands, and are reckoned very fine pieces."

"They are so, indeed," said I; "and they testify that you are well informed."

"There was a succession of noble knights and esquires of that name—There was Sir Henry; and Sir Philip; and Sir Reginalds, two or three.

"The estate was in the possession of Henry Marney, Esq. At the time of the Restoration. His son Reginald went over with James the Second; but returned, after many years, and took the oaths to King William.

"This gentleman did not marry till late in life. He left two sons, Reginald and Henry. The eldest was but nineteen when his father died.

"There was never greater antipathy between the two first brothers, Cain and Abel, than between the two of the name of Marney. Reginald was proud and vainglorious. Henry was brave, generous, and courteous: he was beloved by all the inhabitants of this his native village.

"There was a certain lawyer, whom the father of these youths had taken into his family, to be his steward. He had managed the estate while the squire was in France, and had wormed himself into his favour and confidence, so that he did nothing without consulting him.

"Mr. Longford got on the right side of the young squire, Reginald. Instead of healing the breach between the two brothers, he widened it. Reginald insulted Henry, who offered to fight him: he refused it, but provoked him by insolent language.

"One day, Reginald struck his brother. Henry returned the blow with interest, and beat him severely.

"When Mr. Longford came in, and saw the squire in this situation, he took part against Henry, and advised his patron to turn him out of doors. This was ordered, and executed, the same instant.

"Henry was then under age, and could not demand his fortune.

"Longford was his father's executor, and used his power to distress him to the utmost.

"Thus was this deserving young man thrown upon the world, and obliged to seek his fortune.

"He tried the friends of his family. They were generous of advice, but frugal of their assistance. They put him to a merchant, who sent him abroad to transact his business on the continent.

"Henry Marney behaved so well in his situation, that he gained the affection and confidence of his master.

"When his time was expired, he offered to take him into partnership, if he could bring money sufficient to purchase a share in it; and to settle him in France, as his partner and factor there.

"Mr. Marney came over to London. By his master's advice, he employed a lawyer, to demand the portion his father had bequeathed him.

"Reginald was already involved in troubles. He had set out upon too large a scale: he kept a pack of hounds, a large stud of horses; he loved hunting, shooting, and drinking; he outran his fortune, and Longford supplied him with his own money.

"When Henry's agent demanded his fortune, that villain Longford pretended that there was a flaw in the will; and that it was in Reginald's power to withold his portion, and to pay him as much, or as little, as he pleased; or even to keep back the whole.

"The agent remonstrated on the cruelty and injustice of this dealing—What had Henry Marney done, that he should be disinherited?

"Longford, after much subterfuge and evasion, offered to pay to Henry three thousand pounds. His father's bequest was seven thousand.

"Henry and his friend were informed of this offer; and the honest lawyer advised them to accept it, rather than wait the issue of a law-suit with a man so artful and deceitful as Longford, and so inveterate as Squire Marney.

"Accordingly, they accepted the sum offered; and Henry gave releases of all farther claim upon his brother.

"His master took him into a share of his business: he gave him his daughter in marriage; and sent him over to France again, where he resided till his brother's death.

"Reginald run out his fortune, and had no skill in business; so that he could not look into the state of his affairs. Longford supplied him; and told him, that he would, one day, put him into a way to repay him.

"He saw that his constitution was ruined, and that he declined daily. He took an opportunity of persuading him to make a will, in which he acknowledged a very large debt to him, and left him his whole fortune to discharge it.

"Reginald died at the age of forty; and thus the estates of the family of Marney fell into the hands of the villain who had long laid in wait for them.

"Henry Marney was unfortunate in his business: he lost money every year.

"His father-in-law died insolvent; and Fortune declared against him in all his undertakings.

"As soon as he heard of his brother's death, he made haste to settle his affairs, and to leave France.

"He paid every demand; and, with a small residue, returned to England with his wife and two children. The former was in a deep decline.

"He made no doubt of succeeding to the family estate, and to bring up his son as the heir of it.

"This poor beggar, that now stands before you, ladies, was not always the wretch he now is, though never in a state of independence. My family is ancient, though now fallen to decay.

"I was a clerk and writer in the house of Mr. Compton, Mr. Marney's father-in-law.

"As soon as he came to London, he made enquiry after the remains of this dispersed family; and I was the only person to give him information of it.

"I shall never forget the melancholy scene of my first introduction to him!

"Henry Marney was a fine person, and looked the gentleman all over. His countenance was overcast with grief, which he stifled for his wife's sake: but you saw a noble heart breaking under misfortune.

"He had just heard an imperfect account of his brother's will; but hoped to find it a false report.

"I was unwilling to increase his distress; yet I could not avoid answering his questions: I did with so much caution, that he observed it.

"My friend, you seem concerned for me," he said.

"I am, indeed, Sir," said I; "and heartily wish it was in my power to be of any service to you."

"Will you go with me to Woodlands, to fathom this sea of iniquity?"

"I will, Sir, if you please to accept me as your servant."

"He struck his hand upon his breast, and exclaimed—"Servant! It is for men of property to keep servants: I have none. If you serve me, it must be from pure love and friendship; for I have nothing to pay your services."

"It shall be so, Sir; and, when you recover your rights, you shall repay me by taking me into your service."

"Generous spirit! I wish you a better master!—Let me know where to find you, and you shall hear from me soon."

"I left him, and went home to my dwelling.

"After I was gone, his wife begged him not to leave her, as she feared she should not live till he returned.

"She died in a short time afterwards; and he was overwhelmed with grief and despondency.

"He sent for me the day after, and employed me to give the necessary orders concerning her interment; for, though I was so lately known to him, he had no other person to employ, or to rely upon.

"The day after the funeral, I waited on Mr. Marney, who was moaning over his children, and in the very depth of sorrow.

"Now, Sir," said I, "I am come to offer my company, to go with you to Woodlands. Change of scene, change of air, and attention to business, will dispel the gloom that hangs over you, and restore your health and spirits."

"Oh, Balderson!" said he, "how can I acknowledge your kindness? It is more than I have met with from any man beside. Your regard for your late master induces you to serve all his relations, and that at a time when none of them can pay you for your services. I pray God to reward you!—Alas! I cannot!"

"I expect no reward but your friendship. Let us not speak of it, I pray you, Sir. I have a proposal to make you; which is, to leave your daughter in the care of my wife, while we are absent: she and her children will be proud to wait on her, and to pay her every attention in their power. You may discharge these lodgings, and take young master with us into the country. We will take a lodging somewhere near Woodlands, and try what the country air, exercise, and employment, will do for you both."

"He was scrupulous of being expensive to me; but he had taken such a hold of my heart, that I would have divided my last shilling with him.

"My wife lived in Southwark. She kept a chandler's shop, and sold every thing almost: she got a decent livelihood. I wrote for the shopkeepers, whenever I could get employment; and this was the height of my prosperity.

"The week following, I attended Mr. Marney and his son into the country. We took lodgings at a farm-house in this village. We enquired after the rector of the parish, and his character. Hearing him well spoken of, I advised Mr. Marney to go to him, and tell him his story. "If," said I, "he is what a good clergyman should be, he will pity and befriend you."

"We waited on the Rev. Mr. Dalby, and told our story. He expressed much concern for Mr. Marney's misfortunes, and wished to serve him, but knew not how to do it.

"Mr. Longford is a rich man," said he: "I am a poor one. If I make him my enemy, it will do Mr. Marney no good, but may do me much harm. My good Sir, you must seek relief from the law, and not from the church: wicked men set us at defiance, and care little for our remonstrances. You must employ a lawyer; and he must apply to me, to certify your birth and baptism: this I will do faithfully; and I will give you my best advice beside. While you stay here, you shall be welcome to my table at all times; and I will do all I can, in the way of mediation between you and Mr. Longford, whenever I am called upon properly."

"We thanked the worthy clergyman for his kindness; and asked, if he could recommend us to a lawyer of fortune and character, who would either patronize us out of pity and generosity, or else advise us to give up our hopes at once.

"He said he would consider of it, and let us hear farther in a few days.

"Accordingly we were invited, a few days after, to meet a gentleman, learned in the laws of the land, and to lay Mr. Marney's case before him.

"The gentleman shewed his humanity and kindness. He spoke to this purpose—'I am truly concerned for your situation, and wish it may be in my power to do you service. Mr. Longford knows something of me: I think he will not refuse to confer with me upon the subject. The objects of my enquiry must be, first, Whether the will, under which he holds the estate, is a good one? Secondly, Whether your brother had a right to dispose of all the estates of the family? As to the first, I cannot flatter you with any hope of it. Mr. Longford knows the law too well to bring that into question. Your hopes must arise from the second. I should suppose, that some parts of the family estates may be entailed; and, unless your brother cut them off, which, I think, he could not do without your knowledge and concurrence, you may lay claim to them. But, in case we have nothing to hope from either, I would advise to appeal to his humanity for some assistance for you: the hardship of your case, and the judgment which the world passes upon him, as the man who has deprived you of your inheritance, may, perhaps, induce him to do something for you; at least, we will leave nothing untried to bring him to terms of reason and of justice.'

"And is this all the hope you have to build upon?" said Henry Marney: "then I must appeal to a higher tribunal—I must claim the protection of Heaven for my poor children, and find my own refuge in the grave!"

"Mr. Dalby talked to him: he blamed his despondency, and called upon him to exert the strength and fortitude of a Christian, to bear his sufferings with patience, and trust his cause to

Heaven; that in case his worldly hopes should fail him utterly, he had still a better hope in reversion.

"The lawyer comforted him in the way of his profession; and I could only argue as a friend, and implore him, for his children's sake, to bear up and wait the event.

"I saw that his heart and hopes were sunk; and a gloomy kind of tranquillity was spread over him, which only covered a deep despair.

"The week following, our counsellor waited on Mr. Longford; who received him with politeness, and heard him with patience.

"In reply to the first question, he read the will to him: to the second, he answered—"I know the tenure by which I hold these estates, and I will keep them by it. Henry Marney always behaved ill to his brother; who would have disinherited him, if he had not incurred the debts to me which are acknowledged in the will.—Sir, he is a beggar, and cannot repay your services: if you are wise, you will have done with him and his affairs from this time."

"The counsellor then urged the pleas of justice and humanity. He hinted, that the world believed that Henry Marney was an injured man, in regard to his private fortune bequeathed by his father; and now, a second time, in being deprived of his inheritance: that he was blamed, and Mr. Marney pitied. He urged him by every motive to do something for him; and, at least, to set him above want.

"Longford grew surly and reserved; and they parted with hardly civility."

While we were in this part of the story, my maid Peggy came to seek us, and to tell us that dinner waited for us.

I bade her return, and we would follow her. I then spoke to Balderson—

"I am summoned home to dinner: I cannot invite you to my house, for many reasons; but I will endeavour to assist you."

I took out my purse. I gave him two guineas. The man looked astonished.

"Put yourself and the boy into better cloathing. Meet me here this day se'nnight, at twelve o'clock, and tell me the remainder of your story: I am deeply interested in it, and shall remember all that you have told me. But, before you go, tell me how that boy can be your grandson?"

"Because his father married my daughter."

"What, then, was Henry Marney his father?"

"No; his grandfather."

"I understand you: that son, who was here with his unfortunate father?"

"The very same."

"Farewel, friend. I shall expect to see you this day week."

"Farewel, dear lady!—May God reward your bounty to this wretched orphan and his protector!—Kneel down, boy, and pray for a blessing on your benefactress!"

Miss Elton and I ran home; and we heard these grateful creatures invoking Heaven in our behalf all the way.

We could talk of nothing else the whole day. She desired she might be present at the remainder of the story; and I promised, that she only should partake of this secret, which I should guard carefully from Mr. Strictland.

I had often enquired of Mr. Strictland concerning those five pictures; and he told me, in general terms, that they belonged to the Marneys. I had asked their names, and their history: he grew tired of answering me.

"Will you never have done talking of those pictures? It seems as if you were ready to fall down and worship them."

"No, I will not do that; but I respect them exceedingly."

"Respect a faggot-stick!—You may, as well as an old figure painted upon canvas."

"They are very fine paintings, Sir: good pictures are sometimes highly valued."

"Well, I have heard so before now; and you may set what value you please upon them. I should like somebody else should take a fancy to them, and give me a good sum of money for them: I would take it."

Money was his idol, and his estimate for every thing.

The week rolled round in it's usual course; Wednesday returned; Miss Elton came early; Mr. Strictland went his journey, and we to our appointment.

Balderson and his boy were waiting for us. Their rags were thrown aside. They were drest so tight and tidy, that Mr. Strictland would not have known them. The boy was washed clean; and his countenance was open, pleasant, and manly. I thought I could trace a likeness to the admired picture of Sir Reginald Marney. Miss Elton would not allow it; but rather laughed at the excursion of my fancy.

After the greetings of the day, Balderson pursued his story—

"Soon after the interview I have mentioned, our good counsellor received a letter from Mr. Longford; and we were summoned to hear the contents. In it he acknowledged, that there were some apparent hardships in the case of Henry Marney; that, out of humanity, and pity at his unhappy situation, he offered to pay him one thousand pounds, upon condition of signing a release to all his claims upon the Marney estates, for himself and his posterity; and that this writing should be signed, sealed, and witnessed, properly.

"Mr. Marney refused to sign any such instrument. He said, his health had been declining for a long time past, and he should soon be out of the reach of his enemy's cruelty and injustice: that, though he knew his claim was become a mere shadow, he would not injure his children so much as to renounce it: there might come a time, when they might revive it with better hopes; but, that he should not die in peace, were he to deprive them of it.

"The counsellor, Mr. Dalby, and myself, urged him to accept the offer; as the interest would support himself, and the principal would be an outset for his son, and put him into some genteel profession.

"He would not hear of it, but persisted in an obstinate refusal.

"The counsellor signified his refusal to Mr. Longford: he pitied and excused him.

"In less than a week, a note was sent to Mr. Marney, from Mr. Longford's clerk, to this effect—'By order of Robert Longford, Esq. I write, to desire you to quit this parish as soon as possible; and he sends the inclosed to bear your expences.'

"This note covered another, value fifty pounds.

"Mr. Marney's spirit rose at this order; he would have sent it back; but we joined to over-rule him. He would answer it, however; and it was to this effect—

"HENRY MARNEY considers himself as an injured person, in all respects. In spite of Squire Longford's mandate, he will take the liberty to die in the parish, where he was born: he will lay his bones near those of his ancestors; and his soul will complain to his grandfather's, of the treachery and injustice of his steward towards his heir."

"We all urged him to accept Mr. Longford's proposal; but he was inflexible. He was declining daily, but he scorned to complain. He lived about seven weeks in this village. He gave me the charge of his son; and bade him seek for some employment—he advised him to get into the army, or the navy, as the least unworthy of a gentleman.

"He spoke on this subject to Mr. Dalby, saying, his son must cut his bread with his sword.—'But, what will become of my daughter?—Oh, Sir! My heart bleeds for my dearest Anna!'

"The worthy Mr. Dalby promised to invite her to spend the summer in his family; and he would seek out for some eligible situation for her.

"He took his hand, and kissed it; he thanked him incessantly while he staid in the room.

"Mr. Dalby and the rest of us prayed with him, and he seemed comforted.

"The next day, while he was wishing to see Mr. Dalby, he had a convulsion fit; and, as that gentleman entered the room, he expired.

"Thus died Henry Marney, at only forty-six years of age; a gentleman of a high and generous spirit, and worthy of a better fate—but he is gone where merit is understood and rewarded!

"I cannot say which was the most grieved, myself, or young Reginald. It seemed as if I had lost an only brother. I was rouzed by the necessary attention to the last duties to my friend and master. We followed to the grave, and saw him interred in the church-yard, near the family vault. I ordered a stone to be put over him, with this inscription—

"Here lie the remains of HENRY MARNEY, Esq.
Heir of the honourable family of MARNEY:
Formerly in possession of the Mansion of WOODLANDS,
In this parish.
Now, dispossessed of all worldly property,
He is gone to seek an immortal inheritance,
Where the wicked cease from troubling,
And the weary are at rest."

"I resolved to go to church the following Sunday, and on the Monday to set out with young Reginald for my own dear home.

"The stone was put down one day in the week: and on the Sunday morning I went to weep over it; when, behold! The whole inscription was erased, and the following put in it's place—

"Here lie the remains of HENRY MARNEY,
The last of that family; formerly
Proprietors of WOODLANDS, in this parish."

"I easily guessed from what quarter the alterations came. Mr. Dalby advised me to be silent, for we were not able to contend with the author.

"I had spent the greatest part of the fifty pounds we received, in the necessaries for the funeral, and putting the stone over the grave. On the Monday we set out in a cart, which carried us and our baggage to the next market-town; and from thence, in a stage-waggon, to London.

"Reginald Marney was just turned of fifteen; he was a fine manly youth, with a genteel person, and an amiable disposition.

"I carried him to my own house, and bade my wife receive him as one of our children. I had then living an hopeful son, and two dear and lovely daughters."

Here Balderson stopped to weep. Our tears accompanied him. The past tale was melancholy, and the succeeding promised nothing better.

"If this recital is too painful to you," said I, "let us defer it another week."

"God bless your kind and generous heart, lady!—No; I can now go on—

"My son had a strong propensity to the sea. He had been several voyages; and was now waiting for a ship not quite ready to sail. He took an affection for Reginald Marney, and persuaded him to go with him. I acquainted Miss Marney with Mr. Dalby's kind invitation, and advised her to accept.

"The poor thing wept bitterly: she complained that, after the loss of both her parents, she had attached herself to my family; that she must now be torn from her dear brother, and from the only person that loved or cared for her. I represented, that she would find herself in a better situation at Mr. Dalby's, and live like a gentlewoman there; but, if she preferred our humble dwelling and board, she should stay with us, and be as one of our children. She reflected upon what I had said, and took her resolution to go to Mr. Dalby's; for she could not bear to be an expence to us, who had already done so much for her. She only begged that she might stay till her brother was gone to sea.

"We fitted out young Reginald for a sailor, and waited for the time. My James was three years older than him, and took him under his protection. We had a melancholy parting. We could hardly tear Miss Marney from her brother; but it was necessary, and must be done. I took her from him, and comforted her as well as I could.

"As soon as the first burst of grief was abated, I told her she must prepare for her journey. My wife fitted her out with decent mourning, and other necessaries; and, within a week after, I attended her to Mr. Dalby's.

"I had a melancholy satisfaction in having discharged all the duties and offices of friendship to my beloved and respected Henry Marney. I shed my tears over his grave. I took a tender farewel of his daughter; and, having spent all the money I could raise, I returned home on foot, with just enough to buy my bread, and drank of the running stream. I did not tell my wife how close I was driven, and I returned to my usual course of life. I settled her books, and assisted in her trade.

"Several years we lived in peace and comfort, but what some people would call hardly. We seldom tasted meat, unless of a Sunday. My daughters took in needle-work, when they could get it; for that business, like all others, is overstocked, and is the wretched resource of too many. Of an evening, I wove laces and bobbin,[16] and made cabbage-nets; and, I can truly say, I did not eat the bread of idleness.

"When our sailors returned home, then was our festival. They used to bring all the money they had earned. They lodged together, near us: they threw their share into our mess, and then we lived comfortably. The dear boys denied themselves every thing but necessaries, and were proud to contribute to our comforts and conveniencies: they used to bring home gowns and linen for my wife and girls.

"Miss Marney wrote to us once in a while, and gave an account of herself. By the recommendation of the good Mr. Dalby, she was taken as a companion to a widow lady, who had lately buried her own daughter. Miss Marney did honour to her credentials. She pleased the lady, and became very dear to her. She lived happily there several years.

"Our children grew up to maturity. The young men earned more money, and were able to assist us. Our happiness increased every year.

"Let me be grateful for the good I have received, and patient under the evil!

"But now the passions implanted by Providence in the hearts of men for the wisest and best purposes, began to disclose themselves. Young and amiable persons, of different sexes, can hardly be much together, without feeling the impulse of nature, and the attachment of the heart.

"I may say, without flattery, that both my daughters were

handsome and modest; but the younger was the most engaging in her manners. Reginald Marney loved her before he knew all that love demands. Every return brought an increase of affection; and their greetings were so tender, that we all perceived their tendency.

"I thought it my duty to check it, in respect to the memory of Henry Marney; but still I could perceive that they loved each other most ardently. I advised with my son, and he reproved them both.

"You are neither of you in a situation to think of marriage," said he. "The man who loves honestly and wisely, will wait till he can maintain a wife, before he takes one. I have seen my dear parents wrestle with poverty, and hardly could keep it at arm's-end: I would not wish to see my children in the same situation. Self-denial is a duty which I can recommend, because I practise it. Oh, Reginald! There is a lady in the world, who, if I were king of the globe, I would make my partner: but, far be it from me to wish her to share my homely lot, and to suffer what I have seen those most dear to me undergo. She knows not, she never shall know, the love I bear to her. May she live in the bosom of Peace and Plenty! And, if she meets with a man who can secure it to her for life, I will bless, and pray for him."

"I was proud of my son; I blessed his noble and generous passion; I forbade the lovers to think of marriage, and wished them to dissolve their engagements. Reginald refused to do that, but promised to postpone his marriage till after another voyage.

"A young ship-carpenter courted my eldest daughter. He carried all my children to the launching a ship for the service of the East India Company.[17] He advised my sons to offer themselves to the captain. He said, it was a pity that two such clever lads should go with petty merchants and traders, in small ships, when they might go to India, and perhaps make their fortunes.

"My young men said, they would consider of it, and let him know.

"When they came home, the subject was canvassed among us all.

"My wife and daughters were against it: they could not bear the thoughts of such long absences. But my James spoke like a man of spirit—"It is my ardent wish, and shall be my endeavour, to lift you all out of this den of poverty, and to place you in a comfortable situation. For you I grudge no toils nor travels. I can but just get on, and help you a little; but, if I launch out in a better way, I may, in time, rise to preferment; and, at least, I will leave nothing untried. I trust that my brother Reginald is of the same opinion, and that he wishes to raise the girl he loves to a state of comfort: he would shame to see his children, who must bear the name of Marney, in this poor and sordid situation.—My father, I call upon you to confirm our resolution, and to comfort our dear women—and you, Reginald, must do the same."

"Reginald took his hand—"My dear brother, I will live and die with you; and I will go with you to India."

"My heart sunk at the thoughts of their long absence, and the dangers they might incur; but I should have scorned to let our interest and pleasure weigh against their good, and the generous motives they had urged. I gave a full consent to their going, and reproved the women for their selfish opposition to it. They wept in silence.

"Young Stevens, their friend, called the next day. He said, he had spoken to the captain, who desired to see them.

"They went to wait on him the same day; and they engaged themselves to go with him the following spring; and, in the mean time, they went a short voyage to Ostend, as usual; and they returned in good time for the Indiaman.

"We had a dismal parting. The girls were distracted with grief, and the mother not much better.

"I had a heavy task to conceal my own fears and cares, and to support them; but I knew it was my duty, and I did not shrink from it. I prayed to God for a blessing upon my dear sons.

"Young Stevens was carpenter's mate in the same ship. They all took leave at the same time. They went away in high spirits, apparently; saying, they were going to make fortunes for us all."

I called to Balderson to stop here—"We will meet you here again next Wednesday; and, in the mean time, we will consider how I can serve you and your grandson."

"Oh, Madam! you are too good to us! This child deserves your favour. He is a clever and a towardly boy. I have taught him to read, and he can say the Church Catechism quite perfect."

"That is a good beginning," said I. "May God succeed your endeavours!"

I took Miss Elton's arm, and was followed home by their prayers and blessings.

After dinner, Miss Elton and I consulted about assisting the boy. I said, if I could put him out to any trade, so that he might be a good member of the community, I should be satisfied; and knowing that he could read, made me the more desirous to take him away from that vagabond life, and make him a useful man.

Miss Elton said, the schoolmaster of the village wanted an assistant, and had applied to her father; but she feared young Marney was not capable of the office.

I answered—"No; but he may be made so. I thank you for the thought: I embrace it. Let us go directly to the schoolmaster's. I will ask him to take an orphan child as an apprentice. I will offer to pay him annually, which suits me better than paying all at once. I have it all in my heart. Let us go, my dear friend."

"God bless that generous heart, and make it's power equal to it's wishes! I attend you now."

Away we went, finished our business, and returned to tea.

The schoolmaster agreed to take him at once. I was to pay him ten pounds for the first year; and the salary was to be lessened every year, in proportion to the boy's proficiency, and capability of assisting the master.

It was to be a profound secret who placed him there; and he was to be called Henry Smith, for the name of Marney would excite jealousy and suspicion.

I never was better pleased in my life than with this agreement. This action gave me credit with myself. I used to dream of the Marneys continually, which was not surprising; and I fancied those two fine pictures walked out of their frames, to thank me for my kindness to their descendant.

After every meeting with Balderson, I wrote down all that passed between us. At first, I did it to impress the story upon my memory; and afterwards, I thought it might, one day, be very valuable to young Marney.

It is from this I shall transcribe the particulars I shall send you.

I have sometimes intended to send away my packet; but then it has risen to my mind, that you would be better pleased to have the whole together: therefore I continue my narration.

I promise myself, that the family history of the Marneys will be as interesting to you as to myself.

The boy is my child by adoption, and is become very dear to me. He shares my affection and cares with my own children. I consider him as the right heir of my son's estate, and that we are bound to support and provide for him. Will you, my friend, blame me for this way of thinking? I answer to myself, that you will not. You also have adopted children, and they also shall be dear to me. When we meet, we will investigate these subjects; and, I trust, we shall agree to love all that are dear to each other.

I have written till I am weary, and shall now lay down the pen for a time; but I shall never be tired of telling you, that I am,

Your faithful and affectionate friend,
RACHEL STRICTLAND.

LETTER VIII
Mrs. Strictland, to Mrs. Darnford, in continuation.

I WILL now give my friend an account of my third interview with Balderson, and the sequel of the story of the Marney family. You will always remember, it is Balderson that speaks.

"We passed our time heavily during the absence of our beloved friends. My wife and the girls blamed me for letting them go. My daughter Agnes used to go moping about, and frequently weep by herself. I reproved her for it; but she gave me for answer, that she only lived for Reginald Marney; and, if she was not to be his wife, she did not wish to live at all. My other daughter, Hannah, had a stronger mind, and a more chearful heart.

"In the second year, our sailors returned, in good health and spirits; and then our mourning was turned into joy.

"The lovers were in raptures, and insisted upon being married immediately. My James attempted to persuade Reginald to defer it till after another voyage. He resented it, and they almost quarrelled about it. I pacified them; saying, they should be married as soon as the banns[1] could be published.

"Stevens and Marney went out together the next day; and, in the evening, they returned with licences, and insisted on being married on the morrow. I blamed them for spending so much money, when they might have been married so much cheaper. Reginald said—"What is money good for, but to make us happy?"

"But, we have made no preparations."

"We have done that for you," said Stevens. "We have ordered

a breakfast and a dinner at a public-house, and shall put you to no trouble or cost."

"I shook my head. 'I am afraid you will want the money you thus squander away,' said I.

"They desired I would not cast a damp upon their joys. Reginald sung these lines—

> "Let's be merry, while we may;
> "Life is short, and wears away."[2]

"On the morrow, the weddings were celebrated. It was, indeed, a festival. We threw aside care, and enjoyed our present happiness.

"Stevens had taken a lodging for himself and his wife. Reginald went home with us. They agreed to spend the chief of their time together, and to leave their wives with us during the next voyage.

"Never was there a happier family, during the four months they staid at home. They made preparations for another voyage the following spring.

"I thought I saw, at times, a gloom upon my James's manly countenance. One day, I questioned him upon the cause of it. He said, I had great discernment, and that I had a right to know every thought of his heart.

"During the time I was at Madras, an elderly gentleman, who had long resided there, took a great deal of notice of me. He examined me upon various subjects, and seemed satisfied with my answers. By degrees, he opened his mind to me. He said, he was engaged in a particular branch of trade, independent of the Company; that he had lately lost the person whom he trusted with all his affairs; that he wanted one to succeed him; and that the man he should employ would be able to do well for himself, at the same time that he was serving him. There were three requisites in the man he should chuse—good-sense, courage, and fidelity; "and, I think, I have found them all in you," said he. "Consider of my proposal; and then tell me, whether it is worth your acceptance."

"I said, I was the son of poor, but honest parents, who depended, in some degree, upon the fruits of my labour and industry; that I was unwilling to engage in any undertaking that would remove me out of their reach, and put it out of my power to assist them. He said, that I should be enabled to assist my parents more effectually, and to build a fortune for myself;

that he would settle upon me an handsome salary, and give me an opportunity to trade for myself beside. I said, I would consider of it, and let him know my determination.

"A short time before we sailed, I waited on him. I told him, I was resolved to return home, and visit my parents; that, if they consented to it, and if he was unprovided with such an agent as he wanted, I would enter into his service at my return.

"I have kept this secret in my own heart, because I was unwilling to give you pain unnecessarily; and, as to my mother, I dare not tell her at all, but must leave it to you, to break it to her tenderly after I am gone. My sisters have other men to care for, and to care for them; they can spare me the better; and I hope that you, my dear father, will give me your consent, and your blessing upon it."

"Here James paused, and waited my answer. I paused also, for I knew not what to say. At last I said—"It is not for me to decide a point of so much importance. Judge, and decide for yourself, my son. I may suffer; but I will not oppose your generous and manly designs and undertakings. God direct you for the best, and succeed you in all your doings!"

"I could not help weeping while I spoke. My son embraced me, and shed tears upon my face."

"My father! if you forbid me, I will not proceed in this undertaking!"

"No, I do not forbid you. I should be unworthy of such a son, if I was to check your brave and noble spirit. I will pray incessantly for blessings upon you."

"Thank you, my father! But, remember, you are not to tell my mother till I am gone."

"Do Stevens and Marney know your intentions?"

"No. If Reginald had continued a single man, I would have invited him to go with me; but now that he is married all is over. I shall not tell him till I leave him; and I shall hope to send you letters through his hands. Keep my secret, and make your mind up to my destination."

"My son left me to my own reflections. My heart was oppressed with cares and fears; but I still carried a chearful countenance.

"When they departed for India, my heart sunk within me: all my steadiness forsook me, and I was overwhelmed with grief. I dared not tell my wife the cause, for she was too much affected. She saw that I was more concerned than usual, for I lost my rest and appetite. She forgot her own grief, to comfort me.

"Cheer up, Balderson," said she: "I think you are worse than me." I exerted myself, and overcame it.

"There is a proverb, that says—"God assists those who assist themselves." I found it so; for I recovered my health and spirits. Alas! I had need of them; for my trials were now approaching.

"The autumn following was a very sickly time: an epidemical distemper raged in London and it's environs. It visited my poor family: we all had it more or less, but my wife died of it. I lost an industrious and faithful woman, who was the chief support of us all.

"In the midst of my grief, I was comforted by the reflection, that she knew not of her son's destination; and it became a source of consolation to me.

"My daughters recovered by degrees, and so did I; but we were every day more sensible of our great loss.

"Our business depended upon my wife. People knew and loved her; and they liked to be served by her. My daughters were not equally qualified: they knew not the way of the trade so well.

"I did all in my power; but I was not successful. Our business fell off, we had a severe winter, expences run high, business declined, and we were obliged to break into the money my sons left behind.

"The following spring, in the month of May, my daughter Marney was brought to bed of this dear boy, the object of my hopes and cares. She nursed him with the utmost care and attention. I fancied I saw in him a resemblance of Henry Marney, and I doated upon him. I desired that he might be called after his grandfather; but my daughter, who almost worshipped her husband, insisted upon adding his name: so he was called Reginald Henry, but I always called him by the latter name.

"My daughter Hannah had miscarried during her illness; and she grieved, that she also had not a child to present to her husband at his return.

"The second year rolled heavily over us; and we reckoned the months, the weeks, and the days, when our dear friends were expected home.

"One evening, in the dreary month of November, as my daughter Stevens and I were sitting over an handful of fire, (Agnes and her child were gone to bed, and we were preparing to follow them) we heard a knocking at the door.

"We asked, who was there; and the answer was—"Your

friend and relation." I opened it immediately; and Jack Stevens entered, in deep mourning.

"We embraced and welcomed him: but, as soon as our emotions subsided, we considered his dress and appearance; for his countenance wore mourning, as well as his body.

"Unwilling to forebode farther griefs, I said—"You have heard of our misfortune?"

"He shook his head, and replied—"But you have not heard of mine; that I must, unwillingly, relate."

"My heart sunk—"Ha! what, have you any more sorrows for us?"

"I have," said he: "prepare to hear them with patience and resignation; and may God support you!"

"I shook like a leaf, and felt as if I should faint.

"Hannah said—"Tell us quickly, and put us out of suspence."

"He sighed deeply; and then—"Reginald Marney is dead; and James Balderson is gone up the country, nobody knows where: he had been gone several months before I came away from Madras."

"As I feared the worst, this last article revived.

"You have not heard that James is dead?"

"No, Sir; I have letter from him to you; but it is dated four months before I sailed."

"Thank God for that!—But, tell me, how did Reginald die?"

"Of an autumnal fever.[3] It is a cursed country. I will never go there any more."

"I rejoice to hear that," said Hannah.

"We all were glad that Agnes was gone to bed; and we consulted how we should break the dreadful tidings to her. I made up the fire, and we sat and talked away the whole night.

"I thought there was a coldness and formality in Stevens's behaviour, which I had never observed before; but I imputed it to his concern for the tidings he brought, and his endeavours to conceal it.

"When day-light was come, he went out; and told Hannah, he should call again by and by.

"When Agnes came down with her child, my tears flowed so fast, that I was obliged to conceal them. She said, "I saw a man go by our house, so like Jack Stevens, that I should have thought it was him, if he had been in England." Hannah answered—"I have heard that he is arrived, and I expect him every hour."

"Have you a letter, sister?"

"I have."

"Where, then, are Reginald and James? No letters from them?"

"No."

"Father, what is the meaning of this?"

"I could make no answer.

"She set down the child, and came up to me. I was leaning against the wall, and crying like a child. She looked in my face, and saw my tears. She looked back, and saw Hannah weeping, and both silent. She gave a loud shriek, and fell into a strong fit.

"I will draw a veil over this scene of anguish, for your sake and my own. It was terrible. She was either in raving, or in silent fits, for three days and nights. At intervals, she enquired for her husband. I dared not deceive her. I told her, he was dead, and she must submit to the will of Heaven.

"In the midst of our distress, Stevens came in. He offered to take his wife away from me.

"I called him cruel and ungrateful, to think of such a thing. He said, she could do no good, but only make him and herself unhappy.

"I implored him, for Heaven's sake, to take pity upon me, and help me to support my trials, which were already as much as I could bear. He turned out of the house in anger, and beckoned his wife to follow him; but she had too much humanity to leave me at that dreadful moment.

"She advised me to send for a poor widow, that nursed us in our past illness, and did the last offices for my poor wife. She said, he had taken a lodging, and insisted upon her sleeping there; but she would be with us in the day-time, and wait to see what turn her sister's disorder would take. I thanked her, and followed her advice.

"I had never left my poor Agnes, from the time she was struck down by this fatal news. Nature demanded some repose. I left her to the care of the nurse; I took the dear child with me, and went to rest, which I much wanted. My fatigue served me as an opiate: I slept till a late hour, and awoke refreshed and restored, and enabled to go through the painful duties that awaited me.

"Hannah called upon me at noon. She said, her husband would not allow her to eat or sleep at my house; that he was engaged to work at the Dock-yard at Deptford,[4] and was resolved to settle there; that he wanted to carry her there directly, but she would not go till she saw me through my present distress, which, she saw, bore hard upon me.

"I desired her to tell her husband to send me my son's letter; for my attendance upon Agnes made me forget to ask for it.

"On the morrow, she brought it, and I was eager to peruse it. I was surprized and concerned to find it had been opened, and closed again in a very bungling manner. In it he told me, he was going up the country, on the business he had mentioned to me. He desired me not to be alarmed, if I did not hear from him every year; but it was his wish and intention that I should receive letters from him annually: that he had told his brothers, Marney and Stevens, that he was engaged in a gentleman's service, without giving them the particulars of his employment: that he sent me a remittance by them, and hoped to send me, at least, the same sum annually; he chose to limit my expectations, but should rejoice to be enabled to exceed them.

"The sum was carefully scratched out; but, by turning it about to the light, I discovered it to be fifty pounds. I was struck to the heart at this proof of the baseness of the hands through which this letter was conveyed to me; but I wondered it was not destroyed.

"I now discerned the cause of Stevens's shyness and reserve; and I had still more villainy to apprehend from him.

"I took no notice to my daughters; but said, I took it unkindly that Stevens should shun me because of my poverty and distress: I hoped he would think better, and come to me; for I had many questions to ask him.

"The poor girl promised to use all her influence, to persuade him to come with her the next time; and at last she brought him.

"I saw that he was in confusion, and expected to be questioned on the subject of the letter; but I had determined to attack him where he did not expect it first.

"I asked him, whether he had received his pay from the Indiaman?

"He answered—"Yes."

"Then you received also what was due to Marney and Balderson?"

"No; I did not."

"That is very strange to me: you must know, that both myself and my daughter had need of it."

"I had not a proper power to receive their monies."

"I am sorry for it. I must enquire how and where the seamen's wages are to be paid. In the mean time, you can pay me the remittance my son James sent me, as mentioned in the letter."

"It was not me to whom he gave it."

"Who, then?" said I.

"It was Reginald."

"Was not you with him when he died?"

"Yes; but I was not allowed to take his effects."

"Who did, then, pray?"

"I do not know."

"God grant me patience!" said I; "and may they who have wronged the widow and the orphan, find their ill-gotten wealth grind their hearts in their last moments!"

"Stevens was confused; but he affected to be angry, and went out in a seeming rage.

"After this enquiry, I saw little more of Stevens. My daughter always called once a day, but never ate nor slept at the house.

"After a variety of sufferings, partly bodily, and partly mental, my poor daughter Agnes expired. In all her lucid intervals, she prayed for death, and wished her child would have gone with her.

"Now was I bereft of all my comforts, and left with the charge of this unfortunate child, to struggle through difficulties of every kind. I could only resign myself to the will of Heaven, and pray for strength and fortitude.

"I sent word of the event to Stevens and his wife. She came to me; she lamented my situation, and wished she was allowed to be constantly with me.

"The day after, she came again. She said, her husband was concerned for me, but he could not bear to be present; it hurt him too much; but he had sent me five guineas towards the funeral.

"If it is his own, I am obliged to him; but I fear—I fear, he owes me much more than this: but I leave him to Heaven, and his own conscience."

"She begged me not to entertain suspicions of him, but to take what he had sent out of good-will. I bade her frame what answer she pleased, and give it to her husband.

"She attended the funeral with me; but he declined it. Perhaps he was too much conscience-stricken, to be able to be present: but why, then, did he not make restitution?

"The day after, he came to fetch his wife from my house. He

told her, she must now take her choice, to go with him, or stay with her father: he was going away directly.

"She wept in my arms. I said—"Go, my child; it is your duty to follow your husband: leave me to the protection of Heaven. God bless you! and farewel!—Stevens, do not defy Heaven's justice. May you repent of the wrongs you have done me, and be forgiven!"

"He said, he had done me no wrong; but, that I had abused his good-will. He went away in anger; and his wife followed him, weeping.

"I was left in this disconsolate situation, yet I did not despair. I lifted up my heart in prayer, and said—"Nothing happens without thy permission, O Lord! Do thou strengthen me to support my sufferings, and to rely upon thee to deliver me in thy own good time: thou canst make all these things work together for good to those who love and obey thee."

"The good woman, who did the last offices to my child and her mother, told me there was a man and his wife, who would be glad to take my house and shop off my hands.

"It was a welcome offer, for I was no longer in a situation to carry it on. I treated with them; they took most of the furniture and fixtures.

"I hired an upper-room in a poor house near by. I took a bed, and chairs, and furnished my room; and then went thither with my child, who gave me courage to struggle through my troubles, and rewarded my cares and his innocent smiles. For his sake, I exerted myself; and, if I could provide food for him, I cared not how poorly I fared.

"I wove garters, laces, and bobbins; I sold ballads, and little chap-books.[5] I was a petty hawker and pedlar: I carried a basket before me, and my child at my back.

"I generally earned enough to buy us a supper at night; a loaf, or a few biscuits, fed us all day.

"The poor widow lived next door to us: she used to wash for us, and keep my boy wholesome and cleanly; he throve, and grew to my heart's wishes.

"When the spring came forward, I extended my walks through all the environs. I implored people to buy of me for charity, and in pity to the poor orphan I carried with me. I told no feigned story; my griefs were real, and I sometimes affected my hearers: they would give a few pence to the little boy, and we returned them our blessings.

"As soon as he could speak plain, I taught him his letters: he soon learned to read. I taught him Dr. Watts's Hymns,[6] and made him sing them to such as would give him the hearing.

"I strove to impress upon his mind a strong sense of religion and virtue; of the duties to God, and to our neighbour. I taught him, that a poor beggar was better, in the sight of God, than a rich man without good principles, or the fear of God.

"In a year's time, I became inured to this kind of life. I earned money sufficient for all my wants. I paid my lodgings every Saturday, and had a hot dinner on a Sunday.

"I had still an hope warm at my heart, that I should sometimes hear of my poor James, and receive remittances from him: that I should make use of them to put my Henry out to some creditable trade, and make him a good and useful member of society. These were my wishes, and the only objects of my ambition.

"I used to stroll about all the villages within ten miles, all the summer; but in the winter, I kept within the limits of the triple city, London, Westminster, and Southwark.

"The people knew me, and always kept my lodging for me. The persons who took my house and shop were kind to me; they often sent me victuals, and they were desired to take in all letters for me.

"I expected, when the India ships came home, to hear from my son; but no letters came.

"It came into my mind, that the same person who stopped my first remittance, might intercept any future ones, and also the letters that brought advice of them; yet I dreaded to find my suspicions well founded: I was unwilling to think so hardly of nature, and of relationship.

"One day, when I was strolling through Leadenhall Street, near the India House, a young man, with a pen in his hand, took very kind notice of my child: he gave him six-pence. I was used to observe men's countenances; and, I thought, he looked good and gracious.

"A thought struck me—I asked him to let me speak with him, if it did not intrude upon his time. He bade me speak.

"I stood in the street, and he upon the upper-step of the door. I told him, briefly, that this child was a wretched orphan, who had no friend or protector but myself; that his father was a sailor in the India Company's service, and died at Madras at such a time; that his uncle remained there, and that both of them had wages due to them; and, if he could put me in a way to receive them, he would confer the greatest obligation upon me.

"He wished he might be able to do me this service. He took down the name of the ship, and the men, in his pocket-book, and promised to endeavour to serve me. I gave him my direction, and begged he would let me know his success. I told him the use I intended to make of the money for the child's service, and that I preserved my life for his sake.

"The young man was affected; he was convinced of my veracity. He gave me half-a-crown: I declined it; saying, it was enough to intrude upon his time, and to give him trouble. He put it again into my hand, gave it the grasp of friendship, and went away, saying—"Thou art no common beggar, I am sure!"

"His grasp went to my heart; it filled my eyes with tears. I said—"Thou art no common giver, I am sure!"

"He shut the door, and I went away with my heart lighter than it had been for a long time.

"When the spring advanced, it came into my mind to wander down to Woodlands, and to enquire after Miss Marney, from whom I had not heard of a long time. My own cares and troubles had so much engrossed me, that I could think of nothing else. Very little preparation had we to make. My child began to walk by my side, and I only carried him when he was tired. I bought him a pair of stout shoes, and away we went.

"We passed through Bow and Stratford, and steered away for Epping Forest.

"In the thickest part of it we were overtaken by a violent storm of thunder, lightning, and rain, which I shall never forget. I took shelter in a hollow tree, and it kept me from all it's inconveniencies.

"In the midst of this awful scene, I felt none of those fears which used to attend me in happier days. I had no friends, no property, to lose. I held my child in my arms, and recommended him to the care of Heaven: it seemed to me, as if we were more immediately under it's protection.

"Let the wicked tremble," said I; "we fear God, and he will defend us from all other fears." I felt inexpressible peace and confidence in his mercy; and was, at that awful moment, happier than the man of property, for I had nothing to lose but this earthly tabernacle, and that, I was assured, I should exchange for a better, and my child would share it with me.

"The storm went over towards evening. The Sun shone out in all his glory, and gilded the clouds with a thousand colours;

when a troop of gipsies, or travellers, or beggars, though not of our cast, came running up to my tree.

"They shook the rain off their tattered cloaths; they gathered sticks, and tore down boughs; they struck a light, made a fire, and set on an iron pot with meat to cook for their suppers.

"I came out of my retreat, and was glad to see again human faces. They called out—"A brother! a brother!" and addressed me in all the cant of their knavish trade.

"I was ignorant of their meaning; but told them, briefly, that I was reduced to indigence, and had this child to provide for.

"Like true citizens of the world, they welcomed me, and invited me to partake of their supper. I accepted their hospitality with thanks, for myself and my child. We ate heartily, and one of them had a wooden cask of ale, and cups to drink out of.

"I said, I believed I had made free with their lodging. They all cried out—"Take it, father, and welcome, for this night!"

"They invited me to go with them: they taught me some of their language, if ever I should meet with any of their brethren, for they were a numerous society.

"I thanked them for their civility; but declined going farther with them, as my business led me another way.

"Which way, father?" said the Patrico.[7]

"To a place called Woodlands, in the county of Essex."

"We are but just come from that village," said he.

"Indeed!—Can you tell me any tidings from thence?"

"What family there would you enquire after?"

"That of Squire Longford, who now lives at the Manor-house."

"Who did live there, you mean."

"Well, what did you know of him?"

"What I know is from common report, which calls him a great villain."

"It calls him truly."

"He then told me the heads of the story I have related to you; and added, farther, that the daughter of the late Henry Marney had lived with a widow lady, who loved her dearly—that young Longford had fallen in love with her—that his father was enraged against him and her, and did her ill offices with the lady, her friend—that he promoted a marriage between her and a young farmer, whom she could not like—that the son of the rector of the parish loved her likewise; and was forbidden by his father to think of marriage, as neither of them could support a family, and it would be ruin to both. Young Dalby, being enflamed with love and jealousy, and provoked by opposition, stole Miss Marney away from her patroness, and was going with her to Scotland; but they were pursued, and brought back again.

"Old Longford persuaded the lady to send Miss Marney away from her; and she must have gone to the workhouse, but for the humanity of old Mr. Dalby, who took her into his protection, upon condition that his son should go to Cambridge directly, and not come home till he permitted him.

"All these things had such an effect upon Miss Marney, that she fell into a hasty decline. The lady, her friend, came to see her; she was reconciled to her, and offered to take her to her house again: but she declined it. She confessed that she loved young Dalby, but would not marry him to his ruin—She was going down to the grave, and did not wish to live. In short, she died, and was buried while we staid in the parish."

"Here," said Balderson, "I groaned with anguish. I exclaimed—"Oh, unfortunate family! Unhappy Anna Marney!—Yet, why do I say so, when she is released from a world of misery, while I sustain a life of cares and troubles?—The will of Heaven be done!"

"Can you tell me any farther particulars of the Longfords?"

"All the village mourned over Miss Marney: all cried shame on Longford! People cried out to their children—"There goes the man that ruined the Marneys! Learn to be contented with a little: it is better to be poor and honest, than to be rich and wicked; to be hated and despised, like that man!"

"Some of these things were said in Longford's hearing: whether they touched his heart, or whether the judgment of Heaven followed him, I know not; but it was said, that he was troubled in mind, and he conceited that he was haunted; and so truly he was, by an evil conscience.

"There came a gentleman, who had made a great fortune in trade, and yet bore a fair character, excepting that he was counted very close and covetous. His name was Strictland. Longford sold the estates to him. They said there was some scruple about the title; but, for that, he was obliged to abate of the price. So Mr. Strictland bought it, and Mr. Longford and his son left it immediately.

"Some say, they are gone into a foreign country; and others, that they are gone into the North of England: but, for certain, they have left Woodlands; and, like a candle's end, they went out with a stink."

"I thanked the Patrico, or father of the gipsies, for his intelligence; which had saved me the labour of my journey, and some part of the pain I should have suffered from hearing all these things upon the spot.

"I slept with my child in the hollow tree that night; and the next day, I took my leave of the gipsies, and re-trod my steps back to London, ruminating upon the various fates and fortunes of men.

"If we could divest ourselves of prejudices," said I, "it signifies little to the public, whether particular families rise into affluence, or sink into indigence. We all spring from the same source, and to all there is but one event."

"At my return home, I found a letter from the good young gentleman who had promised to make enquiry after my son's wages. He told me, that a young man, who called himself their brother, had received their wages, and given a discharge for the money.

"This could be no other man than Stevens; his base conduct was proved, past all doubt.

"I looked over my letter from my son James. I found in it a direction to the gentleman, his patron, at Madras, under which I might write to him. This I had not observed before; and I determined to make use of it now.

"I wrote an account of all that had befallen me during his absence, and a minute account of every part of Stevens's conduct; desiring him, in future, to direct to me at the house where I formerly lived: and I sent three duplicates, by as many different ships.

"Thus I went on, from year to year, hoping and expecting to hear from my son; and, though always disappointed, I did not despair of it.

"My mind often ran upon going to Woodlands, and to shew my boy the seat of his ancestors, and all the places adjoining; to shew him his grandfather's tombstone, and to relate his story; to impress these ideas upon his tender mind, and to excite in him a laudable ambition to imitate the virtues of his family, and avoid all that can disgrace it.

"I had another and secondary motive: to try the spirit of the present proprietor of Woodlands, whether he had the charity and generosity to assist me in putting out the unfortunate heir of the family of Marney, so that he might earn his bread in a creditable way; and not lead the life of a stranger and a vagabond, as he had done hitherto.

"These, Madam, were the motives that led me to Woodlands; and these made me send the boy to try Mr. Strictland's charity.

"I was near at hand: and, if he was encouraged, I would have come up and told my story and his; if repulsed, I was at hand to protect him.

"You know all that followed. In your heart, lady, I found all that I wished.

"I was afflicted with an ague, last winter, and that reduced me to a state of beggary. My cloaths were worn out, and I had no money to buy new ones. You have cloathed me and my boy, and enabled us to get on in our former way of life. We humbly thank you for all favours; particularly, for giving a patient attention to my story. May God give his blessing to you and yours!"

Here Balderson ended his story. He bowed, and motioned to retire.

I beckoned him to stay. I had heard him with various emotions, and now could hardly command my voice to speak to him upon the most interesting subject.

"Could you part with your boy?"

"To do him good, I would part with my life."

"Perhaps, it would be a lesser trial, than to be separated from him. However, I will not be so cruel to ask it. I design to answer your secondary motive of coming hither. I will put your boy in a way to earn his living; but he must lay aside his name for a time: I must not be known to be his friend. You must continue in this neighbourhood, and you shall see him once in a week. I will allow you a shilling a week for yourself, and I will see you sometimes. This lady will be my substitute, and she will pay your pension for me. Will you, Balderson, accept my conditions?"

The man trembled with joy and gratitude. He prostrated himself upon the earth; he lifted up his eyes to Heaven, and tears ran fast down his cheeks.

The boy ran up to him, and clasped his arms round his neck—"What makes you cry, grandfather? Henry will not leave you for any body!"

Balderson arose—"Forgive him, lady! I will make him sensible of his obligations to you; and we will wait your commands."

I desired Miss Elton to buy some necessaries for the boy. We agreed, that he should come to her on the Monday following, and that she should go with him to the school. Also, she was to pay Balderson his pension. These matters being settled, they departed, and we returned home.

Every thing that we had planned was executed.

Here I shall leave them for a time, and return to the affairs of my own family.

Mr. Strictland fell into a decline. He grew very fretful; but did not believe himself in any danger, nor would accept of any assistance. He followed his workmen, as usual; not would be persuaded to take any care of himself.

My second son had all the distempers incident to children: the whooping cough came last, and totally destroyed his constitution. He died at three years old.

I grieved for him: but his father's sorrow had more the appearance of anger; and it seemed pointed at me, as if it was my fault.

The year following, I lost my youngest child. She died of teething;[8] and Mr. Strictland was very angry at it. He said it was d——d hard!

The two surviving ones were very healthy and promising.

I taught them to read, as soon as they could speak plain; and their proficiency was a sweet reward for my trouble and attention. They loved me in return; and I spent my pleasantest hours in their company.

Mr. Strictland loved them in his way; but the harshness of his temper, and the warmth of his expressions, made them afraid of him, and checked the affection they would otherwise have felt for their father.

Ill-tempered people suffer more pain than they inflict; and this is a just punishment of Heaven. It is not more our duty than our interest to restrain our passions; our happiness depends upon it.

One day that Mr. Strictland was riding, near Mr. Elton's, he was taken with a faintness that took away his strength. He rung at the gate. The servant came, and saw that he was ill; he helped him to alight, and led him into the house, where he had a fit. The family gave him all the assistance in their power, and shewed every mark of friendship and attention.

After he was perfectly recovered, Mr. Elton took the liberty to advise him to settle his worldly affairs: that it would not hasten his death, but only make a due preparation for it—that he spoke as his parish-priest, who thought it a part of his duty. He also desired him to consult a physician.

Mr. Strictland received his advice properly, and thanked

him for it. He said, he would consider of it: that he had no good opinion of doctors or lawyers; but, in some cases, they might be necessary evils.

They invited him to stay to dinner; but he chose rather to come home.

A short time afterwards, he called at Mr. Southgate's, and had another fit there. Mr. Southgate gave him the same advice that Mr. Elton had done; to make his will, if he had any particular dispositions to make. They both thought him declining very fast, and that he should lose no time.

He desired Mr. Southgate to come and dine with him the first day he could spare; and added—"Bring an honest lawyer with you, if you know one."

Mr. Southgate appointed the Monday following. Mr. Elton was invited to meet him.

I wondered what this invitation meant. Mr. Strictland said, it was upon private business.

He took his guests into one of the other parlours, which was contrary to his usual custom; and, when there, asked them to be his executors.

He said, he hated lawyers: that one of that craft had ruined the family of Marney, formerly proprietors of Woodlands; and he was resolved that none of them should be his executors—that he believed them both to be honest men, and that they would not wrong his wife and children; and therefore he begged them to take upon them this trust.

They both thought well of me; and thought it would be for my service to accept it, lest it might otherwise fall upon strangers, who might give me trouble.

They both promised to accept it, and to discharge it faithfully.

In the afternoon, the attorney came, by Mr. Southgate's order. He took minutes from Mr. Strictland's mouth, and was ordered to get them put into proper form as soon as possible; and, within a week, the will was signed, sealed, and executed, in due form.

It was fortunate that this business was done at the time; for Mr. Strictland did not live above a month after.

He had fainting-fits often: but still he thought there was no danger; yet he grew weaker every day.

One day, he consented to lay down after dinner. I assisted him, and sat by his bedside till I saw him asleep; and then went into the common parlour.

At the usual hour of tea-drinking, I sent Mrs. Gilson to see whether her master was awake. She staid some minutes; and then came down in an odd way, looking frighted.

"Is your master asleep?" said I.

She answered—"Yes. He will never more wake in this world, I believe!"

I was surprized; though we had long expected this awful event.

I went up stairs with her, and found it was even as she had said. Mr. Strictland was departed without a struggle, and lay as if asleep.

I sent immediately for Mr. Elton, and put myself under his direction. I was affected with various emotions, and could hardly understand my own sensations. I felt compassion and concern for the father of my children, thus dying in the prime of his life. I wished that I had loved him more! I wished that he had allowed me to love him! I was awed, and frightened; yet I could not take any blame to myself.

Poor Gilson was deeply affected. She loved him, as a parent loves her child; and excused his faults, as a parent does by a froward one.

Miss Elton kindly accompanied her father, and staid with me till the most distressing scenes were all over.

The next day, Mr. Southgate and Mr. Elton came together. The will was opened, and I found myself joined with these two gentlemen in the executorship, which I had not expected. I was sensible that I owed it to their good offices; and they owned that they had urged it, as it would enable me to receive the rents, and to act for my children.

We united in paying the last duties to Mr. Strictland, and in settling his affairs. I found new business and duties coming forward every day.

I will here conclude this enormous pacquet, and send it to Mrs. Martin, to convey to your hand. I shall soon have another ready. I have matter sufficient for another, before I conclude my story; but what remains will be drawn into a smaller compass.

I have also a farther demand upon you; but this I will enlarge upon in my next pacquet.

Believe me, always, my Fanny,

Yours, faithfully,
RACHEL STRICTLAND.

LETTER IX
Mrs. Strictland, to Mrs. Darnford, in continuation.

MR. Strictland had a mean opinion of women: he had frequently told me so. He said, they were not to be trusted with power, nor with money: for the latter they had no occasion; having meat, drink, and lodgings, provided for them.

"But, then, cloaths and linen, Sir? Have we no occasion for them?" said I.

"Yes; but not for half the quantities you buy, and make up. Men are more reasonable; they seldom have more than are necessary. I never have more than one coat in a year; and I wear them one under another, to spare them."

There was no replying to this argument. "*I do so,*" was a clincher.

Thus thinking, and thus acting, how can I account for his last disposition of his property? Can I do otherwise than impute it to the influence of the two gentlemen, who assisted him in making his will, and to hasten through a disagreeable business?

Thus it was—He left all his landed estates, not less than eighteen hundred pounds a year, to his only son; under the following restrictions. When he should come to the age of twenty-one, he was to be paid a rent-charge of one thousand pounds sterling to begin the world with. He was to be put into possession of the house called Woodlands, and to reside there. The rest of the income of the estates was to accumulate, *from that time*, till he should attain to twenty-five years; and then he was to receive it, with all the remainder of his fortune.

The estates were entailed upon his sons, grandsons, &c. and, failing heirs, to his daughters; failing both, to his sister, in like manner: and all the heirs subjected to the same restrictions.

To his daughter, the sum of six thousand pounds, if she married with consent of her mother and guardians, to be paid on the day of marriage. If otherwise, to be paid three thousand when she should come of age, and the remainder at twenty-five years.

To his widow, six thousand pounds, (somewhat more than he received with her) over and beside her marriage-settlement.

To Martha Gilson, widow, his faithful servant, an annuity of twenty pounds a year, for her life; and ten guineas for mourning.

To every servant in his house, one year's wages.

He appoints his wife Rachel Strictland, the Reverend Thomas Elton, and Richard Southgate, Gent. Joint executors of his will, and guardians and trustees for his children. He leaves an hundred pounds legacy to each of the gentlemen, for their trouble.

He makes his wife the residuary legatee. He empowers her to receive the whole rents and income of his fortune during the minority of his children; that she may provide for the maintenance and education of his children, and that they may be dutiful and obedient to her. But he restrains it by the following conditions—

She is to receive all his income, and to have the care of his children, so long as she remains a widow; but, in case the said Rachel Strictland should marry again, she is no longer the receiver of his rents, or the guardian and trustee of his children: yet, even in this case, he gives her back all her own fortune, in addition to her marriage-settlement; and the children are to be taken from her, and put under the care of the other guardians, who are to be accountable for the rents till his son comes of age; and, in that case, they are entitled to an additional legacy of two hundred pounds each.

He then concludes, and executes this last Will and Testament.

Now, my friend, what think you of this Will? I will tell you my opinion; that it is the most generous, just, and prudent one, that I ever saw or heard of.

I subscribe to the conditions with my hand and heart; and wish more men were as wise as Mr. Strictland, in guarding their property for their children, and restraining their widows from squandering their fortunes, and buying themselves husbands.

I have, at this moment, in my mind's eye, a widow, turned of sixty years of age, in whose hands a too generous husband left the disposal of a great part of his property. This woman, instigated by a passion that, at her years, is a disgrace to her sex, married a man under thirty; settled all her property upon him; wronged, cheated, and insulted her children, and grandchildren; and became the contempt and disgrace of her family, of her sex, and of the world.

It is not our sex only that have played the fool in these cases; yet it is in the power of the other only to lay a restraint upon us and themselves. It would be a wise act of the Legislature, who have limited the time of entering into matrimonial connections, to set limits to the time also when they should cease, and put the superannuated lovers into custody.

It is not easy to describe the situation of my mind at this time, both with respect to the past and the present. I wished to have a grateful sense of Mr. Strictland's generosity and confidence towards me; yet, on the other hand, I had a smarting remembrance of his churlish temper and behaviour. How was I to blend together such contradictory feelings as I could neither investigate nor comprehend!

I resolved not to affect a grief I did not feel, nor yet an indifference that might be deemed disrespectful; but to shew my gratitude by a faithful discharge of the trust he had honoured me with, and a constant and unremitting attention to the interest and happiness of his children.

The gentlemen informed me, that, being named first as executor, the chief of the power resided in me; but they would always be ready to give me their advice and assistance, whenever I should call upon them.

I told them, I should never take any material step without their advice and approbation; and I wished them to know every part of my conduct.

"Permit me, Madam," said Mr. Southgate, "to ask, whether you propose to live at Woodlands, or not; and whether you do not think, in that case, it might be let to advantage, during the minority of your son?

"That," said I, "requires some consideration. I wish to pay all due respect to Mr. Strictland's memory, and to second his wishes and intentions to the utmost of my power. I know it was his design to bring up his son to the same business which he followed himself: he wished him to study agriculture, and to practise it. I would not oblige him to it, against his inclination; but I would give him an opportunity to know what it is, and to make a fair choice. It is more than time that he was put to school; but I should wish him to spend his summer vacation at Woodlands constantly, to see the occupations of the husbandman, and to know the farming business."

"But, in the mean time, who is to take care of the land? There is between two and three hundred pounds a year estate, which Mr. Strictland used to keep in his own hands: who is to take care of that?"

"Why, Sir, I have been thinking of that. I would put in a bailiff, or overlooker of the farm, during my son's minority; and he should give an account of the profits of the farm to you, Sir, who are best qualified to understand it; and, if you would be so kind as to overlook him, I should be ready to make acknowledgment for your trouble."

He seemed displeased with what I had said. I feared I had affronted him by offering him an acknowledgment for his services. But, after he was gone, Gilson told me, that, from things that had fallen from him, she suspected that Mr. Southgate would like to farm the lands himself.

I asked Gilson, where was her son? She said, he was headman to a farmer in the next parish, but would be disengaged at Michaelmas.

I sent for Mr. Elton, and told him the plan I had laid; which was, to take young Gilson for my bailiff and overlooker.

I said, Mrs. Gilson's long and faithful services well deserved a recompence; that I meant to continue her as housekeeper for me at Woodlands, and to give her son's company and protection, which would be making her happy. I could trust the house and furniture to her care and fidelity: I and my children could go and come as it suited us; and they would be always ready to receive us, and happy to see us with them.

Mr. Elton said, my plan was at once benevolent and prudent; but that he had something to propose, that, he thought, would be an improvement to it, and what he was desired to mention to me. He said, there were two farms laid together, and either of them was a sufficient one to employ one overlooker or tenant—that Mr. Southgate wanted to put his eldest son into business, and wished to have one of these farms, which was, in a manner, under his own eye—that he would give me a fair price for it, and refer it to arbitrators chosen between ourselves. He wished to have the land nearest his own—that there was an house upon it, which Mr. Strictland let in tenements to three of his workmen; if I would have that house put into a tenantable state, he would be at half the expences, and in every thing would refer to a third person—that Mr. Southgate was my neighbour and friend, and I might oblige him without any disadvantage to myself, but rather the contrary.

I told Mr. Elton, that I would readily adopt his improvement to my scheme; and that he should chuse a person to be my arbitrator, and both of them should treat with Mr. Southgate.

When I told Gilson my intention respecting her son and herself, she could hardly believe that such good fortune was reserved for her. Her joy and gratitude were extreme. I told her, I was deeply in her debt, for her good offices towards myself, my husband, and my children; and I should study for opportunities to repay them.

Mr. Elton and Mr. Southgate came to our house soon after. They brought with them two eminent farmers, as arbitrators between Mr. Southgate and me. The lands were divided, the terms settled, and men were set to work to ditching, fencing, and laying out the lands. The tenants were warned to leave the house as soon as possible; but I was concerned for them, and enquired after places for their accommodation.

There were five cottages, that stood straggling, with ground behind them: they were destined to be pulled down, rather than be at the expence of repairing them.

Being used to hear these subjects discussed between Mr. Strictland and Mr. Southgate, I had imbibed the opinion, that consolidating farms, and destroying cottages, was a cruel and wicked policy, and had a tendency to depopulate the villages, and destroy the peasantry of the land. I therefore declared myself the protector and patroness of this most useful order of men.

I bought the five cottages, and the ground about them. I ordered them to be put into thorough repair immediately. Three of them were appropriated to the three families that were warned out of the farm-house hired by Mr. Southgate; and they were to be got ready as soon as possible. A fourth I made considerable improvements in, and destined it to a purpose that I shall explain by and by. The fifth was allotted to a reduced family, that I protected.

I could have let twenty cottages, if I had them to dispose of; but I had business enough upon my hands; and I was pleased with, and proud of, my new estate.

In the next place, I had to think of Henry Marney, and to appoint his destination.

I sent for the schoolmaster; and enquired of him, what kind of boy he was, and what proficiency he made.

The schoolmaster spoke very highly of him. He said, that Henry was an exceeding clever youth, and deserved a better education than it was in his power to give him.

"Then he shall have it," said I; "and I thank you for giving me this information."

I paid the master his due, and something more. I ordered him to send the boy to Woodlands in the following week. I determined to examine his capacity and disposition, and to decide for him accordingly.

I put him into decent mourning before I took him into the family. I presented him to my son: I told him, this youth was descended from an honourable family, fallen into misfortunes, and I wished him to love and be kind to him.

To Henry I said—"This youth is to be your patron, friend, and benefactor; and you must love and honour him."

He said—"It is enough for me to know that he is your son."

I answered—"No: you must love him for his own sake."

"But, I must first love him for yours. Can I ever forget what you have done for me and my grandfather?"

"You are right to remember it, my good lad; but, in future, I would wish you to attach yourself to my son: he will have it in his power to be your friend hereafter."

He said, he would obey me in every thing.

My son had never before a companion, except his sister. Young Marney shewed him the plays of boys, in their different seasons: he played with him, and amused him in a way he had never known before.

I had no occasion to tell Jonathan to love his companion: he took a strong affection for him, and was never easy but when he was with him; and his greatest fear was to lose him.

"Pray, mamma," he would say, "don't send Henry away from me again: I cannot spare him."

"But, my child, he must go to school, and you too."

"Then, let us go together," said he; "and then I shall be happy."

"I will consider of it, and let you know in proper time."

I consulted Mr. Elton about a school for them; for I resolved that they should go together, and that I would encourage their friendship, in hopes of it's being of mutual advantage to them. Young Marney had nothing rude or vulgar in his manners. He had conversed chiefly with his grandfather, who had not suffered him to acquaint with other boys of his own degree, but had taught him courtesy and gentleness. He had never had companions till he went to school, where he behaved so well as to be beloved by the master and the scholars.

In two years time, he was much improved: he read English very well, and wrote a tolerable hand. There was a foundation laid, upon which should be raised any kind of edifice that might be judged necessary and proper.

I have not spoken of his grandfather; but, I trust, you will give me credit for my conduct towards him.

You will think, I could not take his darling under my roof, and forget the cares and sufferings of his venerable parent.

It was one of my cares to provide a bed of repose for his old age. It was now in my power to do it, without injury to any one. I had been contriving a place of peace and comfort for his residence.

There were two old women, sisters, who were under a peculiar distress. I had assisted them privately in my husband's lifetime, but now I took them openly under my protection.

They had lived in a miserable cottage, that hardly sheltered them from the weather. One was a widow, the other an old maiden. The widow had a daughter, grown up: she and the sister went out to washing, ironing, cleaning, and every other kind of women's work. The widow was lame: she staid at home, did needle-work, and spun wool.

They were honest and industrious, and got their living; and always paid their rent punctually, which was forty shillings a year. Sickness visited this poor family: the widow was laid by with the rheumatism; the sister and daughter had agues. They were incapable of work, and lived upon the little they had saved to pay their rent. The owner of the cottage, almost as poor as themselves, pressed for the rent. They were going to sell their beds, and to lie on the floor, when Mr. Elton heard of their distress. He made a collection for them; the rent was paid; and they remained in the cottage, which was to them a comfortable dwelling.

Miss Elton made their case known to me. I had a receipt for an ague, of approved efficacy, which I sent them; and also victuals, which were wanting to make my medicine take effect. I sent them warm coverlids[1] for their beds, and ordered the thatching of their house to be repaired.

Between the Eltons and myself, we carried them through a severe winter. In the spring, they recovered, and returned to their work and their wages again.

From this time, I kept my eye upon them, and gave them casual assistances; and with them I intended to place my friend Balderson.

For them I reserved my fourth cottage; to which I made great additions and improvements.

There was an entry with a door on each side of it; a staircase, which divided the two upper rooms; a kind of loft over these, to put lumber in. The best room on the upper floor was for Balderson. I furnished it with a good linsey-wolsey[2] bed and window-curtain; the rest of the furniture suitable and comfortable. In the room below stairs, I put a matt and great chair for Mr. Balderson, and several other necessaries and conveniences.

I set them rent-free, paid them for Balderson's board, and settled them a comfortable and happy family.

I had likewise to reduce and regulate my own family.

At Michaelmas, Mr. Joseph Gilson entered my service. The head-man was very much offended: he said, he was as capable of overlooking the farm as Joe Gilson, and he would not stay to have another servant put over him.

I said, he was at liberty to go, or to stay upon my conditions. He said, that was a poor reward for faithful services.

I told him, he might stay till he could get a place that suited him; and I was ready to give him a good character, which, I thought, was all that was due from me to him.

The man was dissatisfied, and went grumbling about the house.

I thought there was some reason for his complaint, and considered how to satisfy him.

I spoke to Mr. Southgate upon the subject; and he offered to take him as head-man to his son in the new farm. He spoke to him, and engaged him in his service, which made all easy.

I retained no more servants than were necessary for the management of the farm. Mrs. Gilson was to be mistress of them all, and to give me an account of their proceedings. Mr. Southgate promised to superintend the farming business.

Mr. Elton recommended me to a worthy clergyman, his friend, who took twenty youths to educate. He said, they had all the advantages of a public school, without the dangers of one; and, he thought, I could not do better than to place my son there.

I enquired, whether two vacancies were there? I received for answer, that there would be two after Christmas.

I resolved to stay at Woodlands till I should have fulfilled this duty, and then to go to London for a month or two. I solicited Mr. Elton to give me his daughter's company to London. He was very unwilling to comply with my request. He said, London was the place, of all others, the most likely to spoil young people; to pervert their good principles, and give them bad ones instead of them. I promised to take care what company I should carry her into. I returned to the charge so often, that he could not entirely refuse me; but he insisted that she should return on his first notice. He said, he was not certain that London would not corrupt me; that he should judge by me, how far his daughters were to be trusted, and whether they could return to their own station again.

Between Michaelmas and Christmas, I made an excursion through the counties of Norfolk, Suffolk, and Essex, accompanied by Miss Elton and my daughter, and left my boys to the care of Mrs. Gilson. This tour was of service to my health and spirits. I was amused, and enjoyed my liberty without abusing it.

> "Tow'red cities please us then,
> "And the busy hum of men."[3]

I had been so long secluded from these scenes, that it seemed like going into another world; and I seemed afraid of mixing in society.

I was astonished at surveying the trades and manufactures of different towns, and the buz of the number of inhabitants.

I staid not long any where, and returned to Woodlands before Christmas. I thought there was something right in spending my Christmas there. I had not run away from it immediately; I had employed my time usefully; and, when I had sent my son to school, I was free to enjoy that liberty of which I had been so long deprived.

Mr. Elton gave me credit for it: he praised my conduct; and said, it gave him confidence in me in future, and encouraged him to trust his daughter to my care.

The boys were rejoiced at my return, and gave me unfeigned marks of affection and sincerity.

My daughter was offended at being excluded from their plays and exercises; but now, she took upon her,[4] from being allowed to go abroad with me, and to see great towns, and to give account of her travels.

As soon as the holidays were over, I carried the boys to school. I cautioned Henry Marney against mentioning the manner of life he had led with his grandfather; but, at the same time, to avoid telling untruths; but to be discreet, and to know how to keep a secret.

I told the master, that this boy was descended from a good family, but by misfortunes reduced to indigence; that he had lost some time in his education, and I wished him to have additional lessons, that he might recover the ground he had lost. My son ought to have been sent to school sooner; but he was four years younger, and might recover, and overtake the other youths of his age.

Balderson parted with his Henry with a magnanimity that did him honour. He thought any reluctance on his part, would be ingratitude to his and his child's benefactor.

I now prepared for my journey to London. I hired a job-coach, which carried Miss Elton, myself, my daughter, and my maid Peggy.

I promised myself a great deal of pleasure, but found myself as much disappointed as people generally are in the schemes they form, and the expectations they build upon them.

Miss Elton and I were like people dropt from the clouds into a strange land. We knew nobody, nor did any body know us. There seemed to me a strange alteration in the dresses and manners of the people: they were as foreigners to me, and I to them. We saw the new buildings, and admired the magnitude and populousness of the great city. We saw all that excites admiration and surprize; the churches, the theatres, the pantheon, the hospitals, and all that strangers desire to see.

We were, indeed, as much strangers as if we had come from another country; and wanted an interpreter, to make us understand all we saw; for to us it was incomprehensible.

I had been there but once before, Miss Elton never; and we were exactly in the same state of ignorance, wonder, and disappointment.

In the churches, we heard the doctrines of high Calvinism,[5] which I always thought had been confined to the dissenters; and, I was told, all the popular preachers held forth these dogmas. They frightened me, but they did not convince me.

I said something of this kind to Miss Elton. A gentleman-like man, who assisted us to our coach, heard me.

"He said—"You have heard, Madam, that the good people of England like to be told they are ruined. In like manner, they are best pleased with those preachers who send them all to the devil. There is a fashion in preaching, as in every thing else; and these men are now all the fashion."

I thanked him for his information: but I dared not encourage his acquaintance; for, I had been told, it was dangerous to converse with strangers in London.

I was equally disappointed at the theatres. The good old plays, that I was used to admire, were so mutilated, that I hardly knew them again; and the new ones had nothing that interested me.

A third subject gave me serious concern—the increase of criminals, and the improvements in the arts of stealing and picking pockets, house-breaking, and every kind of robbery.

"Surely," said I, "these are not merely conjectures: they are demonstrations of the increase of vice of every kind; and that our laws, or the administration of them, are very defective. There must be great faults somewhere."

We new-modelled our cloaths, but not to the extremes of fashion. I resolved to attempt a medium between them. But fashion loves extremes, and demands unlimited homage from her votaries: to her they sacrifice reason, propriety, and even common sense.

I once saw the following lines written in a lady's pocket-book. If the admonition is good, it signifies nothing who was the author—

> "Let not your form, or inclination,
> "Be govern'd by the harlot fashion
> "Treat her, in manners, and in dress,
> "As handmaid, not as governess."

I honour those who have courage enough to withstand the torrent; and, without affecting singularity, dress within the bound of modesty, and simplicity of manners: it indicates every thing that is right.

Mr. Elton began to remonstrate on our stay in London. We went thither on the twentieth of January, and staid till the end of March. His last letter was more like a command than a request. Miss Elton resolved to obey it, and I to carry her safely home.

We were joyfully received at the parsonage. Mr. Elton confessed I was better than he expected, and returned to his first notice.

My worthy Gilson wept for joy at my return to Woodlands. She said, that I had spoiled her by my kindness and indulgence, and she could hardly endure my absence. I assured her, I should see her often; and that I had not yet determined where to fix my residence in the winter, and in summer I should be chiefly at Woodlands.

I made an excursion in the spring, and took Kitty Elton for my companion. Her father limited the time of my return. Finding he was unwilling to let his daughters be long absent from home, and was in prudent apprehension of their being unsettled, and uneasy in the station where Heaven had placed them, I cast about for a companion whom I might retain with me, and who might assist me in the education of my daughter.

My mind rested upon you, my dear Fanny. I began my chace after you. I went to several places before I could find any means to trace you. At last, I went to W——: there I met with Mrs. Martin and Mrs. Bailey; and, by their means, I got a kind of access to my friend.

You have told me your story; and you have insisted upon mine. I have given it sincerely; and I expect your remarks with respect and apprehension.

And now, my dear friend, I draw my business to a point, and must insist upon a categorical answer.

You ask, what farther I have to ask of you? How far does my curiosity extend? Even to the extent of the limits you have prescribed to it.

You have told me, you are engaged in the service of an unfortunate lady, who wanted a friend, and deserved to find one. You have half promised to relate her story to me.

The story of an haunted house, and a lady deranged in her mind, and restored by your offices, is sufficiently interesting to excite a colder curiosity than mine. But, when I have heard it, I am to judge, whether you can, and whether you ought to leave her.

This brings me to the second point I have to insist on.

When you have told me this story, I must again ask, whether, and when, you will permit me to see you? Shall I come to you, or will you come to me?

If you refuse to tell me this, and conceal yourself from me in mystery and obscurity, I must then give you up to the person who holds you by a stronger tie than a long friendship and disinterested affection.

This I am unwilling to believe. You have told me a great part of your story, and given me reason to expect the remainder.

I wait for your next with no small degree of impatience: it will enable me to decide on many things that are yet in suspence. Hasten it to me as soon as possible, and depend upon my fidelity and secrecy where it is necessary. I am, my dear friend,

Yours unfeignedly,
RACHEL STRICTLAND.

Volume III

LETTER X
Mrs. Darnford, to Mrs. Strictland.

I HAVE received your concluding pacquet, and will now speak to the contents.

I am obliged for your own story, and declare myself highly satisfied with your conduct in trying situations. In some cases it deserves applause, and in others it claims excuse.

It seems to me, that you never loved Mr. Strictland well enough to overlook his faults. I have known some women in your situation, that, by a strong affection, have borne all kinds of ill usage, and still loved their husbands; and others, that knew not when they were kindly treated, but were ungrateful and unjust to the best and worthiest of men. I confess, yours did not go the right way to gain your affections; and that there was great merit in performing all your duties under these circumstances. That he loved and esteemed you, is clear from the last solemn act of his life; and you have done justice to his memory. His will is, indeed, what you have called it, just, generous, and prudent. You have only to observe the duties arising from your situation, to make yourself, and those who depend on you, easy and happy.

I am deeply interested in the memoirs of the Marney family. I respect Mr. Balderson extremely, and think he deserves the epithet which Homer gives to Ulysses—"the much-enduring man." With great sensibility, and warm affections, he is humble, patient, and resigned to the will of Heaven. This is true Christian fortitude, and cannot fail of it's reward, either here or hereafter. Heaven has raised him up as a friend, to support and cherish his old age. He is weaned from the world, and is daily preparing for a better.

I sincerely wish the youth may deserve your patronage and protection: but, remember, the most obliged persons are not always the most grateful. I venture to give you this warning, that, in case you should be disappointed, you may not be surprized.

I honour your noble spirit as it deserves. You have laid in a stock of benevolent actions, that will cheer your heart as long as you live; and may your life be prolonged for the sake of many!

And, now, I must reply to your last paragraph. I am angry with it: it supposes me unjust and ungrateful. How ought I to resent it? If I were indeed so, I should not take much pains to answer the imputation; but I will shew my sense of it by a better way—by fulfilling all the duties that such generous friendship enjoins, and which I have given you room to expect. But I waited to see whether you would urge it any farther. You do urge; you insist upon it; and I am going to obey you.

The lady, my friend and companion, will be happy to receive you here; but it is necessary that you should first know who and what she is. Her story is interesting; her trials have exceeded yours and mine: she has been comforted, and restored to reason, and even tranquillity, by kindness and tenderness; and she is grateful, to enthusiasm, to her friend and servant.

You may remember Mrs. Martin's making mention of a seafaring gentleman, Captain Maurice by name, who first brought a child to be under my care; and afterwards engaged me to take the care of his lady, who was in a state of insanity.

The fatigues of the school had hurt my health. I wanted air, and exercise, and quiet, to restore me.

I was not desirous to undertake this charge: I wished to know more of the lady, and of the gentleman, first; and whether there were any hopes of her recovery. I asked many questions; and Captain Maurice, at last, gave me a perfect information of the particulars.

Captain Maurice was a stout, thick-set man, with a dark complexion, and thick black eye-brows. His looks bespoke courage and assurance; his manners were courteous, and even polite; he spoke Italian, and that was the introduction to our acquaintance. I met him at Mr. Sorling's; and his wife recommended us to each other.

Upon farther acquaintance, I perceived a cloud of care and anxiety, that hung over his brow, which was afterwards sufficiently explained.

I shall make Captain Maurice tell his own story; and, as nearly as I can, in his own words. You are to suppose him such as I have described, walking backward and forward all the time; sometimes turning towards me, and at others going from me—

"I have heard much of you, Madam; and, since I have seen and conversed with you, I have found you to exceed all that I was told. There is so much gentleness and candour about you, that I could tell all my thoughts to you, sooner than to any body else.

"I am a man of many faults, and am now doing penance for them; but I am desirous to repair the mischiefs I have done, as far as lies in my power. I will convince you of this, by telling you all that relates to the lady I have been speaking of.

"I was bred a sailor, under an uncle who was as bold a seaman as ever walked between stem and stern. He was in the merchants service; and went to Naples and to Messina, and was in great credit with the English factories at both places. After the death of one of his patrons, he struck out a new course of life for himself. He had observed, that the Italians were very fond of English goods; particularly hardware, cabinet-goods, toys and trinkets of various kinds, and chairs of walnut-tree and mahogany. Those made in Naples are very rude, and old-fashioned; and it is but of late years that they have discovered the superiority of the goods of other countries.

"My uncle had another nephew, a sister's son, who made two or three voyages with him; he was of a more delicate make, and of a timorous disposition. I was his favourite, because I feared nothing. After our return to England, he bound my cousin to a taylor in London; saying, he was just good enough for that trade, and he wanted no milk-sops to go with him.

"I then enjoyed his favour, without a rival: and, when he died, he left my cousin five hundred pounds, to set him up in his business; and to me he left his ship, and the remainder of his fortune.

"I pursued the track he had marked out for me, and made some improvements upon his plan.

"I was well known, and respected, both at Naples and Messina. I liked the first place by far the best, and I sometimes staid several months there. I made acquaintance with many gentlemen there. I was often invited to dinner at the houses of the principal merchants; and some people of the quality did not disdain to notice me, though they are most of them as proud as Lucifer, and some of them are as poor as Job. They are cruelly oppressed with taxes; and the maxim is, to kick and be kicked.

The nobles insult the lower degrees of men; they abuse, and sometimes kill, their servants.

"I used to brag of English liberty and property. The young men loved to set me on talking; and I, sometimes, was more talkative than wise.

"One young gentleman told me, I was not a Christian. I repeated our Form of Baptism, to convince him that I was. The silly youth told his confessor all that passed between us; and that the English were not heretics, as he had been told. The confessor was in a rage, and threatened punishment to the Englishman who dared to affirm that he was not an heretic.

I had a friend who reported this to me. He advised me to be more prudent in future, and promised to ward off the danger for this time.

"Not long after, the same company tried to get me again upon the same subject; but I had my cue. I told them, I was only a poor seaman, and not a missionary; that I wore my religion in my heart, and would not give offence to any other's, nor would ever again speak upon that subject.

"This behaviour of mine pleased most of the company, and introduced me to the acquaintance of a young gentleman, called Don Antonio di Soranzo; and from that time he sought my friendship."

Here Captain Maurice sighed deeply; he seemed confused; and, after some hesitation, he proceeded—

"This Don Antonio asked me many questions concerning England; it's laws, it's government, it's liberty. Whether Catholics were allowed to enjoy the liberty of their own manner of worship, and were not persecuted, nor molested?

"I told him, truly, that we were of a more liberal spirit, and that every man might serve God in his own way: that your property was well secured; and, if people paid all that was due by law, they could not be injured by any one. I mentioned our trials by juries, and all the precious rights and privileges we yet enjoy; and drew the comparison in favour of my own country.

"Don Antonio desired me to meet him at a certain coffeehouse, and he would trust me with a secret of great consequence to him, and consult me upon a scheme he had formed for himself. He named the time, and I was punctual to his appointment; when he told me his story, as follows—

"You know, that it is the custom of our country to give all the estate to the eldest son, and to condemn the younger to some profession from the hour of their birth. Thus I was destined to the church, without consulting my genius or inclination. I have protested against it repeatedly, but I could hardly be heard. I had an uncle, who had set an example of resistance to all the younger brothers of the family. He disdained the pittance and the appointment, and went, in the train of an ambassador, to Madrid. He travelled all over Spain; then through France, over the Alps, and through Italy. Instead of coming to Naples, he went to Venice. There he made acquaintance with some young men in the mercantile line; he engaged in their house; and from thence wrote to his friends, and asked for his portion, to employ in business. They execrated the meanness of his spirit, in preferring business to the church or the army: however, they sent the money intended for his service, and did not wish to hear any more of him.

"After twenty years absence, he returned to Naples, rich, and a bachelor. These circumstances rendered him a welcome guest to my father: moreover, he declared an intention to leave his fortune into our family.

"This good uncle took my part; and my father, not chusing to disoblige him, kept his views for me in suspense, and left him free to give his advice upon them.

"There was, in Naples, an old lady, whom he had loved in his youth. She was then a widow, and in a declining state of health. He visited her; and, had she been in health, they would have been married; but she declined it upon that account. She had a niece, whom she had brought up from an infant, and adopted for her heir. My uncle proposed, that their friendship might descend to their heirs, and that one of his nephews might marry her niece. My father seized the occasion to marry his eldest son: so Don Girolamo was proposed to Donna Hortensia, the lady's aunt. She, like a true parent, said, if her niece liked him, she should make no objection; but it should depend upon Isabella to accept or refuse him.

"Things were in this situation, when I visited the ladies with my uncle. Don Girolamo had been there, and was permitted to visit, as a candidate for the lady's favour. I liked Isabella from the first minute I saw her: I thought it hard that all the blessings of love and fortune should fall into the lap of the elder brother.

"We Italians understand the language of love better than those of other countries. I loved Isabella; my eyes told her so, and she understood them: her's did not discourage me to proceed. I resolved to try my fortune. If she preferred my brother,

I would give over the pursuit for ever; but, if she gave me hopes of her preference, I would persevere, and my brother should give place to me: I would try to engage my uncle on my side, and I promised myself success. I visited Isabella almost every day: I found opportunities of declaring my passion. She declared, that she would never marry while her aunt lived; and that she would know the temper and disposition of the man she meant to make her husband. She gave me no denial: she permitted me to visit her, as a candidate for her favour; but she had not yet declared her choice.

"I met my brother there one day. He thought there was a secret intelligence between her and me: he was enflamed with rage and jealousy; he took a hasty leave, and gave me looks of anger and defiance.

"When I returned home, he had acquainted my father and my uncle with his suspicions; and I was interrogated, as if I had been before a court of judicature. I confessed the truth; that I loved Isabella, and sought to obtain her favour: that, if she declared a preference for my brother, I would desist immediately; but, if she made choice of me, he ought to do the same.

"My uncle espoused my cause. He said, it was a fair proposal; that my brother's eldership gave him advantages enough; and that I was free to pursue my fortune.

"Don Girolamo was so enraged, that he could hardly speak for passion. My father said, that Girolamo was first proposed to the lady, and I was invading his rights every way.

"I said, the lady was, by her aunt, left free to make her choice; that she had not yet made known, whether either of us was the man: I only waited for that; and I left it to her to decide my fate: I would submit to her decision, but not to any other; and so saying, I left the room. After this, my uncle was desired to use his influence with me, to give up my pretensions. He advised me to travel, as he had done in his youth; and promised to give me a large sum of money, and farther expectations at his decease. I still referred to the lady. I wrote to her, and gave my uncle a copy of my letter. I have also a copy about me; and I will read it to you, Seignior Inglese—

"MADAME,
"My brother has made a great disturbance in my family. My father and uncle have espoused his cause. I am urged, persuaded, and threatened, in order to induce me to give up my pretensions to you. I should not deserve your favour, if I

could not resist such measures. If you will speak the word, I will persevere till death. If you forbid me to hope for the blessing, I will obey your commands. Must I be sent to travel? or must I enter into holy orders? or must I die at your feet?— Speak, and decide my fate!"

"ANTONIO DI SORANZO."

"A few days afterwards, I received the following billet—

"THE fate of Don Antonio cannot yet be decided: it is for his safety that it should remain in suspense. He must not visit so often at Donna Hortensia's; he must not leave Naples for longer than a month; he must not shave his crown; he must neither presume nor despair, but wait patiently an event that depends on the will of Heaven."

"This event is the death of Donna Hortensia, which is expected every day; and I presume to hope, that then Isabella will be mine. If she was now to declare in my favour, I should be exposed to all the effects of my brother's resentment: it is thus that I understand the letter. I have formed a design, that, if she agrees to, will put it out of the power of our enemies to prevent or interrupt our union. And, now, Seignior Inglese, I shall ask your assistance. I propose, as soon as I can prevail on Isabella to bless me with her hand, to come on board your ship, and take a voyage with you to England. Time will abate the resentment of our friends. Perhaps they will invite us to return home. We shall visit your England, and perhaps France, and the Low Countries. We may settle where we please, and be happy in each other's company. You shall be our friend and assistant; and we will endeavour to make amends for the trouble we give you. And now, Sir, may I depend upon you?"

"I answered, that he might," said Captain Maurice; "and that I would wait the issue of this affair, and be his faithful servant.

"About a fortnight afterwards, I met Don Antonio again.

"All is well," said he: "I am now upon firm ground. I no longer visit at Donna Hortensia's; but I see Isabella privately at a neighbour's, who is in treaty with her for the house she now lives in. He is our friend and confident,[1] and will favour our escape, when the time is ripe for it. Isabella has given me her promise, and will be mine. I wait her pleasure, and am resigned to her disposal. I have told my uncle, that I mean shortly to set out upon my travels. My father and brother believe that I have given up my pretensions to Isabella. My uncle will advance me a considerable sum, whenever I call for it. All things are prepared; and I now, indeed, wait on the will of Heaven."

"I prepared for the reception of Don Antonio and Isabella on board my ship, and resolved to devote myself to their service.

"I met Don Antonio every week; and we engaged in a friendship that was to last during our lives, and seemed inviolable on both sides.

"One night, I received a note, to this effect—

"DONNA Hortensia is dead! As soon the last duties are paid, Isabella will be mine. She will go with me to any part of the world that I shall chuse: my resolution holds for a voyage to England; and I depend upon your honour and fidelity.

"A.S."

"After this, I saw Don Antonio frequently. He told me he was making preparations for his departure; that he had acquainted his uncle with his resolution to travel; and was to receive a sum of money from him within a fortnight; that Isabella was turning all her effects into money, for this purpose. She had sold her house to Don Dominico di Rossi, her neighbour and friend, who was commissioned to sell her other estates after her departure, and remit the money to England, for she was resolved not to settle in Naples.

"I advised them to take only sufficient money for present expences; and to remit the rest through the hands of the English Consul, to be paid to them in London.

"All things being prepared, I received a summons from Don Antonio—

"FOLLOW the bearer, who will conduct you to your friend, who waits for your presence to witness his happiness.

"A.S."

"I was conducted to the house of Don Dominico di Rossi; where Don Antonio welcomed me, and introduced me to Isabella, and to the master and mistress of the house.

"A priest came soon after, and the nuptials were solemnized. Present, Don Dominico, and his lady; their eldest son, and daughter; myself, and an old servant of Donna Hortensia's, who dearly loved Isabella, and upon whom she had settled a pension for life.

"After the ceremony, we had an elegant supper, and spent the evening every pleasantly.

"Donna Isabella informed us, that she had seen Don Girolamo yesterday, for the last time—that she had told him often, that she never would be his, but she had then forbid him to see her any more—that he left her in anger; but declared he would not give her up, and uttered menaces against the man she should favour—that she was resolved to put it out of his power to injure her or her husband, and that in kindness to all the parties concerned—and she was now ready to follow Don Antonio to any part of the world.

"I told her, I would do my best to accommodate her on board my ship; and that she might send her baggage as soon as she pleased, and I would see it safely stowed. Don Antonio said, they should send it on the morrow: that he and Isabella should be concealed at Don Dominico's; and, in the evening, he should see me on board the ship.

"Three days after, Don Antonio and his lady came on board; and, on the fourth, we set sail for England."

Here Captain Maurice stopped; saying—"I believe, Madam, I have tired you with my story, though this is only the beginning of it. I will proceed with it another time."

"No, Sir," said I; "*I* am not tired, but *you* may, with talking and walking. Sit down a while, and rest; and proceed at your own time."

"With your leave, that shall be now; for I wish it was done: it causes me many painful recollections. I am used to walk the deck of a ship; and I am more at me ease than if I sat down—

"Donna Isabella, at the request of her husband, put on boy's cloaths before she entered the ship. The sailors were told they were brothers, and she went by the name of Don Giulio.

"We had a brisk gale or two, but a good and quick passage upon the whole.

"We landed at Bristol, and my business detained me there some weeks. My passengers were impatient to see the capital, of which they had heard so much. I sent our baggage round by a smaller ship; and ordered the master to send it ashore at Gravesend, to the house of an acquaintance of mine there.

"As soon as I had finished my business, I attended them to London, by land, in the stage-coach. They were amazed at the accommodations upon the road; and said England was, indeed, a fine country to travel in, but very expensive.

"I carried them to South Lambeth, where I used to lodge, and which was cheaper than London to live in. From thence I used to take a boat to Paul's Wharf; and I shewed them, by degrees, the extent of the great city, which afforded many subjects of surprize and admiration.

"Don Antonio and his lady observed that the people they met were always in a hurry; very different from what they were used to see in Naples—which was natural for them to take notice of; for the Italians walk in a very slow and stately manner, and as if they were telling their steps.

"I shewed them every thing worthy of notice in London and the environs. They were pleased with the country about, which looked like a fine garden, highly cultivated; but, they both said, they should not like to live in London.

"I had my ship laid up; and resolved to devote this year to the company of my friends, and to the enjoyment of my ease in my native country.

It was the beginning of June, the season fine, the days long: I proposed to my friends to make an excursion into the country; to which they agreed.

"We went on a tour through Essex, Suffolk, and Norfolk. They found England greatly superior to the descriptions they had heard of it. I told them, they must expect to see it in a different state in the winter, and prepare to encounter the inclemencies of it.

"In our journey, we stopped in a pleasant village, and laid by in the heat of the day. After dinner, the landlord laid upon the table a printed catalogue of a sale in the village. It consisted of an estate, with a good house upon it; and the conveniencies were specified. Secondly, a farm; with a house, and it's appurtenances. Thirdly, all the houshold goods and furniture, farming stock, and implements of husbandry, belonging to the mansion-house. Fourthly, the goods and stock of the farm.

"We enquired of the landlord, how far off were the premises? He told us, they were only a short mile from the street, as he called it.

"We said, we should like to see them; and he offered to accompany us thither.

"Don Antonio and Isabella went in the post-chaise. I walked with the landlord, and met them at the mansion-house.

"We were told, that these estates had belonged to a gentleman of a respectable family, whose ancestors had resided there, and were a blessing to the village. The last heir left the country, and went to London to see the world. He both saw and felt it to his cost: he entered into all the pleasures and dissipations of it; and, in a few years, run through his fortune. He was obliged to surrender all his effects into the hands of his creditors; and they had commissioned their agents to see them immediately.

"My Italian friends were shocked at these circumstances.

"I said, I was sorry to tell them, that such things were become very common in England. "Then," said Don Antonio, "your virtues and manners are on the decline."

"I could not deny it; but I wished him to think the best of us.

"We went over the house. They liked it extremely.

"I should like," said Don Antonio, "to jump into such an house, ready furnished, and with every convenience about me. What says my Isabella?"

"I," said she, "should think it a paradise."

"If you are in earnest," said I, "this may easily be done. We may attend the sale; and it is probable that it may be sold cheap."

"Don Antonio desired that I would stand forward as the buyer, and give a fair price for it.

"From the mansion-house, we went to the farm, which was another mile. I talked with the farmer, concerning the rent, and the value of the land; and, having gained the lights[2] I wanted, we returned to the inn.

"We talked this matter over. Don Antonio thought the land about the mansion-house would be sufficient for him, and that he should not desire to buy the farm.

"Then," said I, "I will buy that for myself."

"Do so," said Isabella. "You shall marry, and give me a good neighbour there."

"I shook my head, and said, that was not in my power.

"Why not?" said she.

"Because the woman I should have married is dead."

"But, there are others living, that may be as good, and make you as happy."

"Perhaps so, my dear lady; but I may not be worthy of them."

"We must leave this event to time," said Don Antonio; "for Don Francisco will not chuse Isabella for his confessor, I perceive."

"I turned the subject to that of our intended purchases.

"Don Antonio said—"A thought strikes me—Supposing my monies in England should not be sufficient to answer the purchase I meditate?"

"What then?" said I. "Have you not a friend who will be proud to supply you?"

"He grasped my hand: said, I was indeed a friend; such an one, that he should be unable to do any thing without me. Isabella joined in the acknowledgment; and, I believe, there were not, at that moment, three persons in the world that had a more entire friendship and confidence in each other. Oh, happy days, that never shall return!—Days of misery only remain for me!"

Here Captain Maurice groaned, and was silent some minutes.

I desired him to take breath a while. I offered him some refreshment. He drank a glass of wine, sat down, crossed his arms, and looked overwhelmed with melancholy thoughts. At length, he resumed his story—

"We attended the sale. I bought both the estates; which was all of the first day's business.

"I offered the agents to purchase all the stock and furniture of both houses together. They said, notice had been publicly given, and the sale was expected. I then said—"Suppose you put all of them into two great lots; one for the mansion-house, the other for the farm; and let any one that pleases bid against me." After some discussion, this was agreed to.

"The auctioneer made a general valuation; and I bought them the following day. There was only one bidder against me. But then the lots were put up at the full value: they were certainly worth more to us than to any other persons.

"I told Antonio, that I would put him into possession of his purchase, and then go with the agents to London, and pay the first part of the money, and give security for the remainder. He said, he would consent, upon condition that I should stay no longer than was necessary: "for we shall do nothing, nor enjoy any thing, till you return."

"As soon as the business was finished, we left the inn, and took possession of the mansion-house.

"It was pleasantly situated, near a navigable river; and there was a creek that came up within a quarter of a mile of the house. There was a boat there, and every convenience for fishing and for pleasure, in a hut that was built hard by for that purpose.

"Don Antonio and Isabella were overjoyed to find themselves

in a house of their own. We entertained the agents of the creditors, gave them a dinner, and then dismissed them to our quarters at the inn.

"We were next to engage servants for the family. The dairymaid was lately married to a young, sturdy husbandman. I advised my friends to engage them both, for we found them in the house. I desired the farmer's wife to send us a net girl, to wait upon the lady of the mansion. I had a handy boy, who used to wait upon Isabella on board ship: she called him her page; and I promised that she should have him, as soon as I could fetch him from Lambeth, where I left him. I took a farmer's boy, to run on errands, and wait at table, for the present moment. Thus having formed a kind of houshold, I settled them in three days time; and they began to find themselves at home.

"I then took leave of my friends, and went to the inn, to the agents; and, the next morning, set out with them for London.

"Don Antonio had given me an order upon his banker, to receive all the monies in his hands. I made the first payment for him and myself, and gave security for the remainder.

"I sold my monies out of the public funds, and put every thing in train for concluding our purchases. I discharged our lodgings at Lambeth, paid off the servants, and the dues of all kinds. It was above a month before I was free to return to D——.

"I received a pacquet of letters from Italy for Don Antonio; and a remittance from Don Dominico di Rossi, which enabled me to finish the purchases; and I settled all these affairs before I left London.

"I likewise paid a visit to a dear little infant at nurse at Stockwell. This child is now under your care, Madam; and I am happy that she is so well placed, for all her obligations are mine."

"Pray, Sir, allow me to ask, whether she is not nearly related to you?"

"She is, Madam: I have chosen you for my confessor, and will not now shrink back.

"Her mother's name was Charlotte Brady. I dearly loved her, and wished to marry her; but my uncle would never have consented to it. He was an old bachelor; and an enemy to marriage, particularly in soldiers and sailors: he said, they ought not to think of it, till they were wholly retired from their profession. I was dependent upon my uncle, and had only my wages as mate of his ship, and was unable to support a family; but I was under a solemn promise to marry her, as soon as my uncle should die.

"Our amour had the usual consequences. She found herself with child, and pressed me to marry her; which I could not comply with, for the reasons I have given: but I made vows of fidelity, and left the greatest part of my property in her hands.

"I went my voyage. At my return, I found her with my infant at her breast, and in a deep decline.

"Our meeting was very tender. I blamed her mother for suffering her to nurse the child, in her weak situation. I sent for an eminent physician. He ordered the child to be taken from her; and that she should go into the country for the air, and drink cow's milk diluted, which he judged to be better than asses milk.

"I carried her to Enfield, and took lodgings there. We put the child to nurse, to a hearty, strong woman; and Charlotte saw it every day.

"I offered to marry her then, but she declined it, from generous motives. She said, if it had been offered in time, to make her child legitimate, she would not have refused it; but, as that time was past, she would wait till it was quite convenient to me.

"Her mother was a tradesman's widow, a modest, humble woman. She had three more children, and a scanty fortune to maintain them.

"I put out her eldest son to a brazier,[3] and the second to the sea. There was another daughter, who assisted her mother in nursing and attending on my Charlotte.

"I staid with them at Enfield several weeks, and till my uncle wrote to me to come to him at Gravesend, and prepare for another voyage.

"I then offered to put off the voyage, and to stay with Charlotte till she should be perfectly recovered; but she opposed it. She said, I had more expences coming upon me, for herself and the child, and I ought not to lose the means of increasing my property. Beside that, my staying at home might offend my uncle, and injure my interest.

"I took a melancholy farewel of my dear girl, with a foreboding heart that I should never see her alive again. I left all the money I had with her; charging her to take care of her health, as the best proof she could give of her regard for me.

"I went with my uncle, as usual, to Naples, and to Messina. I was absent seven months; and, at my return, found my Charlotte in the cold grave.

"I was deeply affected, though not surprized. Her mother and I comforted each other. I put a stone over her grave, and shed many tears upon it.

"A young carpenter courted the other daughter. They married, and removed to Stockwell: the mother, and the young child, went with them. I paid them well for her board; and she continued with them till I thought it was time to take some care of her education, when I took her away from them, to place her with you.

"And, now, Madam, I must beg you to judge me favourably in this affair; for I could not have acted otherwise than I did."

"I have no right to sit in judgment upon your conduct, Sir: I leave it to your own conscience to decide upon it. But now, I think, it will be right to take some respite. You must be fatigued; and we will postpone the remainder to another day."

"I will do so, Madam, at your desire: I will take leave of you for this evening."

So saying, he bowed, and departed.

And here I will give my friend a respite also for the present; but I will soon resume the pen, and the story.

Adieu! and love me, as I shall endeavour to deserve it.

FRANCES DARNFORD.

LETTER XI
Mrs. Darnford, to Mrs. Strictland.

I WILL now proceed with Captain Maurice's story.

He came again two days afterwards, at the hour when I dismissed my school. As soon as the forms were set by, he renewed his walk, and his story.

"You cannot conceive, Madam, the joy with which I was received at my return to D——. Don Antonio flew into my arms, and held me in his for some minutes. He called me his friend, his brother, and the blessing of his life. He made Isabella embrace me, and shewed every mark of unfeigned affection.

"I told him all that I had done for his service, and gave him the pacquet from D. Dominico di Rossi.

"It contained letters from himself to Don Antonio, and from his lady to Isabella. And also one from Don Antonio's uncle, in reply to one he left to be sent to him after he was gone; excusing his elopement with Isabella, by desiring him to suppose himself in his situation, and then asking, whether he could refuse the blessings of love and fortune, to gratify an elder brother, who neither loved nor cared for him?

"The uncle, in his reply, confessed that, in his heart, he excused him; but that he dared not avow it to his father or brother. That Don Girolamo was like a madman for many days: and, though his rage had subsided, his resentment remained. And that he was of opinion, that it would not be safe for him to return to Naples.

"Don Antonio said, he had no such intention; and that he was as happy here as he could be in any part of the world.

"There is only one thing wanting to make my happiness perfect."

"I asked him what that was, and whether I could not procure it for him? He said, it was a priest of his own religion to visit him, and to perform the duties of the Romish Church for them.

"This I undertook to do in a short time.

"I went to the family of a Catholic baronet, and obtained that his chaplain should attend them at the great festivals, and some of the holidays of the year. This completed their wishes, and there never was a happier family. It was a delightful autumn. I carried Don Antonio with me a shooting. Sometimes we went a fishing in the boat.

"One very fine day, we persuaded Isabella to go with us. The wind was high, and we had some difficulty in landing. Isabella fell into the water. I jumped in after her, and brought her safely to land. She was a good deal frightened, and very wet, but not otherwise hurt.

"I left the boy to bring the boat ashore; and Don Antonio and I gave our whole attention to Isabella. We carried her home between us. She got dry clothes and linen, and met us at dinner.

"She then paid her acknowledgments to me; but said, she would have nothing to do with water-parties from this time forward.

"It seemed as if every circumstance that occurred served to endear us to each other, and to cement our mutual friendship.

"I took possession of my farm. I planned an addition to the house; a new lower room, and a chamber over it. Isabella desired I would make it large enough to receive a wife; and Antonio added his urgency, that I should give them, one day, a neighbour.

"Don Antonio was subject to the cholic[1] constitutionally. I went to a sea-port town, at about twelve miles distance, in the boat; and took with me only the boy I have mentioned.

"I went to a sale at the Custom-house. I purchased a tub of Hollands geneva, a lot of brandy, and some other articles. I stowed them in the boat, and carried them safely home. At my return, Don Antonio was ill with the cholic. I told him I had brought a cure for it; and that, as the weather grew cold, he must take some of it frequently, to fortify him against the approach of winter.

"I mixed it with boiling water, and put some grated ginger in it. He took it, and found relief presently.

"He said, that I foresaw all his wants, and knew how to provide against them. I bade him keep this liquor always in the house, and not to use it freely.

"As winter came on, my friends retreated from room to room; and, at last, settled in the keeping parlour, which was a very warm and comfortable room: and I advised Isabella to have a constant fire in her bed-chamber. With all these precautions, they found the winter less severe than they expected.

"I talked with the hind, and found him able to conduct the farming business. His wife performed the dairy work, and had a peasant girl under her. The houshold was now established, and regularly conducted.

"During the winter season, I taught my friends to understand the English language, and I read and conversed with them.

"In this happy society, the winter wore away imperceptibly: I never knew it so short.

"We welcomed the approach of Spring. I sought for the earliest flowers, to grace the fair Isabella's bosom; the snow-drop, the yellow crocus, and the purple, intermixed with laurustinus. I wove a garland, and placed it upon her head. Antonio was not displeased at my gallantry, but complimented my taste.

"I told them, I must shortly take a journey to London, and to Bristol; and desired them to think of what I could do for their service. They seemed loth to part with me, and bade me hasten my return.

"I was absent between two and three months, on business of various kinds. I brought down with me a master-builder, who undertook my proposed alterations in my farm-house. It was an aukward, irregular building, that looked well enough in front, having two rooms and a passage; but, behind, it was quite in and out, and one quarter vacant; so that it made a kind of triangle. My builder proposed to fill up this quarter, and make it a square house, and to carry the offices down to one side, into the yard.

"I was to have one very good parlour, and a store-room; and, above, a very good bed-chamber and dressing-room, with a separate stair-case. The roof was to be raised, and two good garrets in front; two, not so good, for the use of the farmer.

"The lease expired at Michaelmas. Several tenants offered, and proposed voluntarily to raise the rent. I let it to a responsible man, for one hundred pounds a year, which was ten pounds advanced rent; and conditioned for my own reserved apartment.

"I had every place put into thorough repair, and made a good road from the mansion-house.

"My friends complained, that this undertaking engrossed my time and attention, and that they had less of my company. I observed, that Donna Isabella was increased in size; and congratulated her husband on the prospect of an heir, who should be an Englishman.

"He received my compliment coldly, and turned the conversation. I thought he seemed to think it too great a liberty: I could not otherwise account for his behaviour.

"I thought I saw, at times, a cast of care upon his brow; but he was generally as open as ever. Isabella was unwell, and often retired to her apartment.

"One day, he spoke upon the subject himself. He wished Isabella had some female friend, to advise her in the choice of a nurse, and a midwife. I said, he should consult the doctor in the next town; and he would recommend a nurse, and provide all other conveniencies.

"He desired me to explain my meaning. I could hardly make him understand, or believe, that men attended our ladies in the office of accoucheur.

"He raved against the impropriety and indecency of this custom: said, that the Italian ladies would never permit such things; and that his Isabella should never submit to them. I told him, that I was not able to decide upon the subject: "but, let be good or evil, it is unjust that your resentment should fall upon me, who only answered your questions."

"He seemed to recollect himself, and apologized for his warmth; but I thought his behaviour capricious and absurd.

"The wife of the hind lay in in the house. She was attended by an old woman, the midwife of the parish.

"Don Antonio took occasion to remark upon the subject, and to tax me with falshood. He asked the hind, whether men ever attended in such cases? The man answered, that the gentry always bespoke the doctor; and only poor men, like themselves, employed the old woman.

"This made him more easy. He ordered the woman to attend Isabella, and to give her advice and assistance; and she confirmed the truth of my report.

"He seemed uneasy and unsatisfied in his mind; and said, that it was a kind of sacrilege for any man to approach Isabella in her present situation. He did not like that I should see or converse with her. He said, it was owing to his care and anxiety about her; and always seemed conscious, that his behaviour stood in need of an apology.

"Upon this occasion, it came into my mind, that the dearest and most intimate friends might see too much of each other, and that it would be prudent in me to seek another home; that I would go an excursion, and come over now and then, till my house was finished; that I would reside there some months in the summer, and go to London, or to Bristol, in the winter.

"I took leave of Antonio, who said, he was sorry to lose my company; but his looks said something very different. I had done nothing to forfeit his regard; and I knew not whether I was more angry, or grieved, at his behaviour.

"I desired him to address his letters to be left at the post-house at N——; and, if he had occasion for my services, he might command my return at a short notice.

"He embraced me, and desired me to excuse any thing that I thought amiss in his temper, or conduct; assuring me, that his affection for me was as strong as ever.

"I wished I had not so soon given credit to professions and fair appearances. I repented that I had purchased the farm, and laid out more upon it, and thus fixed my residence near the mansion.

"I went a tour through Cambridgeshire, Lincolnshire, and Derbyshire; and back again, through Nottinghamshire, Lincolnshire, and Norfolk. I should have been happily amused; but I had a thorn in my heart, that would not let me enjoy my own comforts.

"When I came to N——, I found two letters from Don Antonio. In the first he acquainted me, that his dear Isabella had brought him a son, and demanded my congratulations. In the second, he wished for my return; and to consult me on the subject of his farm, as he thought his manager put him to too much expence.

"There was also a letter from my architect, who wished me to see the state of my house, and to give orders for the fitting it up on the inside. I resolved to go thither directly.

"I wrote to my correspondent in London to send me down goods to furnish my apartment, neat, and plain, and fitting for a farm-house. I determined to go into it as soon as it should be finished; and, in the mean time, I should find employment in it.

"I returned to D——, and went directly to the mansion-house. My heart did not beat with joy, as it used to do, when I approached it: but I determined to see how the land lay; and, if I did not like my reception, to take up my lodging at the inn in the village.

"Don Antonio received me as a welcome guest. I thanked him for his letters, and congratulated him on the birth of his son. He seemed more at ease within himself, and more free in his behaviour to me. Isabella brought her child to shew me: her behaviour was free and kind. Antonio's eyes were fixed on her and me; he never withdrew them a moment; his countenance varied often, yet he seemed to conceal the emotions of his mind. I said to myself—"Is not this man jealous? If so, it accounts at once for his late conduct. I know myself innocent of having given cause for it: but that is not sufficient to satisfy a mind tinged with this fatal passion; I will observe him carefully, and come to an explanation with him."

"He behaved in a kind and friendly manner for several days, and in that time he consulted me concerning the management of his farm.

"I told him, that his servant was right; that he ought to be generous to his farm, and that it would repay him seven-fold—That, as he kept a head-man and a boy in the house, that was sufficient; and it was better to hire men occasionally, than to increase the number of servants to be constantly maintained.

"He was convinced by my arguments, and thanked me for my counsel.

"I advised him to make acquaintance with some of the neighbouring gentry, but he declined it.

"He complained of lassitude and inquietude; and said, he never experienced such feelings in Italy. I told him, it was owing to want of society, and want of employment. I recommended the study of agriculture; saying, the greatest philosophers had thought it worthy of their attention. I got books of this kind for him, and he promised to peruse them. I advised him to make an excursion with me; but he excused himself, saying, he could not leave Isabella alone. I said, she would be employed in her nursery duties and employments.

"And who is to be her protector in my absence?"

"She will not want any, for she will not be in danger of any kind."

"I will not trust to that," said he: "I will not leave her."

"As you please, Sir: but I cannot conceive what you are afraid of."

"Within a week, his countenance was altered again, and seemed full of anxiety and suspicion. When he was in full confidence with me, he used to call me *Don Francisco*; or, *Mio caro Amico!* when in this way, it was *Capitano Maurici*; and this, by degrees, became the general appellation.

"One evening, as we were sitting after supper, and Isabella was present, he asked me, whether I never intended to go to sea again?

"I paused some time before I answered; and then said—"I do not know; but I know for whose sake I have staid at home."

"He looked earnestly at me, as if expecting a farther answer.

"I then said—"I thought, Sir, that you had occasion for my services, and that I was obliging you by giving you my company; at least, you gave me reason to believe so."

"He coloured, hesitated, and was so confused, that he could not speak plainly. At last, he said he was very much obliged to me, but he should be sorry that I should lose the great advantages I made by my voyages to Naples and Messina, on his account.

"I answered—"You have made Naples too warm a country for me. But I should be glad to know what you drive at; and I beg you would explain your meaning farther."

"He said, he had no meaning but what was for my advantage.

"You, then, prefer my advantage to your own satisfaction, at this time?"

"Yes, Seignior Capitano; I would not that you should lose your time."

"How comes it that you did not think so a year ago?"

"Seignior, I thought—I believed—I wished that you would not leave us, until—till—till—"

"Till you had no farther need of me. You, then, preferred your pleasure to my advantage?"

"I smiled indignantly, and he seemed to shrink into nothing. He took shame to himself, and was silent.

"Isabella looked at us both. She said—"Don Antonio!—Don Francisco!—what is the matter? I fear you do not understand each other."

"I am afraid I understand too much. I leave you, Don Antonio! I wish you a good night!"

"So saying, I took my hat, and went out of the room, as if I was going up to bed. I bowed to Isabella as I retired. As soon as I had walked a turn in the garden, I resolved to go directly to the inn. I did so. I spent a very restless and uneasy night. I was irresolute how to act in this disagreeable situation; whether to reconcile myself to Don Antonio, or to break with him for ever. I felt, by turns, resentment, pity, and forgiveness. I pitied his jealousy, I resented his ingratitude, and I despised his meanness.

"Thus I spent the night and the day at the inn. In the evening, I received the following note from Isabella—

"Don Antonio is very much concerned at what passed between him and Don Francisco last night: the thoughts of it deprived him of rest. All this day he has been very ill with the cholic, and grows worse every hour.

"Forgive, and forget, the infirmities of a friend, and hasten to our assistance. Be our comforter and physician, as you used to be; and our only friend, as we are yours, truly,

"ANTONIO AND ISABELLA DI SORANZO."

"I doubted whether to obey this summons; but friendship got the better of my resentment, and I resolved to try him once more, and that for the last time.

"I went to the mansion-house. Isabella was told I was come. She came down stairs to meet me.

"You are very kind," she said: "I thought you would not desert us; I was sure you would come. Let us go up stairs, for he wishes and longs to see you."

"I followed her into Antonio's chamber: he was rolling about upon the bed, in agony.

"He lifted up his head, and saw me. He held out his hand, and hid his face in the pillow, as if ashamed to see me. I took his hand, and he grasped mine strongly.

"I said—'Let us make haste, and get the medicine ready.' I

asked for the materials: the servant brought them; and I gave him a strong dose of geneva and boiling water, with ginger grated into it. He seemed to shake with cold. I suspected that it was something of the gout in his stomach, as I had done before; and I had advised him to drink more wine, for that it was necessary in a country so much colder than his own: but he seemed to grudge the expence, and I found him afraid of that in every thing. I was obliged to give him a second dose, and a third. At length it gave way, and the pain abated by degrees.

"I advised him to get some repose, and offered to leave him, but he begged me to stay: so I threw myself into a great chair; and we both took a comfortable sleep, to our great refreshment.

"Isabella left the room; and I fancied he did not like to leave us together. When once a suspicion is gone forth, every trifling circumstance seems to add strength to it.

"I desired Isabella to order some mutton-broth to be made, and that Antonio should eat nothing else. When he awoke, I enquired after his complaint; and he was quite easy. I then took leave of him, in order to return to the inn. Both he and Isabella pressed me to stay; but I said—'When you are well enough, we must have a serious conversation: there are some points to be settled between us, before I can again lodge under your roof. God bless you—and farewell!'

"The next morning, I sent to know how Don Antonio did. The answer was, that he was much better, and desired to see me.

"I went to the house, and into his apartment. As soon as we were alone, I went to the bottom of the subject, and desired him to give me the reasons of the alteration in his behaviour towards me. He was, at first, shy and reserved; but I insisted on a full explanation.

"He confessed, that he had felt much inquietude; but could not well explain the reasons of it. When I was absent, he reflected upon my merit, and the services I had done him; and then he loved me as well, or better than ever: but, when I was present, his inquietude returned, and he was almost ready to wish me away again, though he condemned himself for it.

"I desired him to tell me, if any part of my conduct had given cause for this inquietude; if I had given him any offence? I begged him to be very explicit, for it would oblige me very much; and, perhaps, it would lay the foundation of a right understanding hereafter.

"Again he shuffled and hesitated.

"Speak out, Sir," said I: "either speak like a man, or give me manly satisfaction."

"He turned pale; and, in a strange manner, half willing, and half afraid, he told me, that his servants paid me more respect than they did him, and looked up to me for orders and directions; and—and—and—he thought I meant to live here, and be their master.

"I felt anger and contempt rise in my heart; but the latter kept under the former.

"How could you think so, when you see me making an apartment for myself in my farm-house, and that I am preparing to reside in it as soon as it is habitable?—But go on, Sir: tell me all the rest."

"He said, some part of his inquietude was on account of Isabella. When I was absent, she was always speaking in my praise; that I was so clever, that I knew every thing that was to be done by land, as well as sea; and that I had resources for every thing—that she once said, she believed, if Don Francisco were cast ashore, naked, in a strange country, he could make his fortune there, by being useful to every body that fell in his way—that he feared she might, in time, love me better than himself—that he sometimes made the comparison against himself, finding me so much more useful in society; and that he wished he had made himself capable of doing many things I did; only that, in his country, such things were thought unworthy of a gentleman: but, though he valued me for knowing so many things, he did not like that his wife, or dependants, should love or respect me more than himself.

"Here he paused, and looked ashamed, and yet glad it was over.

"Is this all that you can say or think upon this subject?"

"It is all," said he; "and you have obliged me to say all that I think, or feel."

"Well, Sir, I perceive it has been sufficiently painful to you; and yet I am glad that you have been so explicit with me. And now, Sir, hear me in turn, and hear me patiently. It is necessary to probe a wound before it can be healed; and to know your complaint, is a step towards the cure. It depends upon you only, Don Antonio, to heal your wound, and to cure your distemper. It is called jealousy: that is it's right name; and a worse, or more painful one, is hardly to be found. It makes you unjust to me, and unhappy in yourself. I call Heaven to witness, that I have never injured you, in thought, word, or deed; so may

I prosper in all my undertakings! Thus far with regard to myself.—But you have also injured your wife, who deserves your entire love and confidence. You owe her your repentance, and reparation also. You are guilty of cruelty and injustice. But what shall I say of your suspicions of others, because they pay me the respect they owe me, even upon your account? They are mean and sordid, unbecoming a gentleman, unbecoming a man. I am ashamed of them for you. They have lessened you in my esteem; they have driven me from you: for, after what you have confessed, I can no longer take up my residence in your house. In the next place, Don Antonio, I must inform you, that my fortune is sufficient to live comfortably upon, without going to sea, unless I chuse to do so; and that it belongs to me only to decide that point. I mention this circumstance, to convince you that I never meant to fasten myself upon you, nor to live at your expence. My spirit is too high for that situation; but, while I was of service to you, I thought I earned my board with you; and that is all I ever received from you. I never asked, nor received, any payment for your passage and accommodations during your voyage to England. You professed yourself my friend; you solicited my company in the strongest manner; you said, you could do nothing without me. Deceived by your professions, I thought we had established the most sincere and disinterested friendship, which nothing could break or disturb. Such a friendship is it's own desert and recompence. I would have divided my last shilling with you. Nothing but your own mean and injurious suspicions could have broken ours: and they will poison your happiness, whether I am with you or not; for they will create objects of doubt and distrust, and mix with every thing you do, or think. If I sought revenge upon you, I could not have a greater one: but I advise you, as the last proof of my regard for you, to drive this evil spirit from your bosom, while you are suffering from the pains and troubles it has caused you. Now is your only time; for, to be always fluctuating between right and wrong, is a miserable state. Consult your priest upon this subject: it is a serious matter. You have been ingenuous in your confession to me. I thank you, and forgive you for this reason. May God be your protector! May you be happy and fortunate!—Farewell!"

"While I was speaking, Don Antonio's countenance varied continually. Resentment, shame, and grief, were predominant in their turns. At the conclusion, the last had the ascendancy. When I was going to leave him, he held me in his arms—he wept—he held my cloaths. At last, he fell on his knees, and embraced mine: he implored my forgiveness in the most humble manner.

"I am never pleased with improper humiliation. I never knew a person capable of an abject submission, that was not as ready to offend again. A mind that is conscious of it's own integrity, scorns to say more than it means to perform.

"I felt pity for Don Antonio, but it was mingled with contempt. I raised him from his knees, and begged him to be composed. I told him, I would try the strength of his resolutions in my own way; and, when I was convinced that his mind was cured of it's unjust suspicions, I would be to him all that I had ever been. In the mean time, I must leave him to his own considerations.

"We were called down to dinner. Isabella met us with a smile. She took my hand, and that of Antonio, and joined them together. She said—"May God confirm the union!" Antonio's eyes were full of tears. I bowed in silence; and we sat down to dinner.

"After the servant was retired, Isabella acknowledged my kindness in coming to Antonio's relief. She said, whenever he was uneasy in his mind, these attacks of the cholic came upon him: but, she hoped, all things were now set right between us; and that she should never forget what she owed to my friendship.

"Don Antonio said but little. He sighed often, and seemed full of vexation and care.

"When the evening came on, I took my leave. They both pressed me to stay; but I had taken my resolution, and adhered to it.

"I told them, I was going to London; and asked, if I could do them any service there? Antonio wished me to enquire, if there were any letters for him from Italy. I promised to do so, and was going away; but he stopped me—

"Do not be in so much haste to leave us. Let me ask you a question."

"Do so, and I will answer it."

"Supposing we should wish to make a visit to Italy, when the dear child is old enough to bear the voyage; would you not carry us thither in your ship?"

"It is not in my power, if it was my inclination. I have sold my ship; and, if ever I go to sea again, it will be in a different way."

"That is unlucky!"

"Thus far I can serve you: I can enquire for a ship that is going to some port in Italy, and get you a passage in it, if you desire it."

"I thank you, Sir: but where shall I direct to you in your absence?"

"At Garraway's Coffee-house, Cornhill. If you should chuse to sell your estate here, I dare say, it will be easy to find a customer. It was bought very cheap; and, perhaps, may be sold to advantage."

"I have no thoughts of that, at present; but I will consider of it."

"Again I took my leave; and it was with difficulty I got away.

"I was very uneasy in my mind. I was disappointed in that friendship which I had relied upon as the chief comfort of my life. I was unsettled, and undetermined with respect to my future residence, and could only resolve on spending the winter in London.

"My new tenant took possession of the farm at Michaelmas. It was now the latter end of October. The goods I had ordered were arrived, and my new rooms were getting into a state to receive them. I had pleased myself with the thoughts of the employment I should have in getting my house in order by Christmas, when I intended to inhabit it. My schemes were all overset. I put the goods into the room unpacked, locked the doors of my new apartment, and gave the keys to the farmer. I sent for all my baggage from the mansion-house, packed up my apparel, and set off to N——, and from thence to London.

"I found a letter for Don Antonio at the usual place. I enclosed it in a cover, and sent it to him directly.

"At a coffee-house that I frequented, I met with many seafaring people. A gentleman was going to Antwerp, hearing that the Emperor was endeavouring to revive the trade of that port, formerly so famous. He invited me to go with him, and I accepted his offer.

"We sailed soon after, with a fair wind, and had a good voyage. The captain, who was likewise the chief owner, staid some time at Atwerp; but I visited all the principal towns in Brabant. From thence I went through Flanders, and at last came down to Ostend. I laid plans, in my own mind, for establishing a trade hereafter. Finding a ship ready to sail for Harwich, I returned home in it, having been absent between four and five months.

"I found, at the coffee-house I frequented, three letters from Don Antonio.

"The first contained an acknowledgment of the receipt of his letter from Italy. It brought an account of the marriage of Don Girolamo, his eldest brother; and that his resentment against him was as strong as ever—that his uncle was now of the party against him, and had promised to make Girolamo his heir—that there was, therefore, no encouragement for him to return to Naples again.

"The second gave an account of the sickness and death of his son—that Isabella was inconsolable for his loss; and he was obliged to stifle his own grief, and to be her comforter.

"The third was an enumeration of the wants of the family, and a commission to send them stores of all kinds. He was surprized that he had not heard from me, but supposed I was absent, and hoped to hear from me as soon as I was returned.

"Now, this commission I wished to decline; for he had honoured me in the same way whenever I went to London, but never once offered to repay me the money I had laid out for him; and I began to wish to withdraw from all connection with him.

"I answered his three letters in one, as briefly as possible. I condoled with him on the death of his son, and wished the loss might be repaired. I advised him to send for his family stores to N——, which was but little more than ten miles, rather than from London, which was an hundred, as the best oeconomy. I wished him and Isabella health and happiness, and so concluded.

"My farmer sent me a letter also. He wished me to come to D——. He had some farther improvements to propose to me; and he would have my apartment aired and got ready upon my first notice.

"I sent word, that I would be with him on the twentieth of May; and I was exact to my time."

Here Captain Maurice stopped to take breath; and I desired him to postpone the remainder of his story till another day.

He said, he would do so; for, he believed, I was tired, as well as himself; and what followed would be very painful for him to relate: but he was resolved to make full confession of all his sins, relying upon my honour and secresy, and hoping I would accept it as a pledge of his sincere penitence, and his resolution to make every atonement in his power.

And, now, my dear friend, I will conclude this letter. Make it known to your children, that the friend of their mother is theirs also; that she longs to embrace them, and to tell them so.

Donna Isabella di Soranzo salutes you. She promises you her friendship. She invites you to visit her, as soon as you are fully informed of her past sufferings, and her present situation. She will soon lay claim to your tenderest pity and affectionate regards.

My adopted children present their respectful compliments to Mrs. Strictland, and her young people. They hope to be, in due time, their friends, playfellows, and humble servants. I am

Yours truly and affectionately,
FRANCES DARNFORD.

LETTER XII
Mrs. Darnford, to Mrs. Strictland.

HUMAN Nature is undefineable. Man vainly strives to investigate it. Some believe it naturally prone to evil: others, that it is equally susceptible of good and bad impressions; and this is the most reconcileable to reason, and to experience. Man is born liable to sin, but not incapable of virtue: yet he must be continually on his guard against the dangers that surround him; or present pleasure, or present passions, will weigh down the hope of future recompence. Even men of good principles, and moral conduct, are liable to fall, by insensible steps, into crimes that, at first, they shudder at.

I fell into these reflections while I was preparing to continue the history of Captain Maurice for your perusal: a man of a mixed character, such as compose the bulk of mankind; for very few are absolutely good, or atrociously wicked.

Captain Maurice, at his next visit, continued his story as follows—

"I came to my farm on the twentieth of May, as I had promised. I brought with me some books on the improvements in agriculture, which I recommended to my tenant's perusal. I talked with him upon his proposed alterations, and we were mutually satisfied with each other.

"The day after my arrival, I sent a message of enquiry after the health of Antonio and Isabella. They sent an answer, desiring to see me as soon as possible.

"In the evening, John Roberts, whom I had placed with them, came with a second message, desiring my company to dinner on the morrow. After he had delivered his message, he desired me to hear what he had farther to say, on his own account.

"He told me, that Don Antonio was a very odd-tempered man—that he was pleased and displeased without any reason—that he had long been tired of living with him, and that he had given him warning, six weeks ago, to leave him at the month's end; but his master either could not, or would not, understand him, nor would he let him go—that, hearing I was expected, he staid till I should come to D——, hoping that I should make his master hear reason, and that they should part upon good terms.

"I promised to settle matters with his master. He asked me, whether I intended to go to sea again? If I did, he hoped I would take him with me. I said, it was uncertain; but, if I did not myself, I would recommend him to another ship-master. He was full of complaints of his master's jealous and suspicious temper; but I cut him short, and sent him home.

"The next day, I went to dinner at the mansion-house. Don Antonio received me with formal civility, but not with the warmth of friendship. Isabella was more frank and open in her behaviour. She was full of grief for the loss of her son, and told me every circumstance of his sickness and death.

"I said all that I could think of, by way of consolation, both to her and her husband.

"After dinner, we conversed on various subjects. I took occasion to mention John's complaints; particularly that, after having given him the usual warning, he refused to let him go. I said, perhaps he was not fully informed of our laws and customs: that servants here were as free as their masters; and, in case of dislike on either side, they were equally free to separate, either giving the other the usual warning, or a month's wages. He was angry. He said, the lower sort of people had too much liberty in England; it only made them saucy and ungovernable. I would not enter into the subject with him: I only told him, such were our laws and customs, and they must be complied with.

"He supposed, I would take him again into my service. I said, that was uncertain; and, after he had fairly left him, it was of no consequence to whom he should offer himself. He seemed displeased with me, as well as with John. I turned the subject.

"Isabella told me she had received several civil messages from the rector's wife, on account of the child's sickness and death. I wished she had encouraged her acquaintance; and she might, then, have acquired a neighbour, and, perhaps, a friend.

"Antonio said, he could not bear the idea of a married priest. I answered, that married priests were much less dangerous, among men's wives and daughters, than such as took a vow of chastity, which they never wished nor intended to keep.

"He was offended; but seemed to check himself, as if afraid of affronting me. Again I changed the subject; but we could not agree in opinion on hardly any point: and I no longer paid attention to his humours, as formerly, but spoke with an honest and manly freedom; yet not rudely, nor merely to gratify my own temper.

"I invited Antonio and Isabella to dine with me, in my new apartment, and wished them to name a day. Antonio seemed to demur, and doubt whether to accept my invitation. I smiled; and, I fear, it was rather contemptuously: for I said—'As I know your engagements and occupations are very numerous, I leave you to consider and resolve upon this important subject.' I turned to Isabella, and said—'When Don Antonio has determined on the day, be so good to let me know as soon as possible, that I may get something for you to eat.' She answered, that she hoped I would not take too much trouble upon myself on that account.

"Antonio looked sullen and reserved. I asked him to lend me the boat, and I would endeavour to get some fish for him. He said, it was always at my service. I took my leave.

"The next morning, I sent to desire Don Antonio would let John go with me a-fishing. I was answered, that he was wanted at home, and could not be spared. Jack slipped a note into the boy's hand, and in it were these words—

"It is all nothing but ill-humour and crossness; for master could spare me if he would. Sir, your friend and servant,

"J.R."

"No matter," said I: "he shall not provoke me to do any thing to blame myself for hereafter. I will bear with him for a while; and he shall not drive me away from my own house."

"I took my tenant's boy with me. I caught a good many fish. I sent half of them to the mansion-house, and had the rest dressed at home.

"Mrs. Ringrose, my tenant's wife, was a clever and managing woman. They had five children; three daughters, and two sons.

"The eldest daughter was about eighteen years old; a neat and well-looking girl, healthy, and chearful. I meditated whether she would not be a suitable wife for me, but was not resolved on making the offer. I only mention it to you, as a proof that I never had a thought of seducing Antonio's wife: but one inducement to marriage was, the hope it might cure him of his jealousy.

"One day, the following week, they dined with me; and I desired Mrs. Ringrose to do the honours of my table. Antonio was displeased at it; and, after she was retired, he mentioned it as an affront to Isabella. I explained to him the difference between an English farmer and an Italian one, who is only the vassal of his lord, and does not presume to eat of the wheat which he sows and reaps. I told him, that his husbandman was a better man; "for he is a freeman, and your Italian vassal is a slave." He was not pleased with my explanation: but I defended my assertion; and, upon that ground, my setting the farmer's wife at my table.

"I visited Antonio about once a week. He seldom came to me. He was reserved and abstracted in his manners, except when he wanted my advice and assistance; and then he was free enough. We frequently differed in opinion, and I spoke my own sentiments freely, and sometimes ventured to touch him in a tender part; but I did it to cure him of his eternal jealousy and suspicion.

"Once, when he was talking of returning to Italy, I asked him how he should like that Isabella should be attended by a Cicisbeo?[1] He was much offended at it.

"Nay," said I, "but you must submit to the custom of your own country. I do not say this, to dissuade you from returning to Italy, for I really think it is the best thing you can do. But, how will your countrymen receive you, if you oppose, or blame, the system of Cicisbeism?"

"He was very angry, and went out of the room. I confess, that I was to blame to urge him on this subject, knowing his weakness in this respect; but, when he was blaming the manners of my country, it was natural to advert to those of his own.

"It was my intention to stay in the country all the summer and autumn, and then to take a trip to the Continent, and winter there. I was likewise meditating on a scheme for establishing a trade at some port in Flanders.

"Antonio grew daily more reserved and uncompanionable; and, in consequence, I went seldomer to his house. I behaved with a general civility, but with less familiarity than ever. Isabella seemed concerned at it; and this increased her husband's chagrin and ill-humour: she knew not what he would have; nor, as it seemed, could he have informed her.

"I was never of an idle disposition, but loved always to be doing something. I used to employ myself, of an evening, with making a net. As soon as it was finished, I wanted to use it; and, the next morning, I went out, with intention to go a-fishing, and I promised Mrs. Ringrose some fish for her dinner. When I had got about half-way to the creek, I met Don Antonio. I had my net coiled about my left arm, and a crab-tree stick in my right hand. I just touched my hat to him, and passed on: he crossed the path, and intercepted me.

"So, Sir," said he, "you are going a-fishing?"

"I am, Sir."

"You might, at least, have let me know it."

"To what purpose, Sir? Did I ever use your boat without sending you a share of the fish?"

"No!" he believed not.

"Then be satisfied with your fisherman, or else he will serve you no longer."

"I said this between jest and earnest; but he turned pale with anger. I never loved *pale anger,* for it shews a malignant heart; but I had not the least suspicion of the malicious intention of Antonio.

"While we were talking, I coiled up the net upon my arm, and left my right side unguarded. At that instant, he stabbed me with a dagger, which he held in his hand unperceived by me. I turned quickly. I seized his hand, wrenched the dagger from him, and threw it to some distance. My passion rose above my governance.

"Traitor!—Assassin!" said I: "is it thus you repay my services?"

"I seized him by the collar, with my left hand, and shook him till he gasped for breath. I thought not of my wound. I took my stick, and laid upon him; I beat him unmercifully from head to foot, and upon every part that came in my way.

"It is thus," said I, "that an Englishman resents the injury done him by an ungrateful and treacherous Italian!"

"When I let him go, he fell to the earth, as in an agony of pain. My passion abated, and I began to feel an emotion of pity for him.

"Go home," said I, "and wash yourself with vinegar, and lie

a-bed a few days. I did not seek your life, though you have mine. I will now take some care of myself; but, whatever happens, remember that you were the aggressor."

"I took my pocket-handkerchief, and put it against my wound. I wound the net about my body as tight as I could, and turned about to go home. I saw Jack Roberts at a distance; I hallooed to him—he came running. As soon as he came near, I said—'Jack, take care of your master; he has met with an accident, and so have I. Lead him home directly, and put him to bed. We have fought. Say nothing to any body; but take him home directly, or he will not be able to go. I am bleeding. Ask your master who has wounded me. God be with you!'

"He went to raise his master, but was not able. I went to his assistance: we raised him. He leaned upon John's shoulder, and moved slowly, groaning bitterly.

"I walked slowly towards my own home, and began to find myself grow weak and faint with loss of blood; for, though my wound was not deep, I lost a good deal.

"When I entered the house, I sat down on the first chair I met with. Mrs. Ringrose and her daughters came about me, and enquired what was the matter? I told them, I had met with an accident; but bade them not be frightened, for I should soon get the better of it. I begged they would let a man-servant help me up stairs, and put me to bed. Mr. Ringrose assisted me himself. As soon as I was undressed, I made a pledget[2] of linen, and dressed my wound, tying a napkin round my body. My tenant was frightened at the sight of my shirt; but I charged him not to speak of it. He helped me to put on a clean shirt, and then I went into bed. He would fain have sent for a surgeon, but I would not suffer it. I wished this affair to be known to as few people as possible. I took some wine and water, and endeavoured to compose myself. The family paid me every kind of attention: they made me broth, and ordered one of their servants to sit up with me.

"I had a tolerable night, and was pretty easy the next morning. About seven o'clock, Jack Roberts came to visit me. He was very desirous to know all that had passed between his master and me. I told him the whole, but enjoined him to secresy.

"Jack told me, he was in great fear, both for me and his master. "You have laid it on very heavily," said he; "and he cannot stir. I have anointed him well with vinegar; but I am really afraid of the consequences."

"Did he send you here, to enquire after me?"

"No, indeed," said Jack; "but he has not told his lady. He said, he had a fall, and was very much bruised. As for the rest, he thinks of nobody but himself."

"Does he shew no concern for me? does he say nothing about me?"

"No, Sir; but he sighs and groans bitterly, and seems very unhappy."

"I begged of Jack to come in the evening, and dress my wound for me. He said, he would make some excuse, and come to me, if possible.

"He did come, and was convinced of the malicious design of his master; but he expressed fears of his doing well. I had no doubt of his recovery, and gave directions how he should be treated. I bade him say nothing of me, unless his master enquired after me; and, in that case, to tell him the truth.

"My wound was now in a very fine way, and I hoped to be well in a few days. I resolved, as soon as Antonio and myself were well, to leave the country, and go to London for a time. I proposed to write to Don Antonio, to endeavour to make him ashamed of his behaviour; and to advise him to sell his estate here, and to return to Italy, for he would never be an Englishman.

"Thus I proposed schemes for my future conduct. Alas! they were all counteracted by unforeseen circumstances and events.

"On the third day after this unfortunate meeting, Jack Roberts came about noon-time. His looks were ominous.

"What is the matter now, Jack?"

"Matter enough!" said he. "In addition to your dressing, which was sufficient for him, Don Antonio is seized with the cholic. His sufferings are so great, that, I am sure, you would pity him."

"That I do sincerely!" said I.

"Thank God for that!" said Jack: "that is kind and charitable in you. But, Sir, will you come and help him?"

"That I will not do."

"I am sent to beg that you will come to him."

"Who sends you?"

"Both my master and mistress. He calls on you incessantly; and my lady begs you will come without delay."

"She knows not what has passed between us, or she would not urge it. Beside, it would be dangerous to me, on more than one account. If he should not do well—if our encounter should be known—I should incur danger from an enquiry. I will not administer any medicines to him. You may give him some gin and water, as I have done; but I will not see him again, if I can help it."

"Jack tried all the arguments he could think of; but I remained inflexible, and thought myself justified in my refusal. After he was gone, I had a great many anxious and uneasy thoughts. If Antonio should die—if the bruises upon him should be imputed to me—if a coroner's inquest should sit upon the case—all these *ifs* were uncomfortable to me.

"I confess, that I likewise felt sorrow and remorse for the blows I had given him. But he was the aggressor. He had a design upon my life. I had none upon his: I only meant to chastise him. But, supposing that passion and resentment, on my part, should have the same, or worse effect, than enmity and malice had on his, could I acquit myself of his death? Wretched is the mind that is obliged to undergo such conflicts: torn between self-accusation, and self-acquittal; always arguing with itself, but never satisfied with it's own decision!

"The next morning, Roberts came to my house, and put me out of doubt, at least. As he entered the room, he said—"All is over!—Don Antonio is dead!"

"I shuddered and groaned, but could make no answer.

"He told me, that he lay in the most violent pain for two days—that Isabella had not been in bed, nor took off her cloaths, all the time—that, whenever she touched him, he screamed out, being sore with the bruises he had received—that she was quite exhausted with grief and watching, and fell into fits—that the old nurse was sent for, and she was carried into another room; and that she had miscarried, as Mrs. Cob had told him, and was confined to her bed—that Antonio's pains abated about ten o'clock, and he composed himself to sleep—that Isabella was told he was better, and she went to rest—that he sat in his master's room, and fell asleep, and did not wake till day-light. Then he went to the bed-side, and observed that his master lay in the same posture he left him in. He touched his hand, and then his face, and found that he was dead. The first thought that occurred to him, was, to come to me, and beg me to go home with him, and give orders what should be done. "We are a distracted family, Sir," said he; "and it would be very imprudent to let strangers come into the house, especially considering all the circumstances that are known to you and I."

"I started up—'You say true, John. The case requires presence of mind. I will go with you directly. There is no time to lose. May I depend upon you, John?'

"You may, Sir. I will be true and faithful to you."

"Now, then, I am ready."

"I drest myself as quickly as possible. He came on horseback. I mounted the horse, and he walked by my side. When we came to the house, I took Mrs. Cob, the husbandman's wife, into the parlour. She looked frightened.

"Your master is dead, as John tells me. I am deeply concerned: but we must not sit down and grieve, till we have done our duty. Do not let your mistress hear a word of this sad event, till she is better able to bear it. Charge the nurse to be silent and careful. Let no one go near her but you two. John and I will see to what is necessary to be done above stairs; and do you keep away all impertinent intruders of every kind."

"I left her, and went up stairs; and John followed me. We went into the room, and my heart sunk within me at the sight. Antonio was already turned black, almost all over; and it was necessary to put the body into a state to be removed.

"I paused some minutes. John said—'What shall we do, Sir?—Who shall lay him out?'

"That office must be done by you and me, John. Nobody else must see him at present. A thought strikes me! In Italy, they bury their dead in the cloaths they wear when living. We will dress Antonio in the cloaths he wore last, lay him straight, and then send for the carpenter to make his coffin. The women need not come about him. We will perform the last sad offices."

"Accordingly, we performed this melancholy duty. We took off the bed and bedding; we dressed him as we proposed; we then wrapped the body in the under sheet, and laid the upper one over him.

"I then sent John to the carpenter, and bade him not return without him. He came directly, and measured the body. I told him, it was the custom in Italy, to be buried in their cloaths; and that his lady would think it a mark of disrespect to do otherwise.

"I bade John, before the carpenter, go to the parsonage, and acquaint the rector with his master's death, and give notice that he was not to be buried in woollen; that we were ready to pay the penalty, half of which would come to him, as the informer.

"I told the carpenter, that the gentleman died of a mortification in his bowels; and that he must be buried as soon as possible. He promised to make the coffin immediately.

"After he and John were gone, I went down stairs, and into the garden, where I had a kind of fit; for my heart was sorely oppressed, and I was almost suffocated. The idea of self-defence, which is said to be one of the first laws of nature, came to my relief; it supported me through scenes that I cannot, even now, look back upon without horror, and still wonder how I went through them: yet I thought it would be unjust, that I should come into hazard of my life, for a man who would have killed me, and against whose life I had no premeditated design.

"I ardently wished to get the funeral over before Isabella should know of his death; which would prevent all future enquiry.

"The next morning, the carpenter brought home the coffin. Assisted by John and myself, the body was laid into it. We carried it down stairs, and set it into one of the parlours. After which, all the servants were permitted to see it; and then it was screwed down, and set ready to be interred.

"Antonio died on the Wednesday, and was buried on the Sunday following: it would have been dangerous to keep him longer. All the servants attended the funeral: but I had not spirits to go; and, as I was known to be his most intimate friend, I was excused, and commended for my sensibility.

"Isabella was told he was better, every day; and she did not know the whole truth till a week afterwards.

"When she was told by her nurse, she was in agonies of grief and despair, which threw her back; and she was feverish and delirious several days. Nature, at length, got the better: she ate and slept, and enquired into the particulars of her husband's death and burial.

"She was told, that I had taken upon myself the last duties and offices, and had performed them with great concern and attention. I took this for an indication that I might be seen; and, as soon as she was well enough to sit up, I took the liberty to pay my respects to her.

"She had a burst of grief, upon the first sight of me; but, after a flood of tears, she began to question me—

"Why did you not come time enough to be of service to my Antonio?"

"Because I was very ill myself, and confined at home; and, when I did come, I was fitter to be in my bed."

"Why did you bury him so soon?"

"Because it was impossible to keep him longer. He died of a mortification, and the body was putrid: it would have been enough to breed a contagion to keep it longer."

"Where is he buried?"

"In consecrated ground—the church-yard of this parish."

"Alas! he had no priest to attend him!"

"The circumstances were too sudden to admit of it, or I would have sent for one: but the funeral rites were performed with every kind of decency and propriety."

"I thank you, Sir, for the trouble you have taken, when I was unable to attend to any thing."

"I am always ready to do you service, Madam; and I desire you will command me at all times."

"Pray, Sir, where do you take up your residence?"

"At my own house, Madam; but I come here every day, to receive your commands."

"I thank you, Sir!—Oh, my Antonio! he is lost for ever!"

"Here she fell into a paroxysm of grief. I retired, fearing to make my first visit too long, but glad that the ice was broken. I ordered all the bills to be sent in, and they were given to Isabella. She gave me the key of the escritoire, and desired me to take money to pay them. I thanked her for this proof of her confidence; but declined it, unless she would go with me, and see what money was there. She did so; and we were both surprized to see what Antonio had accumulated within three years: it proved his sordid and avaricious mind.

"I took an account of the money, and gave her the copy. I paid the bills, and brought her the acquittances.

"This was the last of those employments which were so painful to me, and which have left a weight upon my mind, never to be removed. And now, Madam, I will relieve you and myself, and will postpone the remainder of my story till another day."

Here Captain Maurice took his leave; and it was a relief to me, for I felt too strongly all the dismal circumstances of the story he had told.

I will not anticipate your judgment upon it; but leave it to your candour, and to your pity.

Adieu, my dear friend. I am, always, Yours faithfully,

FRANCES DARNFORD.

LETTER XIII
Mrs. Darnford, to Mrs. Strictland.

I WILL now proceed with Captain Maurice's story, in his own words—

"In regard to what is past, Madam, I lay claim to your pity and candour; in what is to come, I expect your disapprobation and censure. I have owned myself guilty of many faults, and only implore your compassion as a penitent desirous to atone for his crimes.

"During Antonio's life, I never entertained a thought, or a wish, to obtain the love of Isabella; but, from the time that the funeral was over, and she seemed returning to health and tranquillity, I fixed my mind upon this expectation, and determined to be her husband.

"She received my services with gratitude; she never denied me her company. If I staid away from her house a day, she always sent to know how I did, and desired to see me on the morrow. These circumstances encouraged me to persevere in my pursuit. I only knew her situation. I was her friend and servant. I resolved to be her affectionate husband, and her faithful steward. I was not over forward to declare my wishes: I never mentioned them till between three and four months after the death of Antonio——"

I interrupted him, by saying—"I think that was much too soon."

"If you consider our intimacy, Madam, perhaps you may change your opinion. We were then upon such good terms, that it seemed as if nothing but the question was wanting."

"Was Isabella of this opinion, Sir?"

"No; she was not. From the moment I declared myself her lover, she fell into reserve and sullenness. Sometimes she left the room, and would see me no more that day; but, when I asked for her the day following, she came at the first word. She would talk freely with me upon business; or, in short, upon any subject but one—that one which engrossed all my attention.

"After the ice was broken, I obliged her to hear me often. I thought on the old saying—"Faint heart never won fair lady." I teazed her continually: I persecuted her with my addresses. Sometimes she burst into an agony of tears; sometimes she exclaimed aloud—"Oh, my Antonio!—Oh, my Giulio!—Why are not you here to protect me?"

"And had you no pity for her?" said I.

"Yes; I more than pitied—I adored her."

"That was not the kind of pity she wanted."

"My passion grew by opposition. I suffered as much as she did. I have kneeled, and prayed, and wept; but in vain."

"Poor lady!" said I, "what must she have suffered!"

"I thought you would pity her, and blame me. But, no matter. If I can engage your pity for Isabella, so as to induce you to take the charge of her, I care not what becomes of me."

"What a mixture of strange and generous sentiments!—Proceed, Sir: I will not again interrupt you, if I can help it."

"One night, that I had been very urgent with her to give me her hand, she broke from me, and ran up stairs; and I saw her no more.

"The next day, her servant told me, that she went into the chamber where Antonio died, and she would not come out of it. She threw herself upon her knees, against the bed; she invoked Antonio's name; she implored him to help her. After doing this some time, she seemed as if speaking to some person actually present: she waited for his answer, and then replied again, and so continued in talk with him. The servant intreated her to go to bed in her own apartment. She answered—"No: I will not sleep any where but in this room. Here I have found my protector, and here I will remain!"

"The woman urged her to go. She bade her go to her own bed; for, if she staid all night, she would not leave the chamber.

"Mrs. Cob and her husband were gone to bed; so was the boy; and there was nobody up but Susan Dobbins.

"I should have told you, Madam, that the young woman who waited on Isabella was married, and gone away, just before Antonio's sickness and death. There was in the parish a young widow, who had lately buried her husband and child: they died of the small-pox. The woman had it, and recovered. Finding she could not support herself, she resolved to go to service. She was recommended to Isabella, who took her into her family. She was an honest and tidy woman, but very vulgar and clownish; and Isabella was disgusted with her, and did not like her about her person. I had offered to enquire after another; but wished to see Isabella more composed, and more reconciled to my wishes, before a stranger was admitted into the family.

"This Susan Dobbins perceived my design; and, like a true gossip, whispered it to every one that came near her, that I was to marry her mistress as soon as the year was out, as she phrased it. I thought this would forward my scheme, and therefore did not contradict it; but I charged Susan not to hint it to her mistress.

"Isabella did not see me for two or three days after; and, when she did, there was a wildness in her eyes that surprized and shocked me.

"I enquired tenderly after her health. She said, she was better, and should be better still.

"I told her, I was glad to hear it; for that I was informed, that she neither ate nor slept well.

"Oh, yes," said she, "I eat and sleep enough."

"Can I do any thing, Madam, to promote your health and happiness?"

"Why, yes; I believe you can, Sir. I am resolved to go to Italy; and you must carry me in your ship, Sir. Antonio will be with me; and he will protect me from you, and from every body."

"I do not understand you, Madam: Antonio is dead and buried."

"Yes, I know that too well; but he will be with me, for all that."

"How can that be? I cannot understand or believe you."

"No matter. I know what I say. I know where to find him; and he comes to me whenever I call him."

"Strange fancy!—This is all conceit, Madam: you dreamed it."

"Yes, I dreamed it, both sleeping and waking: no matter how. I do not want you to know all that I do—only take care how you insult me again, for I have a friend that will resent it."

"Insult you, Madam! I would not, for the world, do any thing to offend you. You kill me with your cruelty; and this fancy is assumed, to distress and mortify me!"

"No, I do not want to kill you, or distress you. I would only keep you at your proper distance; that is all, Sir."

"What, then, can I do, and not displease you?"

"Be humble, and modest, and keep your distance; and only come here when I send for you. That do, and I will thank you."

"You use me very ill, Madam. I never staid away from your house, that you did not send for me the next day; and now, you would throw me to a distance."

"I did once think you my friend, Sir. I thought I was obliged to you; but I have forgot why I thought so. Sir, you may stay to dine here, but I shall not dine with you."

"Then I shall not stay. I do not want a dinner. I shall wait your commands—when you know your own meaning!"

"I took my leave in anger, and went home vexed and unhappy.

"I could not understand, whether her head was affected, or whether she feigned herself thus, in order to drive me away from her; but my mind rested upon the last opinion.

"Two days after, I received a message, that Madam desired to see me. I went directly. John met me with a smiling countenance—

"I am glad you are come, Sir: I hope you will be our master at last."

"God knows!" said I; "but I saw nothing like it when I was last here."

"Never mind, Sir. "Women's minds waver," says the proverb."

"I shook hands with him, and went into the parlour.

"I waited above half an hour before Isabella appeared. I bowed respectfully, and enquired after her health. She curtsied, and thanked me. She was silent, and looked serious. I waited her motions, but she said nothing.

"At last, I spoke—"I came hither, Madam, in obedience to your commands."

"Did you, Sir?—Oh, now I recollect, I had something to say to you! They tell me, I was rude to you when you was here. I ask your pardon, Sir!"

"I bowed to her—"You have it, Madam. I thought you unkind; but I feared you were not well, and I excused it."

"I am not well," said she; "but I do not know what ails me. I have lost my memory. I do not recollect any thing. Sometimes, I am very happy for a short time; but then, again, I feel very miserable. I do not know how it is."

"I am glad to see you better, Madam. I now ask you to forgive any thing I may have done to offend you." [I kneeled to her.]

"Yes, Sir, I forgive you, and all the world!"

"If I stay, will you give me your company at dinner?"

"Yes, if you desire it; but I cannot eat, and I hope you will excuse me."

"She gave me her company at dinner, but she neither ate nor spoke. She drank a little wine and water, and she seemed thirsty and feverish. As soon as the dinner-things were taken away, she curtsied, and withdrew. I walked in the garden, fretting at her behaviour, and doubtful of how to act.

"Susan Dobbins came to me, laughing like an ideot—"So, Madam sent for yow agen; but te' moight bethank me!"

"I do not understand you," said I.

"Why, I tould her, as how that yow were affronted, just as John tould me, and that yow would never come agen, except she sent for yow; so that made her oneasy, and so she sent for yow to come to-day."

"I dare say, you meant it well: but I earnestly desire, that you will say nothing of this kind to your lady in future."

"Well, I 'on't, then. If yow understand one another, that's enough."

"Pray, tell me, does she still fancy that her husband is with her?"

"Aye, that she do, sure enough: she hold long talk with him, and spake so natural, that I am sometimes sort of afraid, that there is somebody else in the room beside ourselves; or else, that her poor head ha' got a crack in it."

"Well, do not speak of it out of the house: do not let her be long alone; watch all her motions, and let me know how she does every day. Try to amuse her from thinking too much; try to excite her to eat; make her broth, and get her every thing she can ask or wish for. Go to her now. I will see you again in a few days."

"Thus we went on for several weeks. I called every day, but did not stay dinner except she asked me.

"One day, she seemed better, and she entered into conversation with me. She asked me to go with her to Italy.

"And what will you do there, Madam?"

"I would go and board in a convent for a time; and, if I liked it, I would stay there always."

"This would be a dismal and uncomfortable life for you."

"I do not think so: perhaps, I might be happier there than here."

"What hinders you to be happy here?"

"I do not know," said she: and was silent.

"I will carry you to Italy, upon one condition: give me your hand, make me your husband, give me a right to be your protector, and I will go with you all the world over."

"No—no—no!" said she; and rose to go away.

"I took her hand—"Stay a minute longer—hear what I have to say. Perhaps, I have urged you too soon. Let us compromise. I will not again urge you on this subject, till your year of widowhood is fully expired; but, then, I must hope you will receive me more graciously."

"I kissed her hand, and released it. She went away from me,

and ran up stairs. I went home, chagrined, and out of spirits. I was wholly unsettled, and took no pleasure in any thing, but the hope that she would one day be mine."

"Surely, Sir," said I, "it would have been wiser in you to give over the pursuit, when you found the lady so averse to it."

"Perhaps so, Madam: but I did not give it over, as you shall hear.

"I continued my attentions to the lady, without mentioning our marriage, till the year was completed, and the fatal day had passed over us; which I kept with many sighs, and some tears.

"Isabella did not reckon the days and weeks, as I did. She knew not the anniversary of her loss, and I was glad that she did not: but she continued in the same strange way, talking with the idea of her husband, and telling him every thing that happened.

"I now resumed my addresses and importunities. I urged her to be mine, to turn her thoughts from fancies and conceits, and meet her happiness in her lover's arms.

"She was, for the most part, silent and sullen; but sometimes broke out into fits of passion, and even frenzy. I flattered myself, that if once she found herself married to me, she would be reconciled to her situation and to me, and a new scene of happiness would arise to us both.

"With this in view, I contrived to dress John as a priest of the Romish Church, and prepared him to read the ceremony to us. I besought her to consent to it's being performed. I begged, prayed, soothed, and threatened, in turn. I tried to frighten her into a marriage; and, when she should be reconciled to her situation, I always meant to have it solemnized in a legal way.

"Many distressful scenes followed: I cannot recite them all to you; yet I must, in my own behalf, assure you, that I never attempted to use violence, not to commit any act of indecency.

"One evening, when I had tried all the arts of persuasion, I bade Susan call in the priest. When John entered, she fell into hysteric fits. I said, it must be now or never, and bade him perform his office.

"When she recovered, she found her hand in mine, and the supposed priest giving the nuptial benediction. She gave a shriek, and went into fits again.

"Susan and I supported her. I poured some water down her throat, and she revived again.

"As soon as her senses returned, I said—"I thank you, father, for your good offices. When Isabella is better reconciled to her situation, we will hope to see you here again."

"He went away, wishing us happy together.

"I then said every thing soothing and comfortable. I told her, I was entirely at her command, as before; and that I would take no advantage of the holy rites that made her mine—That she was free to retire to her own apartment whenever she pleased.

"From that time, I took possession of the house. I slept there, but in a distant part of the house from Isabella's apartment. She was in passions of grief and frenzy all the night; but, in the day-time, she composed herself by her ideal conversations with her husband.

"Susan told her, that I was her husband. She denied it, and called upon Antonio, to witness to the contrary.

"I enjoyed no advantage from this supposed marriage, but that of being acknowledged by the servants as their master. They told it through the village, that we were married; and it was believed by all the inhabitants of the parish.

"From the time of our supposed marriage, Isabella gave me very little of her company. She refused to come down stairs to dinner. She would sometimes come into the library, or walk in the gallery; but, if she heard any body coming, she retreated into her chamber. I sometimes came into the gallery, and conversed with her as she stood in the library; but, if I offered to come any farther, she went into the bedchamber, and locked the door.

"I have argued with her by the hour, beseeching her to leave that part of the house, and come into her former apartment; yet she would never listen to it, but always said, in that chamber she had a friend that would protect her.

"Susan slept in a couch-bed, in the library. I ordered her to sleep in the chamber with her mistress; but she said, she could not—that she was scared out of her senses, and conceived that something more than themselves was in the room, and especially at night.

"This notion gained ground daily, and the under-servants reported that the house was haunted; which gave me concern, and I cast about how to put an end to it; which I was certain, could not be done, without obliging Isabella to quit that chamber, and then to shut it up entirely."

"Surely," said I, "you could not be so cruel. It was enough to drive her to distraction and desperation."

"I expected, Madam," said he, "that you would interrupt me."

"It is with difficulty I have refrained speaking so long."

"Have patience a little longer. You may blame me; but, when you have heard all, perhaps you may pity me."

"My pity is engrossed by the poor sufferer."

"Already are you biassed? What must I expect hereafter?"

"I hope there is nothing worse, to make me execrate you?"

"Worse, or better, you must hear all; or you will think worse of me than you ought. I did not go the lengths that you suppose."

"You went much farther than I can approve, or allow."

"I went far enough to spoil my peace; and, if I had been more resolute, perhaps I had suffered less. He who is a compleat villain, suffers less than he who stops short of the last extremities, both in regard to himself and others."

Here I will finish this sheet; and subscribe myself,

Yours, always, and equally,
FRANCES DARNFORD.

LETTER XIV
Mrs. Darnford, to Mrs. Strictland.

THOUGH Captain Maurice had forfeited my good opinion, I was desirous to hear the rest of his story; and to know how far it might be in my power to be of service to this poor afflicted lady, whose sufferings proceeded from real grief and unfeigned misfortune.

I desired the strange man to proceed with his narration.

"I resolved," said he, "to try fair means to get her out of that fatal chamber, which I shuddered at approaching. Having encouraged myself with a bottle of wine, I followed her one night into this room. Susan Dobbins was present. I only meant to conduct her to her former apartment, and to leave her there.

"At the sight of me, she shrieked loudly; and ran to a corner of the room, as if for safety. There stood an old-fashioned high-backed great chair: she had hung upon it a suit of cloaths of Antonio's, and buttoned it over the chair; and her disturbed imagination represented to her the idea of Antonio's being present there. She threw the sleeves of the coat over her, and then composed herself.

"There! There! Now I am safe!—He dares not take me out of your arms!"

"My dearest Isabella," said I, "let me persuade you to leave this room, and return to your own apartment. I swear to you, that I will leave you to your repose!"

"I do not mind his foolish talking—no, my love, I am yours only. Do not be uneasy; I promise you, I will never marry any other man."

"Hear me, Isabella! It is for your sake I ask you to go from this chamber: it is this place that disturbs you, and makes you thus; you will never be well while you stay here."

"Let him talk on," said she; "do not mind him. I will never leave you, my Antonio; no, never! Maurice, begone!"

"Again, on my knees, I besought her to come away.

"Oh," said she, "you must not fight! I will hinder that—He is not the man we once thought him. You were in the right, my love; but I was very wrong, to take his part against you: that was very wicked of me, but I have been punished for it.—Go, man! get away from me! Are you not ashamed to come here?"

"Susan Dobbins then spoke—"There, Sir! you have heard her with your own ears; I hope you will believe me another time."

"I was provoked, and ashamed, to be thus got the better of. I advanced towards her, intending to take her into my custody. She rose up, without fear, but animated with strong resolution—

"Maurice, if you approach a step farther, you will meet your punishment! Antonio dares to fight you; for all you have said is false."

"She stood, as if interposing between him and me. Sometimes she went to him, as it seemed; sometimes she came towards me. She talked incessantly to one and the other. She said the strangest things that can be imagined. She raised a kind of terror, that subdued me: and, at last, she said—"No, I do not believe that Maurice killed you, because you lived three days after—But, how could he hurt you, and leave no wound?"

"My heart smote me: I was struck with horror; my knees knocked together, and I retreated slowly out of the room. I went backward; and, as I came past the bed, I fell over a chair that stood in my way; and, crawling upon my hands and knees, slunk away, baffled and shamed, and went to my own apartment, where I spent a wretched night, without sleep or composure.

"I am naturally bold and intrepid; but never was a man's

courage more compleatly subdued than mine, on that fatal night. I never shall forget it while I live!

"The next day, I was almost in a state of distraction; alarmed, ashamed, incensed, unable to form a resolution, yet unwilling to relinquish my pursuit.

"I got on horseback, and rode for several hours: came home to dinner, and afterwards slept in a great chair for a considerable time. I enquired after Isabella, and was told, that she did not go to bed till day-light, but had then a comfortable sleep of more than five hours. Susan told me, she dared not sleep in her chamber, but brought her bed into the library, and slept there.

"Things remained in this state several weeks. I went into the room opposite to Isabella's, on the other side of the library, where I watched her motions. She asked Susan where I was; and she said, she could not tell certainly, but believed I was walking in the garden. "Then I will walk too," said she.

"She came through the library, and went to walk in the gallery. I snatched the opportunity. I sprung through the library, double-locked the door of her chamber, and put the key into my pocket.

"When she returned, she was surprized and grieved. She tried at the lock, and found it fastened against her. She called to Susan, who protested she knew nothing of the key. She fell into a passion, stamped and tore; and, having exhausted her strength, fell into a swoon.

"I then stepped forward; and, assisted by Susan, carried her into the dressing-room, between the two chambers in the gallery, and there left her to the care of Susan; but waited within hearing, in case she should want any farther assistance.

"When she returned to life and her senses, she raved against those who had locked her out of her own chamber, and asked who it was.

"Susan said, she believed it was her master.

"She exclaimed—"What master?"

"Captain Maurice, Madam."

"You have no master!"

"Yes, I have. Captain Maurice is my master, and yours too."

"She raved against me till her strength failed her, and then fainted again, and continued several hours in this way. At length, she grew quieter; and Susan, with Mrs. Cob's help, put her to bed.

"She called on Antonio, and her son Giulio, incessantly; till wearied Nature took pity on her, and lulled her into repose."

"Yet you took no pity on her," said I, unable to keep silence.

"Yes, I did," he answered. "I was clear she would never recover so long as she staid in that chamber, fatal to her and me."

"We went on thus for a few days; when Mrs. Cob complained, that Susan and she were quite worn out, and they could not support the fatigue of their daily work, and watching all night with their mistress. I asked what she would advise me to do?

"Sir," said she, "there is a person in the neighborhood, that is used to nurse people that are out of their right mind. She is just now at liberty, and came here to offer her service yesterday, while you were gone out; so I bade her come again today, and she is now in the house."

"I will come and speak to her," said I; and went to her immediately. I enquired where she had been, and who was to give her a character. She shewed me a written one, from the surgeon and apothecary in the next parish; signifying that she had been employed in several families where he attended, and that he would be answerable for her honesty and fidelity. I told her, she might come directly; and desired her to treat the lady with the utmost attention and tenderness. She bragged of her knowledge in such cases; and said, she must be left to her own method.

"Mrs. Burton entered upon her office immediately. I introduced her to Isabella, who was sitting in the dressing-room. Susan was standing by her; and she seemed quiet, and half-asleep.

"At the sight of us, she started, and looked angry. She held up her hand in a threatening attitude. I approached her, and spoke—

"My dearest Isabella, I have brought a gentlewoman to wait on you, to nurse you, to comfort you, and to make you well."

"She looked disdainfully on her, and on me. She held up her hand, as before. I drew near her; I took her other hand, and kissed it. She gave me a blow with her right-hand, that surprized me: it made my face glow for a long time after.

"Mrs. Burton said—"Oh fie, Madam! Is this your behaviour to your husband?"

"She looked at her scornfully, and held up her hand, in defiance.

"I said—"You must be gentle and obliging to her."

"She smiled—"I can perceive that you have been too gentle to her; and I see how she returns it. You should be more resolute with her."

"Not so," said I; "nor will I suffer any one to treat her roughly. Observe what I say, Mrs. Burton, or you will not stay here."

"Very well, Sir," said she: I will endeavour to oblige her and you."

"Isabella stamped with her foot, and shewed signs of impatience. I withdrew, and left her to the care of Mrs. Burton.

"As I found the sight of me discomposed her, I only saw her by stratagem, now and then trying whether she would endure it more patiently; but every experiment I made, served to confirm me in opinion, that she never would love me, nor admit me to the privileges of an husband.

"After Mrs. Burton had been some weeks in the family, Susan Dobbins was often hinting to me something that she feared to explain. I desired her to speak out, and fear nothing.

"After much prefacing, she told me, that, in her mind, Mrs. Burton used her mistress very ill; but begged I would not let it be said that she had told tales of her: that was her way of speaking.

"I determined to know the truth of it, and to discharge Mrs. Burton the first opportunity.

"A few nights afterwards, as I was going to bed, it came into my head to listen at the door of Isabella's room. I heard Mrs. Burton speaking in a loud and insolent tone of voice—"You shall, Madam—I tell you, you shall do as I order you—What, do you think to make a fool of me, as you do of all the rest?—I know better how to manage you—I have broken a higher spirit than yours—Lie still, and go to sleep, or——"

"At that moment, I tapt at the door. Mrs. Burton came, and opened it.

"How dare you speak in that manner to the woman I love as my soul?"

"Oh, dear Sir! is it you?—They tell me, that, though you have been married to her many months, you have not had courage enough to bed her. Come in, Sir; and I will bring her to your lure, I warrant: you shall go to bed with her now, if you please, upon condition that you give me a pair of gloves, and a favour, tomorrow morning."

"I made her no answer, but went into the room. I saw the dear saint lying like a lamb under the hand of the butcher. My heart smote me, and I felt as if a dagger was run through me. I kneeled by the bed-side, and begged her to speak to me.

"Oh, my Isabella! give me your hand, and speak one kind

word to me, and I will send this woman away from you! she shall never approach you more!"

"She lay with her face into the pillow, and I feared she would be suffocated. I offered to take her hand.—Oh, Madam! how shall I speak it?—Her dear hands were tied behind her, and her feet tied together! I felt as if my heart was bursting. "Oh, vile woman!" said I; "brute!—monster! is it thus you treat the fairest of women?—Run up stairs, and call Susan this moment; and come not again into my sight!—I will speak to you to-morrow."

"She began to apologize.

"Get out of my sight this moment, or I shall do you a mischief!"

"She ran up stairs, and sent Susan in a few minutes.

"I cut the strings that tied those fair hands. I begged her to pardon me for giving that woman the charge of her. The moment her hands were at liberty, she rolled herself up in the bed-cloaths, so that I could not see her face, nor any part of her. Susan came down. I bade her take care of her mistress, unfold the bed-cloaths, and put her to bed, and stay with her all the night. "I am not going to bed. I will come again in an hour, to know how she does. If she should drop asleep, come to my room, and let me know it."

"I retired to my own room, in a violent agitation of spirits. My heart was touched. I reflected upon the trouble I had given that sweet and amiable woman. I had wished a thousand times to have her at an advantage; but, when that moment came, my heart would not suffer me to avail myself of it: I was not so hardened a villain. That vile woman's wickedness awoke my compassion and remorse. I felt the most true compunction for the part I had acted by her, and the most ardent wish to make atonement for it.

"As soon as I was alone, I threw myself upon my knees. I prayed to Heaven to restore her, and to forgive me. I vowed that I would no more insult her with my importunities, but would do every thing in my power to serve and save her. My heart was softened to such a degree, that I wept like a chidden infant, and found my heart relieved by it.

"After some hours spent in this way, I returned into the gallery, and tapt softly at the door. Susan came; and, in a whisper, told me, her mistress was not asleep, but that she lay quieter. I laid my finger on my lip, shut the door, and went back to my own chamber. I had no call to sleep. I walked about the whole night, ruminating on the past, and planning schemes for the future.

"As soon as I heard Cob and his wife stirring, I went down stairs. I told them what had past with Mrs. Burton, and ordered them to call me as soon as she came among them. They did so, and I went down to speak to her. In the interim, I considered that it was best to part with her upon good terms, lest she should make bad reports about the neighborhood; that I would pay her handsomely, and send her away satisfied.

"She would have argued with me, on the propriety of her method of treating the lady; but I desired her to say no more, only make her demand. She did so, and I paid her something more; and told her, if we had any farther need of her service, we would let her know it.

"I felt some relief to my mind, after I had dismissed Mrs. Burton. I then wished to find a person of good heart and character, to whom I could trust the care of this unhappy and innocent creature, and ease my mind of the burthen it laboured under; for I resolved to use the power I had acquired over her, for her benefit in future.

"The house was grown melancholy and disagreeable to me. I was so depressed in mind, that I took no pleasure in any thing.

"John Roberts took the liberty of advising me to go abroad again, and to give up my pursuit of Isabella, which, he said, (very truly) had only made her miserable, and myself too. I told him, I had already resolved upon something of this kind; and, as soon as I could meet with a proper person to take charge of Isabella, I would go to the Continent. John desired to continue my servant, and to go with me. I readily accepted his offer, and prepared to realize this plan.

"In the course of this year, Madam, I had placed my Charlotte under your care; and was pleased with, and proud of, her improvements.

"I now went to Mrs. Sorling's, and consulted her about putting my wife (so I called her) under your care. She said, if you would accept the charge, I might think myself a fortunate man; but she doubted whether I would undertake it.

"Now, Madam, I will add a few particulars, in the hope they may induce you to do it—

"Isabella is generally melancholy and sullen; yet she has sometimes fits of frenzy, but is never mischievous to herself, or others. She sometimes refuses her food; but Nature resumes her rights, and then she eats greedily. She is thin and emaciated: she seldom speaks; but she prays often, and mostly mentally. There is a poor woman who assists Susan in the care of her. If she is refractory, Susan threatens to send for Mrs. Burton; and that makes her comply with whatever she desires. She is also afraid of me, and I cannot prevail upon her to endure my company; but, when I am absent, she is quiet and patient.

"This, Madam, is the true account of our situation. And now, let me implore you, for pity's sake, to accept the charge of this poor, unhappy lady!—I preserve the appearance of a power over her, only for her service: she might otherwise be subject to worse treatment.

"I will make you my tenant at the mansion-house: Isabella and my Charlotte shall be your boarders. I will settle the money I leave in the funds upon Charlotte irrevocably; and I will request you to accept the office of her guardian. I will give you a power to receive the rents of my farm during my absence. When all these points are settled, I will go abroad, and try to recover my health and my peace. Deign, Madam, to accept this kind and charitable office!—I will pray to God to influence your mind in my behalf!"

He kneeled down, and lifted up his eyes, which were swimming in tears: I could not refrain mine.

"You are moved," said he: "thank God for it!—You will do nothing to repent of!—Your goodness will be rewarded, both here and hereafter!"

He stopped, and wept in silence.

After a pause, I said—"Sir, I do not promise to do what you require: I fear it may be too much for my health and spirits."

"You can but try, Madam. If you find it so, you need only see that poor Isabella is used well by her attendants, and direct what is to be done for her service. Do not refuse this, I beseech you!"

"Well, Sir, I will consider of it. But I should wish to see the house, and the lady, before I give a decisive answer."

"You shall do so, Madam. I will attend you whenever you please."

I promised that I would take this journey; and the unhappy man was cheared by it. He went away, thanking and blessing me.

It came into my mind, that this poor lady had never been attended by any person that could be her companion or comforter. I resolved to see her, and to judge whether there were any hopes of her recovery, by proper treatment, and the company of a friend. This idea I kept to myself, and determined to try the experiment.

I proposed to Captain Maurice, that Charlotte Brady should go with us; and that she should be his companion, while I attended on Isabella. He gladly consented to it.

The following week, we set out on this journey. My next letter will bring you an account of the success of it.

In the mean time, I will send away this pacquet.

Ever yours faithfully,
F. DARNFORD.

LETTER XV
Mrs. Darnford, to Mrs. Strictland.

I IMPLORE your mercy and compassion in behalf of Captain Maurice. Do not be too severe in your judgment of him. Though he has been very wrong in his persecution of Isabella, and though her sufferings were the result of his perseverance, it was not his intention that she should suffer; and accidental circumstances had a share in it.

But, look upon him in another, and more favourable light—as a man who had one object in view, which he had long pursued with unceasing assiduity—that object in his power, and passion pleading for it's gratification. Behold him struck with sorrow and repentance; not light and momentary, but deep and serious! he foregoes all his purposes, and studies to make atonement by every means he can think of. He settles his affairs; provides for the welfare and comfort of the persons most dear to him; gives up the greatest part of his property, and goes, with a heavy heart, to seek a new destiny in a foreign land!

Let these circumstances have their due effect upon your mind. Consider that human nature is frail, and liable to error. There are few people who have not some secret faults, that are concealed from the world's knowledge, and that prey upon the heart in it's deepest recesses, for which there is no other remedy *"than the heart's sorrow, and a clear life ensuing."*[1] To this, and to the mercy of Heaven, I leave this unhappy man; and shall now give you an account of my first journey.

Captain Maurice, Charlotte Brady, and myself, went in a post-chaise to N——, where we slept one night, and reached the end of our journey by noon the next day.

We were met, within a mile of the house, by a clown driving a chaise-cart, into which we got with our trunk. Captain Maurice took the reins; and the man walked before us, and opened the gates for us. He drove us round to the front of the house. It is a very pretty one, sashed and modernized, and pleasantly situated. It looked light and chearful, and had nothing ominous nor melancholy in it's appearance. He rung the bell, and a woman-servant came to the door.

"So, Mrs. Cob," said he; "did your husband receive my letter?"

"Yes, Sir; and we have done all that you ordered."

He said—"I have brought this lady to visit your mistress, and in hope that she will take the charge of her when I am gone abroad. She understands how to treat people in her unhappy situation."

The woman shook her head, as if afraid he had brought another Mrs. Burton.

We went into the hall, which is, indeed, too large for the house. It is decorated with stags heads, hunting-horns, and other emblems of the chace. I suppose, it's former owners were hunting squires.

Captain Maurice shewed us the parlours, and a large store-room. He then led us up stairs. Over the hall and the store-room were three good-sized rooms, two bed-chambers, and a dressing-room. There was a gallery the whole length, at the end of the library, which has been often mentioned; and a chamber on each side of it.

I was struck with the sight of a new door on the outside of the door-case. I looked at Maurice, and he changed colour.

"That is the door," said he, "that leads to the chamber——"

"I understand you, Sir."

"No, not quite," said he. "While Mrs. Burton was here, I made them bring all Isabella's cloaths, linen, and every thing, out of this room. I took away the bedding, and every thing likely to be of use to her. I then caused a new outside door to be put up; and, instead of a lock, it is screwed into the door-case, so that it cannot easily be opened. Now, that it is wholly shut up, there is an end to all the foolish talking that I have told you of."

"In my opinion, Sir, it was likely to be the more talked of."

"I do not find it so, Madam. I am convinced that room was the cause of Isabella's losing her reason; and it had liked to have turned all the heads in the family. It shall never be opened again, while I have any power in this house."

I said no more; and he seemed glad to get away from the subject. We returned into the gallery, and he tapt at the door of the dressing-room. A woman opened it.

"Susan," said he, "how is your mistress?"

"Much the same, Sir. She is frightened now, at your knocking."

"I have brought a lady to visit her, who understands her case.—Here, Madam, I leave you. Charlotte and I will go down stairs."

I followed Susan into the room. There sat the poor lady in a great chair; her face reclined against the side of it. She had on a white loose morning gown, tied round her waist; and a rosary by her side. She was the wreck of beauty; pale and emaciated, but finely made; and, thus simply dressed, she looked like a person of superior degree and consequence. At my appearance, she started, and threw her handkerchief over her face, as wishing to hide herself from every body.

Susan went and bawled in her ear, as if she was deaf—"My master ha' brought a lady to visit yow, and he pray you to behave kindly to her."

She threw back her hand, as if to forbid my approach. I felt an aukwardness about me, as if intruding myself upon her. She would not deign to look upon me, but sat in all the silent majesty of woe.

I sat down near her, and spoke to her in the softest tone of voice—"My dear lady, I am not come hither out of impertinent curiosity, but to try whether I can be of any service to you. I shall not stay, if you forbid me. But see me, and know me, before you reject my services."

She waved her hand for me to leave her.

"I know, and pity your misfortunes, Madam. I, too, have suffered; and, being a child of Sorrow myself, I can sympathize with you; and, perhaps, may be enabled to be your comforter."

She clapped her hands together, and seemed to pray mentally.

I went on—"I am not come to assume any authority over you, but to see that every one does their duty to you. Deign, Madam, to look at me; and accept my intentions, though you should refuse my personal attendance on you."

She sighed deeply, and again waved her hand to me.

"Cannot you persuade the lady to look at me, and hear me?" said I.

Susan spoke to her in a vulgar and cajoling manner. She called her, her pretty dear, and behaved with a disgusting familiarity.

She stamped with her foot, and pointed to the door.

I said—"I will withdraw for the present; and, when your lady is disposed to see me, I will wait on her.

"Consider, my dear lady, that you want a friend and a companion; and do not drive away from you the person who comes only to assist you."

So saying, I left the room, and went down stairs to Maurice and his Charlotte, where I told him all that had passed.

After dinner, I made a second attempt to gain her attention; but with no better success. I left her in the evening, and walked in the garden till it grew duskish.

There was a long terrass-walk, from whence you descended to the garden, which was all upon a declivity; and, at the bottom, a piece of water. It was surrounded by a good wall, with fruit-trees planted against it. The ground was divided into four quarters, bounded with espaliers;[2] and, within, full of herbs and roots, for the use of the family. On the opposite side, the ground rose; and there was, on all sides, an agreeable prospect, and great capabilities of improvement.

Captain Maurice went to his farm-house, for he had not slept at the mansion since he resolved to give up Isabella. Charlotte and I slept together in a room out of the gallery, and we rested comfortably in our new lodging.

As soon as I was dressed the next morning, I desired to speak with Susan, and enquired whether her mistress was willing to see me.

She told me, that Madam had not forgot my visit; that she asked, whether I was not Mrs. Burton in disguise. Susan told her, that I was quite another person.

"I thought," said she, "that the voice was not like Mrs. Burton's: but she might alter that, you know."

"The only way to know that, was to look at her," said Susan.

She said, she was afraid I should get her into my power; but, if I should call again, she would look at me.

I bade Susan tell her, I was come again, and desired she would see me.

In a quarter of an hour, Susan came to conduct me to her. I went with more courage, and pleased that she recollected me.

When I entered the room, she was sitting in her chair, as before. She held her hand partly over her eyes, as if the light was painful to her; and looked earnestly at me. I curtsied to her, wished her a good morning, and hoped she was better to-day. She was silent.

Susan said—"My dear creature, why don't you speak to the lady?—Pray, do, my dear."

"I think you treat the lady in too familiar a manner," said I: "as your mistress, you ought to shew her more respect."

"Respect!—Lord help us! I have all the respect in the world for her! I loves her, and pities her; and I humours her like a child."

"So I think, Susan: but she requires to be humoured as a woman, and as a lady very much your superior, notwithstanding her unfortunate situation."

"Lack-a-day! I don't mean any disrespect, not I."

"I dare say, not. I have heard that you have been very faithful to her, and I think very well of you: but still I wish you to pay her a little more respect; for, I think, she would like you the better."

I took a chair close to her. I took her hand in mine. She gazed at me till she abashed me. I spoke to her again, and asked her, whether she saw any thing in my face that displeased her?

She spoke—"No, I think you are not Mrs. Burton, nor yet Mr. Maurice; but, who are you, Madam?"

"My name is Frances Darnford; and I wish to be called your friend. I am come to visit you, and to comfort you."

"Who sent you, pray?"

"I heard of your ill health, Madam: and I hoped it might be in my power to assist you; and, perhaps, to make you well."

"No, never; never more shall I be well!" She sighed deeply.

"Do not despair of it. Sometimes, Heaven permits a heavy cloud to pass over us; but, if we remain patiently, and trust in God, we shall, in time, recover the daylight again."

"That is very pretty; I like it. Are you a Christian?"

"I hope so, my dear lady; I endeavour to be so."

"I am glad to hear it. I have not been among Christians a great while."

"Lord ha' mercy!" said Susan, "how can you say so? We be all Christians here."

"We will speak farther on this subject another time.—Will you, Madam, permit me to breakfast with you?"

"I have nothing to give you," said the poor lady; "I have none for myself!"

"You may have what you please," said Susan: "you need only tell me what you please to have."

"No, I have none—I want none—I have left off eating—it don't agree with me."

"Ah, but you can eat a sly bit in a corner, sometimes," said Susan.

"You are very indiscreet to say so. You should not speak of these things before her——Will you order the breakfast to be brought into this room—And will you, Madam, permit me to make tea here?"

"If you please, Madam. It was very good of you to bring some with you: there was none in the house."

I humoured this thought, and begged her to partake of it.

The tea-equipage was brought, and I made tea. I desired Susan to tell the young lady, to wait till the gentleman came, and to breakfast with him.

I told the lady, that I had a young person under my care with me; but, as she was averse to company, I had left her belowstairs. She bowed to me. I intreated her to partake of the breakfast. She would not eat; but she drank a cup of tea, and thanked me for it.

I told her, if she would invite me, I would stay and dine with her. She wished she had any thing to give me; but said there was nothing in the house but poverty and misery. I answered for the dinner; but she cared not to speak of it.

When the breakfast-things were taken away, I offered to stay with her, till her servant had taken her's, and desired she would come then and relieve me. I tried to engage her in conversation; but she answered me only Yes, and No.

I kept silence some time. She looked at me—

"Pray, talk again; I like to hear you."

"I accept the omen!" said I: "it gives me hopes, that you will often hear me with pleasure."

I talked away; and she listened attentively, but said little.

When Susan returned, I took my leave, saying, I would wait on her at dinner. She shook her head, but seemed not displeased with my visit.

I retired to my room, and considered with myself, whether I should give hopes to Maurice of her recovery. It was not impossible that he might resume his former designs upon her. I resolved to be very cautious of what I said to him upon the subject.

When I saw him, I told him, that the lady had endured me in her sight; and I did not despair of one day rivalling Susan in her favour. He asked, what I thought of her; and whether he might encourage any hopes of her recovery?

I said, it was impossible to form any judgment upon so short a knowledge of her, but that I perceived she was sensible of both good and ill treatment; that she still feared Mrs. Burton, and dreaded her return.

I enquired, where was his servant, John Roberts? He said, he had sent him to Harwich, and ordered him to wait for him there.

I walked over the grounds with him and Charlotte, and returned to dinner. I told him my intention of eating in Isabella's room, in order to excite her to partake with me; and he thanked me for the thought.

I tried to persuade her to eat, but she refused me. After I had dined, I sopped a piece of bread in a glass of wine and water, and gave her a few pieces thus moistened; she swallowed them, and drank the liquor. Soon after, she laid her hand upon her heart, and seemed cheered by it.

I sat with her till Susan had dined, and came back to her. Then I left her, and I saw her no more that day. I wanted to see whether my company was wished for or not. The next day, Susan told me she had asked, when that lady would come again. She feared she had behaved rudely to me, and that I would come no more.

This experiment answered to my wishes; and I resolved to make another, that would be likely to enable me to decide the question, whether I should take her under my care, or not.

I sent word, that I would wait on her to dinner, if agreeable. The answer was, she should be obliged, if I would bring my dinner with me.

I went, when the dinner was ready, with the hopes that she would expect me some time. She did so; and was uneasy that I came no sooner.

She rose to meet me, and I embraced her. She opened her eyes wider than I had seen them, for they were commonly half-closed. She looked pleased at my coming, and I seemed rejoiced to see her. Dinner was served up. I asked no questions, whether she would eat, but fed her from my own plate: she ate several morsels of meat thus, and I gave her sopped bread as before.

As soon as the dinner-things were removed, and Susan was gone down stairs, I tried my second experiment.

I drew my chair close to hers, took her hand in mine, and spoke to her in Italian. I asked her to accept my friendship, and give me her's in return, which I intended to deserve of her.

She was surprized, and gratified. Her heart heaved with sighs. She leaned her head upon my shoulder, and burst into a passion of tears; the happy proof that I hoped to receive of her sensibility, and of the probability of her recovery. She shed torrents of tears, that relieved her over-burthened heart; mine accompanied them, and mixed with them, as they flowed into her lap.

After they were abated, I spoke. I said all that I could think of, to comfort and compose her mind. She saw me weep with her, and looked at me with tenderness and gratitude.

When she was somewhat composed, I asked her, whether she should like that I should come and stay some time with her, and be her companion and friend?

She said—"Oh, yes, yes, yes!" it would be the greatest consolation this world could give her—"but, if Maurice should know it, he would take you away from me."

I seized the opportunity of telling her, that Maurice was soon going abroad, and that I would come to her when he was gone.

She listened to me attentively, and was pleased with the intelligence I gave her. Susan returned, and was surprized to hear us talk in a language she could not understand.

When I offered to leave her, she besought me to stay, and never leave her again. I told her, that I must return home to my friends, and settle my affairs; but I would certainly return to her, after some time—That I should see her every day while I staid in the village, and that I was not going immediately. She was very unwilling to part with me. I told her, I must leave her then, but would see her again on the morrow.

She desired me to come sooner than to-day, and I promised to do so.

When I returned to Maurice, I told him that I had spoken to Isabella in Italian, and that she was reconciled to my company, and was not unwilling that I should come and stay with her.

He took occasion to urge me to promise him to accept the charge of her. I said, if I saw nothing worse than I had seen, I would, and that she was the most patient sufferer that I ever knew.

He said, she was impatient enough whenever she was opposed. I observed, that proved the necessity of indulgence to her, and that I should use no other method. He thanked me for my compliance.

Isabella grew every day fonder of my company. I promised her, that I would come and stay with her, upon condition that she would oblige me, in complying with what I desired, in regard to eating, and doing what was good for her health. She promised to do all that I should require of her.

I ordered Susan to bring her, every morning, half a pint of milk, warm from the cow, and put a tea-cup of hot water into it; and, if she did not chuse to take it immediately, to leave it in her room till she did. I saw her take it several mornings, and begged her to continue it.

I introduced Charlotte to her, and desired her to pay her great attention, and endeavour to make herself agreeable to her. She supposed her to be my daughter; but I assured her, she was only my ward. I asked her permission to bring Charlotte with me when I should come again.

She said—"Any friend of yours will be welcome; but you must bring your own provisions."

I undertook to provide for us and the family. She thanked me for my goodness.

"Pray, tell me your name?"

I did so.

"Pray write it down, for I have no memory."

I asked, if she had not a pocket-book?

She did not know.

Susan found it, and I wrote my name in a leaf of it.

She was pleased with it, and read it over and over—"Frances—Francisca—Francesina. Shall I call you Donna Francesina?"

"Call me what you please, so you add the name of friend to it."

"La cara Amica Donna Francesina!" Darnford she made a strange word of; but I was glad to see her amuse herself with any thing.

I wrote down the name of Charlotte Brady, and desired her to remember that also; and Charlotte begged her, very prettily, to do her name the honour to remember it.

In short, we amused her with such trifles, and took off her attention to her own melancholy thoughts, and the recollections of the causes of her sorrows.

Captain Maurice brought his tenants, Mr. And Mrs. Ringrose, to pay their respects to me, one afternoon. He had told them every thing that could prepossess them in my favour, and also his design of going abroad, and leaving Isabella in my care. He desired Mr. Ringrose to overlook Richard Cob, and see that he did his duty during his absence. Before them, he gave me the power to dismiss all, or any of the servants, whom I should disapprove; and he repeated it to all the servants.

Mr. Ringrose promised to do me every service in his power—and his wife said, she hoped I would neighbour with her; for that Don Antonio, and his lady (now Mrs. Maurice) were too proud to take any notice of them, and they thought it too great an honour for her to sit at the same table with them.

Maurice said—"That is past; let us say no more of it. Mrs. Darnford will, I am sure, acknowledge and return your good offices."

I assured them, that I should be glad to have such good neighbours, and promised to return their visit before I went home.

They drank tea, and poor Isabella sent Susan several times to see what was become of me. She was told I was gone out on a visit, and would come to her in the evening. After they were gone, I sat with her till supper-time; and then came down to Maurice and Charlotte. He went away at ten o'clock, and we went to our rest.

I returned the visit to the farm-house in the morning. Maurice shewed me his apartment, which is indeed a very good one. He consulted me about letting it. I advised him to keep it in reserve, for he might one day wish to return to it; and, beside, there might be disagreeable inmates to the family; and, upon the whole, it was better to leave it in the care of Mrs. Ringrose. She was pleased with what I said; and it was settled accordingly.

We staid twelve days at the mansion-house; and I had every reason to hope that my undertaking would be crowned with success.

Isabella was very loth to part with me; but I told her it must be so. But I purposed to return it in a month; and desired her to keep an account of the days, that she might observe my punctuality.

Mr. Maurice earnestly begged that he might see Isabella once more, before he took an eternal leave of her. I was averse to it.

"If she sees you with me, I shall lose all the ground I have gained; and, if you go alone, she will think I have told her nothing but untruths."

"Cannot I see her while she sleeps? I would not disturb her for the world."

He ordered Susan to tell him when she was asleep. He put on a long black cloak of mine, and Susan's bonnet upon his head. Susan went softly into the room—I was in the gallery. He put his head into the room: he clasped his hands together, and gazed at her in silence. He sighed and groaned inwardly. He stood till she started, and then came away, and Susan shut the door. I persuaded him to go down stairs; and he saw her no more. He lamented the alterations in her person and intellects, and kept his resolution with unshaken steadiness.

The next morning we returned to N——; and from thence went home to W——, where I staid a month.

You know all that passed between Mrs. Martin and her family and myself.

Maurice sent me two writings, properly signed and executed. The first was a lease of three years of the mansion, and the ground adjoining: the other was a power of attorney to receive his rents, and the interest of his money in the funds, during Charlotte's minority.

These points being settled, I returned to the mansion-house; and arrived there on the day that my appointed month expired. I carried with me Charlotte Brady, and Patty Martin, as my companions and associates, with whom I hoped to form a pleasant and chearful society, and that Donna Isabella would make the fourth in due time.

The lady gave me a joyful reception; but it suffered some abatement on account of my two companions. I told her she would find them very amiable and good girls, and they would amuse and entertain her: that they were likewise very ingenious, and would shew her many curious works. By degrees, she was reconciled to them; but she was rather jealous that I should love them better than herself, and deprive her of my company, and bestow it upon them.

My first act of power was to discharge the supernumerary servant, hired to assist Susan; my second, to throw her to her proper distance, and reduce her to her proper station, that of an house-maid.

Myself and my young people took her place about Madame di Soranzo. Our business and exercises became her amusement: we shewed her how to nett,[3] to knot, and to weave laces and bobbin. She had never been used to do any kind of work; but these were so like play, that she was persuaded to try her hand at them.

I found Cob and his wife honest, sensible, and discreet persons; and I put confidence in them. I regulated the houshold, and put every thing into an easy method; so that every servant might do their work with ease, and yet have time for themselves.

Our manner of life was this: At seven o'clock in the morning, our half-pint of milk and water was brought to Donna Isabella and myself—we both found it of great benefit to us. At nine, we breakfasted in the dressing-room; and afterwards pursued our works and our lessons till twelve. I then walked with the two girls till half after one; when we returned home, and dressed before dinner: for I used them to make some alterations, that they might not grow careless and slatternly. We dined at two, or a quarter after: at first, we ate in the dressing-room, but afterwards in the parlour.

Isabella was sometimes capricious and fanciful: we then suffered her to dine alone in the dressing-room; and we left her with Susan. But she was too sensible of the value of our company to let us stay away from her: she soon recollected herself; and, sometimes, would apologize for her behaviour.

By degrees, I persuaded her to walk a little; for she had used herself to sit altogether, which had almost disabled her. She told me, that Mrs. Burton would not let her go out of her own apartment; and that Maurice desired her to stay there. I easily conceived the reason of this prohibition—while they were cleaning her former room, and putting up the new door—but I thought it was now time that she should use her legs, and that her health should be promoted by exercise.

We persuaded her to walk in the gallery: sometimes she leaned upon me; at others, upon Patty; and Charlotte desired she might not have her offers of service refused.

I shut the door into the library, and left it to her to make the discovery of the alterations there. She often looked at the door, stopped, and sighed: at length, she said—"Will you allow me, Madam, to open that door?"

"Certainly, Madam. I would not offer to restrain you in any thing but what was likely to be hurtful to you."

She opened the door, and looked in. She started at seeing the new door. "Santa Maria! what do I see! Is there no admittance into that chamber?"

"No, Madam. Captain Maurice ordered that room to be cleared of all it's furniture; and then shut it up, as you see."

She kneeled down at the door, and prayed. She chanted, after the manner of the cathedral service—"Saint Antonio, Ora pro nobis! Santa Catherina, Ora pro nobis!"[4]

"Come, my dear lady, this room is not good for you. Others, beside Mr. Maurice, think that chamber did you harm: you indulged fancies there that ruined your peace and comfort. Now that you are getting better, you will listen to advice; and, when your reason gets it's full strength, you will be convinced that it was a kind action to take you away from it."

She wept, and trembled. "Oh, that room! the scene of all my joys and all my sorrows! I cannot see it without emotion—Must I never enter that room again?"

"No, I hope not," said I: "but you shall use yourself to see that door, till you think no more of it than of any other; for you ought not to be a prisoner in your own house any longer. Let us go back to your dressing-room; and you shall come here again another day."

She leaned upon me, and we returned back again. She wept, but her mind was relieved by it. We talked on various subjects; and she soon recovered her usual composure.

After this, she visited the library every day; and, by degrees, was familiarized to it: but always said a prayer, or sung her "Ora pro nobis!" before she returned to her own apartment.

Her appetite returned. I never urged her to eat more than she chose. Nature requires but little food. Most of our disorders arise from repletion. I gave her only simple and plain dressed meats, with a proportion of vegetables; and left the rest to nature.

Isabella had a closet out of her bedchamber, where she used to pray several times in a day. I would now and then throw out a hint, that we all worshipped the same God, and acknowledged the same Saviour and Redeemer. As she grew better, she was more sensible of the difference between our mode of worship and her own. I insisted upon it, that we were Christians; and that she ought to allow us to be so, as we allowed her to be one.

I said, that the Christian church was divided into many branches, yet all springing from the same tree; namely, the Gospel—that every nation had it's own church, and had a right to it's own form of worship. That way in which a man thought he could best serve God, and secure his own salvation, that was the best to him. "God is the Father of all his creatures, and his tender mercies are over all his works. As such, I adore, love, and obey him; but I could not love him truly, if I thought he was the Father of only one small part, or one society only, and the Step-father of all the rest. I believe my national church to be a good and a safe one; but I do not believe it the only one in which I may obtain salvation. Compare my opinion with your own; and remark which has the most charity and benevolence, and which is the nearest to the charity of the Gospel, and the Spirit of it's Divine Author; who declared—"*By this shall all men know that you are my disciples, if ye have love one towards another.*"[5]

"You speak very well," said Isabella; "but I am not convinced by what you say. I do not think every one has a right to chuse his own religion, but that all should conform to the Mother Church. How can you be Christians, that pay no honour to the Mother of our Lord, not to any of the Saints?"

I answered this, by adverting to our Lord's treatment of his Mother: a circumstance that one of our most celebrated divines attributes to his foreknowledge of the abuses of the successors of the Apostles, and that she would one day become the object of idolatrous worship. "It is from himself that we must learn every circumstance concerning her; and, from him, how far she is to be respected, but not worshipped. "*Who is my mother, and who are my brethren? Behold, he who doeth the will of my Father in heaven, the same is my brother, and sister, and mother.*"[6]

She was offended. She asked how I knew that our Saviour said so? I told her, we had free recourse to the Scriptures; and they were in the hands of every one that could read.

She doubted the translation. I told her, that the many sects into which Christianity was divided, were constantly watching each other, which prevented the corruptions and interpolations of any.

I asked whether she had now any priest to attend her? She was uneasy, at times, that she had not; but believed that Maurice had forbidden the person that used to visit her: which I thought very likely, though he said nothing to me upon the subject.

Thus I laboured to enlarge her charity, and to make her think favourable of Christians of all denominations, without trying to make her dissatisfied with her own church. I acknowledged the Pope's supremacy in Italy; but would not allow it to reach any farther. I told her, that a great man of our country had said, that Providence made the Italians Catholics, and the Dutch Protestants, for the benefit and convenience of both.

Every evening, before we went to supper, I called the family together, and read the evening prayers of the Church; concluding with a prayer of the excellent Bishop Hoadly: and sometimes gave them a brief exhortation on the greater and lesser duties of all those who call themselves Christians.

Isabella did not, at first, give us her company: it was near the expiration of the first year before I carried this point with her. But it gave me inexpressible satisfaction when she did join with us; and she now never misses it. She confesses that she has found great comfort to her own heart in performing this duty.

At the end of the first year, I returned to W——, according to my promise. I staid a month with Mrs. Martin; settled all her affairs; saw my friends in that neighborhood; and then returned to Donna Isabella, who was very impatient of my absence.

I wrote to Captain Maurice from time to time; and gave him an account of Isabella's gradual amendment, and the prospect of her perfect recovery, in consequence of a mild and gentle treatment, and proper attention to her bodily health. His answers expressed his pleasure in hearing such good tidings; and his gratitude to Mrs. Darnford, for her care of the two persons most dear to him of any in the world. He informed me, that he was engaged in a mercantile society, and was going a voyage to the West Indies.

I wrote also to my worthy friend, Counsellor M——; and acquainted him with my present situation, and my success in it, which gave him great satisfaction.

In the second year of my residence here, I lost that dear, that inestimable friend, whose generosity extended beyond his life. He left me five hundred pounds: a noble legacy, which secured me a competency for life.

Mrs. Langston gave me an invitation to her house; but I excused myself, and gave a power of attorney to a clerk of my benefactor, to receive my legacy, and employ it in the funds, and to receive and transmit my interest-money to me.

Isabella recovered, by degrees, her health and spirits; and she has often declared herself happier since I came hither than at any period of her life.

When I thought her sufficiently recovered, I asked whether she thought herself the wife of Captain Maurice? She said, she supposed that the marriage-ceremony had been performed, after our manner, while she was in fits: but she never could think herself his wife, unless it had been celebrated after the manner of the Church of Rome; and that could not be done without her consent, which she never would give as long as she lived.

I then ventured to disclose the welcome secret, that she was not married at all; and that she was entirely her own mistress, and that of this house, and the lands belonging to it.

She screamed for joy. She embraced me. Then recollecting herself—"Are you sure of what you tell me?"

"Very certain of it."

"Yes—I believe it! You could not, would not, deceive me!—But how do you know it? Who told you?"

"He who best knew—Mr. Maurice confessed it to me. Moved by a generous remorse and repentance, he told me every thing that could give me full information of your case, and enable me to give you hope of future quiet. You may depend that he will never more persecute you: he leaves you to enjoy your own comforts, and will never more disturb your repose."

"Then he is not so bad a man as I thought him."

I took up Maurice's cause, and pleaded for her pity and forgiveness; which, after some time, she allowed me to send him, in her name.

When he returned from his voyage, I transmitted this welcome news; but conditionally, that he should never more approach her: otherwise, she would declare to every body that she was not married to him, and would expose him to the censure and contempt of the world.

I shewed Madame di Soranzo two books I had made; in one of which I had set down all the money I had received on her account; in the other, all that I had expended for her. I told her, I had hitherto been her faithful steward; but was ready to resign my office whenever she pleased, and to quit her house whenever she thought she had no farther need of me.

She had hardly patience to hear me out. She changed colour: she wept—"Surely, you could not be so cruel to leave me! If you did, I should relapse into the miserable state in which you found me. Oh, my dear friend! you must never, never leave me! You have been my comforter, physician, priest, companion, and counsellor—I can never forget my obligations to you—I can never be happy without you!"

"I am not going to leave you, unless you should desire it."

"So far from it, it would be the greatest misfortune that could befal me. Be still my steward, my manager, my governess—All I have is yours; and I am yours to the end of my life!"

I assured her, that I had no thoughts of leaving her, unless upon some extraordinary occasion.

With her health, Madame di Soranzo has recovered her beauty; and she is at this moment a most interesting person, equally capable of inspiring love, and of conciliating friendship.

My two pupils are amiable girls. Patty Martin is remarkably ingenious in all manner of needle-work. I had her taught to make gowns. We have modernized Donna Isabella's wardrobe; and I have dressed her hair in a medium style, between fashion and simplicity, but in a manner extremely becoming to her form.

When first I heard from the dear friend of my youth, I read your letters to Madame di Soranzo. She grew extremely jealous, lest I should leave her, and go to live with you. I told her, I would state the case fairly; and I could trust to your equity to decide in her behalf, though against your own wishes.

And now, my dear friend, you see the bands that hold me; and I am sure you will think that this lady has most need of my company and assistance. The two girls likewise depend upon me. Under these circumstances, I have thought on a plan that will bring us together. In the name of Madame di Soranzo, I invite you to visit us here, as soon as you can conveniently. I propose to myself the greatest pleasure I can enjoy, in making my personal acknowledgments for your generous and steady friendship. You must bring with you your daughter, and a servant to attend you here, for we have only the honest and vulgar Susan Dobbins; but I hope to get soon a more handy and suitable attendant. In your next, you must fix the time for your journey. I will meet you at N——, and conduct you safely to D——.

With the most ardent wish of embracing you shortly,

I am,
FRANCES DARNFORD.

LETTER XVI
Mrs. Strictland, to Mrs. Darnford.

THANKS, many thanks, are due to my dear friend, for all her communications, and her most kind invitation in the conclusion.

Poor Isabella! her sufferings have been great indeed! I have felt them for her most truly. Oh, that vile Maurice!—how can you excuse him!—how can you vindicate him! I hate and detest him, and never can forgive him! And yet you have persuaded the poor lady to pardon him, and to let him know it! When I come, I will reckon with you for all your superlatives.

I want to consult you upon many subjects; principally, on the education of my children. Shall I send my daughter to a good school, or shall I take a governess into my house? Shall I send my son to a public or a private school, or shall I give him a tutor at home? I have a scheme of this kind in my head, which I shall lay before you.

I have had my boys with me lately; and they are just restored to school again. They are very much improved; but Henry Marney has the superior talents. No matter for that: if my boy is virtuous and amiable, I am satisfied and thankful.

What strange, inconsistent creatures, we are! Woodlands, that was formerly my prison, is now become pleasant to me. I can spend the summer months here very comfortably; but I mean to winter in some large town or city. On this head I shall consult you also; and you shall be my Apollo.

Mrs. Elton's eldest son is a very ingenious young man: he is chosen a Fellow of his College. He means to offer himself as a governor to some young man of fortune. He wishes to travel, and to instruct himself and his pupil at the same time. Whether travelling does most good, or harm, I am not competent to decide. Tell me your opinion of it.

I have regulated my family very much to my satisfaction; and all my servants acquit themselves well in their several stations—my worthy Gilson and her son at the head of them.

Present my respects to Madame di Soranzo: tell her, I hope she will admit me into the number of her friends. I am preparing to pay my acknowledgments, in person, for her kind invitation. I shall pay court to her good opinion; and shall do all I can to persuade her to return my visit at Woodlands. I shall open a plan of spending most part of our summer together; and, according to my success with you both, I shall make my visit longer or shorter—Take notice of that.

On Monday next I set out on my journey. I hope to sup with you at N—— on Tuesday night. I suppose you will come in your chaise-cart to meet me. I shall put Peggy and our luggage into your vehicle, and you shall step into mine. On Wednesday, I shall proceed with you to D——. Heaven send us all a happy meeting, and all the following blessings of friendship and select society! So prays,

> Your sincere and affectionate friend,
> RACHEL STRICTLAND.
> WOODLANDS,
> July 5, 1780.

LETTER XVII
Miss Elton, to Mrs. Strictland.

MADAM,

IT is cruel to interrupt your happiness, in the society of that dear friend, whose noble and amiable qualities you so truly love, and so justly esteem: but, as you have honoured me with the office of your almoner, and your substitute, with respect to your pensioners and paupers, it is incumbent on me to acquaint you with something that has passed here, which has excited our expectations and our wishes.

In your absence, I have always called upon old Balderson once a week, at least, and desired him to call on me as often. On Monday last, he came to me, with a letter in his hand; and he trembled as he gave it me to read, and seemed much agitated. I send you here a copy of it—

"MR. SAMUEL BALDERSON,

"I SHOULD be glad to know, speedily, whether you are dead or alive; for Mr. Grant, your old friend, says, he had not heard from you a great while; and he says, beside, that he has heard tidings of a friend of yours in India, and that there is some money for you in his hands. I write to you, at his desire; and, as soon as we know that you are alive and well, you shall know farther particulars.

"I am your old neighbour and friend,

> JOHN MULLINS."
> SOUTHWARK,
> July 20.

Mr. Balderson had neglected writing to Mr. Grant, having given over all hopes of hearing from India. He had told him of his happiness in your protection, and that of his dear Henry Marney; and, after that, he wrote very seldom, having nothing farther to wish, or to hope, in this world.

My father thought this letter of great consequence; he offered to answer it himself. He certified the writer, that Samuel Balderson was alive and well, and very desirous to be informed of the farther particulars as soon as possible; desiring him to address his next letter to Balderson, at the Parsonage.

On the Friday we received the second letter; which I copy—

"MR. BALDERSON,

"WE have received an answer to our letter, from the Rev. Mr. Elton, rector of your parish, and are glad to hear you are alive and well; but it would have been more satisfaction to have had it under your own hand.

"You must know, that John Mullins's son, who was thought dead, is lately returned from India, with a great deal of money; and he says, that your son, James Balderson, was alive and well when he came away from Madras; and he sent home a hundred pounds for you; and he said, he had always sent that sum to you, every year, for a great many years past. He says, that Mr. James Balderson is coming home soon, and wants very much to know the situation of his family.

"I send you herewith a Bank-note for fifty pounds; and desire you will acknowledge it directly, and with your own hand, if you are able, and then I will send the remainder.

"Take care of your health, and keep up your spirits, for you may expect to see your good son one of these days. So God bless you, and farewel!

"Your old and true friend,
"MICHAEL GRANT."
SOUTHWARK,
July 27, 1780.

This Mr. Grant lives in the house formerly inhabited by Balderson, and he was charged with the care of all letters to him. The poor old man is overwhelmed with joy, but mixed with doubts and fears. My dear father kindly supports him; he calls upon him for fortitude to bear prosperity, as firmly as he has done adversity, and strengthens his mind by religious considerations. We visit him every day, and send him what we think is good for his health and spirits.

"My father is of opinion, that Mr. James Balderson is actually arrived, and takes this method to prepare his aged father to see him. If so, you shall soon hear farther from, dear Madam,

"Yours, faithfully, &c.
"ANNE ELTON."

LETTER XVIII
Miss Elton, to Mrs. Strictland.

August 1, 1780

MY dear father's penetration had been truly justified. I am, even now, hardly composed enough to tell my dear friend all that has happened: I will, however, attempt it.

Last Thursday, old Balderson dined with us: my father made him sit down with us, though his modesty would have declined it. In the afternoon, a stranger knocked at the door. Does not your heart tell you, already, who this stranger was?

The tears gush from my eyes; I cannot describe the affecting interview.

He asked a few questions concerning Mr. Balderson. The old man knew him; he fainted away in his son's arms. Never did I behold such manly, such affecting tenderness, as James Balderson's!

"Oh, God! spare my father, that I may have somebody to live for!"

He was in agonies, lest the discovery should be too much for him; and we were in fear that he would not revive.

My father fetched a bottle of choice Madeira wine, reserved for great occasions. He said, in the words of the Wise Man—*"Give strong wine to him who is ready to faint; let him drink and forget his poverty, and remember his misery no more."*[1] He gave it to him with a tea spoon, with the utmost care, and he revived by degrees.

My father begged Mr. Balderson to restrain his joy, and to appear composed.

The old man gazed wildly on his son—he embraced him. The tears ran down the cheeks of them both, and ours accompanied them.

The old man recovered his voice; and his first words were ejaculations of gratitude to the Supreme Benefactor—"Praise be to God for all his mercies!—O Lord, make me truly thankful for this blessing!—Now will I say, like old Jacob to his beloved Joseph—*"Now let me die, for I have seen they face once again!"*[2]

My father, in order to compose the minds of both, began a recapitulation of all that old Balderson had suffered, till the time of his being received into the protection of Mrs. Strictland. He enlarged upon her goodness to him, and to his beloved Henry Marney.

While he was relating many instances of this lady's benevolence and bounty, Mr. James Balderson kneeled down, and invoked Heaven to shower down it's blessings upon herself and children.

He then asked, where this excellent lady was to be found: he would go a journey as far as to India, to pay her his acknowledgments. My father desired him to have patience, and remain where he was: that the time Mrs. Strictland had proposed to be absent was nearly expired, and that he might soon pay his respects to her at her own house; and he would answer, that she would give him a hearty welcome, and a gracious reception.

My father would not let old Balderson go home that night. His son sat by his bed-side, and watched him with true and pious filial affection. The next day, he was perfectly recovered. His son went home with him, and he spends most of his time with him, though my father had got him a lodging in the village.

And now, Madam, I am desired to remind you, that your proposed time is nearly expired, and that your return is impatiently wished; and I am authorized to speak my own wishes in those of others.

Oh! but I have not told you, that Mr. James Balderson is a fine, manly, sensible-looking man; tall, and well made; with an open aspect, that speaks courage, frankness, and benevolence! His countenance is bronzed over, by a warm country; but his honest, generous, and affectionate mind, shines through it.

Accept, Madam, the compliments and regards of all those who bear the name of Elton; and I presume to ask you to present mine to all your friends at D——.

In hopes that Woodlands will soon be illuminated by your presence, (it is very dull without it) I am, dearest Madam,

Your faithful and obedient servant,
ANNE ELTON.

LETTER XIX
Mrs. Strictland, to Mrs. Darnford.

THE voice of joy and gladness resounds throughout this house. I have been obliged to listen to raptures of praise and gratitude. I fear, lest vanity should induce me to take too much to myself; therefore I am retired to my own apartment, to offer the incense of praise and thanksgiving to that Power to whom it is due, and to thank him for enabling me to comfort and assist so many worthy hearts as are now under my roof.

This duty paid, it is incumbent on me to pay my acknowledgments to my dear friends, Donna Isabella, and Donna Francesina, for their kindness and hospitality to me and my daughter. My dear Rachel sends her thanks to the ladies, and her love to Miss Brady and Miss Martin, and wishes to have them live with her always; for, sure, Woodlands is big enough for us all. Pray observe and remember this, and make no scruple of coming—all of you. I can always make room enough for such dear friends.

Mr. James Balderson is one of *your gentlemen* of God's making: he gives the lye to all exclusive pretensions of birth and fortune. He has the spirit of a prince, and would make me such presents as are only proper for those of the highest degree to wear. He has obliged me to accept of some jewels of high value—one diamond, of a large size—and I must have quarrelled with him, if I had returned them to him. The man pays me a kind of homage that is little short of adoration!

You must know, that his chief traffick has been in jewels; and he has been engaged in journeys of much danger, between the settlement at Madras[1] and the mines of Golconda.

When his patron died, he left him one-third of his fortune, and the remainder to his relations in England. This honest factor transmitted accounts of every thing to them; and employed a third person to divide the property, and to settle between them. He remitted all that was due to them, before he took measures to secure and remit his own property to England.

He has detected the fraud and treachery of his brother-in-law, Stevens, who intercepted all his remittances to his father, and suffered that worthy man to endure penury and want, while he was spending the money that would have procured him and his grandson all the comforts and conveniencies of life. He is little less angry with his sister. He says, though she had not the command of much money, she could have relieved her own father in many respects; and, at least, she might have given him pence and twopences, as others did, from no other motive than merely charity. "I renounce such children and relations! I will never more have any intercourse with them!"

He lamented the loss of so many dear relations, whom he had hoped should have shared his fortune; but, still more pathetically, he deplored the fate of his adored Anna Marney.

You may remember the noble self-denial of this generous lover. If you do not, turn to my Letters, and to Balderson's history of himself and family. "If I had known her situation," said he, "I would have provided for the man she loved; and he should have been my friend and brother during my life."

By these traits, you may judge of the heart of this noble fellow, who deserves all that fortune can bestow on him.

He was impatient to see his nephew. I sent for both the boys, the day after I came home: for Jonathan would have thought me unkind to leave him at school, while Henry came home; nor would I have lost the pleasure of my son's company.

There was a fresh effusion of gratitude on seeing his nephew dressed, educated, and treated, like my own son. He was charmed with the person and behaviour of the boy; and swore he should be provided for, like the heir of the house of Marney. He is not much less fond of my son: he thanks him for his affection to his nephew, and hopes it will last all their lives.

But you would be delighted with Henry Marney's behaviour to his grandfather. Though he sees his uncle in a situation to provide for him nobly, and with a heart and will to do it, all his attentions are to the old man; he is even jealous, lest he should think he can love any body equal to himself. He stands close to him; he throws his arms round his neck—"How are you, my dear grandfather? You have not spoken to me a long time! Tell me, that you are well and happy."

When his uncle was speaking of his obligations to me, the boy said—"I am sensible of all I owe to this dear lady; and to you, my honoured uncle: but still more than these are due to my grandfather—he bore me in his arms when I could not walk—he begged for me—he almost starved himself for me! Oh, that I may live to shew my gratitude to all my friends, but especially to my grandfather!"

"Dear, dear boy!" said the old man, "how am I rewarded!"

"You did more than all this, grandfather! You taught me to fear God, and to read his holy word, and to keep his commandments. It is from knowing these, that I am sensible of all my duties: first, to God; and, secondly, to my neighbour. All other kinds of learning are as nothing, when compared to these!"

"God bless thee, and direct thee in his ways!" said old Balderson; "and make thee a blessing to others, as thou art to me!"

These worthy creatures are here every day. I cannot forbid them—I cannot limit them. Their visits are the incense of gratitude, and the emanations of sincere affection.

James Balderson is already laying plans for his nephew. "Since this estate is gone for ever from the family of Marney, I wish to build a house for Henry in this neighbourhood. I want to purchase some lands for this purpose. I wish him to be near you, Madam; and to be still the friend and companion of your amiable and beloved son. How shall I do this, without your assistance?"

I answered—"Consult Mr. Elton, and he will direct you better than I can do. I wish the dear boys to be always each other's first friend."

He wanted me to sell him my cottages, and the ground about them; but I refused to part with them. They are consecrated to the service of the deserving and the unfortunate—they shall never be alienated from this purpose—I will secure them to it.

The Eltons are with me every day. I am very much obliged to them for their good offices during my absence.

How greatly preferable is this society to that of the world at large!

I am making alterations in my house. I have cleared out the old apartment on the first floor, had the tapestry taken down, and the old tattered velvet bed. The doors are new-hung and lifted; and they no longer chatter of a windy night. The rooms are to be hung with a light paper: they are already new-washed and painted. The picture of the cross Old Lady I have sent up another flight of stairs; and she is in a room on the second story, where they are nearly as good as the first. In one room, I have put up a light green morine[2] bed; in another, two canopy beds, for single persons, of printed cottons. The middle one is to serve as a dressing-room to both. They are all to be new-furnished; and I intend this apartment for you and your friends. Never fear crouding my family; for, as Rachel says, "Woodlands is big enough for us all."

I expect you next month. The autumn season is the favourite one with me. I desire you not to defer your coming. I have hopes of procuring you a servant, such as you wish for, to wait on Donna Isabella and yourself; therefore you need not bring Susan Dobbins with you to Woodlands.

The Eltons long to know and converse with you. I mean to make your residence here so agreeable, that you shall have no wish to leave it in haste.

Suppose I should ask Mr. James Balderson to build a house for you near us? You shall be his tenants, and my guests every day.

> "I prattle out of season; and I doat
> On mine own comforts."
> SHAKESPEARE.³

You can allow for all my flights and fancies. There is not a thought in my heart that I wish to conceal from you. For

I am always your's truly,
RACHEL STRICTLAND.
WOODLANDS,
August 21, 1780.

LETTER XX
Mrs. Darnford, to Mrs. Strictland.

I SHARE in all your joys and comforts, my dear friend! To be the minister of Heaven—to dispense it's blessings all around us, is the greatest honour a human creature can receive. You have a right to enjoy the sweet reflections arising from these actions. It is thus they raise us to the view of eternal bliss, far above all that the world can give or take away.

I had written to Captain Maurice, upon his return from the West Indies, acquainting him with our present situation, and desiring him to release Donna Isabella from all engagements to himself, by declaring, to all those who suppose them married, that his marriage was not a legal one, and that they are both free to contract another engagement, in case they should chuse it.

I have received his answer, since you left us. He is displeased with me for urging this point, because it will hurt his character in this neighbourhood, where he has avowed his marriage. To her, and to me, he freely owns the deception; but he wishes to conceal it from the world. He has no wish to contract any new engagement, but desires to know, whether she has any thoughts of that kind: he confesses, it would give him pain to see her the wife of another; but, if she will tell him she wishes it, he will come over and release her.

There is nothing in this world that she dreads so much as the sight of him; and she would rather remain in the state she is. I shall urge him again, to release her by a written instrument; and represent that, in case she should like to dispose of her estate here, she cannot do it without his concurrence. I have hopes, that I shall prevail upon him to perform this act of justice, and to set her free to act as she pleases.

I have letters from my friend Mrs. Langston. She urges me to stay some time with her, the ensuing winter. She has been robbed and cheated by her servants; and she begs of me to come and regulate her houshold, and she will follow my orders in her conduct towards them, in future.

She tells me, that Lady B—— returned home, a widow, near a year ago; that she has resided since at her country-seat, in L——; that Lord A—— has been her visitor and comforter; and, report says, they are soon to be married. I think, she is much too good for him, and wish the tattling gossip, Report, may be a liar.

I wish I could engage some sensible and discreet woman, to take my place with my friend Isabella; that I might visit all my friends, and go and return to her as it might suit me. I wish this person to be a Roman Catholic; not a bigot, but one that would allow other Christians to go to heaven, as well as those of her own church.—Do you think such a Catholic is to be found? In that case, I would engage a priest to visit them, who knows nothing of Isabella's story; who should make her mind easy, and perform all the duties of her own church for her.

Is my scheme practicable, or is it not? I will consult your Mr. Elton. The vicar of our parish is an impertinent, gossiping man: I do not like him well enough to consult him on this subject.

And now, my dear friend, let me warn you of a danger, which you are not aware of. Your new friend, Mr. James Balderson, is a fine person, endowed with a noble mind, and enriched by the gifts of fortune.

My friend is, in person, a most desirable woman, not past the age of conquest. *"He pays her a kind of homage, little short of adoration!"* He opens his heart to her; consults her upon all his plans, for himself and his nephew. His gratitude gives him a fair pretence to pay his homage continually, and neither of them suspect it for any thing more. From a friend, thus admitted, thus encouraged, how easy is the transition to a lover! Think of it, and be prepared for whatever may happen. I shall not be surprized at it.

We purpose to visit you next month, unless any thing should happen to prevent it; in which case, you will give us timely notice.

Donna Isabella sends her best regards, with those of

Your ever faithful and sincere friend,

F. DARNFORD.

LETTER XXI
Mrs. Strictland, to Mrs. Darnford.

OH, Donna Francesina! you are a witch!—I will carry you before Mr. Elton, and have you weighed against the Church Bible. You are so light, that the experiment may be dangerous. It were a good deed to make you believe, that all your prognostics are fulfilled, and that you are invited to be a bride-maid. How comes it, that I cannot bear the idea of being lowered in your opinion for one hour; and that I dare not deceive you?—

> "There is a virtuous magic in your eye,
> That, wheresoe'er it casts a beam of light,
> Creates a blessing."
> SHIRLEY.[1]

So I must tell you the truth, whether I chuse it or not.

James Balderson has thrown himself and his fortunes at my feet.

I suffered him to say all that was in his honest heart, before I offered to reply to him; and then, without a blush, without coquetry, or evasion, I answered him—

"I am extremely sensible, Sir, of the honour you have done me; it is the greatest you could pay me, and demands my sincere acknowledgments. I am so circumstanced, that I cannot accept your generous offer; but, though I forbid the lover, I wish to preserve the friend. Listen to me, while I tell you the particulars of my situation."

I then told him all the particulars of Mr. Strictland's will; and that I should forfeit the care of my children, and their fortune, by a second marriage. He had hardly patience to hear me out. He swore that my fortune was no object with him; and that he wished I had no fortune at all, that he might prove it.

I begged him to hear me farther. I had only told him the circumstances that bound me, with respect to the world; but that I was with-held by much stronger and dearer ties—that I would not relinquish the care of my children, to be crowned the queen of the richest country upon earth—that it was incumbent on me to justify Mr. Strictland's good opinion, and to entitle myself to the love and respect of my children—that, if all these considerations could be set aside, I had resolved, for reasons respecting myself, never to marry again. "And now, my good Sir, it remains with you, whether to promise to give up all expectations of this kind, and to continue my friend, or to oblige me to forego your company."

"Oh, that is a cruel alternative!" said he. "Surely, I was born to be disappointed in all my wishes!"

"Not so, Sir," said I; "you have been fortunate in your virtues, and in your use of them; and none knows them more than I do."

"Oh, Madam! you have crushed all my hopes and wishes in the bud!—You know not yet all that is in this aspiring heart; but I fear to utter what remains."

"After what you have said, Sir, you need not fear to say any thing. Let me, then, hear what remains: I will attend to it, and either encourage it, or give you good reasons to the contrary."

"You dash me down with one hand, and raise me with the other. I must have some object in view, on which to build my future hopes, and exercise my faculties.

"You see my nephew, Henry Marney, a fine promising lad. You have destroyed my first wish; my second rests upon him. I did wish, I did presume to hope, that, when his education should be finished, and he had attained to manhood, you might one day give him the hand of your fair daughter, and make him your son in earnest. I had intended, on that day, to divide my fortune with him; and I am still ready to fulfil that intention, if you will deign to encourage this, the now favourite wish of my heart."

"My dear Sir! this wish is surely premature. Consider the age of these children, and the uncertainty of all sublunary schemes—but I am unwilling to crush all yours; I will wait to see whether time will promote them. If the young people should like each other, I will not refuse my consent to their union."

Balderson kneeled, and clasped his hands together—"May the Almighty ratify and confirm this engagement!—I thank you, Madam: you have given me a subject for my mind to work upon; and now I will not repine at any thing. I shall still be allowed to be your friend, and that of all your family."

"One thing, Sir, I must insist on, that you keep this treaty secret, and not mention it to any one—least of all, to the youth concerned—for it would be likely to destroy the means that should lead to the accomplishment of your own wishes."

"Only one exception let me make, Madam. Suffer me to give a glimpse of this hope to my venerable father: it will be like a ray of the setting sun to illuminate a distant prospect; and it shall be under the strongest injunctions of secrecy, which I promise, for myself and him, shall be truly preserved."

"I accept this promise; and here let this subject rest. Let us now study how to compleat the education of the two youths under my care.

"I am weighing in the balance, whether to send them to school again, or to take a private tutor into the house, and to trust them under his care. I shall consult you, Sir, in every step I take for your nephew's service."

"I shall agree to whatever you propose, Madam. We are already too much obliged for your kind offices to him; and you must take the lead in whatever relates to him."

Here I thought proper to put an end to our conference; and I have since treated Mr. Balderson with more reserve, but not less respect and politeness.

The worthy man perceives that I am steady in my refusal of his offer, and that I keep him at a greater distance. He understands, and submits to it.

He staid away from the house two days. On the third, he came to enquire after my health, and that of all the family. He asked me to let the two boys walk out with him. I gave leave; and invited his father and himself to dine here the next day. Mr. and Mrs. Elton met them. After dinner, I introduced the subject of public and private education. Much was said, that had often been said before; and Mr. Elton concluded, that a public school was more likely to produce eminent men, but a private education best calculated to bring up men for a private station, well instructed in the social and domestic virtues.

I wished Mr. Elton to decide for me with respect to my son: but he referred it to me; saying, both these methods had succeeded in some instances, and failed in others—that it belonged to me to decide in the present case.

I decided in favour of the private scheme. I asked Mr. James Balderson's opinion. He said, he entirely approved mine, and hoped his nephew would partake of the benefits of it. He said, he was ashamed that I should have had all the expences of Henry's education; that he was able to sustain them, and equally ready to do it; that he insisted on repaying my part of it, and of taking the whole upon himself in future.

I said, I took it very ill that he should wish to deprive me of the merit of having served Henry Marney for his own sake: that I would hear nothing of the past; but I would allow him to be an equal sharer with me in all the expences on the account of the youths from this day forward.

He bowed, and was silent.

I then asked Mr. Elton, whether his son George was engaged? He was not, he said.

"Then I engage him to take the care of our two young men. Mr. George Elton is an ingenious young man; he has had a liberal and expensive education. It is requisite that his time and attention should be properly estimated. Will you, Mr. Balderson, allow me to speak for you and myself?"

He bowed, and laid his hand upon his heart.

"Then, Sir, you shall pay him an hundred pounds a year, and I another. He shall be at home, in this house, and I will directly fit up an apartment for him and his pupils: and, as soon as it is ready, he may enter upon his office."

Mr. Elton bowed low, and looked as highly obliged. Mrs. Elton took my hand, and dropped a tear of gratitude upon it.

These silent emanations of the heart are more eloquent than words, and more sincere—

> "For, in the modesty of silent Duty,
> I read far more than in the rattling tongue
> Of saucy and audacious Eloquence."
>
> SHAKESPEARE.[2]

James Balderson broke the interesting silence—"You told me, Madam, that you would allow me an equal share of the young man's expences; but you are a monopolizer—you take to yourself theirs and their tutor's board, and many other things. I protest against it."

"Have patience, Sir; they will not always be at their lodgings here. I intend they shall make excursions in the summertime, and get acquainted with their own country, before they see others."

"That I entirely approve," said Mr. Elton—"And will you, Madam, allow me to propose an addition to your plan?"

"Certainly, Sir: you will do me an essential service."

"It is, that the young gentlemen shall visit every county in

England and Wales; observe the produce and the soil of every one; the trade and manufactures of every great town, the beauties and the defects of it; and thus be acquainted with more than the surface of things. After this tour is completed, I would have them go all over Scotland and Ireland, in the same manner, and inform themselves of every thing worth their knowledge through the whole extent of the British empire."

"Sir, I approve your plan entirely, and I will adopt it."

"In the mean time, Madam, I would have them study the laws, the government, and the constitution, of their country. I would have them read Blackstone's Commentaries,[3] and learn to comment upon them. I would wish them to understand thoroughly whatsoever regards the welfare of their own country."

"I thank you, Sir: it will be my pride to second your instructions."

"By G—!" said James Balderson, "it shall be at my expence, not your's."

"I will absolve your oath," said Mr. Elton, "and accept your offer."

"I thank you, Sir. You will hear reason; but that lady will not."

"I will hear it for her, Sir; and will engage for her compliance with it."

We smiled; and the subject was imperceptibly changed to another.—And thus, my dear friend, are these important points settled.

I am now employed in fitting up an apartment on the second floor for Mr. George Elton and his pupils. There is a very large room that I intend for a family library. It is to be shelved all around, and furnished properly by Mr. Elton's assistance. I shall appropriate a sum yearly for this purpose. There is a good bed-chamber for the governor; another for the pupils, with two single beds in it, and suitable furniture.

Mr. Elton informs Mr. James Balderson, that the proprietor of a farm in our parish, having heard that he wishes to purchase, has offered to sell it for much more than it is worth.

"I will purchase it," said Balderson, "at any price."

"It will be as wise not to tell him so," said Mr. Elton. "Will you trust me, Sir, to treat for you?"

"Most readily, Sir: only do not let it slip through your fingers."

"I will take care, Sir; and will do my best for you."

"But do it, Sir, as soon as possible."

James Balderson is erecting a monument in the church, to his father's honoured friend, Henry Marney, Esq., another to his son Reginald and his wife, and to his sister, Anna Marney.

I have now to tell you, that your apartment is quite ready to receive you. There are fires in it every day; and the windows are open from sun-rise to sun-set.

Woodlands will soon be fully inhabited. It looks like a different place to what I once knew it. I have got you a servant; and she is in training under my Peggy.

You are to bring Donna Isabella, and both your adopted children. Who knows, but more future alliances may be schemed out? I could speculate upon the subject with much pleasure.

Let me know when you set out, that I may reckon the hours till your arrival.

Ever your's, faithfully,
RACHEL STRICTLAND.

LETTER XXII
Mrs. Darnford, to Mrs. Strictland.

I Thank you truly for your last favour. I mind not your threats nor your coaxings. I never distrusted your judgment, nor your prudence; and your late conduct has justified them both.

I am pleased with the plan for your young men's education, and I am thankful for all your communications. It was right that I should know all these things before I came to Woodlands. I have now to tell you, that Mrs. Langston is infallible in her intelligence. The marriage I mentioned in my last, is announced in the public papers. I have only to wish it may be happy.

Mrs. Langston urges me to come to her, as soon as I conveniently can. She throws out hints of her intention of settling her affairs, and making her will, and appointing me her executrix. I wish she had not mentioned these things: they will give an interested appearance to all the attentions I shall pay her, and I shall be the less forward to accept her favours.

We cannot make people behave as we wish them. Let us, then, take the world as it goes, and make every allowance for the defects and mistakes of it. All of us have had our respective trials. You and I, Donna Isabella, and your truly venerable Balderson. We have all worked our way through them. I trust, that we are all the better for them; and we certainly have the better title to the blessings that remain to us.

Let us enjoy them with gratitude and humility, and with resignation and adoration to the Power that gives and takes away, as it pleases him; and hold ourselves in readiness to surrender them back again, whenever it pleases Him to call for them. Yet, we may firmly believe and trust; that all things work together for good to those who truly fear, love, and obey God. We purpose to set out on our journey next Monday, and hope to be with you in the course of the week. Isabella begs we may go but short stages. She is fanciful, and supposes great fatigues in travelling to any distance.

The girls are all joy and gratitude for your very kind invitation. They reckon the hours, and minutes, till they shall enjoy Miss Strictland's company.

I have ordered the double door to be opened during our absence. The room is to be new white-washed and painted. The old escritoire and bureau are to be sent up another pair of stairs, and the room furnished as a dressing-room. I have ordered a strong lock to be put on the outward door. When we return, I shall try the experiment. If Isabella should return to her whims and fancies, it will be locked up again, and the key will be lost; but I hope for better things.

She has left off praying to Saint Antonio, and seems to be in a sound state of mind; and, I hope, will continue so.

I will have no more haunted rooms here, any more than you have at Woodlands. The virtuous have nothing to fear. "*The wicked flee when none pursueth; but the righteous are bold as a lion.*"[1] This belief is the best antidote to all unreasonable fears.

I long to see and converse with all your friends; and to tell you, in person, how much, how truly, I love and respect you.

I am, my dear friend,
Yours, most sincerely and affectionately,
FRANCES DARNFORD.

FINIS.

APPENDIX
Emendations

THE FOLLOWING EMENDATIONS, IDENTIFIED BY PAGE AND LINE numbers, have been made in this edition. The letter (D) indicates that the emendation has also been made in the Dublin edition of *The School for Widows*.

VOLUME I

French and Italian She said] French and Italian. She said (D)	12.00	76.18
extrvagantly] extravagantly (D)	24.00	88.08
appartment] apartment (D)	60.00	101.18

VOLUME II

Miss Elton and I tan home] Miss Elton and I ran home (D)	91.00	277.17

Notes

Preface

1. *A Sentimental Journey Through France and Italy* (1768) written by Laurence Sterne (1713–1768), chronicles protagonist Yorick's European travels, focusing on his sentimental experiences, and mingling light-hearted comedy with sensibility. Here Reeve may also be alluding to Henry Mackenzie's (1745–1831) sentimental novel *The Man of Feeling* (1771), in which the hero, Hartley—often weeping copious tears—displays feelings of sympathy, benevolence, and pity, and is thus represented as an ideal of sensitivity and virtue.
2. I will keep the spelling of the possessive pronoun (it's) formed at the end of the sixteenth century and retained until the beginning of the nineteenth century. Reeve regularly uses this spelling.
3. Consisting of or relating to ideas.
4. In her earliest novel, *The Triumph of Virtue* (1777) (later retitled *The Old English Baron*), Reeve used her hero Edmund to embody this "ennobling sensibility."
5. Reeve misattributes this quotation. It is from the younger Seneca's *Dialogue on Providence*, in which the author refers to the noble suicide of Cato the Younger.
6. Reeve explains this idea of the novel's function at greater length in her dialogue *The Progress of Romance* (1785).

Letter I

1. *Hamlet* (I.ii.76). "I know not seems," Hamlet tells his Gertrude, refusing to relinquish the dark clothes that are the outward symbol of his grief for his father. Reeve has Rachel echo Hamlet's words here, but with a very different meaning. Interestingly, Rachel shows a disregard for conventional bereavement and appearances that is unusual for women of the period. Reeve thus voices nonconformist ideas through one of her most clearly virtuous characters.
2. The law of entailment secured the inheritance (money, title, household effects) for a predetermined male line of succession, almost without exception.
3. A legal document that usually ensures that part or all of the property that the wife brings to the marriage will belong ultimately to her, and will revert to either her or her children in the case of the death of her husband. A

marriage settlement can also ensure that the children of the union inherit a certain guaranteed minimum amount.

4. A clergyman engaged for a stipend or salary, and licensed by the bishop of the diocese to perform ministerial duties in the parish, as a deputy or assistant of the incumbent; Reeve's father and grandfather were both curates.

5. Genesis 39:15.

LETTER II

1. A parson or incumbent of a parish whose tithes are not impropriate. In modern use the term also sometimes applied to the holders of ancient chapelries and perpetual curacies.

2. A travelling carriage, usually having a closed body and seating between two and four people, with the postilion or driver riding one of the horses.

3. *The Double-Disappointment; A Farce* (1755) by Moses Mendes (d. 1758). The allusion is to the "Irish" song sung in act I, scene I of the ballad opera, in which fortune-hunting Irishman Phelim O'Blunder bellows,

> Wherever I'm going, and all the Day long,
> At home, or abroad, or alone in a Throng,
> I find that my Passion's so lively and strong,
> That your Name, when I'm silent, still runs in my Song.
> Sing Balinamone o-ra, Balinamone o-ra,
> Balinamone o-ra, A Kiss of your sweet Lips for me.

LETTER III

1. Slight alteration of lines 58–67 from Dryden's translation of the latter part of the third book of Lucretius, "Against the Fear of Death" (1685).

2. Reeve's idealization of country life and her championing of agriculture was typical of many late-eighteenth-century novels, such as Charlotte Smith's *The Young Philosopher* (1798).

3. Genesis 39:6. Again Reeve quotes from a chapter concerning Joseph.

4. A number of gold coins made up into a cylindrical packet. In *Grose's Dictionary* (1796) the number of guineas therein is given as "from twenty to fifty or more."

5. Misquotation from Shakespeare's *Timon of Athens* (II.ii.156–57). The actual passage reads,

> —The world is but a word:
> Were it all yours, to give it in a breath,
> How quickly it were gone.

6. A company, band or assemblage of persons (usually spelled *rout*).

7. Here Reeve echoes Pope's description of Belinda at her toilette in *The Rape of the Lock* (1712–1717): "Here Files of Pins extend their shining Rows, / Puffs, Powders, Patches, Bibles, Billet-doux." (I.37–38).

8. *Hamlet* (III.ii.37). Hamlet tells the players, "I have thought some of Nature's Journey-men had made men, and not made them well, they imitated human nature so abominably." Reeve substitutes *disgraced* for *imitated*.

9. A variation of what was considered the most prestigious and socially acceptable of card games in Great Britain between about 1750 and 1900, when it was supplanted by bridge. In whist, four people play, two against two as partners. The cards are dealt in clockwise rotation, one at a time, face down except for the last card—the trump card—which is turned face up. The trump card becomes part of the dealer's hand just before he plays to the first trick. The object of the game is to win tricks, with each odd-trick counting one point. In England, the game was won by the first side to earn five points (Charles Goren, *Goren's Hoyle Encyclopedia of Games* [Chancellor Hall, 1961, 180–88]).

10. Hairdresser.

Letter IV

1. A private commercial establishment for the lending of books; the borrower paid either a fixed sum for each book lent, or a periodical subscription.

2. Jean-François Marmontel (1723–1799), protégé of Voltaire, philosopher, historiographer, dramatist, Frenchman of letters. His *Contes Moraux* (1786) promote sensibility, toleration of husbandly/wifely faults, and the idea of perfectibility through moral influence. In the *Conte Moral* to which Reeve refers—"*La Femme comme il y en a Peu*" [usually translated as "A Wife of Ten Thousand"]—Meliodor, a Darnford-like philandering spendthrift and aspirer after the life of a man of "quality", is reformed by his angelic wife Acelia. Like Darnford, Meliodor becomes greatly indebted to a duplicitous friend, and Acelia saves the day by taking her husband's debts into her hands, reforming the household expenses, installing the family in the country away from the temptations of Paris, and generally showing Meliodor the superior pleasures of a virtuous life.

3. The idea for Southerne's 1694 play (as for his *Oroonoko*) was taken from a story by Aphra Behn. It was very popular and was a stock piece throughout the first half of the eighteenth century. David Garrick presented a revised version in 1757 as *Isabella; or, The Fatal Marriage*, and it is probably the slightly abridged version of *Isabella*—with which Sarah Siddons made her extraordinary comeback in 1782—that Reeve describes here.

4. Sarah Siddons (1755–1831) was born Sarah Kemble into a family of actors. She worked in the provinces as an actress, there marrying her husband William Siddons. She was soon noticed by David Garrick and became one of the greatest tragic actresses at Drury Lane after years of hard work. Her performance as the tragic Isabella, a woman who inadvertently brings about the death of her beloved husband and then kills herself, was said to be so electrifying that the audience was completely silent as the curtain fell.

5. *The Fatal Marriage* I.iii.205–210. The unforgiving Count Baldwin refers to Isabella's flight from a nunnery and unsanctioned marriage to his now-deceased son, Birón.

6. Thomas Southerne (1660–1746) was considered to show extraordinary sensitivity to women's concerns in his plays, especially in *The Fatal Mar-*

riage, and in his understanding portrait of a woman caught in a disastrous marriage, *The Wives' Excuse* (1692).

7. Edward Moore's (1712–1757) popular middle-class tragedy, first performed at Drury Lane in 1753 with David Garrick in the starring role as the unfortunate Beverly. Frances chooses her play well: Moore attacks the "prevailing and destructive vice" of gaming through the tragic tale of Beverly and his noble, virtuous wife. The idea that the theater could affect those whom the pulpit could not reach was a common one among dramatists like Moore who were writing domestic tragedies. (Frances, ever-optimistic, seems to be of the same opinion).

8. Hamlet's words to his mother (III.iv.158–59). Reeve substitutes *better* for *purer*.

9. This spelling of "seemed" traces its roots back to as early as 1250.

10. The holding of property to the joint use of a husband and wife for life or in tail, as a provision for the wife in the event of her widowhood.

11. Fawning flatterer or sycophant. Originally this word referred to the servant of a charlatan, who was employed to pretend to eat toads (commonly thought to be poisonous) in order to enable his master to display his great skill in counteracting poison.

12. A *made dish* is composed of several ingredients. For example, a made gravy is one which is artificially compounded, rather than merely consisting of the juices given off from meat when it is cooking.

Letter V

1. Samuel Johnson of Cheshire (1691–1773), playwright, violinist, dancing-master, composer and wit, whose "craziness"—eccentricities including his great fear of old women and his habit of making horrible facial contortions while singing—did not prevent him from being a popular guest at fashionable London dinner parties. His first work, *Hurlothrumbo: or, The Super-Natural* (1729) is an exuberant mix of drama, music, and humor. It tells the tale of three noblemen—Urlandemy, Darony, and Darno—who rebel against their beneficent king, Soarthereal, finally forcing him to suppress the rebellion. Hurlothrumbo, the supernatural superhero, is on the side of the rebels, and thus is crushed along with them. The quotation is from a conversation between Hurlothrumbo and Dologodelmo (I.i), servant to the King; the latter is speaking in reference to the conspirators.

2. A covered conveyance, usually for one person, used in India and in other Eastern countries, consisting of a large box with wooden shutters, and usually carried on poles by four or six men.

3. A farmer; a man who tills or cultures the soil.

4. A set of three.

5. The King's Bench was a former court of record and the supreme court of common law in Britain. King's Bench Prison was a jail formerly designated for debtors and criminals confined by the authority of the supreme courts.

6. A four-wheeled coach-for-hire, drawn by two horses, and seating six people.

7. A phrase which occurred in numerous legal documents. Similar terminology is used by Laurence Sterne a few times in *Tristram Shandy* (1760–

1767); According to Melvyn New, Sterne was amused by the play of *appurtenance / purtenance* ("an appendage" / "the 'inwards' of an animal"— *OED*). See the Florida edition of *Tristram Shandy,* Bk. I, Ch. 7, Melvyn and Joan New, eds. (1978). Reeve also seems to have had a liking for the word, which occurs several times in *The School for Widows.*

8. Garraway's Coffee House, Exchange Alley, Cornhill. Famed as one of the chief auction houses of London, Garraway's started in 1669 and was not closed until 1872. It figures in several of Dickens's novels as well. (*The London Encyclopedia*, ed. Ben Weinreb and Christopher Hibbert, London: Macmillan, 1983).

9. *La lingua batte dove il dente dole.*

10. A light open carriage for one or two persons, drawn by between one and four horses.

11. From Irish dramatist George Farquhar's (1678–1707) comedy *The Twin-Rivals* (1702). In act I, scene I, the Elder Wou'dbe, speaking to Subtleman, the lawyer, accuses, "Thou art the Worm and Maggot of the Law, bred in the bruis'd and rotten Parts, and now are nourish'd on the same Corruption that produc'd thee."

12. Personal goods or belongings.

13. Rumford, alternately spelled Romford, was a small market town in Essex where such famous inns as the Blue Boar, the Swan, and the White Horse were located. (*A New Historical Geography of England*, ed. H. C. Darby, Cambridge University Press, 1973).

In 1592 known as Cup Field and Purse Field, Lincoln's Inn Fields take their name from the Inn of Chancery, and were open spaces where people could walk and take the air. At one time the site of executions, in the later seventeenth and early eighteenth centuries Lincoln's Inn Fields became known as a fashionable neighborhood (William Kent and Godfrey Thompson, *An Encyclopaedia of London*, London: J. M. Dent and Sons Ltd., 1970), 329–33.

14. The type of annuity to which Frances is referring is an investment of money whereby the investor becomes entitled to receive a series of equal annual payments which include the ultimate return of both principal and interest.

A security was a document held by a creditor as a guarantee of his or her right to payment.

Letter VI

1. *The Spectator* was a periodical published in London by Richard Steele and Joseph Addison from 1 March 1711 to 6 December 1712, and revived by Addison in 1714. It dealt with political and topical subjects, and was purportedly designed to "enliven morality with wit, and to temper wit with morality."

Stéphanie-Félicité de Genlis (1746–1830), French educator and fiction writer. She was popular and influential in England, where she was admired primarily for her pedagogy. Married at 16, she was governess to the daughters of the Duc de Chartres, and later became the duke's mistress. *Theatre of Education* (1779) consists of short plays, many of which are for girls.

2. *Tales of the Castle, or Stories of Instruction and Delight* (1785) and

Adelaide and Theodore, or Letters on Education (1784) both tell improving tales of children who live in the country under the sole influence of their mother, whose entire life consists of educating them and bringing them up to the best of her ability. Like Frances, she recommends reading lists to her children, and advocates very selective reading of novels (*The Feminist Companion to Literature in English*, ed. Blain, Grundy and Clements, 1990).

3. James Fordyce's (1720–1796) *Sermons to Young Women* (1766) was one of the most popular conduct books of its time. Fordyce emphasizes domestic and religious duties, and wives' submission to their husbands.

Dr. John Gregory's (1724–1773) influential conduct book, *A Father's Legacy to his Daughters* (1774) defines a "natural" woman as possessing vanity, a love of admiration, a retiring delicacy, and the like. According to the prescribed role given women by Dr. Gregory, a distinguished university professor, if they display such qualities such qualities as humor, learning, wit, or excessively good health, they will appear "unnatural" to men.

Thomas Percival, MD (1740–1804) wrote *A Father's Instructions* (1781) for his own children purportedly with the design of promoting "the love of virtue, a Taste for Knowledge, and an early acquaintance with the works of nature." In order to "refine the feelings of the heart," Dr. Percival focuses on such varied topics as: Cruelty to Insects, Taking of Bird Nests, Respect and Deference due to the Aged, and Idleness and Irresolution.

Anne Thérèse, Marquise de Lambert (1647–1733), French advice writer who ran a distinguished Paris salon. Her essay *A Mother's Advice to Her Son and Daughter* (1729) was written with the object of "awakening in the youthful mind the most noble sentiments, and stimulating it to the grandest pursuits of virtue." Typical subjects addressed include the duties of society, the necessity of possessing friends, and the danger of displaying wit at the expense of others.

One of the Bluestockings, Hester Chapone (1727–1801) was a self-educated poet, essayist, and translator, well respected by Johnson and Richardson, among others. Her most famous essay, *Letters on the Improvement of the Mind* (1773) fits in well with Frances's program in that it is a series of letters originally written to the author's niece, which outline a practical course for a young woman's self-education, including ambitious recommended reading lists.

4. *The Spoiled Child* (1779) is a two-act comedy by Madame de Genlis, written as part of her *Theatre of Education*. Dorina, the title character Lucy's music and drawing mistress, does nothing but alternately flatter and ignore her young charge, contributing to the girl's waywardness.

5. It is not clear how Frances could have rebuffed her husband with evidence from Plutarch, whose account of the story of Cato the Younger's sharing of his wife Marcia with his friend is much like Darnford's. Plutarch does emphasize that Hortensius's main desire is for a child, and that once Cato's wife has brought him a son, he will "restore her" to her husband.

6. This appears to be a misquotation of a stanza from Ambrose Philips's (d.1749) Sixth Pastoral poem (written sometime before 1708), the original text of which reads:

> Come, Rosalind, O, Come! For, wanting thee,
> Our peopled vale a desert is to me.
> Come, Rosalind, O, Come! My brinded kine,
> My snowy sheep, my farm, and all, are thine.

The lines are spoken by Hobbinol, one of three shepherds who are given voice in the poem. Samuel Johnson describes Philips as a zealous Whig, a "witty and political" man whose pastoral poems were, unfortunately for him, "too much commended" (*Lives of the Poets*). (Cambridge: Cambridge University Press, 1910), 52–62.

7. Anna Letitia Barbauld (1743–1825), teacher, editor, critic, and poet. Her *Lessons for Children* (1788) is a book of behavior, adapted to the comprehension of children between two and three years of age. It includes elementary lessons such as counting to three, the five senses, the colors, the body parts and what they do. The author also emphasizes sensibility; for example, a child is exhorted to feel pity for a "poor sparrow" caught in a cat's mouth.

8. Hannah More (1745–1833) was best known as a writer of popular tracts and educator of the poor. She was friends with David Garrick, who produced a few of her plays. In her work she defends traditional values, and the education that she advises for the poor is one that would reconcile them to their poverty (i.e., Bible-reading, catechism, skills fitting their station). Her *Sacred Dramas* (1782) are poetic interpretations of Biblical scenes (*Belshazzar, Daniel, Moses*) and *The Search After Happiness* (1773) is a short "pastoral drama for young ladies," written to be performed in boarding schools with the aim of "promoting a regard to Religion and Virtue."

The Lady's Preceptor; or, Letter to a Young Lady of Distinction Upon Politeness (1743) was translated from the French by the Abbé d'Ancourt, and addresses the proper behavior in such matters as letter-writing, table manners, going to court, and the like, and warns against such peccadilloes as affectation, "mimicking others", and "appearing absent in company."

The Compleat Geographical Grammar (1699) by Patrick Gordon is a short, comprehensive analysis of the world, divided into two sections: "A General View of the Terraqueous Globe," and "A Particular View of the Terraqueous Globe." Its stated design is to "present the younger sort of our Nobility and Gentry, with a Compendious Pleasant and Methodical Tract of MODERN GEOGRAPHY" and it includes many tables and maps.

A Short History of England. Questions and Answers. This is a common title for general English history books written for children and youths during the eighteenth century. One example of such a work is J. Maddern's *Short History of England, from the first landing of the Romans under Julius Caesar . . . down to George II* (1760).

Oliver Goldsmith (1728–1774), Irish poet, playwright, novelist, translator, and essayist, also made forays into history. His two-volume *Roman History, from the Foundation of the City of Rome to the Destruction of the Western Empire* was published in an abridged edition for children in 1772.

Frances refers to Goldsmith's *Grecian History, from the Earliest State to the Death of Alexander the Great*, another two-volume work published in 1774.

A Treatise on Self-Knowledge (1809, 2nd edition) by the Reverend Mr. John Mason (1706–1763) proposes that "the great end of philosophy, both natural and moral, is to *know ourselves*, and to *know* GOD" (viii). Mason writes his treatise with the aim of benefiting youth, particularly those who are to be future members of the clergy.

Though Moore claims in his preface to his *Fables for the Female Sex* (1744) that he is writing these tales merely for the amusement of his audience, he has a clear moral purpose in mind. Using characters from the animal kingdom, Moore satirizes flaws such as flattery, pretence, and vanity, while advocating knowledge, sense, taste, and above all virtue.

Nathaniel Cotton's (1705–1788) *Visions, for the Entertainment and Instruction of Young Minds* (1751) calls upon young women to be men's saviors, pleading, "Save us, ye fair, or we're undone; / Maintain your modesty and station, / So women shall preserve the nation" (p. 6). Each poetic "vision" addresses a different subject, such as friendship, health, slander, and marriage, advising prudence and virtuousness in all aspects of a young woman's life. Cotton was a physician as well as a writer, and is perhaps best known today as the proprietor of the private madhouse to which poet William Cowper was sent after his attempted suicide.

Les Aventures de Telemaque, fils d'Ulysse (1699) by Francois Fenelon (1651–1715) is the story of the political and moral education of a young man, Telemachus, by his virtuous and wise tutor, Mentor. Philosopher, writer, and royal tutor for ten years, Francois Fenelon was ordained a priest in 1675, but fell into royal and religious disfavor for his ideas. Louis XIV read *Telemachus*, for example, as a satire on the ostentatious luxury and militarism of his reign.

Xenophon's history of the Persian king Cyrus was translated into French many times during the eighteenth century. The 1736 edition *Histoire de Cyrus le Jeune, et de la Retrait des Dix Mille, avec un Discours sur l'histoire Grecque*, translated by J. A. Pagi, was a popular version.

Sarah Trimmer (1741–1810) was one of the England's most prolific children's writers. She published lessons to help children learn English and Roman history, and her two volumes on the scriptures (1804) make up the "Sacred History" to which Frances is referring.

The Guardian was begun 12 March 1713 and continued until 1 October. Of 175 numbers, 53 are from Joseph Addison's pen, although the original conception of the journal was Steele's. Like *The Spectator* and *The Tatler*, *The Guardian* was designed to reform society and to regenerate literary taste.

The Rambler was a twice-weekly periodical (published 1750–1752) in which Samuel Johnson published essays on subjects as varied as literary genres and marriage. Johnson's stated intention was to "inculcate wisdom or piety," and his essays are much more serious in tone than those published in, for example, *The Spectator*.

John Hawkesworth (1715?–1773) started this periodical (published 1752–1754) in imitation of his friend Johnson's *Rambler*. In fact, Johnson himself contributed twenty-nine essays to *The Adventurer*, during the course of 1753. Hawkesworth was also Johnson's successor as compiler of parliamentary debates for the *Gentleman's Magazine*.

Johnson's 104 essays written for *The Idler* (1758–1760) were lighter in style and tone than his *Rambler* essays, and were not as greatly admired. They include, though, such accomplished essays as the famous number 84, in which Johnson praises autobiography over biography.

Spectacle de la Nature; or Nature display'd, being discourses on such particulars of natural history as were thought most proper to excite the curiosity, and form the minds of youth, (published 1736–1748) was originally written in French by Noel Pluche (1688–1761). It is a multi-volume work of large scope, attempting to cover such varied subjects as childhood exercise, the structure of a plough, marriage, the origin of society, and carpet-making.

Elizabeth Carter (1717–1806) was a poet, scholar, essayist, and translator, and widely believed to be one of the most learned women in England during the eighteenth century. Her good friend Samuel Johnson made her the famous left-handed compliment that she "could make a pudding as well as translate Epictetus from the Greek; and work a handkerchief as well as compose a poem" (*Encyclopedia of British Women Writers,* ed. Paul Schlueter and June Schlueter, NY: Garland, 1988), 84–85. Frances is likely referring to Carter's second volume of poetry, *Poems on Several Occasions* (1762), which includes her "Ode to Wisdom"—originally published as part of Samuel Richardson's *Clarissa* (1747).

9. In ancient Rome the word was used to refer to a servant whose business it was to inform his master of the names of persons, particularly when engaged in canvassing for office. In general a nomenclator is one who announces, or imparts to another, the names of persons or guests.

The Red-Book was a popular name for the *Royal Kalendar; or Complete . . . Annual Register* (published 1767–1893), which comprised a list of the nobility and gentry, with their town and country residences, and other information.

10. John Elwes (1714–1789), member of Parliament and nephew and heir to Sir Harvey Elwes. Like his uncle, John Elwes was known for his wealth and his avaricious nature.

11. "The School-Mistress" (1737) was the best-known poem by William Shenstone (1714–1763), poet, amateur landscape gardener, and collector. The poem is a commemoration, in Spenserian stanzas, of Sarah Lloyd, who was Shenstone's first teacher at the village school.

12. In Ben Jonson's (1572–1637) *Explorata,* "Oratio Imago Animi," he writes, "Language most shews a man: Speak, that I may see thee . . . No glass renders a man's form, or likeness, so true as his speech" (*The Complete Poems,* ed. George Parfitt [New Haven: Yale University Press, 1975], 825–26.)

13. John 2:25. 1 Corinthians 1:27.

14. Psalms 119:46.

15. Line 15 of Alexander Pope's "Epistle to Burlington" (1731).

Letter VII

1. A reference to Timon "the misanthrope" who supposedly lived in the time of Pericles, and today is primarily known through Shakespeare's tragedy *Timon of Athens.*

2. One who deals in meal (the finely-ground edible part of any grain, commonly understood to exclude the product of wheat).

3. A small group of peasants.

4. Ale brewed in October.

5. From Milton's *Poems on Several Occasions* (1673), sonnet xix.

6. Tables made of fir or pine.

7. Artificial.

8. Here Reeve refers to Horace Walpole's *Castle of Otranto* (1764), the prototype of the Gothic novel. Reeve admired the work, but had reservations about its imaginative "excesses." The alluded-to instance—the ghostly ambulation of the subjects of paintings hanging in a room in Otranto—

influenced Reeve's representation of the "haunted chamber" in *The Old English Baron*.

9. This sentiment echoes that of the oppressive, squirrel-killing Mr. Munden, husband of the title character of Eliza Haywood's (1693–1756) novel *The History of Betsy Thoughtless* (1751). Like Strictland, Mr. Munden thinks of his wife as an "upper servant."

10. A man who assists women in childbirth; a male midwife.

11. Ephesians 3:26.

12. A now-obscure variant of skein, namely, a large quantity of thread, yarn, silk, or some similar material, wound upon a reel, and often gathered up in a loose knot.

13. An annual sum allotted to a woman for personal expenses, usually in dress. The term seems to be a loose one, as many women were made to purchase not only their personal clothes and incidentals, but also household necessities with this often trivial sum of money.

14. A commodity no longer in demand; something (or someone) that has lost its value.

15. Also spelled sennight. A week from (this day).

16. A bobbin was a finely weaved cord used in haberdashery. Cabbage-nets were small nets used to boil cabbage.

17. Formerly called the English East India Company (1600–1708) and the United Company of Merchants of English Trading to the East Indies (1708–1873), the East India Company was formed in order to exploit trade with the east. It was incorporated on 31 December 1600 by royal charter. From 1773 on, the Company exercised political power in the East, and had chief part in the administration of the affairs of Hindustan (until 1858 when the government was assumed by the Crown). Its political influence was destroyed by Pitt's India Act in 1784, and its commercial influence steadily declined in the years immediately afterward, until its final expiration in 1873. The history of the East India Company is "central to the British experience of trade and territorial expansion overseas . . . Its longevity . . . and critical role in bringing India and other eastern lands into the British empire mark the Company as unique in the nation's history." (*Encyclopaedia Britannica*, 1995 and *The East India Company: A History*, Philip Lawson, London: NY: Longman, 1993, viii). *The New Encyclopedia Britannica*. Vol. 4. 15th Ed. Chicago: Encyc. Britannica Inc., 1977. p. 329.

Letter VIII

1. The proclamation or public announcement given in church of an intended marriage, in order that those who might know of any reason for preventing the marriage should have the opportunity of voicing their objections.

2. Possibly a variation of an air by William Shenstone, the first verse of which reads, "Awake! I say, awake, good people! Come, let's be merry; stir the tipple; / How can you sleep / Whilst I do play?" (1773).

3. This term likely refers to a malarial fever. Continued severe fevers with stupor or coma were in the medical world of the late eighteenth century often called typhus, and the adjective "typhoid" was often given to fevers that were not truly typhus, but were typhus-like. Daniel Drake, renowned North American geographer, wrote of the "typhoid stage of autumnal fever,"

by which he probably meant what we might today call pernicious malaria (*The Cambridge World History of Human Disease,* ed. Kenneth F. Kiple, Cambridge: Cambridge University Press 1993), 1078–79.

4. Deptford, now part of the London Borough of Lewisham, was a metropolitan borough south of the Thames. The famous Deptford Dockyard, founded in 1513 by Henry VIII, was closed in 1844 (*An Encyclopedia of London,* eds. William Kent and Godfrey Thompson, London: J. M. Dent & Sons Ltd. 1970), 245.

5. The term applied to works of popular literature that were circulated by chapmen, or itinerant salesmen. They consisted mainly of short pamphlets containing tracts, treatises, popular stories, and ballads.

6. Isaac Watts (1674–1748) was the English Nonconformist minister widely regarded as the "father of English hymnody." Among his most famous hymns are "Our God, Our Help in Ages Past" and "Jesus Shall Reign." The preface to an 1818 edition of Dr. Watts's hymns attests to their being "so generally esteemed and extensively circulated" that no apology or explanation is necessary for the attempt to facilitate their use. Besides writing great hymns that are still popular in many Protestant churches today, Watts had the fourth largest number of separate editions of his works published before 1800 (The first three are John Wesley, Shakespeare, and Daniel Defoe). In his later life, Watts spent much of his time writing, and finished his book on logic (*Logic, or the Right Use of Reason in the Enquiry After Truth*) in 1725 (Encyclopedia Americana. International Edition. Vol. 28: Danbury, CT: Grober, 2001), 501.

7. A priest or parson, patrico is often a term of disparagement, like hedge-priest, which refers to an uneducated priest of low status.

8. Eighteenth-century physicians erroneously believed that teething was a cause of serious infantile illness (cough, vomiting, convulsions, and the like) (*Encyclopaedia Britannica,* 1999).

Letter IX

1. A variant of coverlet, the topmost covering of a bed.
2. A variant of linsey-woolsey, a textile material woven from the mixture of flax and wool.

Matt: a piece of coarse, braided fabric intended to lie, sit or kneel upon, or for a protective wall/floor covering.

3. Line 117 of Milton's "L'Allegro" (1645).
4. "My daughter . . ." and so forth: Reeve seems to be using the phrase "took upon her" to refer to the girl's gaining a feeling of self-importance through her travels and experiences.
5. The High Calvinists differed from both the Arminians (who believed in universal redemption) and the Moderate Calvinists in their views on free will, grace, and atonement. They interpreted the scriptures as evidence of God's confining his love to the "elect" only (*Atonement and Justification; English Evangelical Theology 1646–1790,* Alan C. Clifford [Oxford: Oxford University Press, 1990], 111–24.

Letter X

1. Variant spelling of confidant, frequently used during the eighteenth century.
2. Illumination; full understanding or realization.
3. A person who works in brass.

Letter XI

1. A variant spelling of colic, a term which is applied to severe stomach pains due to difficulties of the bowels, or other parts.
Hollands geneva was a spirit distilled from grain and flavoured with the juice of juniper berries. Its shortened form, gin, usually denotes an imitation of the original Dutch spirit.

Letter XII

1. In Italy, the name formerly given to the *cavalier servente* or acknowledged gallant of a married woman.
Cicisbeism was the practice of attending a married woman as cicisbeo.
2. A small compress of absorbent cloth, often steeped in some kind of medicine, to be used as a bandage.

Letter XV

1. Shakespeare's *The Tempest* (III.iii). The lines are from Ariel's curse against Alonso, Sebastian and Antonio, the enemies of Prospero:

> Lingering perdition, worse than any death
> Can be at once
> Shall step by step attend
> You and your ways; whose wraths to guard you from—
> Which here, in this most desolate isle, else falls
> Upon your heads—is nothing but heart-sorrow
> And a clear life ensuing.

2. The stakes upon which fruit trees or shrubs are trained.
3. To make or weave nets.
4. "Saint Anthony, pray for us! Saint Catherine, Pray for us!"
5. John 13:35.
6. Mark 3:33–35.

Letter XVIII

1. Proverbs 31:6–8. The words are spoken by King Lemuel, but he is repeating the wise advice of his mother.
2. Genesis 46:30.

Letter XIX

1. Madras is the shortened name of the fishing village Madras Patnam, where the East India Company built a fort and trading post in 1639. Madras eventually became the administrative and commercial capital of the occupying English in southern India.
    Golconda was the old name for Hyderabad (capital of the Andhra Pradesh state, in southern India), which was formerly famous for its diamonds.
2. An obsolete form of moreen, a sturdy woolen or woolen and cotton cloth, often used for curtains and bed coverings.
3. *Othello* (II.i.208). The exact quotation is, "I prattle out of fashion, and I dote / In mine own comfort."

Letter XXI

1. Poet and playwright James Shirley (1596–1666), one of the leading dramatists during the ten years before Parliament's closing of the theatres in 1642. Shirley wrote verse, five masques, and a moral allegory, in addition to his thirty-one plays. The latter are largely satirical, and concerned with fashionable London life in the time of Charles I. Reeve cites lines, however, from Shirley's *The Gratefull Servant* (1629), a romantic comedy brimming with nymphs, satyrs, and Italian noblemen. The lines are spoken by the Duke of Savoy to Cleona, the woman with whom he has fallen in love, mistakenly believing his lover Leonora to be dead. Reeve alters the words somewhat; the original lines read, "There is a virtuous Magick in your eye, / For where soere it casts a beame, it does Create a goodnesse" (II.i.260–62).
2. *A Midsummer Night's Dream* (V.i.101–3). The words of Theseus to Hippolyta are, more precisely, "And in the modesty of fearful duty / I read as much as from the rattling tongue / Of saucy and audacious eloquence."
3. Sir William Blackstone (1723–1780), barrister, judge, and member of Parliament, was the author of *Commentaries on the Laws of England* (1765–1769). Blackstone's work was the most widely known description and explanation of English legal doctrine, and it became the basis for English and American university legal education. Blackstone's purpose in writing is to describe the state of the legal system in England in the mid eighteenth century, and he does so in a clear and systematic way. (*Encyclopaedia Britannica*, 11th ed. Vol. IV. Cambridge: Cambridge University Press, 1910), 25–26.

Letter XXII

1. Proverbs 28:1.

Select Bibliography

WORKS BY CLARA REEVE

The Phoenix; or, The History of Polyarchus and Argenis. Translated from the Latin of John Barclay (*Argenis*, 1621). London: Printed for J. Bell & C. Hetherington, 1772.

The Champion of Virtue. Colchester: Printed for the author by W. Keymer, 1777. Republished as *The Old English Baron.* London: Printed for E. & C. Dilly, 1778.

"Letters of Aza." *The Lady's Magazine* (June 1778): 284–85.

The Progress of Romance. Printed together with *The History of Charoba, Queen of Aegypt.* Colchester: William Keymer, 1785.

The Exiles. London: T. Hookham, 1788.

The School for Widows. London: T. Hookham, 1791.

Plans of Education. London: T. Hookham & J. Carpenter, 1792.

The Two Mentors. London, 1783.

Original Poems on Several Occasions. London, 1769.

Destination. Dublin: T. Burnside, 1799.

Reeve to her publishers, September 1802. British Library, London, MS Reading Room. *Original Letters Collected by William Upcott of the London Institution. Distinguished Women,* 4.

Reeve to Thomas Percy, Jr., 23 April 1785. Bodleian Library, Oxford, MS Percy.C3, Fol.32.

Reeve to John Nichols and John Bowyer Nichols, 1786. Bodleian Library, Oxford. MS Eng.let.b.15, Fol.181.

Reeve to Joseph Cooper Walker, 1790–1804 (11 letters). Trinity College Library, Dublin, MS 1461.

OTHER WORKS

Alexander, William, MD. *The History of Women, from the Earliest Antiquity to the Present Time.* Dublin: A. J. Hibbard, 1779.

Alliston, April. *Virtue's Faults: Correspondences in Eighteenth-Century British and French Women's Fiction.* Palo Alto, CA: Stanford University Press, 1996.

Armstrong, Nancy. "The Rise of the Domestic Woman." In *The Ideology of Conduct: Essays on Literature and the History of Sexuality,* eds. Nancy

Armstrong and Leonard Tennenhouse. (New York: Methuen, 1987): 96–141.

Astell, Mary. *A Serious Proposal to the Ladies for the Advancement of Their True and Greatest Interest.* London: Printed for R. Wilkin, 1697.

Ballaster, Ros. "Contexts, Intertexts, Metatexts: Eighteenth-Century Prose by Women." *Eighteenth Century Fiction* 11:3 (April 1999): 347–58.

Barbauld, Anna. *The British Novelists,* Vol. 23. London: Printed for F. C. & J. Rivington, 1810.

Barker-Benfield, G. J. *The Culture of Sensibility: Sex and Society in Eighteenth-Century Britain.* Chicago: University of Chicago Press, 1992.

Boswell, James. *Life of Johnson.* Edited by G. B. Hill and L. F. Powell. Oxford: Oxford University Press, 1934 (vols. 1–4), 1964 (vols. 5–6).

Brophy, Elizabeth Bergen. *Women's Lives and the Eighteenth-Century English Novel.* Tampa: University of South Florida Press, 1991.

Butler, Marilyn. *Jane Austen and the War of Ideas.* Oxford: Oxford University Press, 1999.

The British Critic. (Dec. 1793): 383–88.

The Critical Review. 2 (1791): 476–77.

Cole, Richard Cargill. *Irish Booksellers and English Writers, 1740–1800.* London: Mansell, 1986.

Doody, Margaret Anne. *The True Story About the Novel.* London: Fontana, 1998.

The East Anglian Miscellany, upon Matters of History, Genealogy, Archaeology, Folk-Lore, Literature &c., Relating to East Anglia reprinted from the *East Anglian Daily Times,* (Ipswich, 1940) Nos. 10, 735–10, 755.

Ehlers, Leigh. "'A Striking Lesson to Posterity': Providence and Character in Clara Reeve's *The Old English Baron.*" *Enlightenment Essays* 9 (1978): 62–76.

The English Review. 19 (1792): 70–71.

Foster, James R. *History of the Pre-Romantic Novel in England,* 186–224. New York: Modern Language Association, 1949.

The Gentleman's Magazine 55 (Sept. 1785): 454.

———. 56 (Jan. 1786): 16.

———. 56 (Feb. 1786): 117–18.

Goldsmith, Elizabeth C. "Authority, Authenticity, and the Publication of Letters by Women." In *Writing the Female Voice: Essays on Epistolary Literature,* edited by Elizabeth C. Goldsmith, 46–59. London: Pinter, 1989.

Gordon, William. *The Plan of a Society for Making Provision for Widows by Annuities for the Remainder of Life.* Boston: Joseph Edwards and John Fleeming, 1772.

Griffin, Dunstin. *Literary Patronage in England, 1650–1800.* New York: Cambridge University Press, 1996.

Grundy, Isobel. "'A Novel in a Series of Letters by a Lady': Richardson and Some Richardsonian Novels." In *Samuel Richardson: Tercentenary Essays,* edited by Margaret Anne Doody and Peter Sabor, 233–36. New York: Cambridge University Press, 1989.

Hecht, J. Jean. *The Domestic Servant in Eighteenth-Century England*. London: Routledge, 1956.

Hemlow, Joyce. "Fanny Burney and the Courtesy Books." *PMLA* 65 (1950): 732–61.

Historical Manuscripts Commission. *Report on the Manuscripts of Lady Du Cane*. (London: Ben Johnson & Co., 1905): 238.

Hufton, Olwen. "Women Without Men: Widows and Spinsters in Britain and France in the Eighteenth Century." In *Between Poverty and the Pyre: Moments in the History of Widowhood*, edited by Jan Bremmer and Lourens van den Bosch, 122–51. New York: Routledge, 1995.

Jeaffreson, J. Cordy. In *Novels and Novelists, from Elizabeth to Victoria*, 269–75. London: Hurst and Blackett, 1858.

Johnson, Claudia L. *Equivocal Beings: Politics, Gender, and Sentimentality in the 1790s: Wollstonecraft, Radcliffe, Burney, Austen*. Chicago: Chicago University Press, 1995.

Kelly, Gary. *English Fiction of the Romantic Period, 1789–1830*. New York: Longman, 1989.

———. *Women, Writing, and Revolution, 1790–1827*. Oxford: Clarendon Press, 1993.

Kievitt, Frank David. "Clara Reeve's *The School for Widows*." *Mid-Hudson Language Studies* 3 (1980): 73–84.

Leranbaum, Miriam. "'Mistresses of Orthodoxy': Education in the Lives and Writings of Late Eighteenth-Century English Women Writers." *Proceedings of the American Philosophical Society* 121 (1977): 281–301.

Mayo, Robert. *The English Novel in the Magazines, 1740–1815*. London: Oxford University Press, 1962.

Madoff, Mark. "The Useful Myth of Gothic Ancestry." *Studies in Eighteenth-Century Culture*. 8 (1979): 337–50.

Mellor, Anne K. "A Criticism of Their Own: Romantic Women Literary Critics." In *Questioning Romanticism*, edited by John Beer. Baltimore: Johns Hopkins University Press, 1995, 29–48.

Mellor, Anne and Richard Matlak, eds. *British Literature, 1780–1830*. New York: Harcourt Brace, 1996.

Monthly Mirror. (Dec. 1807): 451.

Monthly Review. 5 (1791): 466–67.

More, Hannah. *Coelebs in Search of a Wife*. Edited by Mary Waldron. Bristol, UK: Thoemmes Press, 1995.

Morgan, Marjorie. *Manners, Morals and Class in England, 1774–1858*. New York: St. Martin's Press, 1994.

Mullane, Janet and Robert Wilson, eds. *Nineteenth Century Literature Criticism*. Detroit, MI: Gale Research, 1988).

Munter, Robert. *A Dictionary of the Print Trade in Ireland 1550–1775*. New York: Fordham University Press, 1988.

Napier, Elizabeth. "Clara Reeve." In *Dictionary of Literary Biography*, edited by Martin C. Battestin, 374. Detroit, MI: Gale Research Co., 1985.

Owen, Margaret. *A World of Widows*. London: Zed Books, 1996.

The Petition of the WIDOWS, in & about London and Westminster for a Re-

dress of their Grievances, London 1693. Ann Arbor: Microfilm, University of Michigan, 1982. Early English Books, 1641–1700; 1292; 4.

Roberts, Bette B. In *The Gothic Romance: Its Appeal to Women Writers and Readers in Late Eighteenth-Century England,* edited by New York: Arno Press, 1980): 60–83.

Schnorrenberg, Barbara Brandon. "A Paradise Like Eve's: Three Eighteenth Century Female Utopias." *Women's Studies* 9 (1982) 3: 263–73.

Scott, Sir Walter. *Lives of the Novelists,* vol. 2. Paris: W. Galignani, 1825.

Spacks, Patricia Meyer. "Female Resources: Epistles, Plot, and Power." In *Writing the Female Voice: Essays on Epistolary Literature,* edited by Elizabeth C. Goldsmith, 63–85. London: Pinter, 1989.

Spencer, Jane. *The Rise of the Woman Novelist: From Aphra Behn to Jane Austen.* Oxford: Blackwell, 1986.

———. "Clara Reeve." In *A Dictionary of British and American Women Writers, 1660–1800,* edited by Janet Todd, 266–68. Totowa, NJ: Rowman & Allanheld, 1985.

Staves, Susan. *Married Women's Separate Property in England, 1660–1833.* London: Harvard University Press, 1990.

Sutton, David. *Location Register of English Literary Manuscripts and Letters.* London: British Library, 1995.

Thurston, Bonnie Bowman. *The Widows: A Women's Ministry in the Early Church.* Philadelphia: Fortress Press, 1989.

Trainer, James, ed. *The Old English Baron.* London: Oxford University Press, 1967.

Turner, Cheryl. *Living by the Pen: Women Writers in the Eighteenth Century.* New York: Routledge, 1992.

Van Sant, Jessie Ann. *Eighteenth-Century Sensibility and the Novel: The Senses in Social Context.* New York: Cambridge University Press, 1993.

Warner, William. *Licensing Entertainment: the Education of Novel Reading in Britain, 1684–1750.* Los Angeles: University of California Press, 1998.

OHIO UNIVERSITY LIBRARY

Please return this book as soon as you have finished with it. In order to avoid a fine it must be returned by the latest date stamped below. All books are subject to recall after two weeks or immediately if needed for reserve.

CF